"A superb read about helplessness, power, wealth, honesty, and truth—nightmarishly compelling." —*Booklist* (starred review)

"Perfect reading for the last lazy golden days of September. . . . Lundrigan maintains the pace and keeps the tension and suspense right to the end and there are some really good twists." —*The Globe and Mail*

"From the enticing first pages to the shocking last lines (don't peek!), Nicole Lundrigan's *An Unthinkable Thing* explores the trauma of loneliness and the power of belonging, through the eyes of a tender, unforgettable young narrator. You'll be deeply moved by this thoughtful and atmospheric page-turner." —**Ashley Audrain**, *New York Times* bestselling author of *The Whispers*

"In Nicole Lundrigan's *An Unthinkable Thing* we meet eleven-year-old Tommie Ware, whose life is forever changed by the dark secrets of the wealthy family his estranged mother works for. Gothic horror meets literary suspense, this novel showcases Lundrigan's impressive talent for crafting a story that is propulsive yet measured, never giving up its mysteries too easily. Flawlessly captivating, this is the book I've been waiting to read all year." —**Karma Brown**, #1 nationally bestselling author of *Recipe for a Perfect Wife*

"In *An Unthinkable Thing*, Nicole Lundrigan goes deep behind the glittering curtain of a *perfect* family, skillfully revealing their darkest secrets one shocking layer at a time. Expertly paced, with a voice that's both tender and innocent, this twisted suspense story's jaw-dropping events kept me glued to the pages until the ultimate satisfying surprise. A must read."
—Hannah Mary McKinnon, internationally bestselling author of *The Revenge List*

"I read *An Unthinkable Thing* with my heart in my throat. Nicole Lundrigan masterfully sets the stage with a nostalgic late-1950s backdrop, then ratchets up the tension as she slowly reveals that nothing is quite what it seems. This slow burn mystery builds to an inferno that will keep readers riveted until the final, satisfying page. Five enthusiastic stars!" —Nicole Baart, bestselling author of *The Long Way Back*

"A magnificent example of all the elements of fine fiction—an engaging narrative voice, a profound evocation of time and place, a complex braiding of plot lines—converging to create the perfect tale. Add to this enticing mix a deeply compelling mystery that doesn't wholly reveal itself until the final page, and what more could any reader ask for?" —William Kent Krueger, *New York Times* bestselling author of *This Tender Land*

Praise for *HIDEAWAY*

"Authentic, disturbing and unbearably tense, *Hideaway* will leave you reeling." —Shari Lapena, #1 bestselling author of *Everyone Here Is Lying*

"A terrific psychological suspense story hinging on the spellbinding character of Gloria, the mom from hell. . . . Just when you think you have it all figured out, Lundrigan's plot swerves. This book has to be saved for a binge read." —*The Globe and Mail*

"In elegant, stylish prose, Lundrigan captures the bewilderment of childhood when it's set against the backdrop of how awful adults can be. If ever there was a book that will hook you with hatred and love, *Hideaway* is it. With a great, tense finish, you'll be desperate for the right characters to win. I loved Maisy as much as I do Scout Finch, and that's saying something." —Roz Nay, internationally bestselling author of *Our Little Secret*

"*Hideaway* is a potent exploration of abuse, desperation, coming of age, and broken trust. . . . With her latest novel, Lundrigan proves she's hit her stride." —*Quill and Quire*

"This is a great book for those who love a good suspense or thriller. . . . [*Hideaway*] is amazingly written, Lundrigan doesn't rely on cheap twists or strange thriller plots . . . it's all character." —CBC Books

"Lundrigan's second thriller is a well-crafted dive into narcissistic manipulation and betrayal that, despite being set in the American suburbs, evokes the mood of Scandinavian noir."
—*Booklist*

"Lundrigan is a fearless writer, and has created an unforgettable, psychologically complex, smart, dark story in *Hideaway*. Questioning ideas of safety, truth, and responsibility, it's a bone-chilling tale that goes places you'll never expect—your heart will be racing by the final, shocking climax and you'll never stop cheering for the irresistible child heroes Rowan and Maisy, even in the darkest moments." —**Grace O'Connell, author of *Be Ready for the Lightning***

"Haunting, harrowing, and beautifully written, *Hideaway* splendidly showcases the unique talents of Nicole Lundrigan." —**Ian Hamilton, bestselling author of the Ava Lee series**

"There are few better at writing familial claustrophobia than Nicole Lundrigan, and in *Hideaway* she uses it to drive the suspense in a thriller about the idea of home, its comforts and entrapments." —**Andrew Pyper, bestselling author of *The Residence***

AN
UNTHINKABLE
THING

AN
UNTHINKABLE
THING

NICOLE LUNDRIGAN

PENGUIN

an imprint of Penguin Canada, a division of
Penguin Random House Canada Limited

First published in Viking original trade paperback
by Penguin Canada in 2022.

Published in this edition, 2023

1 2 3 4 5 6 7 8 9 10

*Publisher's note: This book is a work of fiction. Names, characters, places
and incidents either are the product of the author's imagination or are used
fictitiously, and any resemblance to actual persons living or dead, events,
or locales is entirely coincidental.*

Library and Archives Canada Cataloguing in Publication

Title: An unthinkable thing / Nicole Lundrigan.
Names: Lundrigan, Nicole, author.
Description: Previously published: Toronto: Viking Canada, 2022.
Identifiers: Canadiana 20210239557 | ISBN 9780735242692 (softcover)
Classification: LCC PS8573.U5436 U58 2023 | DDC C813/.6—dc23

Book design by Emma Dolan
Cover images: (pool) © Andras Meszlenyi, (broken glass) © hayatikayhan,
(lemons) © igorr1, all Getty Images

Printed in the United States of America

www.penguinrandomhouse.ca

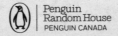

Penguin
Random House
PENGUIN CANADA

Another one for my three.

Sophia
Ella
Robert

And Leonard, too.
Who cannot be left out.

"The trees were full of silver-white sunlight
and the meanest of them sparkled."

—*Flannery O'Connor*

PROLOGUE

When I was a young boy, my aunt often told me a lie makes things worse. But she never explained that the truth can, too. I learned that lesson on my own during the summer of 1958, when I was eleven years old.

Before that, I'd had a fairly regular childhood. I was raised by my aunt Celia, and we lived in a small walk-up apartment on a potholed street in Lower Washbourne. Like most of our neighbors, we didn't have much, but we managed. A nice old couple named Mr. and Mrs. King lived directly below us, and my best friend, Wally, was in the building across the street. When it was warm, Wally and I would bike to the lake to hunt frogs or catch fish with string and safety pins. And children were always outside skipping rope and playing kick the can. School was decent, too. My teacher, Mrs. Pinsent, often told my aunt I was bright but distracted. Apparently, I had a fondness for daydreaming.

But in the weeks before the end of that school year, a shift happened. Not a change I saw or heard, but more something I felt. My easygoing aunt, who'd cared for me every single day since I was born, was different. She'd grown more *intense* about everything. All at once, she was bothered by the stray cats in the alley and the chips on the rims of our cereal bowls. She began to complain about the looping staircases we had to climb to reach our apartment. She spoke repeatedly about wanting a house with a fence and a yard.

I blamed those changes on the new man she'd been seeing. He was one of her patients from St. Augustine's Hospital, where she was a night nurse. I suspected him of making promises he'd never keep. I suspected her of believing them. Even though I hadn't met him, I recall having a damp awareness that he was not a good person. I'd hoped she'd forget about him, like she had with all the others, and everything would return to the way it was before. But it never did. Instead the worst possible thing occurred, upending my life in ways I could not have fathomed. I was forced to leave our apartment and taken to stay with my birth mother. She was a live-in housekeeper and worked for the Henneberrys, Washbourne's wealthiest and most respected family. I soon discovered nobody had a clue who they really were.

Three decades have passed since that hot August afternoon when the Henneberrys—mother, father, and son—were murdered. While that may seem like long enough for the memories to dull, I occasionally wake up during the night and I'm still there. Standing on that manicured lawn. The gun is going off. Once, twice, three times. My shirt is sprayed with their blood and my tongue tastes of metal. When I look up, my mother is beside me. Her maid's uniform has a red smear across the line of buttons. She grips my arm. "Thomas? Listen to me!" I can't meet her eyes.

Then comes the slow crunch of tires over the gravel driveway. The doctor has arrived, but the dozens of pill bottles he carries in his black bag can't change what has already happened. "Hurry!" my mother cries. She's yanking off my soiled clothes. "I need to wash your—"

The car door slams. Even now I can recall the exact dilemma that swirled through my child's mind. He is coming toward me. I only have a moment to decide.

Am I going to tell the truth?

Or am I going to be good and brave. And tell the lie.

Greenlake Chronicle
March 17, 1959

TRIAL BEGINS FOR 11-YEAR-OLD ALLEGED TRIPLE-KILLER

A hush came over the courtroom in Greenlake today as opening statements began in the trial against 11-year-old Thomas Leon Ware. Ware stands accused of the shooting deaths of Washbourne's most prominent family, Muriel Henneberry, 36, Dr. Raymond Henneberry, 41, and their son, Martin, 16. Muriel was the only daughter of millionaire businessman and philanthropist Martin Oliver Gladstone. Ware has pleaded not guilty.

Prosecutor Clay Fibbs said in a statement, "The Henneberrys' sole mistake was opening their door to a dangerous individual. Thomas Ware is the illegitimate son of their housekeeper, a boy with a troubled history. But still, they welcomed him with open arms. And violence, unspeakable violence, was the result of their generosity." When asked for comment, Defense Counsel William Evans said, "Nothing's as neatly cut as Mr. Fibbs would have you believe. But we'll try this case in the courtroom. Not on its steps."

If found guilty, Ware will be the youngest person ever convicted as an adult for a capital crime in our country. Testimony begins tomorrow, with Muriel Henneberry's personal physician, Dr. Arnold Norton, taking the stand.

CHAPTER ONE

On June 14, 1958, my worst problem was the smoke in my eyes. Wally and I were on the fire escape of my apartment using his wood-burning kit. He'd brought me a thin board, and I was moving the hot metal point to form the letters of my name. The *T* was squiggly, but the *o* was turning out better. When it was finished, I planned to hang it on the bedroom door, even though it wasn't just my room. I shared it with my aunt. If I had time, maybe I'd burn her name, too. Tommie and Celia.

I was about to begin the first *m* but Aunt Celia was screaming. Again. "Tommie? Get in here! Quick, quick!"

"What's she on about?" Wally said. He rubbed the fuzz on top of his head. The day before, Wally's mother gave both of us identical end-of-school haircuts with her black clippers. Wally's hair was now a shadow of orangish blond and mine was plain brown. He had freckles and a gap between his front teeth. I had neither.

"Probably a bug," I said.

"She cuts people open and she's scared of a few more legs?"

I laughed and handed him back the wood burner. "Nurses don't cut people open, Wally. They sew them up."

I stepped over the electric cord and climbed through the kitchen window. Sure enough, when I got to the bathroom, I found my aunt standing on the toilet seat, her fists pressed into her chest, and an enormous orange earwig in the bottom of the sink.

"It crawled right up the drain," she said.

It was trying to escape, but it kept slipping. I reached in and cupped it inside my hands.

My aunt shuddered as she stepped off the toilet. "You always take care of me, Tommie."

I did, or I tried to, anyway. As much as I could. Scraping the dishes or bringing her breakfast when she woke up after her shift, or brushing the dirt off her best shoes with the silver buckles.

She turned back to the bathroom mirror. "Now can you get rid of it? And tell Wally he needs to go. Your mother'll be here soon, and you still haven't scrubbed your face. Or behind your ears." She leaned in close to her reflection and dotted lipstick on her mouth. Then she wiped it off with toilet paper. "I look old, don't I?"

"You're only thirty-three."

"Shush, Tommie. Twenty-nine. No, I'll be twenty-eight. Twenty-nine sounds like such a fib."

"Okay," I said, though I didn't get it.

She applied her lipstick again and then glanced at me. "You've got a ring around your neck, too."

The earwig's legs were tickling my palms and my stomach knotted up. I frowned.

"Why that face? Don't you want to be clean for your mother? With your birthday tomorrow, I know she's excited to see you."

I doubted that very much. My mother was a stranger to me. When I was only two hours old, she'd given me to my aunt and gone right back to work at the Henneberrys'. They all lived together in an enormous house in Upper Washbourne, and I heard they had a pool and a beach and plenty of woods for roaming. More grass than a whole park. Barely twenty minutes away by bus.

When I was smaller, I spent a lot of time dreaming about that place. In my head, it was like a picture out of a magazine. The Henneberrys even had a son who was a few years older than me, and I was certain he'd show me around. But in my almost eleven years, my aunt and I had gone to visit exactly zero times.

Aunt Celia got closer to me. Her mouth was moving. Then I heard her say, "I swear sometimes I'm talking to air."

"Sorry." I couldn't help it. I got distracted a lot. Like my teacher said.

I carried the earwig outside to the fire escape and opened my hands to show Wally. Instead of running away though, it stayed on my palm. Never budged. I think it was staring at us. Or maybe it was stunned. Going from a gunky drain to all that sunshine had to be a shock.

"He's jumbo," Wally said, and backed away. "Good thing your aunt's got us men around to protect her."

"Sure is." Wally didn't like bugs either, but I wasn't afraid. And even if I was, I'd never show it. I shook the earwig off and it skittered away.

"Hurry up, Tommie," Aunt Celia called from the bedroom. Then she peeked around the doorframe. "And goodbye, Wally."

Wally packed his kit into the box and climbed down the metal stairs to the street. He crossed the street and disappeared through the glass front doors of his building. His apartment was also on the third floor, but it had three bedrooms because he had a little sister named Sunny. If we caught each other at the right time, Wally and I would wave from our windows. Aunt Celia and I were on a waiting list for the next two-bedroom available, but when we moved, I was really going to miss waving at Wally.

As I went back inside, Aunt Celia was changing her blouse again.

"Why are you fussing so much?"

"Because I want to fuss." She fixed a pink scarf around her neck. "What's wrong with looking nice for my sister?"

I knew Aunt Celia's efforts had nothing to do with my mother and everything to do with her new boyfriend. He was the worst one yet. Whenever they had plans, Aunt Celia waited on the front stoop. I often spied on her from the fire escape. She just stood there, hands clasped, even when it was raining. And when the man finally drove up in his dark car, he barely slowed down. He would sound his horn and she'd dash off the bottom step, her skirt swishing back and forth. Sometimes as he drove away, he'd hang his arm out the window. I always stared at his hand. His fingers. White and fat and ugly. I worried they'd made those five tiny bruises I'd seen on the top of Aunt Celia's arm. I counted them while she was asleep.

"Tom?"

I'd bet a nickel she was going out to see him once my mother had gone.

"Tommie? Can you hear me?"

"Huh?"

"Get ready, I said, and then go downstairs and greet her."

"Greet?"

"Say hello when she arrives. You know. Look sharp."

I'd never done that before. Gone outside to wait. I brushed my teeth and swiped a soapy facecloth on my neck. Then I walked down the three flights of stairs. I had to squeeze past Mr. Pober who was sitting on the stoop of our building. He was the tenant from the bottom floor and he was there every single day, even when it was storming. My aunt told me he'd "gotten unhinged" during the war and he didn't have any family to care for him. He couldn't even hold a job bagging groceries. Aunt Celia said he was forty-four, but I would've guessed he was a hundred and ten. His bald head was covered in spots and his chin needed a shave. There were yellow stains in the armpits of his shirt. I had to hold my breath as I waited because the hot day made him smell even worse.

In the street some kids were playing hopscotch and others were drawing with chalk. I wished I could join them. Mrs. Pinsent said I was the best artist in her class. When we'd made self-portraits with colored pencils, everyone else's were the same, but I made my face with triangles. My mouth and eyes and the bones in my cheeks. Even my hair was all skinny triangles. I'd seen the whole thing in my head like a snapshot and I just copied it down. A few of my classmates snickered, but Mrs. Pinsent told them it was the most creative of the lot. "Demonstrates an advanced distortion of concept," she'd said. I had no idea what she meant, but it sure shut everyone up.

When a lady from another building strolled past our stoop, I could hear Mr. Pober muttering dirty things. About her legs. Her panties. What he'd do if he caught hold of her. She hurried past and brought her purse close to her stomach. I turned around and saw his white tongue poked out between his lips. Whenever he said nasty stuff, which he did constantly, it always made me feel squeamish. And angry. So many times, I imagined grabbing his tongue with my fingers, yanking and yanking until the whole slippery muscle came loose. It would curl and twitch in my fist, and Mr. Pober wouldn't be able to say another filthy word ever again.

"We really ought to feel sorry for him," Aunt Celia had said when I complained. "Think about it. He's got no one to love. No one who loves him. Nothing to fill him up. I'd guess he's an empty sort of fellow, don't you?"

"Not even close," I'd said. He wasn't empty. His entire skull was full of blowflies and moldy garbage. When he called me "a little bastard" because I didn't have a father, my aunt told me to ignore him. She said I was too special to have a father. She said I'd just appeared in the world in a big sploosh. I used to believe her, but then I learned the facts. There was no *sploosh*. Wally and I discovered a book in his apartment, hidden on the top shelf behind all the other books, with drawings of men and women. And it clearly showed babies required a father. That meant mine hadn't wanted me. Same as my mother.

Just then the kids started moving off the pavement. A sparkling mint-green convertible was making its way down the street, swerving left and right to avoid the deep ruts. It pulled up outside our building. Two men were in the front, and my mother was tucked in the back, a polka-dotted kerchief tied over her head. The man in the passenger side hopped out and flipped his seat forward. He was tall and thin and tanned.

"Delivered without a hitch," he said as he offered his arm to my mother. She stepped onto the road. Then he reached into the back and lifted out a stuffed paper bag. She took it from him.

"Thank you, Mr. Fulsome. And thank you, Dr. Henneberry. I hope it wasn't too far out of your way."

"Of course it's out of my way," the driver said. His fingers opened and closed around the steering wheel. "But you're here now."

My mother lowered her head.

"You're such an old grump, Ray," the other one said. He smoothed his wind-ruffled hair back in place. "Ignore him, Esther. We're happy to be of service." He grinned at me as he clambered back into the car. Sunlight bounced off the side of it. The chrome was spotless; not a speck of dust or a splash of muck.

I heard my aunt's voice from above me. "Yoo-hoo!" she yelled out. "Yoo-hoo!"

She was leaning out our bedroom window, one arm stretched high in the air and she was waving. I felt a jolt of fear she might topple over the brick ledge. The pink scarf was knotted on top of her head now, and the color of her lipstick was brighter, redder.

My mother never seemed to notice. She shuffled toward me with the paper bag in her arms. She was shorter and heavier than my aunt, and there were streaks of gray in her brown hair. Even though my aunt worked all night long, it was my mother who had shadows beneath her eyes.

"It's nice to see you, Thomas," she said.

"You, too."

"You've grown."

"Have I?" I guess I had. Unless my pant legs were shrinking.

The car began driving away. The kids circled back to their hopscotch and drawing. A few of them clustered together, deciding who would be cops and who would be robbers. As we climbed the steps past Mr. Pober, Aunt Celia was still hanging out the window and waving. At somebody. I searched up and down the sidewalks, but I couldn't see anyone there.

EXCERPT

Testimony of Dr. Arnold Norton, Greenlake Family Practice
Direct Examination by Prosecutor Clay Fibbs

Q. Dr. Norton, can you tell us where you were last year, on August 19th at 4:00 p.m.?

A. Arriving at the Henneberry residence. For my weekly appointment with Muriel Henneberry.

Q. Weekly?

A. Yes. Muriel worked especially hard to stay on top of her health.

Q. Can you describe what happened as you were coming down Roundwater Heights? Before you reached the Henneberry estate?

A. I was driving slowly.

Q. Why?

A. Mrs. Henneberry valued punctuality, and I was early. So I was lingering a little. When I was about halfway down the street, I heard a loud sound. Several sounds, actually.

Q. Can you describe the sounds?

A. Three bangs, sir. Like large branches cracking, one after the other. It startled me at first, but I assumed an automobile was backfiring.

Q. Please carry on, Dr. Norton.

A. Exactly a minute before four, I drove in and parked. As I got out with my bag, I saw Esther Ware, their housekeeper, dashing up over the lawn at the side of the house. She had an armload of clothing.

Q. What did you do next?

A. I took a few steps and peered down over the slope. I wanted to see why she was running like that. And then I saw them.

Q. **Saw who, Dr. Norton?**

A. The Henneberrys, Muriel and her husband. Down by the pool. I thought it was a trick of the light, all that red. I called out, but neither of them got up from their chairs. I hurried down to them. The top of Mrs. Henneberry's dress was soaked with blood. She had this—a bullet wound in her neck. Dr. Henneberry was slumped forward. I could see the back of his skull, and part of it wasn't there, Mr. Fibbs. It simply wasn't—

Q. **Please continue, Dr. Norton.**

A. Then I realized young Martin was on the bottom of the pool. There was a cloud of blood in the water around him.

Q. **Was anyone else present?**

A. That boy. Right there.

Q. **Let the record show Dr. Norton has indicated the defendant, Thomas Leon Ware. Can you describe what Mr. Ware was doing?**

A. At first he was standing stock-still beside the pool. Then as I approached, he went over to Mrs. Henneberry. Started nudging her, as though he were trying to wake her up.

Q. **What was he wearing?**

A. Not much. Just a pair of blue briefs. At first I thought he'd been injured as well, because he had so much blood on him. But his eyes were clear.

Q. Did you speak to the defendant?

A. No, sir. I was too concerned with Muriel. I took off that
   hat she was wearing and checked for a pulse. I
   checked Dr. Henneberry, too. I wanted to get Martin
   out of the pool, but I can't swim, you see. I can't
   swim. I searched for the gun.

Q. And did you find one?

A. No.

Q. Thank you, Dr. Norton. Now, both Mr. Ware and his
   mother made statements to the police that they'd
   witnessed a man arriving in a black car. They both
   claim this mystery person was the one who shot the
   Henneberrys.

*Defense Counsel: Objection, Your Honor. Is Mr. Fibbs
   testifying?*

The Court: Just ask your questions, Mr. Fibbs.

Q. Sure. Thank you. Dr. Norton, did you see a man
   leaving the property?

A. No, sir.

Q. Did you encounter anyone on your drive down
   Roundwater Heights?

A. Well, yes, I did. James Fulsome drove past me as I
   was making my way. He and Dr. Henneberry were
   friends, I believe. But that was definitely before I
   heard those bangs. Beyond him, there was no one
   else. It was notably quiet.

Q. What happened next, Dr. Norton?

A. I told that child to stay put, and I hurried up to the
   house to alert police.

Q. After calling police, did you see or hear anything out of the ordinary?

A. Yes. Water splashing. I found the housekeeper in the laundry, and she was leaning over a bucket.

Q. What was in the bucket, Dr. Norton?

A. Water. Reddish water. And clothes.

CHAPTER TWO

Once we were inside the apartment, my mother handed me the paper bag. "These are for you," she said.

She always arrived with something for either me or my aunt. A piece of cake wrapped in waxed paper. A leafy handful of mint from the Henneberrys' backyard garden. A storybook that seemed brand new but wasn't. This time, she'd brought a pile of folded shirts, pants, and underwear that used to belong to Martin Henneberry.

"Thank you," I said, even though I always felt odd taking his clothes. He wasn't my brother or my cousin. I didn't know him at all.

My mother sat down at the kitchen table. I sat across from her. Aunt Celia was at the counter making coffee.

"Do you want me to find some music on the radio?" I asked.

"Actually, I'm enjoying listening to the children. It's too quiet at the Henneberrys'."

Laughter was coming in the open window. Wally was probably out there. I heard a tin can being kicked along the road. Someone had a game going.

"Are you excited about your birthday?" she asked.

"Kind of. Aunt Celia's making a double-decker cake."

My mother cleared her throat. "Do you have any summer plans, Thomas?"

"Tons. With Wally." We were going to build a soap box car. Catch tadpoles and swim in the lake. I'd help him babysit Sunny. We'd watch movies Wally's father projected on an old bedsheet.

"Wally's your friend?"

"My best friend."

She smoothed the tablecloth. "It's good to have a best friend."

I smoothed the tablecloth, too. It was white with flowers made of thick red thread. Mrs. King from downstairs had sewn it. "Do you have one?"

"A friend? Mrs. Henneberry, I suppose. Her family has always been kind to me. They've given me a home and a livelihood when I had nothing. I owe them a lot."

My mother and Aunt Celia never talked about what happened when they were teenagers. They'd taken a boat over from England in 1940. They were supposed to go back, but their parents were killed in one of those bombings, and they had no other relatives. The church placed my mother, who was thirteen then, with the Gladstones. They were Mrs. Henneberry's mother and father. But Aunt Celia, who was two years older, got bumped around because there were too many children and not enough families.

"You work there," I said. "I don't think she can be your best friend."

"No?"

"What about when you were in school?"

"I barely remember that. So long ago."

On a tray, Aunt Celia brought two cups of coffee and a glass of milk for me. She went back for a tin and three small plates, and finally sat down. She pushed the tin toward my mother. "Try one of these. Tommie and I made them this morning."

That was a fib. Mrs. King made them. An hour earlier, the smell of baking had wafted up through the floor. Within minutes, she was opening our door with two dozen warm peanut butter cookies, crisscross patterns on their tops. Mrs. King did things like that all the time.

My mother took a bite. "Delicious, Cee. You'll have to give me the recipe."

"Sure. If I can find where I poked it." Aunt Celia wrapped her hands around her cup. "Well, you certainly turned some heads, Esther. Dropped off in such style."

"Dr. Henneberry and Mr. Fulsome were headed into Greenlake." My mother had said Dr. Henneberry was supposed to be the best dentist in town. He owned his own practice. "I preferred to take the bus, but Mrs. Henneberry insisted I tag along."

"I'm sure Dr. Henneberry was happy to oblige."

My mother laid her cookie on a plate. "I'll be taking the bus back. Which gives us"—she peered at her watch—"forty-seven minutes to catch up."

"Well, I do have something to share." Aunt Celia

reached up and touched the knot in the scarf. "I've been spending time with someone special."

My mother's hand went to her cheek. "Oh, that's wonderful, Cee. Tell me everything. How did you meet?"

"At the hospital. A while back."

I kicked my feet back and forth beneath my chair. I'd already heard every detail of that lame story more than once. She'd treated him during her night shift at St. Augustine's after he'd hurt his big toe. Nothing was broken, so she drilled the "tiniest of holes" into the nail to release the blood trapped beneath it. "You might think I'd done magic, Tommie, the way his face relaxed. And then he asked if I was free."

"Free?" I'd said the first time she told me the story. "You're not free." To which she replied she certainly was. "Free and clear to go out if I please."

Since that night my aunt had gotten sneaky. She was going to work earlier and coming home later. Sometimes she snapped at me. I figured she wasn't getting enough sleep.

Then my aunt said, "Can you believe a paperweight brought us together?"

My mother's coffee cup stopped in the air. "A paperweight?"

"Yes. That's what he dropped on his foot. And I cured him." She laughed. "This time, I've caught myself a proper gentleman, too, Esther. A man of means."

I chewed my cookie and tried not to listen anymore because I knew my aunt wouldn't recognize a proper gentleman if one jumped up and bit her. Mrs. King had already explained it all to me. How to charm a girl with flowers or chocolates. Holding open the door. Angling the umbrella so she didn't get wet when it was raining. But the men my aunt invited up kept their shoes on. Called her "dolly." Slurped soda through their teeth. One took our Sears catalogue to the toilet after he'd eaten supper and didn't bother to shut the door. My aunt seemed blind to it.

"Well, what's his name?" my mother said. She put her cup down on the table. "How well do you know him?"

"You needn't be concerned. I won't be making the same mistakes. I know what I'm doing this time."

"Still."

"Really, Esther. Not sure why I mentioned it. It's only been a few dates. I don't want to get ahead of myself."

With her hand, my mother twisted the half-empty cup around and around. "But you are. I can tell by the glint in your eyes. I want you to be careful, is all."

"Careful?" Aunt Celia wagged her finger. "I won't marry him tomorrow, Esther. When that changes, I'll dial you first."

"You know what I mean."

"I do. But that's enough talk about me." Then she said in a singsong voice, "And how's Mr. Vardy?"

My mother flushed.

"Who's Mr. Vardy?" I dipped another cookie in my milk.

"Oh, a man your mother knows at the Henneberrys'," my aunt said to me. "Her very own Mr. Green Thumb."

"What's a mister green thumb?"

"Means he's sweet on her. If half of what your mother tells me is true."

"Celia!"

"When are we going to meet him, Esther?"

"No time soon, I can assure you." She reached over to slap Aunt Celia's hand. But at the same time, she had a wide smile. I could see the dimple on her left cheek. Just like mine. And just like my aunt's. "How I regret telling you anything, Cee. You're going to confuse the boy."

I wasn't confused. I already knew all about how that business worked. Wally and I studied every page of his parents' book. I never got distracted once.

I slipped off the chair and went to get my pencils and my notepad. Even though I wanted to, I wasn't allowed outside until the visit was over. According to my aunt, that would be rude. I sat on the couch, balancing the paper on my knees, and I sketched them side by side. I gave them enormous mouths because they were talking nonstop. About the warm weather and how my aunt wanted something called a kitten heel. Who would've guessed a seaweed bath would do wonders for the skin? Or that Hungry Man's Casserole was the best recipe from May's issue of *Family Circle*? Then a sharp barking came up through the floor, and my aunt explained that Mr. King's cough was getting worse every single day.

"Did you hear?" my aunt said then, in a much softer voice. "They found another one."

I lifted my pencil from the page.

"That's three now?" my mother asked.

"If you can believe it. Same as the other two. Not much in the newspaper, but one of the other nurses told me she was brought to the woods. And just left." I had to strain to hear. "With not a stitch on."

My mother pushed her hand into her chest. "Who could possibly do such a thing?"

"He'll be caught soon enough, no doubt. They're calling him the Greenlake Predator, you know."

She didn't need to whisper. I'd already read about it in Wally's father's newspaper.

"I don't like you taking the bus at those hours, Celia."

"Oh it's fine."

It was fine. My aunt had already said so. She took the bus straight to the hospital and then straight back home to me.

"Is there no one who can give you a ride?"

My aunt bit her lip. "Sometimes my friend is able to drop me."

"Well, he should be collecting you as well. For the time being."

"You needn't worry, Esther. I'm perfectly capable of taking care of myself."

My mother clucked her tongue. "We shouldn't talk too much." When she glanced over at me, she wore an odd expression on her face. As though she were examining a deep sore. With curiosity but also concern that it might get infected or leave a scar. Then she turned her wrist and tapped her watch. "How can time race by like that?"

Both my mother and my aunt stood up at the same time. "I have to get going as well," my aunt said and began to clear the dishes from the table.

I dropped my notepad. "Going where?"

"Hospital. They asked if I could come in early."

"What? They never do that."

"Well, they did today."

I folded my arms across my chest and pouted. I wished she was a day nurse instead of a night nurse. Six evenings out of seven she put on her ironed uniform and white shoes and disappeared out the door. When I was younger, Mrs. King would visit until I fell asleep, but by the time I was seven, I spent most of my evenings alone. I usually woke up a lot, to double-check the door and the windows, but I was never afraid. Not really.

"You should've told them to stuff it," I said.

"Watch your language, young man."

"I didn't say anything wrong."

"Mrs. King's bringing up your supper. And tomorrow we'll spend the whole day together."

That made me feel better.

"Sorry, but I really have to go," my mother said, her hand on the front doorknob.

"We'll walk you down," my aunt said. "Won't we, Tommie?"

I slid off the couch. "Sure."

It always seemed frantic when my mother's visits ended. Even with minutes to spare, she was worried she'd miss the bus back to Upper Washbourne. We followed behind as she clipped down the stairs, her hand skimming over the handrail.

Mr. Pober was still on the front step, but I was glad he was napping. His chin had slumped onto his chest. His neck was like a chicken's.

My mother hugged me first. "I'm sorry I can't be here for your cake." Her mouth turned down. Just a little.

"It's okay," I said. "You came today."

She hugged my aunt and then she scurried down the street. She waited only a moment at the corner before the bus chugged up and stopped.

"Why don't we ever go out there?" I asked my aunt as the door closed behind my mother.

"Not this again, Tommie. The people your mother works for are very important, you know. I'm sure she has her reasons."

"What reasons?"

Aunt Celia put her hand on my shoulder. "Things might change in that creaky old house. Maybe then we'll go visit."

"Change how?"

She brought her head closer to mine. "Mrs. Henneberry. She's not all there, you know. Your mother says a doctor comes every week to treat her."

"Treat her how?"

"With pills, Tommie. Too many pills."

"Oh." I didn't understand. Weren't pills supposed to make someone better?

As the bus turned the corner, my mother waved her hand behind the dusty glass. She didn't look happy, and she didn't look sad. She looked like a photograph, but with all the feelings drained out. And I wondered, like I always did, why she was so nervous about getting back on time. I wondered if she liked being with us in our cozy apartment. I wondered if I should've asked her to stay.

EVIDENCE REPORT

Office of the Coroner, Greenlake
Analysis: Gunshot Residue

Method used: Dermal Nitrate Test (Diphenylamine)

Sample #98 – Paraffin wax molds of hands – gunshot
residue detected near fingertips of right hand
Sample #102 – Paraffin wax molds of hands – gunshot
residue not detected
Sample #103 – Paraffin wax molds of hands – gunshot
residue detected on right palm, back of right hand,
thumb of left hand

Summary:
*Weak positive noted from Dr. Arnold Norton (Sample #98)
indicates secondary transference or contamination (attend-
ing to victims or touching surrounding area).*

*Negative result noted from Esther Ware (Sample #102)
indicates she was not in the vicinity when a firearm was
discharged, or gunshot residue had been removed through
activity (such as hand washing).*

*Positive result noted from Thomas Ware (Sample #103)
indicates he discharged a firearm, was in close proximity to
someone discharging a firearm, or had both left and right
hands in the environment where a firearm was discharged.*

Date of Report: 09/09/1958
File: GLCC9-9-58

CHAPTER THREE

Aunt Celia emerged from the bedroom just before lunchtime. She came into the living room in her long, green silky robe and kissed the top of my head. "Happy birthday, darling!"

"Thanks," I said.

"How does it feel to be a whole year older?"

"Pretty much the same as yesterday."

She yawned, then tilted her head toward the open window. Somewhere outside a band was thumping. A drum. A trumpet, maybe. A man was singing in a deep voice.

"It's already started."

"The music? That's for me?"

"It absolutely is. But it's for everyone else, too. It's an initiative."

"What does that mean?"

"An endeavor to lift our spirits, they're calling it." She laughed. "Some paper pushers thought just living in Lower Washbourne is enough to give us the blues. We're fine as we are, but we won't turn down free Sunday concerts."

My aunt drank a cup of black coffee and ate one of Mrs. King's cookies from the tin box. Then she took the pins from her curls, put on a lemon-colored dress, and covered her lips in red lipstick. I wore one of Martin Henneberry's cotton button-up shirts from the paper bag. Dampened my short hair to smooth it.

We filled our picnic basket and off we went, strolling arm in arm along the streets, then down a path toward the lake. Along the edge of the water there was a wide strip of worn grass. The ground was already crowded, but we found a small area in the shade of an oak tree. I spread out our blanket and smoothed the wrinkles. Then my aunt knelt down and unpacked egg salad sandwiches, two glass jars filled with peach juice, and a cherry coconut square cut into two pieces. We sat side by side, our legs extended. The entire time we ate, my aunt was watching the musicians as they played their brass instruments. She was wearing her navy shoes with the buckles, and she kicked them off, wiggled her toes. Her shoulders tilted forward one at a time, making her brown curls shake.

"You look pretty," I said. Mrs. King told me it was important to give compliments. "Even if you were drenched in a storm, you'd still be pretty."

"Oh thank you, Tommie. And you look handsome. Even if you got spun around and spit out of a tornado, you'd still be handsome." She wrapped her arm around me and pulled me toward her. "Isn't this a birthday treat? Isn't it, though?"

It was. Half our neighborhood was there, but it still felt like just the two of us.

A skinny man wearing a baggy suit and crumpled hat stepped among the blankets, stopping now and again. From inside his front pocket, he withdrew colored balloons, stretching them between his hands before bringing them to his mouth. Fingers nipping and twisting, and I winced waiting for the pop, but it never came. Two balloons made a hammer. Four balloons made a dog with short legs. When he stopped in front of my aunt, he winked at her, and from a pair of pink balloons he made a circle and then attached two rounded ears.

"I could be one of those mouse girls," she said as she eased it over her hair. "Wouldn't that be fun?" She gave him a nickel, even though he didn't ask.

My aunt was the first one up to dance. Swaying side to side. Her fat mouse ears bobbing on top of her head. When the pace of the music increased, she spread her fingers and waggled her hands, her feet kicking out. "Come on, Tommie." Her mouth was wide, and she was breathless.

I lowered my head.

"Don't be shy. You're my main squeeze."

I hesitated, then stood. "I don't know how. I don't know how to dance."

"Nothing to it." She slid alongside me, leaning slightly at the waist. Sunlight caught in her hair and in her smile. "Snap your fingers, Tommie."

"Like this?"

"Close enough. Then side to side."

I went side to side.

"Now bend your knees. Up and down. Up and down. Easy as apple pie."

I tried, but my body didn't want to move the way hers did.

She spun me around and grabbed my fingers. Shook them. My arms rippled right up to my neck. "Oh, you're so stiff, darling."

When she let me go, I fixed my arms like I was a wooden puppet with hinges. I changed positions in short slow bursts, opening and closing my jaw. She was laughing and laughing, in the best way. It made me forget all about the man she'd met at the hospital. Forget about those nights she left early and came home late. Her happiness filled me up. I never wanted that laughter to stop.

When she finally caught her breath, her eyes were sparkling. "You've got moves," she said. "You surely do." She imitated me, and then she lifted the mouse ear balloons off her head and pushed them down on mine. "You never know, my love. It could just catch on."

Hot dogs and warm buns and an iced ginger cake with eleven candles. "Hurry up," Wally shrieked. "Make a wish!"

Eleven tiny yellow flames. Everyone was watching me. My aunt. Mrs. King. Wally. I heard my mother's

voice in my head. *I'm sorry I can't be here for your cake.*
I saw her waving at me as the bus was taking her back
to that perfect place I'd never been. Then my wish was
there, and I squeezed my eyes shut and my mouth
shut. *I want to see where my mother lives. I want to
swim in the Henneberrys' pool. I want to run on their
beach and climb their trees and open their refrigerator
and get lost in—*

"Alright, alright." Wally poked my ribs. "How long
does one wish take?"

I grinned and poked him back.

After I'd blown out all the candles, my aunt cut generous slices of the cake and passed them around.

Wally finished his in ten seconds. "I'm stuffed." His
lips were covered in icing.

I shoved the last forkful into my mouth. "Me, too.
Just busting."

Mrs. King said, "The crumb on the cake is especially
fine, Celia."

"I do love those box mixes." Aunt Celia gathered up
the dirty plates. "Makes life so much easier, and they're
nearly impossible to ruin."

Beside the cake, there were two wrapped presents. A
pale blue cup towel covered a third. "Can I?"

"I guess it's time," Aunt Celia said. "But Wally's
mother already called him home. Open his first."

I ripped the paper off Wally's gift. It was a Slinky. I'd
had one before but it got twisted in five minutes and I
couldn't fix it.

"Thanks! It's great."

"We'll have races, okay? Down the stairs."

"I bet you a penny I'll win."

"Don't do it, Wally." Aunt Celia put her hands on her hips. "He doesn't have a single cent to spare."

Wally shook his head. "It's okay, Miss Ware. My father says I'm not allowed to make bets anyway. He says men can lose a lot like that."

"They sure can," Mrs. King said. "Smart boy."

"I was only joking." I worked the Slinky back and forth between my hands. "Be like taking money from a baby."

Wally punched me in the arm and ran out the door. Within seconds, the slap of his feet as he ran across the street came in through the open window.

"You can open our gift now," Mrs. King said. She shifted her chair closer. "From Mr. King, too. He's sorry he couldn't be here."

She handed me a wrapped box, and I tore away the paper. "Thank you, Mrs. King. I've always wanted one!" A View-Master.

"There's extra slide things, too. Mr. King insisted. Taped on the bottom. One with animals. And I think another with big cities. Or landmarks."

"I love it. I really love it." I lifted the lid off the box. A shiny brown Model E, same as Wally had, and it had a big white knob on the side to shift the photographs. I slid in a cardboard reel. When I brought it to my face and peeked through the eyeholes, I could see a field of yellow grass. A lion was yawning. His sharp teeth were right in front of my face. "Whoa," I whispered.

"You need good lighting to see all the details," my aunt said. She reached over and flicked the light switch. The white glass ball over the kitchen table glowed.

"Double whoa!"

Then Mr. King's coughing was coming up through the floorboards. Mrs. King scraped back her chair. "I should go check on him. But this evening's been lovely. A real treat."

My aunt pushed my arm gently. "Don't forget your manners, Tommie."

"Oh, yeah." I hopped up and hugged Mrs. King. The apartment door was propped open, so cool air would come in. "Thanks again for the present. Tell Mr. King thanks, too. I really love it."

She squeezed me into her soft chest, and then held my shoulders. "I just wish it was more."

"How could it be more, Mrs. King? The whole world's in there!"

She closed her eyes for a second, and when she opened them, they were watery. She let go of me and went out into the hallway.

My aunt flopped down on the couch. "Where do you get that, Tommie?"

I glanced at my hands. "Get what?"

"That ability. Knowing exactly what to say, and when to say it."

"I do?"

"Yep. You didn't get it from me. And you most certainly didn't get it from your mother."

I smiled. *Maybe I got it from my father, whoever he was. Maybe he had all the right words.* "Can I see what's under there now?" I pointed at the cup towel on the table.

"Are you certain you're ready for this?"

"I am."

"Just so you're aware, both your mother and I decided on this. You know she hates to miss these special occasions."

I took the corner of the cloth and yanked it off. A perfect orange goldfish. In a round glass bowl. Swimming in slow circles.

I could barely say a word. I went to the couch and hugged my aunt.

"Are you ready for pet ownership?"

I nodded. "It's one hundred and ten percent exactly what I wanted."

"You've got to be careful not to overfeed. Apparently, that little guy can grow to horrifying proportions."

With careful steps, I carried the bowl over to the coffee table. I couldn't take my eyes off him. His beautiful orange fins, like a sunrise. "Hi there," I said. His mouth opened in a circle like he was surprised, too.

"What're you going to name him?"

"Not sure," I said. "What about George?"

"Perfect. George is an upstanding name."

I lay down on the couch. It was the best birthday I'd ever had. My aunt placed a blanket over my legs and told me a story where George ate constantly and grew to "a tremendous size." He moved from bowl to sink to bucket to bathtub. When I peered at him, he recognized me, darted up through the water to bite my hand. He was a greedy bugger, my aunt said, always asking for more food. Soon word spread through Lower Washbourne, then Upper, then Greenlake, and Slipton County, and finally the whole country. My fish became world famous. My aunt and I wrestled him into a specially made glass bowl, and a crane lifted him onto the flat bed of a truck. We drove all over, the pair of us, selling tickets to show him off. "We got so rich," my aunt said. "Dollar bills were spilling out of our pockets." Everyone loved George the Gigantic Goldfish.

My eyes grew heavy, and with each blink it was harder to stay awake. Aunt Celia was sitting in the chair with a book in her hand. But she wasn't reading. Instead she was watching me as I dozed on the couch. At some point, I dreamt the phone rang. When I opened my eyes, I realized it wasn't a dream at all. Her shoulder was curled around the receiver and her hand cupped the mouthpiece. After she hung up, she moved about the apartment, quietly opening and closing drawers. The clothes hangers clattered softly. She tied her bright pink scarf around her neck. I must have fallen asleep again. When I woke, she was pulling the blanket up to my shoulder and tucking the edges in around my back. She smoothed her hand over my face and kissed my forehead. She might have whispered in my ear that she loved me. Loved me best of all. Or maybe I was imagining that. I didn't know for sure.

EXCERPT

Testimony of Mr. James Fulsome

Direct Examination by Prosecutor Clay Fibbs

Q. How long, Mr. Fulsome, had you known Dr. Henneberry?

A. Since we were in grade school. Climbing trees and stealing candy.

Q. So it's safe to say you two had a long friendship?

A. Yes, sir. He was like a brother to me. Closer. We never fought like brothers might.

Q. You were stationed together during the war?

A. That we were. Ray was the dental officer. Martin was a newborn when Ray shipped out, and he was missing that little guy something fierce. Missing Muriel, too. We kept each other's spirits up. We looked after one a—

Q. Thank you, Mr. Fulsome. I know this is difficult, but I'd like to talk about the day the Henneberry family was killed. You visited them, is that correct?

A. Yes, sir.

Q. And how would you describe that visit?

A. Nothing out of the ordinary. Clear skies, the sun was shining. Ray and Muriel were relaxing on lawn chairs by the pool. Muriel was wearing this huge brimmed hat, and she had to lift up the front every time she spoke. I teased she was pretending to be a movie star.

Q. Did they invite you to stay?

A. They did, but I already had dinner plans. I took a glass of lemonade that Esther, their housekeeper, brought

down to the pool. I talked to Ray some about getting
out for a round of golf before the weather turned.
Then he darted up to the house and came back with
his newest prized possession.

Q. And what was that?

A. A Colt Python. Ray was something of a collector. Had
a cabinet of guns in his study. He wanted to show off
his latest addition.

Q. Did you handle the gun, Mr. Fulsome?

A. No, sir. I just admired it. I'm not an enthusiast like Ray
was, but this one had a beautiful blue-steeled finish.

Q. Did you know whether or not the gun was loaded?

A. I did not. And I didn't ask.

Q. What did he do next?

A. He put it down. On the table beside the lemonade.

Q. He seemed unconcerned about it?

A. I was about to leave, so I suppose he wanted to shake
my hand. I figured he'd lock it away as soon as I'd
gone. Ray was responsible.

Q. Did you see Martin Henneberry on your visit?

A. No, sir. Muriel said he was off with friends.

Q. And what about Thomas Ware? Was he in the
vicinity?

A. Not at first, but then I noticed him near the edge of
the woods.

Q. Standing there?

A. Not quite. He was weaving among the trees. Twice I
saw him lean his forehead against a birch. Then pull
his head back and let it bang. Pretty hard, I'd say.

Q. **Hurting himself?**

A. Sure did seem that way. I thought to ask Ray if the kid had gone off the deep end, but Ray didn't seem fazed. And Muriel, I dare say she was having a snooze under that ridiculous hat.

Q. **Did you have any direct interaction with Mr. Ware? Exchange any words?**

A. No. Not a squeak. He was just meandering toward us. Edging closer, I'd say.

Q. **And closer to the table where the gun and the lemonade were?**

A. That too. Yes, sir. His head looked raw.

Q. **Did you think this behavior was odd?**

A. I thought it was plenty odd. I don't know why I got up and left. I should've stayed . . . I'm sorry. I . . .

Q. **Mr. Fulsome?**

A. I lost everything that day. Ray. And Muriel. I lost everything I loved.

Q. **One last question. Did you pass anyone as you were leaving?**

A. That doctor. Dr. Norton. He was slinking along the road in his car, like some, like some sort of—

Q. **Some sort of what, Mr. Fulsome?**

A. Nothing. He was heading to his appointment with Muriel.

CHAPTER FOUR

I awoke from a deep sleep in the gray just before sunrise. Still on the couch with the blanket over me, George circling around in his bowl. Our apartment felt hollow. I went to the bedroom door and checked the bed. Aunt Celia hadn't come home yet.

A warm breeze, smelling of garbage, came between the curtains. Bottles of milk tinkled. A cat hissed. Footsteps, then, on the sidewalk below. Not my aunt's, though. I didn't even need to check. My skin turned to goose bumps, and I wasn't sure why, but I had a sick taste in my mouth. Maybe too much birthday cake, and I'd forgotten to brush my teeth again. Half the cake was still on the counter. Uncovered and drying out.

I waited and waited. Gradually the sun came up. I was supposed to be getting ready for school, eating breakfast, rinsing my bowl, putting my pencils and scribblers into my bookbag. I went to the kitchen and shook my metal lunchbox. My aunt always made my sandwich when she came home from her shift, but there was nothing inside. Where was she?

Part of me was worried and I wondered if I should go tell Mrs. King that my aunt was really late. But another part, a much heavier part, was angry. She was with that man who'd smashed his toe, and she'd forgotten all about me. She'd done this twice before and dashed in at the last minute with hasty apologies about working late or getting caught up in conversation with the other nurses. Which were lies. I paced around and around the apartment, thinking of all the nasty things I'd yell at her when she tried to sneak through that door.

From the bedroom window, I watched the road. On the pavement below, someone had drawn a life-size cowboy with a hat and two pistols in his holster. The street was filling up with kids. Parents, too. Men dressed for work. Women with baby strollers. Everyone going where they needed to go on a Monday morning. Except Mr. Pober, of course. His head was leaning against the railing. Some days he stayed that way until noon, snoring and puffing air. There was no sign of my aunt.

Wally was coming out of his building with his sister, Sunny. He noticed me in the window. "Hey, Tommie! Want me to wait?"

I crouched down so he couldn't see me anymore. I wasn't going anywhere until Aunt Celia got home. I didn't even care if I got into trouble.

"Tommie!" he yelled again.

Then I heard his mother. "We need to get going, Wallace. I'm sure he'll catch up."

My stomach grumbled, but I wasn't going to eat a single thing, either. I had to feed George, though. I walked over to his bowl, and when I opened the package of food, he swam to the glass. "Only as much as the size of his eye," Aunt Celia had told me. "Otherwise things could get out of control." I really wanted to ask her how big his eye was, just to make sure, but she still wasn't home. George tapped against the glass. He was probably starving. I sprinkled in some flakes and he darted up to eat.

Where was my aunt?

I paced some more. Then the tinny ring of the telephone. It cut through the air and the fright of it made my hands tingle. I picked up the receiver and brought it to my ear, but I didn't say hello. On the other end of the line, someone was breathing in, breathing out. A clacking, like a typewriter. I pressed the phone harder against my skull. *Aunt Celia?*

"Miss Ware?"

My hope deflated. I recognized Mrs. Pinsent's voice from school. Recess had come, and she must be calling from the office. "Thomas is tardy today, Miss Ware. You need to send that boy on his way. Are you there?" I laid the receiver down in its cradle.

As I sat on the couch, I watched George and then watched the door. My head was getting hot because I was getting angrier and angrier. I got up and pushed the back of a kitchen chair under the doorknob. A clever trick I saw in a movie once. When she finally returned, she'd try her key, but she wouldn't be able to open the door. She could knock forever, but she'd have to stay out there in the hallway. Until I was good and ready. Maybe, after a while, she'd begin to cry. She was probably going to be tired from whatever she'd been doing. I'd bet it was something from that book at Wally's place. Drawings of a naked man lying on top of a naked woman. Mr. Pober would know, too, and he'd soon be saying worse stuff.

Just before lunchtime, I heard a bunch of footsteps climbing the stairs. The doorknob rattled. Then tapping. I jumped up. She was home. Maybe she'd brought him, too. Thinking I wasn't going to be there. *Well, I fooled her.* The chair was still blocking the way. How long was I going to wait? More tapping. Harder this time. "You're in trouble," I yelled. "You're in big trouble!"

But it was Mrs. King who called through the wood. "It's just me, Tom, love. I rang the school and they said you were absent. Can you—can you unlock?"

I counted to ten and then pressed my ear into the door.

"In the woods near the hospital." A man was talking. "Newlywed couple out for a stroll. Saw her leg in the bushes."

"It can't be." Mrs. King's voice was faint. ". . . sort of mistake."

"Panties twisted around—"

"Ernst." A different man. "C'mon. We got a lady here."

What are they talking about?

More banging. "Thomas! You need to open this door at once."

My hand was moving in slow motion. I watched it reach out and pull back the chair and open the door. Even though I told it not to. Like my mind knew something horrible was on the other side, but my muscles didn't realize.

"Finally," Mrs. King said. She stepped inside and held on to the top of my arm. Both of the men were wearing gray suits. One had a blue-and-yellow-striped tie and a mustard-colored shirt. The other had a burgundy tie. When he put his hand on his hip, I could see his burgundy suspenders.

"Am I in trouble?"

"No, dear. No, of course not."

"I skipped school."

"Never mind that now. Have you heard from Celia?"

"No," I said. "She's not home yet from her shift. And I know I should've got ready by myself and went with Wally, but I was so mad, Mrs. King, I had to wait and give her an earful."

"It's okay, Tom, love." She had her palm against her cheek. "Um, this is Detective O'Connor. And his partner, Detective—"

"Detective Miller, ma'am."

"I'm sorry. I forgot."

"Not a worry."

She tugged me over to the couch and pushed in right next to me. The side of her body was warm. "These gentlemen need to talk to you, dear." She took my hand in hers, smoothing it, like water over a stone. "About your aunt Celia."

Detective Miller went to the kitchen table and turned a chair so he faced me. Detective O'Connor stood behind him with his arms folded.

"Thomas, is it?" Detective Miller said.

"Or Tommie."

"Tommie. Gotcha. That your fish?" He pointed at the coffee table.

"Yeah, he's George."

"Lot of bother keeping the bowl clean? Any smell?"

"Not so far," I said. "I only got him yesterday."

"I was thinking about getting one for my boy. About your age. Teach him a bit of responsibility and all."

"Sure, yeah. He's a good pet so far."

Detective O'Connor started tapping his foot. He wiped his nose with the back of his hand. "Chuck? Can we lighten up on the chitchat?"

Detective Miller reached inside the front of his suit and took out a notepad. "Okay if we ask you a couple of questions, Tommie?" He flipped open the cover. "Your mother took the bus to Greenlake last night?"

"My mother?"

"No, no," Mrs. King said. "Celia Ware is his aunt. His mother lives out at the Henneberrys'. She works there, and the two of them—"

"Muriel and Raymond Henneberry?" Detective O'Connor said. "In Upper Washbourne?"

"Yes, sir. That's the family."

Hands deep in his pockets, he swayed back and forth on his heels. "That's some fine people right there. Fine, fine people."

"I think we catch your drift, Ernst," Detective Miller said. "Now, Tommie. Your aunt, then?"

"She's a nurse," I said. "At St. Augustine's. Sometimes she works real late, though. Or goes out after her shift."

"Goes out with friends? Other nurses?"

"No." I scrunched my toes into the carpet. "A man."

Detective Miller wrote on his notepad. "What man?"

"Aunt Celia says he's a proper gentleman. But he's not, is he, Mrs. King?"

Mrs. King was nodding. "Not by my estimates. He never once came in to introduce himself. I don't have a good feeling about him, but she's smitten."

"Anything else you can tell me? His name? Where he works?"

I shrugged. What could I say? He drove a black car? At the end of his wrist was the whitest hand? Then I remembered. "He hurt his foot with a paperweight."

"That's exactly right," Mrs. King said. "She treated him at the hospital. That's how they met."

"We can certainly check into that."

"Yeah," Detective O'Connor said. "Maybe some of the other nurses knew who she spent her nights with."

Mrs. King straightened her back. "She has not *spent* her nights with anyone, sir. Other than those patients at St. Augustine's."

Detective Miller cleared his throat. "He meant we'll ask around at the hospital, ma'am. They'll have records of recent patients."

I tugged my hand away from Mrs. King's. "Detective Miller? I called there too many times and now I'm not allowed to unless it's an emergency. But you could call, right?"

"Well, Tommie, we agreed you'd have a conversation with Mrs. King here. It's better to hear—"

Suddenly Mrs. King was sobbing. She clamped a hand around my shoulder. The other hand covered her mouth. Her back shook. "I can't. I don't believe it."

My mouth went dry. I'd never seen Mrs. King so upset, and my heart became a rabbit thumping in my chest.

"I understand, ma'am. Awful hard to wrap your head around it." Detective Miller leaned forward in his chair. "Sonny, can we have a man-to-man?"

"Um? Yes, sir?"

"It's about your aunt."

By the lines between his eyebrows, I could tell he was going to say something terrible. I tried to force my mind to drift away. I watched the other detective as he wandered into the bedroom. He opened the drawers of our dresser. He shook the pages of the paperback on Aunt Celia's night table. He flipped through her daily calendar. She said people should never touch others' belongings without permission. He didn't have permission.

"Sport? You with me?"

I was, though I didn't want to be.

"Your aunt got hurt last night. Hurt real bad."

Mrs. King sobbed even louder.

"Like she fell down? Broke something?" I asked. That was why those newlyweds saw a leg in the woods. She'd slipped.

"No. Not like that. I'm sorry, I really am, to tell you this."

"Tell me what?"

"That you've lost her."

Officer O'Connor whistled. I turned back to the bedroom door. With pinched fingers, he lifted a bra that was on the end of our bed. "Can't fathom why any woman would be strolling around Greenlake at night. No common sense, really."

"Ernst, will you get out of there?"

I tried to stand up, but Mrs. King wouldn't let me go. "But we can find her again, right? You can. You're the police. Heck, you guys can find anybody."

"No, sport. We can't. A different kind of lost."

What other kind of lost is there?

Mrs. King took a tissue out of the fold of her sleeve and blew her nose. "Don't worry," she croaked. "Your mother's coming soon."

Everything was confusing. Why couldn't Mrs. King watch me until Aunt Celia came home? All three of them were staring at me. In a blink, a hundred pounds of rocks pushed on my spine, wanting to flatten me, but I shoved against Mrs. King again. I was on my feet. Teetering back and forth. "I don't want my mother!"

"Steady, boy." Detective O'Connor took a step closer. "Mind your tone."

"Leave him be, Ernst. He's upset." Then to me, "You're going to be okay, sport. We're going to make sure you're well cared for. Do you understand?"

I was filling up with white steam and the pressure was getting tighter and tighter and I needed to yell. As loud I could. "She's with him. She's got to be with him."

"Calm yourself, now. Try to calm yourself down."

I was gasping. "She'd never go into in the woods! Never ever! Not without me to protect her. There are—"

Bugs. Crawling around in the dirt.

She's afraid of them.

Trace Analysis Report Summary – Hair
Division of Medical Examiner's Office

Overview:

Nine hairs, recovered during the Henneberry investigation, were submitted to the lab for analysis. Two were matched to the victims. From the remaining seven unknowns, two were removed from Raymond Henneberry's shirt (lower front left panel). Four were recovered from Muriel Henneberry's dress (two from front skirt hem, two from front right chest). One was recovered from the wash bucket.* Microscopic analyses were performed on the seven unknowns and compared to known Samples GL1-GL4 provided by Greenlake Police Department (see below for identification).

Evaluation:

Both hairs on Raymond Henneberry were consistent with Sample GL2. Two of the hairs on Muriel Henneberry were identified as non-human, belonging to a canine.** One hair was consistent with Sample GL3. One hair was inconsistent with samples provided. We were unable to evaluate the hair found inside the wash bucket. It was damaged due to prolonged exposure to water and chemical cleaners. No reliable match could be identified.

Identification of Samples:

Sample GL1 – Arnold Norton
Sample GL2 – James Fulsome

Sample GL3 – Esther Ware
Sample GL4 – Thomas Ware

----

*Wash bucket used by Esther Ware to clean clothing on the date of the crime.

**Reports indicate Martin Henneberry, at one time, was in possession of a black dog.

File: GLCME1-1-58

CHAPTER FIVE

Late afternoon, my mother came to collect me from the apartment. Her face and eyes were red and swollen, and she held me for a long time. Even though she said "Don't be worried," her scratchy voice was heavy with it.

"I'm not." I knew it was all a stupid mistake. Any second Aunt Celia was going to barrel through that door and flood the room with all her brightness. Her hair would be messed, and she'd have an excuse that would make me scowl. She'd tell me to "Wipe that nasty look off your mug," and she'd rub her hands all over my face. My mother would be flustered over her wasted afternoon. I'd be angry, but I wouldn't be able to keep it up for long.

My mother sniffed. "We best get on with things. So we don't miss the bus."

She made me wash, and while I was scrubbing my neck, she ironed the creases from one of Martin Henneberry's shirts. She packed some of my clothes in Aunt Celia's blue suitcase, and when I asked her what else I could take, she said nothing. "There isn't much room there."

"Yeah, there is." I imagined the Henneberrys' property. "There's tons of room."

She unplugged the iron, wrapped the cord around the body. "No, Thomas. There isn't."

"What about all my stuff?" My drawings. My books. The crocheted blanket Mrs. King had made me with my name in blue thread. My brand-new Slinky and View-Master.

"Later," she said.

"When later?"

"I don't have all the answers, Thomas." Her forehead was glistening. She flipped down the metal tabs on the suitcase, pushed with her thumbs until they clicked.

I pointed at the coffee table. "George is coming. He can't manage without me." He was swimming around his glass bowl. As he circled past, I thought he slowed down to gape at me. No way could he fend for himself.

"No pets," my mother said. Her hands were on her hips. "We need to be practical."

"But you picked him. You and—" Her name stuck in my throat. Like a hair I couldn't cough out.

"I'm sorry. We can't."

My hands turned into fists. I wanted to run at her and punch her. "Then I'm not budging."

"Thomas, don't be—"

"I'll sit here and wait for her to come back." Tears were running down my cheeks. I could taste the salt. "What's she going to think when she realizes I'm gone? She's going to be mad."

My mother sighed and then she went to the kitchen and cut a piece of plastic wrap for the mouth of the bowl. She popped a rubber band around it to secure it in place.

I carried George's bowl and she carried the suitcase down the flights of stairs. It banged against her leg. As we went by Mrs. King's apartment, she came out into the hallway. She told my mother how sorry she was, and then squeezed me again. I breathed her in and kept her smell in my lungs. I didn't want to let it out.

"Come back and see me, okay?" she whispered in my ear.

"I won't be gone long," I told her, and then my mother waved her free hand.

"Thomas?"

We stepped past Mr. Pober on the front step. His head was still against the railing and his mouth was hanging open. He opened one eye and yawned. The corners of his lips were cracked and yellow. Then he sat up and glared at my mother.

"Pretty one's finally done with the kid, huh?" he said. "Who's she dallying with this time?" He grinned, and his squinty eyes got even squintier.

"No one," I said through clenched teeth. "She's at her job."

"Don't talk to that man," my mother said as she stepped onto the sidewalk. "Should be ashamed of himself."

"Dirty girl. Dirty, dirty girl."

"She is not!" I screamed this time, twisted fast and kicked Mr. Pober, full force, in his shin. George's water splashed against the plastic. "She's not dirty. And she's not a girl, idiot! She's thirty—she's twenty-eight!"

He opened his mouth and snickered. "You got a feisty one there, lady."

"Thomas!" My mother grabbed my arm and I lurched off the step. "You can't act like that. Apologize!"

"I will not. You can't make me. He said—"

"I don't care what he said. I care about how you act. You can't be like that where we're going."

I pressed my lips together and jammed George's bowl into my rib bones until they ached.

"Fine," she said. "Forget it. If we don't hurry, we'll miss our ride."

Wally came running up to me. School was already out. "Why'd you skip today?"

I shrugged.

He pointed at the suitcase. "You going on a trip?" He began to trail along with us to the bus stop.

"Sorta."

"When're you coming back?"

"Soon. Real soon." I pretended not to hear my mother sigh again.

"Good. We got to finish our nameplates. My father says I can't start another piece of wood until I get that done, and I want us to make them together."

"Okay. I'll come get you."

"Cool," he said.

My mother and I got on the bus. As it puttered away, I glanced back at my street. There were ropes of laundry and plenty of potholes and the sidewalks were cracked and covered in chalk. Mr. Pober was rubbing his hand over the spot where I kicked him. That made me feel better. Wally waved, and I waved back. *Soon*, I told myself in my head. *Real soon*. Once the police sorted this out, I'd come home.

The air inside the bus was thick with the stench of exhaust. I leaned my head against the rattling window and closed my eyes. My head felt woozy, but I needed to keep everything straight. My aunt had gone to work. On her way home, she'd gotten hurt. And now she was lost. I was with my mother and we were on our way to the Henneberrys'.

Then all at once I remembered my wish. My birthday wish. The bottom of my stomach dropped, and I pulled my knees up to my chin.

I knew. Some part of this was my fault. I'd gotten exactly what I wanted. But I hadn't meant for it to happen this way.

As we drove away from apartment buildings and noisy streets and sour smells, everything outside the window started to change. More grass. More trees. No trash blown into corners. Big houses with white fences. Kids with shiny bicycles. Dogs that didn't have their ribs sticking out. I guessed we were now in Upper Washbourne.

After a while, the driver hollered, "Last stop!"

"This is us," my mother said. I followed her off the bus.

The air was different. Calmer, quieter, cleaner. A white wooden signpost read "Roundwater Heights," and we began walking down a smooth, wide road. High overhead, leafy branches wove together, giving us shade. Every now and again we passed an enormous house that was set back from the road. Properties were outlined by metal fences with spiked tops, or tall cedar hedges cut into sharp rectangles. Nothing was out of place. I wanted to break a branch or rip off some leaves and throw them on the ground. Everything was too perfect.

"Please don't dawdle, Thomas," my mother said over her shoulder.

I tried to hurry, but I had a pebble in my shoe, and George's water kept splashing and leaking out around the plastic cover. All this jerking about, I didn't want him to feel sick. What if he vomited in his water? And that vomit got trapped in his gills? When the road curved slightly, I finally saw something that didn't belong. A black car with muck-splattered sides. A front light was smashed out. It was stopped in the middle of the road, idling. As my mother walked past, the driver put the car in gear and drove away.

I rushed to catch up to her. "Who was that?"

"I don't know. People come around constantly. To dream, I guess."

My mother turned and went between two black iron gates that were held open with spikes stuck in the ground. After walking partway up a long gravel driveway, she paused. Set the suitcase down and took a handkerchief from her purse to dab her face.

"This is where I work," she said.

This was the Henneberrys'? This was where my mother lived? It was even grander than I'd pictured. More like a small hotel than a home. A dozen tall windows lined both the top and bottom floors. The entire structure was made of gray stone, and a bright white porch went across the front. I counted eight massive pots overflowing with vines and red flowers. Mowed grass rolled down in soft slopes until it hit a dense green forest. Nearer the woods on the left side, a rectangular pool sparkled.

If I hadn't been standing right there, I wouldn't have believed it was real. *How can someone have so much?* Aunt Celia had told me it was plain old luck. Mr. Gladstone, Mrs. Henneberry's father, had owned several factories, and as certain items were needed during the war, he'd made a "ridiculous amount of money."

Clouds skittered across the sky, making me feel as though the house was falling forward. I held George tight to my chest. I saw my mother take a deep breath. Then another.

"Thomas?"

"Yeah?"

"You need to be careful here. Do you understand?"

"You mean mind my manners?"

"That, too. But I mean stay close at hand, okay? Where I can find you." She shifted from one leg to the other. Then she picked up the suitcase and said, "We'd better go inside."

As she took quick steps up the driveway, I tried to stay beside her, like she'd asked. We were nearly at the house when I heard sharp tapping. Like a bird's beak striking glass. I leaned my neck all the way back and saw a shape in one of the upper windows. A boy. Older than me. That had to be Martin. At first he was smiling, but then he turned his head and pressed the side of his face against the window. He slumped his shoulder an inch or two so that his eye stretched, and his open mouth twisted. I lifted my hand, but he just stayed there. Half of him. Distorted and perfectly still.

My mother hurried along a stone walkway around the left side of the house. As I followed her, I looked at the pool again. The water was crystal blue and not a single person was swimming. If I raced down the slope and leaped, I'd be splashing about in two seconds.

"This way, Thomas," she called, and we went through a door that was beside a white rosebush. The hallway was dimly lit. I stayed close to her as she walked through a kitchen, and then into a huge area that seemed entirely for laundry. Piles of folded towels and sheets sat on a long table, and damp shirts hung from pipes along the low ceiling. My mother went past an electric washer and dryer, and into another room.

It was a cramped bedroom, not much larger than a closet. The floor was linoleum, and the walls were dingy white. A single bed was pushed into a corner. Beneath the windowsill on the far wall, an army cot had been set up. There was a wooden dresser and a sink with a mirror. "The bathroom's through there," my mother said, pointing to a door. I peered inside, saw a green toilet and a green bathtub that was half the size of our bathtub at the apartment. Across from the tub was a square window up high. No curtain covered it, but green branches from a shrub pressed against the glass, blocking out any light. Outside the larger bedroom window, the shadows had turned long and gray. I shivered.

"Mr. Vardy brought in the cot for you," my mother said. I remembered that name. Her Mr. Green Thumb. "I'll get a sheet and blanket later," she continued. "Though it probably won't be as comfortable as you're used to."

"It doesn't matter," I said. All my curiosity about my mother's world had dissolved. Now I was just itching to go home.

"It does matter. I want you to be okay." She ran her hand over a wrinkle on her bed. Her skin hitched on the fabric. "Mrs. Henneberry said you can stay for the summer."

"What? The whole summer? No way!" I sat down on the cot, George's bowl balanced on my lap.

"Thomas, please."

"I'm not," I said. I picked off the rubber band, the wet plastic, and shoved them into my shorts pocket. "You can't make me."

My mother straightened the lamp on the night table. She didn't smile or nod in agreement, like I wished she would. Instead, she said, "Put your things away. I've emptied the two bottom drawers." Then she went into the bathroom and closed the door.

I placed George's bowl on the windowsill. Then I took my clothes—Martin's clothes—from the suitcase and jammed them into the dresser. As I looked around the barren room, it hit me. Beyond these few possessions, my mother owned nothing else. Not a square of grass or a tree or a single stone on the house. All these years I'd thought she lived a certain way, but I was wrong. My aunt and I had so much more.

My mother emerged wearing a light yellow dress with a white collar. A row of buttons went down each side of the front panel. She pulled a white apron around her waist, tied it behind her back in a bow. Her face was so much like my aunt's. But also different. Something was missing but I wasn't sure exactly what. Loneliness crawled up my legs, through my intestines, into my stomach. I tried to pinch it away, telling myself this was only for a little while. Aunt Celia was lost and hurt, but soon enough she'd be found. Then this garbage adventure would be over.

My mother held my upper arm as we wound our way through a maze of hallways and entered a huge room. The air was stuffy, and the ceiling went up to a point. The walls were made of dark wood, and there were shelves packed with books and board games.

I counted four people. Two I recognized as the men who'd dropped off my mother in front of our apartment. Mr. Fulsome was playing solitaire at a table in the corner, and Dr. Henneberry was sitting on a dark pink sofa, reading a magazine. Next to him was a thin lady. That had to be Mrs. Henneberry. Her blond hair flipped up near her ears and her face was coated in dull beige powder. The boy from the upstairs window was spread on the floor in front of a television.

My mother stood behind me. She coughed, but none of them budged. "Thomas and I are back. I thought I'd bring him to meet—"

"I'm quite certain about it, really," the woman said in a slow, sleepy way. "There's a nest of hornets outside that very window." Her hand was frozen in front of her. Smoke quivered up from the cigarette burning between her fingers. She tilted her head. "Can't you hear them drumming at the glass?"

I twisted to look up at my mother. Her mouth was set tight.

"Nonsense, Muriel. Hornets don't drum." Mr. Fulsome

AN UNTHINKABLE THING   65

swiped his cards to the side and stood up. He came over to us.

"Thomas, is it?"

I nodded.

He put a heavy hand on my shoulder. "You'll be well cared for while you're here. The Henneberrys are quite hospitable."

"Declared the guest who never leaves." Dr. Henneberry lifted his magazine to cover his face.

Mr. Fulsome smirked. "I'm going to ignore you, Ray. If I didn't feel welcomed, you'd never see me again." Then to my mother, "So sorry to hear about your sister, Esther. What a nasty, nasty business."

My mother's shaky breath spread across the back of my neck. I waited for her to explain it was all a mix-up. That there was no "nasty business." But instead she said, "We're handling things as best as we can. Thank you, Mr. Fulsome."

"I'm livid about it, really," he said. "Aren't you, Ray? I mean, what in heck's name is going on over there in Greenlake?"

Dr. Henneberry lowered his magazine. His eyes were cold blue, and his hair was combed tight against his scalp. He glared at Mr. Fulsome over the rim of his glasses. "I'm rarely there in the evenings, Jim."

"Still. You got enough scruffy types lazing around in broad daylight. Those vagrants don't go *poof* after dinner. The cops should round 'em up."

Dr. Henneberry crossed one leg over the other. His leather slipper began to tap the air.

"They are drumming, James. Don't you hear them? It's almost"—Mrs. Henneberry's arm wavered and the smoke curled in the air—"musical."

The boy, who never took his eyes off the television, said, "That's just my show, Mother. I'm watching *Gunsmoke*. A guy's playing piano in the saloon."

"Oh. Is he?" She giggled, and a clump of gray ash dropped into the ashtray on her lap. "I do hope no one's bothered by it, Martin, dear."

Paper crackled. Dr. Henneberry turned a page. "Dr. Norton's been by again, I see," he said. "Keeping you well stocked with all your favorites."

"Oh, he is, Raymond. All these house calls, so attentive. He's very careful with what he prescribes."

"Careful? How can he be careful when he doesn't know his arse from his elbow?"

"Now, Ray," Mr. Fulsome said. "Such coarse language."

My mother cleared her throat. "Can I offer anyone a cool drink? A sandwich?"

"Of course not." Mr. Fulsome now had his hand on my mother's back. "We already enjoyed that delicious cold supper you set out. Why don't you and the boy rest up. You've both been through an ordeal."

"Yes." Mrs. Henneberry yawned. "You're so right, James. Dr. Norton says rest will serve me well. I must adjust to these summer temperatures."

"Good idea," Dr. Henneberry said. He snapped the spine of the magazine. "Go sleep it off."

Mrs. Henneberry gripped the arm of the couch and tried to stand up. The ashtray was slipping off her lap, but Mr. Fulsome rushed to catch it. He tugged the cigarette from between her fingers and stubbed it out. Then Mrs. Henneberry noticed I was there. "Oh," she said. Her eyes were nearly closed. "Such a beautiful boy. Do you want to help me to my room? I don't trust my legs. On all those stairs." Her hand swung toward me, but then it fell back and bounced off her thigh.

"I can't hear my show with all this yapping," Martin yelled.

"I'll help you, Muriel." Mr. Fulsome cupped Mrs. Henneberry's elbow, and he guided her as she shuffled toward the doorway.

"Should I look in on her later?" my mother asked.

"No need," Dr. Henneberry said. "Doubt she'll wake before morning."

I imagined what Aunt Celia would think of their family room. She'd laugh, I bet, at all the pointless furniture. The games and books that looked unopened and unread. The wall-to-wall carpeting that was so plush I felt unstable, even though I was standing still. I'd have to remember every detail so I could tell her about it.

Martin sat up then, crossed his legs. He glanced over his shoulder, gesturing for me to come and join him. An invitation to watch *Gunsmoke*. But my mother whispered

in my ear, "Come along, Thomas. This is not our place."
As I turned to leave, Martin scowled. Cranked a knob on
the television as far as it would go. The sound of gunshots filled the room.

CHAPTER SIX

My mother led me back to the kitchen. While she stood at the counter slicing bread, I went down the hallway to the side door. A breeze was coming through the screen and I put my face against it and inhaled. The wire mesh smelled like old dust. The sun was nearly down. All around the edge of the property, the woods were dark and the black branches shuddered with the wind. They almost seemed to be alive, growling very softly.

"Thomas?" My mother was behind me. "Are you hungry? I made chicken salad. And sliced some tomatoes."

I hated chicken salad. And sliced tomatoes made my mouth itch. Aunt Celia knew that.

"I'm not hungry."

"Still." She rubbed her hands together. "You should come and eat."

In the glass section above the screen, I could see the reflection of the hallway behind me. Near the end, a lamp glowed. But mostly it was just darkness. How could I ever have wished to come here? To this eerie, empty place.

A strange cry fluttered in through the screen. As though someone was injured out there in the shadows.

Or maybe calling out a name. A shiver went up my spine. "What's that noise?"

"Only Mrs. Grimshaw," my mother said. "She's out for her walk in the woods."

I strained to see. Was she that grayish shape beside those bushes? Then it went further along, appearing and disappearing. Like a sheet or towel or a ghost weaving among the trees.

"Why is she sneaking around?"

"She's not sneaking. She lives next door. She's quite old, and her husband died a few years ago. Sad, really. She wanders about calling his name. Sometimes she doesn't recognize a soul."

"Even if you know her?"

"Even if. Mrs. Henneberry's very distressed by it all. Mrs. Grimshaw keeps coming onto their property."

"To visit?"

"No, not to visit. The two families never got on well. Mrs. Grimshaw and Mrs. Henneberry's mother, Mrs. Gladstone, they couldn't tolerate one another."

"Then why's she over here?"

"I guess some days she doesn't remember where she is. Or where her land ends and the Henneberrys' begins. If you happen upon her, please don't bother her, Thomas."

My eyes had adjusted, and I could see her more clearly now. "She's got no shoes on."

"Maybe not. But when you're as wealthy as she is, as the Henneberrys are, you can do what you please."

"Oh," I said. I wondered what that would be like.

Doing whatever I wanted. If I was allowed, I'd leave right away. I'd grab George and hop on a bus to St. Augustine's and find my aunt. Then we'd take a shiny taxi back to our apartment and Mrs. King and I would look after her. We'd bandage whatever cuts or scrapes or broken bones she had. It would take time, but things would return to normal.

"Martin says he hates Mrs. Grimshaw. But to be honest, I think she scares him when he's clowning around in the woods."

I stayed on a stool at the counter, pushing the sandwich around my plate, until it was completely dark. Then I tiptoed through the laundry to the bedroom I had to share with my mother. I felt along the side of the wall until I found the light switch. I turned it on and my heart jolted. Martin Henneberry was sitting on my mother's bed.

"Didn't mean to startle you, pal. Sorry about that."

I scratched my neck. "Um. It's okay."

He grinned, stood up. "Thought I'd drop by to say hello. We didn't get a proper introduction earlier." He stuck out his hand. "Martin," he said. "Martin Henneberry."

Shaking it, I replied, "Tommie Ware."

"Good to meet you, Ware."

He was wearing a round hat over his blond hair, and a fluffy raccoon tail hung down the back of it. He wandered about the room, twisted the sink faucet on and off. Peered into the bathroom. Yanked opened the dresser drawers and sifted through my clothes.

"Do you hate wearing my old stuff?" he asked.

I shrugged. "It's not too bad."

"If I were you, I'd hate it."

He knelt on the cot beside the windowsill. With his fingernails, he clicked the outside of George's tank. His face was so close, his breath clouded the glass. Then he stuck his middle finger into George's water and made a swirling motion. George swished against the current, brushed the sides, brushed the pebbly bottom.

"Hey!" I said.

"Hey, hey," he said back. He removed his finger and faced me.

"That's not safe for him."

"Really? Wouldn't want to hurt the little guy."

"I mean . . . It's probably not a huge deal, but don't do it again, okay?"

"Roger that." He wiped his dripping hand in the middle of his T-shirt. "Did you notice, Ware, that my mother's got a crush on you?"

"A crush?"

"Yeah. She called you a beautiful boy."

I didn't understand what he meant. "So what?"

He laughed. "Well, don't get too comfortable with it. Her little amusements never last long."

"What little amusements?"

He lifted his hands up, showing both palms. "Forget I ever mentioned it, alright? Don't worry, though, I've got you covered." Then he marched out of the bedroom, into the gloom of the laundry room.

I closed the door. Martin's joke was weird, but he was probably just trying to be nice. And I was grateful for that. Perhaps we could hang out tomorrow while I waited for news about Aunt Celia. If she'd been found. How bad she was hurt.

In the bathroom I changed into my pajamas. They were covered in green cowboys, and had also belonged to Martin. Above me a fat fly circled and buzzed and hit the light. I looked out the square window across from the bathtub. The one without a curtain. The view was blocked by the leafy branches but I knew the driveway was out there. Leading down to a road that led from Upper Washbourne into Lower. If I snuck out and didn't stop running, how long would it take me to reach our apartment? Would my aunt already be home? Waiting in her silky bathrobe with the scooped sleeves? Would she have her hair in pins? Would she kiss my face when I opened the door and hurried inside?

I sat on the edge of the bathtub, lowered my head into my hands. I was so tired. Besides George, nothing around me was familiar. I wanted to see Aunt Celia. I wanted to see Mrs. King. I wanted to see Wally. I started to weep. As quietly as I could.

My mother came into the bathroom. She stood beside me. I wanted to embrace her so that she would feel my bones. My soft spots. But my body wouldn't rise up, my arms would not lift. She didn't know what to say to make me chuckle. She didn't know that I liked licorice more than caramel. Or that, in sixty seconds flat, I could finish the letter jumble in the newspaper.

She was my mother. She was also a stranger.

"Am I even going to school tomorrow?"

My mother slowly shook her head.

I wept harder.

"You're overwhelmed, Thomas," she said.

With the hem of my pajama shirt, I wiped the wet off my face. "Why is it taking them so long?"

"Who?"

"The police. To track her down."

My mother opened her mouth, and I stared at the O of her lips, afraid of what might come out. Her chest was rising and falling fast. Her nostrils flared out. After a long time, she closed her mouth and swallowed hard. She blinked fast. "We can talk about this later, okay? Finish getting ready for bed."

At the sink, I squeezed toothpaste onto my brush and cleaned my teeth. Then I crawled onto the cot. The springs squeaked as I lay down. My mother unfolded a blanket and placed it over me. She sat lightly on the very edge, and with her fingertip, she moved strands of hair off my forehead. That sensation calmed me, even though her skin was sandpaper. "Things'll get better," she whispered. "Mr. Vardy says we'll figure it out."

Mr. Green Thumb, again? What does he know?

I was too tired to say a single word. Even though the window above me was open, the air still smelled stale.

In the moonlight I could see George circling in his bowl. *Doesn't he ever get tired?*

My mother went into the bathroom. I heard water splashing. Then the springs of her bed squeaked. After a few minutes, the tumble dryer outside the door stopped thumping, and everything was silent. I thought my mother might be crying, but soon she was breathing softly. A couple of times she whispered a word or two. *Knee. Bent, yes. Fix the zipper.*

George hovered near the bottom of his bowl now, his fins barely moving. I hated that they'd both fallen asleep before I had.

EXCERPT

Testimony of Detective Chuck Miller

Direct Examination by Prosecutor Clay Fibbs

Q. You and your partner were first on the property, is that correct, sir?

A. No. Local police got there first. Upper Washbourne's finest. But once they'd assessed the severity of the crime, they called in the Greenlake Division. When we arrived, we took over the investigation.

Q. Thank you for clarifying, Detective Miller. Now in your report you outline a theory about the order of the killings?

A. Yes. Based on my observations, Mrs. Henneberry was shot first. Ignoring the bullet wound in her neck, she appeared to be relaxed, reclining in a lawn chair, and was taken by surprise. We determined Dr. Henneberry had reacted to his wife's assault and was killed in a sitting position. The boy in the pool, Martin Henneberry, he was the last.

Q. With this information, what did you conclude about the aggressor?

A. There were no signs of struggle, sir. No furniture knocked over. Preceding the attack, no one had engaged in a confrontation or fight.

Q. What exactly does this indicate, Detective?

A. The Henneberrys weren't fearful of their assailant. This individual was able to be on the property, obtain the gun, and shoot them while they were completely unaware of his intentions. We concluded early on that the Henneberrys were familiar with the killer. Not only familiar, but comfortable with him.

Q. **Not a stranger. Would you say a guest?**

A. You'd get up to greet a guest, wouldn't you? No, we determined this was a person who moved among the Henneberry family unnoticed.

Q. **Where was Thomas Ware when you arrived?**

A. Sitting on the grass close by.

Q. **Can you describe his physical state?**

A. He was unclothed. And covered in blood, sir.

Q. **Did you communicate with him?**

A. I tried to calm him down. Calm myself down too. It was horrific scene, and seeing a child smack in the middle of—

Q. **Did you ask Mr. Ware any questions?**

A. I did, sir. But he kept repeating the same thing. A man in a black car came and shot the Henneberrys.

Q. **Did he offer details?**

A. Not much else. A tall man. Slender, he said. Wearing a hat and a coat.

Q. **And did—**

A. And he also mentioned a woman named Mrs. Grimshaw. Said she'd been injured.

Q. **You looked into it?**

A. Yes, we sent two officers straight over to check on her. In case the gunman had reached her. We didn't know what we were dealing with.

Q. **How was Mrs. Grimshaw?**

A. Perfectly fine. Not a spot on her. Her biggest com-
    plaint was the bird population in the woods. Too many
    of them, she said. Overbreeding.

Q. **Just a couple more questions. Prior to this investiga-
    tion, had you ever met the defendant, Thomas Ware?**

A. Yes, sir. Under sad circumstances, I'm afraid.

Q. **And what were those?**

A. His aunt, Miss Celia Ware, was a victim of the
    Greenlake Predator. We went to the young lady's
    apartment to notify next of kin, and Thomas was there.

Q. **Was he upset about his aunt's death?**

A. Deeply. He was yelling and flailing. Thought I'd have to
    restrain him. I didn't want him to hurt himself. Or hurt
    someone else.

Q. **Would you describe his behavior as explosive?**

A. I know what you're driving at, Mr. Fibbs, and I'm going
    to stop you right there. What I saw at that apartment
    was a boy experiencing anguish. Trying to process
    news that was incomprehensible. Nothing more and
    nothing less.

CHAPTER SEVEN

Time ticked by the next day, slower than I ever thought possible. My mother told me I could stay in the kitchen while she cooked, but I waited on the cot near George. I missed my things. My drawing book and my spin top. My Slinky was still inside its box. Soon enough, it'd be time to return to the apartment. I'd hidden the rubber band and plastic for George's bowl underneath the thin mattress. The suitcase was leaning against the wall. My toothbrush was in a glass beside the sink. I could be packed and ready in ten seconds flat.

In the afternoon, my mother found me still in the bedroom. Instead of telling me to gather my stuff, she handed me a shoebox. I opened the lid. It was full of matchbox cars, some brand new in their packaging. "You like those, right?" I nodded. "You can't stay in here forever. Fresh air will do you good." She directed me outside. To a patch of soil beside the rosebush. Not far from the side door, a stone pathway led down to the pool. The water was a smooth blue sheet. I could dip my feet in, lie back, and stare at the sky. Think about all the things I'd do once I got home. As though she'd read my mind, my mother said in a stern voice, "Stay right here, Thomas. No roaming about."

For the next hour I made humps of soil with narrow trails. I plucked leaves from the rosebush to make parking spots. As I drove the cars around the dusty mini-roads, there were frequent accidents. One smashed into another. A red tractor zoomed off into the grass, and a sea-blue station wagon hit a fallen twig and flipped over and over.

"The roof's demolished. Pull her out onto the ground."

"The boy. Is he safe?"

"That rotten man—happy to report he won't survive, Officer."

"Oh, we must hurry, she's nearly gone."

I stared at the upside-down car, and then I dug around in the shoebox. There were so many shiny cars, but no miniature ambulance that could screech up, sirens blaring, to take the dying woman away. I needed to save her, but there was nothing I could do. Then I brought my knees up to my chin, and I started to cry. My tears were sucked into the dry soil.

What if what that detective said was true?

"What's wrong with you?"

I jumped. Martin Henneberry was standing behind me. He was smiling, and his blond hair was sticking up. He had a sore red mark on his forehead. Like he'd pressed it hard against something.

"Nothing." I sniffed. "Poked my thumb on a thorn."

He edged closer. "Hey, my T-shirt looks great on you."

"Does it?" It was yellow and white stripes. "Thanks."

"And I don't mind you having my cars. You can keep them."

I was holding a miniature milk truck with two working doors. "You don't want them back?"

"Nah. I'm too old for kiddie toys." He tucked his shirt into his shorts and tightened up his belt. "I'm a generous guy, Ware, even though you're messing up my routine."

I swallowed. "Sorry." I didn't know what routine he meant. "Um . . . thanks for the cars." Wally was going to insist on having half of them. As soon as I saw him, I'd dump out the entire pile, let him choose first.

"Wait right here," Martin said. "You and me are going to have some fun."

He ran around the corner of the house. A minute later he was back, holding a rifle with a wooden handle and a long gray barrel. He nudged my thigh with his shoe. "Get up. Let's go."

"That's a gun," I said.

He smirked. "Sure is. Belonged to my grandfather. But it's just pellets, Ware. We can't kill anyone with it."

I stood up. "I should tell my mother—"

"Why? You need permission to take a walk?"

I shrugged. I didn't need permission. I'd climbed down the fire escape plenty of times and met up with Wally. We just had to be home for supper.

Side by side, Martin and I walked down the stone pathway. We passed the pool. Further on was a small wooden structure. It had shingles and windows and concrete steps. A painted door with lights on either side.

"Does someone live in there?" I asked. Perhaps Mr. Green Thumb.

Martin grinned. "You're hilarious, Ware."

I chewed my lip. It didn't seem like a funny question.

Martin found a gap in the bushes and we went into the cool woods. Dark green leaves shivered with the breeze, and up above, birds were chirping and bees were buzzing. Beyond a few small patches on the ground, the sunlight was mostly gone. After about a dozen steps, Martin threw back his head and hooted really loud, "Martin's Woods!" Then he turned to me and said, "When my grandfather died, he gave me this land, too. Along with the gun."

"Wow." I glanced around. The trees went on and on and on. "That's some kind of gift."

"Sure, but I'm his grandson. I was named after him, you know. Martin Henneberry and Martin Gladstone." He pointed the tip of the gun into the air and went "*Pew, pew, pew!*"

We walked along a narrow path until we came to a hollow. Martin set a large pine cone on a stump. Then he came back to where I was standing, pumped the lever on the gun, and aimed. A loud crack in my ears, but the pine cone was still there. Martin pumped the gun a second time. Still no luck. A third. A fourth. Then he spat on the ground. "Barrel's gummy," he said. "Probably needs to be cleaned or calibrated."

He shoved the gun toward me. It was heavier than I thought it would be. I pulled down on the lever like he'd done. Then I put my hand under the wooden part on the barrel, brought it up to my shoulder, and aimed. I squeezed the trigger. *Bam!* A rush went through me and the pine cone flew off the stump and plopped to the ground.

"Beginner's luck," Martin said. He ran over and placed another pine cone on the stump. I aimed a second time, and again the pellet struck the pine cone.

"Damn, buddy. You're a regular Annie Oakley. I should take you on the road."

I pumped the lever. I was ready to go. This was actually fun. When I got home, I'd have to tell Wally about it. Maybe one of us could get a Red Ryder and try it out in the woods near the apartments. Wally's mother likely wouldn't buy one, but my aunt might if I bugged her enough.

Martin was about to set me up again when a gray-and-white bird fluttered down and stood on the stump. It had a black cap of feathers on its head, and it pecked at the wood.

"Quiet," Martin whispered. "Go slow."

"Go what?" I whispered back.

"Before it takes off."

My arms felt weaker. Like the gun had turned to lead.

"What're you waiting for?"

I lifted the gun. I aimed. The bird stuck its chest out, rolled back its head, and chirped. "I can't."

Martin grabbed the gun from me. I closed my eyes and heard the crank of the lever and then the crack. When I opened my eyes again, the bird was on a clump of dead leaves beside the stump. One bent wing twitching in the air. *Chirp, chiirp, chiii-irp*. Like a wound-up toy getting slower. And slower.

Then it stopped.

"Lookit," Martin said. "Got myself a sharp eye when it counts."

My throat squeezed. It was only a bird, I told myself. Cats caught birds all the time. They broke their necks on windows. That bird didn't have a family. Nobody would miss it. It was just a dumb bird.

"I'm done." Martin slung the gun over his shoulder and punched me in the arm. "This is boring. You can stay here if you want. You're allowed."

He started stomping out of the woods. His woods. The trees were thick, and I didn't want to get turned around, so I followed a few steps behind. When we came out into the yard, he was whistling a snappy tune. He darted up the stone walkway and disappeared.

I walked up the slope to the door with the rosebush. My mother was outside, cleaning up the matchbox cars. She pushed the shoebox underneath some branches.

"Where have you been?"

"With Martin."

She drew her lips in over her teeth. All around her mouth was white.

"Exploring around," I said.

Her mouth relaxed. "Okay. Come in now. Your supper's on the table."

CHAPTER EIGHT

"Want to go swimming? It's crazy hot out."

Martin appeared, the same as he'd done the day before. Strolling around the back corner of the house, rubbing at his forehead.

I looked down over the lawn. The pool waited there. A glittery rectangle of blue. Just an hour earlier, I'd seen a man setting up candy-colored lawn chairs. He stabbed two striped umbrellas into the ground. The door to that perfect wooden house shimmered, like it was given a fresh coat of paint.

Martin scuffed his foot. "Well, do you? I'm not going to stand around all day while you decide."

"I don't know how." Wally and I splashed around at the lake sometimes, but I'd never learned proper strokes.

"Really? Your father didn't take you?"

"No. He didn't." I usually tried not to think about him. Aunt Celia had several different stories, and when I'd asked Mrs. King, she said my father was probably a "fly-by-night." I guessed that meant someone who didn't stick around. "Look," she'd said. "You've got oodles of people who love you. That man's not worth a second mention, Thomas."

Martin was laughing as he started walking away. Over his shoulder he yelled, "Well, you better stay in the shallow end, Ware. I haven't finished my life-saving course yet."

He jogged down toward the pool, and I hurried behind him. When he reached for the doorknob to the small house, I said, "Shouldn't we knock?"

"It's a place to change. You can't actually think someone lives in here."

Inside was dark and it smelled a little like mold. Martin peeled off every stitch of his clothing, tossed it in a heap. After grabbing a towel for himself, he slapped a second in my direction before strolling out the door. I took off my shorts, then my T-shirt. I hesitated. Then, like Martin, I reached down to take off my underwear. I ran my hands over my ribs and pinched my soft stomach. Baby fat, Aunt Celia had called it.

"Come on, Ware!" Martin's voice was clear as day. As though he were inside the room, hiding in one of the corners near the ceiling. Like a spider settled in its web.

When I came out into the light, he was on the grass beside the tiny house. He grinned at me before he bolted toward the pool, leapt with his knees pulled up, and struck the water with a huge splash. I sat on the side, slowly inched my body lower until my toes found the bottom. The tiles were slippery.

While I stayed near the edge, Martin swam laps back and forth. On his front at first, then rolling onto his back. His body was lean and tanned. He had a smooth chest, but thick dark hair in that area beneath it. I shuffled around slowly, unsure where the shallow ended and the deep began. Did the depth change gradually, or was there a sudden drop? As I moved, water flushed against my parts. It wasn't a cold shock like from the lake, or a hot bath where I forgot where my skin ended. In the warm pool, I was comfortably aware of every inch of myself.

"What do you think?" Martin asked.

"Good," I said. "Nice."

"Told you so."

I put my elbow up on the border of tile at the edge. "Do you always swim with nothing on?"

"Sure. At school we do. For the team. Mother likes me to wear trunks at home, but there's no one around, so why not? If anyone drives in, you can hear as soon as their car hits the gravel."

"But what about that lady?"

"What lady?"

"The one in the woods. She—"

"That wacky old hag from next door? She thinks evil birds are out to get her."

"Evil birds?" I said. "That's kind of crazy."

"You're telling me, Ware." He rolled his eyes. "If you want my opinion, it's old Grimshaw's lucky day if she gets a glimpse of these ripples." He flexed his arm muscles and I chuckled. Maybe this was what older boys were like. I was just too used to Wally who was scared of stepping on a sidewalk crack in case he hurt his mother. I decided I liked Martin Henneberry.

"Yeah," I said. "Her lucky day." I tried to flex my arms too, but nothing changed.

"I'm part of a crew team, you know."

"A crew team?"

"Rowing. Me and my buddy Skip. Can't you tell?"

"Sure." Martin was watching me, waiting for more. "Your shoulders are pretty big, I guess."

"Exactly. We've been out three times now. I mean, it's made a huge difference to my shape. It's obvious in the mirror."

"I can see it too," I said. *Sort of.*

He dove under, cutting through the water until he reached the side. Then he dragged a small plastic boat into the pool and pulled it closer to me. "Get in," he said. I scrambled over the edge, and when I was inside, I held tight to the handles.

"Don't worry. I'm not going to flip it."

"That's good," I said, though I hadn't thought that he might.

He shoved the end of the boat and it cut through the water. I lay back and crossed my feet at my ankles. The boat rocked and bobbed, and the sun drifted down on my wet skin. Martin floated on the surface next to me. He spurted water out of his mouth. I closed my eyes and for little while, I forgot about my aunt being lost and hurt. I forgot about feeling upset. I forgot about how bad I wanted to leave.

"I like swimming," I said when we were lying down on the warm cement surrounding the pool.

"You like the water, you mean."

"Can you teach me later?"

His blond hair had fallen into his eyes. "That's real swell, Ware. But I don't think so. I got crew practice and stuff. So I'm a busy guy."

"Oh." I'd wanted to surprise Wally at the lake.

"But hey." He jumped up and wrapped the towel around his waist. "Let me show you something else."

I followed him over to the house where we'd changed.

"Do you have a big mouth?"

"No," I said. "Of course not."

"Good. Because this is secret." He got low to the ground and pointed. "Put your eye exactly right there."

I knelt beside him, positioned myself in the correct spot, and saw Martin's discovery. A thin crack running up from the bottom of the wall. It was dark inside.

"Is that a leak?" I said.

"You're kidding, right? Did your school have a pointy hat with 'Ware' written on it?"

"No?"

"I'm just joking around, pal." He punched my arm lightly. "Can you see right in?"

"Yeah, but why'd you want to do that?"

He was smirking and shaking his head. I leaned forward and peeked a second time. My vision adjusted to the black, and then I noticed my sneakers side by side on the floor. The clump of my shorts and T-shirt on the bench. Then I understood. He'd watched me get undressed. My stomach flip-flopped. But I shook it off. We had the same parts. What did it matter? It wasn't like he was spying on a girl.

"Get your stuff. My show should be on. I can't miss it." Then he said in a slithery voice, "By golly, I never saw a man so set on anything in all my life."

"Why're you talking like that?"

"It's Doc. From *Gunsmoke*. Don't you know it?"

"Yeah. I just forgot for a second." But I didn't know it at all. Aunt Celia wouldn't let me watch those sorts of shows. And if I tried sneaking one while she was at work, Mrs. King was at the door in a flash. Mr. King hated the sound of shooting. It was boring seeing the pictures without hearing anything, so I didn't bother. I said to Martin, "Want me to grab your clothes, too?"

"Nah. Your mother'll find them. She always does. Sometimes I hide things. Behind a plant, or stuffed up in the bookshelves in Father's den. Then they show up back in my closet, clean and ironed." He snapped his fingers.

While we walked up to the massive house, I hoped Martin would invite me to join him for his program, but he didn't. He scrambled up the steps to the tall front doors, turned, and called out, "We're chums now, right? We get along?"

"Yeah," I called back. "We are." I'd never had a friend who was fifteen before. I stretched my spine, trying to make myself a little taller.

"Cool," he said. "Catch you later, then."

I waved goodbye as he went inside, and kept going to our door by the rosebushes. My mother was standing behind the screen. Her mouth was tight again. As I shuffled in around her, she said, "You were spending more time with Martin?"

I nodded.

She took a deep breath. "Get out of your damp clothes. Leave your things in the basket."

"Okay," I said. I couldn't tell if she was angry because I'd done something wrong or if she was just tired.

After I'd dried off and gotten changed, I went back to the kitchen and sat on the same stool. My mother put a sandwich and a glass of milk on the counter in front of me. I lifted the top slice. Pink ham, cheddar cheese, and mustard. At least it was better than chicken salad. I ate while she peeled apples in the sink.

When she was finished, she wiped her hands in a cloth and turned to face me. I thought she was going to tell me some news about Aunt Celia, but she said, "Did you enjoy yourself?"

"Yeah. Martin asked me to go swimming."

Then she came close to me and she put her hand on my shoulder. The hair on the back of my neck stood up. In a low voice, she said, "Do you know he was named after his grandfather? Martin Gladstone?"

"He told me. And he owns all the woods, too. His grandfather gave them to him."

"I don't know anything about that."

She leaned even closer to me. There was tea on her breath. "They look alike, you know. And I think they're alike in nature, too."

"His grandfather was fun, then? A good swimmer?"

She glanced at the hallway that led deeper into the house, and whispered, "I want you to tread lightly around him, do you understand?"

"Tread what?" I whispered back. My heart went up in my throat, making it hard to swallow the mouthful of bread.

"I just—I don't know. Just be careful." Then she smiled, but the smile was only on her lips. Not in her eyes. "It's better not to make a friend, Thomas. These days here will come and go quickly. I wouldn't want you to miss him."

CHAPTER NINE

On Monday morning, there were voices in the hallway. I peeked around the corner from the kitchen and saw my mother in her yellow uniform. Two men were standing beside her near the door and I recognized them. The same detectives who'd come to the apartment. They couldn't be there for the Henneberrys as Mrs. Henneberry had taken Martin on a summer trip the day after school was let out and Dr. Henneberry had already gone to work. So it had to be about Aunt Celia. I held my breath and listened.

"And she never showed up?"

"No, ma'am." Detective Miller was frowning. "She didn't go in to work that evening."

"Wasn't even scheduled," Detective O'Connor said, "according to the head nurse."

"I'd assumed she had a shift," my mother said.

Lifting his eyebrows, Detective O'Connor said, "Well, seems she had other activities on her calendar."

Detective Miller cleared his throat, took out his notepad, and flipped through the pages. "Her neighbor

Mrs. King mentioned a sweetheart. Is it possible she was planning to meet him in Greenlake?"

"Perhaps," my mother said. "I wouldn't know."

"We'd sure like to chat with him. Clear things up. Did your sister share a name with you? Any details?"

My mother's chest was rising and falling. "Wouldn't there be a record at the hospital?"

"We've already looked into it. Followed up on a couple of foot injuries, like your son mentioned. But no one's connected to her. Or admitting to it anyway."

"That doesn't make sense."

"Apparently some nurses are less than stellar with their paperwork. Especially if the issue is relatively minor and the shift is hectic."

Shaking her head, my mother said, "She wouldn't get involved with anyone dangerous anyway, Detective. My sister was smart. Whoever that man is, I'm certain he didn't—"

"I just find it all a bit odd," Detective O'Connor said slowly. "Nurses at St. Augustine's said your sister used to chitchat up a storm, but since she got tangled up with that new fellow, they couldn't pry a word out of her."

Detective Miller cleared his throat again. Louder this time. "I'm sorry we don't have a clearer picture yet, Miss Ware. We weren't able confirm if she actually took the bus. Or if she met her gentleman friend. Or at what point she encountered the perpetrator."

"So not a single lead?"

"Nothing concrete as of yet." He closed his notepad. "But we're going to catch this guy. We won't rest until the Greenlake Predator is behind bars."

Detective O'Connor unwrapped a stick of chewing gum, pushed it into his mouth. Then said, "Before we leave, ma'am, there's the issue of her remains . . ."

"Yes. Um." My mother fiddled with the collar of her uniform. "A cardboard casket. You can tell them. I can't aff— That will have to do."

At the mention of a casket, something happened to my knees. The joints went loose. I leaned against the doorframe.

Detective Miller had a sorrowful smile. "Thank you, Miss Ware. We'll certainly pass that along."

Both detectives nodded and stepped backward. The door closed slowly and didn't make a creak. My mother stared outside for a while. A black-and-orange butterfly fluttered closer and landed on the outside of the screen. She reached up, touching the same spot, but on the inside. After it flew away, she turned around and her hands leapt into the air. I was standing right behind her.

"Why'd you do that?" I screamed. "Why?" I wanted to push past her. But my legs were too wobbly.

"Do what, Thomas? What did I do?"

"You know!"

"About the casket? I didn't have a choice. I can't manage a fu—"

"They said she was hurt. She was lost."

"Thomas. Stop."

"You should've told them to keep trying!" Tears sprung from my eyes. "You're just jealous because she's nicer and prettier and way, way happier than you'll ever be." My mother's mouth twisted and quivered. "She's lost and no one is looking for her. What if she took the wrong bus? Or hit her head like in that movie and forgot everything. You don't know for sure. You don't—"

My mother gripped my shoulders. Then she shook me. "I can't let you pretend any longer. I can't—"

"Let me go!" I screamed louder. I tried to wiggle away, but she held me tight. "Let me go! Let me go!"

She shook me again, hard enough that my head jerked. "Thomas Leon Ware! You need to listen. Celia is not lost in the woods. She's not trying to find her way home. She's dead. Do you hear me? Dead."

"She is not!" The air was thick in front of my face. I couldn't breathe it in.

"Some vile man took her away. Took her away from you. And from me, too. What's done is done. She's gone and she's not coming back. And we need to cope with it. We're together now." She was sobbing, too. "I'd trade with her if I could, Thomas. You have to know that. If only I could."

I hated my mother. Hated her shiny skin and puffy eyelids. Hated every nasty word that oozed out of her mouth. I twisted hard and she gasped, her arms dropping. I kicked open the screen door and raced over the grass. She was calling out to me. "Thomas! Thomas!

Please wait!" But I ran past the pool with its still, blue water. Past that little house where no one lived, with the peeping hole in the wall. Past the bushes with the green leaves. Then I was among the trees. In the sudden coolness, I slowed down. *Martin's Woods.*

I kept stepping along a worn footpath, deeper and deeper until I came to the hollow Martin had brought me to just a few days ago.

I didn't want to look, but my feet were stepping in that direction. Toward the stump. With my fingertips, I touched the old saw marks. Light green shoots had sprung up around the base of the stump. When I bent down, it only took a minute to find it. Tucked between two thick brown roots, the remains of the bird Martin had killed. Tiny black ants were climbing all over its body. I nudged it with my knuckles. Beneath the feathers, it was solid and light. I picked it up, cupped it in my palm. "I'm sorry you got hurt," I told it. "I'm sorry your family didn't find you."

I knelt down with the bird in my hand and cried for a while longer. I could feel the weight of my mother's words slowly sinking into me. Aunt Celia wasn't stuck at work for a whole week. She wasn't waiting at our apartment. She hadn't forgotten who she was. Or who I was. She was gone. And she was never coming back. The man my aunt had treated at St. Augustine's Hospital had hurt her. He'd crushed her lungs and left her sleeping on the floor of a forest. No, not sleeping. My stubborn brain wanted to pretend again.

With a flat rock, I scraped out a hole in the soft soil near the trunk. I placed the bird in the hole and pushed the dirt back over the top and pressed it down. I felt the slightest bit better. At least it was covered up. At least somebody said goodbye.

A sharp crack sounded behind me. Martin? I hopped up fast. But when I turned, it wasn't him. It was that old lady, Mrs. Grimshaw, the one who'd lost her marbles. Only a few feet away from me. She was wearing a baby blue dress with most of the buttons undone, and her bra was on the outside.

"What're you poking at over there?"

I wiped my face with the back of my hand. "Nothing," I said. "I dropped a penny."

She took a step toward me. Tufts of her gray hair were sticking up. "Have you been here long?"

"I don't know."

Another step. "Did you see a gentleman come by? Handsome, you know. Touch of white at his temples."

I shook my head. "No, I didn't."

"Well my husband went for a stroll ages ago. I'm getting concerned."

I had no idea what to say. I knew where her husband was. The same place as that bird. The same place as my aunt.

"Would you help me, young man?"

She reached her hand out. I stared at the brown spots, the thick knuckles. The golden wedding band.

What harm could it do? "Sure," I said. "Sure, I can help."

"Oh, you're such a nice boy. He can't have gone far."

She linked her arm through mine and we walked side by side along a different path. Sometimes she called out, "Abel? Abel, are you there?" Then she'd slow, a hand cupped around her long ear.

After a while she asked, "What's your name, young man?"

"Thomas," I said.

"Thomas," she repeated. "That's a good, strong name. Tell me, now. Why were you really sitting there? No one cries that hard over a penny."

Mrs. Grimshaw sort of reminded me of Mrs. King but her hair was grayer, and the top of her spine had a hump so that her chin nearly touched her chest. They talked the same way, though. Their words bouncing at me, and I had to pay attention.

"I'm mad at my mother," I said.

"Oh, I remember those days. Mine's long gone, but I was mad for years."

"Why?"

"Haven't the faintest. But it keeps you together sometimes, doesn't it? Being angry at the person who has to love you." Mrs. Grimshaw slowed her steps. "Who's this mother of yours?"

We'd come to a lake, and she let go of my arm. Water lapped up over the yellow sand with a line of clean white foam. The lake was so bright with sunshine, I had to squint. Even though it was the same water, this was much nicer than the beach near our apartment. "Esther Ware," I said. "Over with the Henneberrys."

"Oh, you're teasing me, dear. Young Esther couldn't possibly be. And you must mean the Gladstones. She's always been with them."

Maybe she'd forgotten that my mother was grown or that the house belonged to the Henneberrys now. And that the Gladstones, who owned it first, were gone. My mother once told my aunt that Martin Gladstone had died from sickness in his brain, cancer or a tumor, and then three years later Mrs. Gladstone choked on a pink chicken bone candy.

"Such a shame the church placed her with them. They're despicable people, you know. After what they've done to her."

"What do you mean?" During her visits, I could always hear my mother talking with my aunt. Not that I tried to eavesdrop. The walls were just thin, the vents large. And she'd never said a bad word about the Gladstones. Maybe Mrs. Grimshaw was mixed up about that, too.

Mrs. Grimshaw put a hand to her eyes and looked up and down the beach. "Abel's not here," she mumbled. Then she started walking back up the path. She moved fast for an old lady. I hurried to keep up.

"What did they do to my mother?"

"And who's that, dear?"

"I mean Esther. You said the Gladstones did something?"

"Oh yes. Well, they brought her in to lift Muriel's spirits, I suppose. As a friend. A distraction. Muriel had been in a delicate state, unstable, you might say, since what happened with Alexander."

My hands were sweating. I wiped them on my T-shirt. Who was Alexander?

Mrs. Grimshaw wormed her arm through mine again. "If only Muriel had been more sensible. But really, you can't leave a child alone with someone so irresponsible. She always was a flighty girl."

"What child?" I asked.

"Alexander. Muriel's baby brother. Poor thing drowned in that very lake behind us. Only three years old. They said he made it all the way through the woods and Muriel never even noticed he was missing. Can you imagine?"

"I never knew that," I said.

"It ruined that girl, it did. What a tragedy when you're only a teenager."

I remembered Mrs. Henneberry sitting on the couch in the big family room like a marble statue. Her cigarette right in front of her face as though it was glued there.

"Ruth Gladstone never forgave Muriel, of course. Was determined to send her away to a hospital, but Martin brought in those sisters instead. Esther and another girl. A bit older. Well, Muriel picked out Esther, and they sent the sister back. That seemed to do the trick."

A dull pain spread through me. The back of my nose stung like I'd sniffed pepper. In a box on the shelf in our apartment closet, Aunt Celia had a photograph of the two of them taken shortly after they'd gotten off the boat. Side by side, eyes wide and no smiles. Their hands were clasped together, and they wore identical woolen coats. Name tags clipped on their lapels.

Muriel picked out Esther.

They sent the sister back.

Like she was a sweater that didn't fit, or a hamburger with a burnt bun.

"How did it do the trick?" I whispered.

"Esther lifted Muriel's dark mood, didn't she? That girl clings to Esther, won't give her a moment's peace." Mrs. Grimshaw kept walking. "I don't mean to gossip, dear. I shouldn't say anything more."

That was fine by me. I didn't want to hear any more. There wasn't enough room to fit any more sadness inside my heart.

The path forked, and we went to the right. "Abel? Abel, dear? Can you hear me?"

After we'd made our way back to the hollow, she turned to me. "And what's your name, young man?"

"Um. I already told you. Thomas."

"That's a good, strong name." She waggled the tip of her finger inside her ear. "And who's your mother?"

"She's— I've got to go now."

I wanted to get away from her. Mrs. Grimshaw wasn't like Mrs. King at all. Mrs. King never told me things that made me more miserable. She never forgot a single thing, either, even when I wanted her to.

"I'm sorry," I said when I returned to the kitchen. My mother pulled her head out of the oven. She was wearing bright orange gloves.

"What was that?"

"I'm sorry I said mean stuff."

"I understand, Thomas." She sat back on her heels and put her orange hands in her lap. "I didn't want to accept it either, but in the long run it only hurts worse. You going to be okay?"

I'd been so selfish. Not once had I considered what it was like for my mother. Separated from her big sister when she was only thirteen. Now pulled apart for good. I wanted to hug her.

"Thomas?"

"I think so." Though I knew I wouldn't be. I knew I'd never be okay again. She probably wouldn't be either.

She got up off the floor and tugged the gloves from her hands. "I have an idea. Why don't you make a paper chain?"

"A what?"

"Me and your—" She folded and unfolded her gloves. "It's a craft I did with my mum. When I was a girl in London. I'd make a chain of paper loops to count the days if there was an event in the future. Every day I'd rip one off and the chain would get smaller and smaller."

"Why would I want to do that?"

She lowered her head. "So summer won't seem like forever, I guess." Sunlight was coming in through the window and making her face glimmer. "You can see how we're getting closer to a solution."

"You mean, leaving here?"

"Exactly. When we figure things out."

I wasn't ready to ask what she was figuring out. What if she was figuring in the wrong direction? When the only possible way was going back to Lower Washbourne. To the apartment. Even though Aunt Celia wouldn't be there, I could still see Wally. And Mrs. King would be downstairs. Everything was waiting for me.

"What do you think?" my mother asked.

I thought it was an activity for first graders, but I said, "I suppose I can try."

"Really?" She sounded happy. Then she went to the laundry area and returned with a pad of construction paper, colored pencils, and a small tub of school paste.

I climbed onto my stool at the counter. "How many days?"

"Well, we've got eight left in June, including today. Then sixty-two for July and August combined. So that makes seventy in total?"

Seventy. That seemed like an impossibly long chain, but I set to work. Cutting narrow strips of paper with kitchen scissors. Inside some, I made drawings. The tabby cat that sometimes appeared on our fire escape. An earwig in a bathroom sink. My birthday cake with eleven candles. I wanted to draw a picture of my aunt, but all I could see was a low leafy shrub and a veiny blue leg sticking out from underneath. I tried to blink it away.

"Thomas? Might I have a few?"

"Sure." I pushed a bunch toward her.

"I'm not much of an artist, but I can write notes. My mum used to do that. Put in secret messages to brighten my day."

When we'd finished, I mixed them all up and then twisted the tin lid off the paste. I brushed gunk on one end of each strip and looped each one through the next.

"Well done," my mother said when I was finished. "We can hang it under the cupboards." With pieces of Scotch tape, she fixed the paper chain to the wall. "It really adds some dazzle, doesn't it?"

The chain went across a full wall and halfway along a second. Red and blue and yellow and green. So many links.

"If you made one for today, you can go ahead and rip it off."

I went to the beginning and took the first loop. The glue was still soft, so I peeled it open. My mother's neat handwriting was on the inside. *Everything will turn out okay.* I folded the strip over and shoved it into my pocket.

"Should we take a blanket outside and have supper on the grass?"

"Sure," I said. My voice seemed far away. "That sounds nice."

"I think so too," she said.

—

In the days that followed, we never left the Henneberry home to go to a funeral. I was afraid to ask my mother if my aunt was buried in the ground or burned to ashes. Part of me didn't want to upset her. Part of me didn't want to know.

Most mornings, I'd play with Martin's matchbox cars by the side of the house. My mother didn't want me in the woods or going near the pool. Several times I saw the gardener, Mr. Green Thumb, drive up in his truck. He'd mow the lawn or trim some bushes and then disappear again. Every so often I'd catch sight of Mrs. Grimshaw slipping in and out of the trees. On the breeze, I could hear her calling out, "Abel? Your tea's getting cold." She sounded sad, but also determined. Sometimes I wished I could be like her. Still believing, still hoping Aunt Celia was alive. But my mother was right. The grief was unavoidable. Hiding from it was only making it worse.

Testimony continues today in the trial against eleven-year-old Thomas Leon Ware, charged in the triple murder of the Henneberrys, an affluent family from Upper Washbourne. On the stand this afternoon is Detective Ernst O'Connor, and he has revealed that the suspected weapon used in the murders, a 1958 Colt Python, was not recovered at the scene. Home and property were searched to no avail. Sources say the gun belonged to victim Dr. Raymond Henneberry, who was an avid collector of firearms.

Detective O'Connor spoke with our reporters at the courthouse. "More than a dozen officers combed through the brush," he stated. "Even used some of those metal detector contraptions." He indicated a search of the water was challenging as officers wading in the lake affected visibility. "But we're confident the accused managed to stash the weapon somewhere," O'Connor continued. "A clever spot, to be sure."

Mr. William Evans, defense counsel for Thomas Ware, told reporters, "This only lends further credibility to my client's account. What happened to the gun is simple. The man who shot the Henneberrys took the weapon with him when he left."

Only time will tell what the jury decides.

The trial continues tomorrow.

CHAPTER TEN

The weekend was nearly over when Dr. Henneberry returned from what my mother had called a "little getaway." Mr. Fulsome was with him.

I was in the kitchen with her when the front door slammed. "Esther!" Dr. Henneberry hollered. "We need ice."

My mother straightened her spine, picked at a spot on the front of her apron. "I wasn't expecting him home yet," she said. "I don't have anything prepared."

"We got plenty." Our supper was in the oven.

"Tuna casserole won't do, unfortunately."

"Esther?" he yelled again. "Hurry up. Jimmy needs a drink."

Laughter bounced down the hallway. "Don't listen to him, Esther." Mr. Fulsome was slurring. "Ray's the demanding bastard."

My mother removed the metal ice tray from the freezer, pulled back the lever. Piled the cubes into a crystal bowl. Lay a tiny set of silver claws on top. I trailed behind her down the hallway. We passed two doors, then she turned left at the third. I lingered outside, watching through the gap near the hinges. The room was bright with afternoon sunlight. Mr. Fulsome had dropped into a brown leather chair, head lolled back, legs spread. I heard Dr. Henneberry say, "Quit fussing, Esther. I'll make them myself."

"Not to trouble you," Mr. Fulsome said as my mother passed in front of him, "but any chance of something salty? Salami, say? Or cheese?"

"I'll put a plate together," she said. "Won't take a minute or two."

"You are an absolute doll, Esther. And underappreciated, I might add."

Dr. Henneberry grunted as he sat in the leather chair next to Mr. Fulsome.

My mother brushed past me, hurrying back to the kitchen. I wasn't sure whether I should follow her or wait by the door. Since coming to that house, I'd found it difficult to know where I belonged.

"Can you believe it's nearly July?" Mr. Fulsome said. "Think we'll fit in another boys' weekend?"

"Haven't the faintest, Jim. Got more important things on my mind."

"True. I've been ignoring that."

"Ignoring it won't make it go away. I thought I had our little issue solved, but my entire plan's gone to pot."

"Surely it's salvageable? Whatever it was."

"Nope. Not in the least."

Whistling, then. "We're into it, aren't we, Ray? Up to our necks."

Ice clinking against glass. Dr. Henneberry said, "I saw him out front, you know."

"Who?"

"Don't play dumb, Jimmy. He was sitting in his car on the road. Piece of junk, I might add. He's been monitoring the house."

"Monitoring? C'mon, Ray. You can barely see the end of your drive from here. Let alone recognize a man in a car."

"You don't forget a mug like that. Has he come by yours?"

"Nah. Wouldn't notice if he did."

"Yeah, you wouldn't heed an elephant if it was sitting on your sofa."

"I might if it had lipstick on." Mr. Fulsome laughed.

As they spoke, a sharp pain arrived in my stomach. I'd seen the man, too. In a black car, the same day I arrived. As soon as my mother and I got closer, he'd revved his engine and driven away. My mother said he was likely dreaming about a better life for his family, but what if he had something to do with my aunt? What if he was the same man who made her wait on the front step of our apartment? What if he'd followed me because he thought I'd seen him from our apartment window?

I hadn't noticed his hand. I hadn't noticed his face. I was so focused on balancing George, I wasn't paying attention.

I gazed through the gap again. Dr. Henneberry was reading a newspaper now, the pages open in front of his face. Mr. Fulsome was leaning forward in his chair, using his finger to twirl the ice in his empty glass.

"A round tomorrow, Ray?"

"No time for golf. I've got back-to-back appointments all week."

"Later in the afternoon, then. Nothing wrong with a few hours of leisure."

The paper cracked as Dr. Henneberry flipped a page. "Some of us have to work, Jim."

"Hey, hey, now. I work."

"Doing a few deliveries here or there doesn't count."

"It's enough," he said. "I'm comfortable."

I willed them to talk more about the man.

"You're becoming quite dull company, my friend," Mr. Fulsome said as he crunched a piece of ice. "Quite dull indeed."

Dr. Henneberry cracked the pages again. It was an angry crack this time. He crossed one leg over the other and tapped the air with his foot. *Tap. Tap. Tap*. Then his slipper dropped to the floor. He was not wearing a sock. His bare foot moved through the sunlight. Was that a shadow? I pushed harder against the wood frame. No, it wasn't a shadow at all. The largest toenail was dark purple and blue. As though he'd hurt it. As though he'd dropped something on it.

A paperweight.

My mouth went dry and my heart began pounding so hard in my head, everything went fuzzy. I stared at his injured foot. It wove its way down, poking about until it found the opening of his slipper. He cleared his throat and snapped the paper. Slipper back in place, he tapped the air again. *Tap. Tap. Tap.*

"You're free to find better, Jim," he said. "I don't have you handcuffed."

Mr. Fulsome shook his head. "Tetchy, tetchy."

I rushed back to the kitchen, jumped onto my stool, and gripped the wooden seat with both hands.

It's a stupid thing to think.

It's a really stupid thing to think.

I make stuff up. Mrs. Pinsent tells me that all the time. She says, "Thomas Leon Ware, that noggin of yours floats all over my classroom without permission." Wally's supposed to poke me so I come back. But Wally isn't around. I need Wally.

At the counter, my mother was arranging a plate of finger foods. Rolled-up cold cuts and slices of cheese. Green olives with pimento. Peeled boiled eggs from the refrigerator. And pieces of toast with the edges removed. Her cheeks looked warm and some of her hair had fallen out of its clip.

"Thomas?" she said when she saw me. "Why are you shaking?"

"I got cold." My teeth were clanking. "It's chilly in here."

"Oh, it can be." She picked up the plate. "Even on the hottest summer day, some corners never get warm."

—

That night, I couldn't sleep. When my mother came into the room, I still hadn't dozed off. Even though I was mostly certain Dr. Henneberry didn't know my aunt, the house felt even scarier now. The place was enormous, but suddenly it seemed cramped. Like the air was gone. The feeling reminded me of that afternoon Wally and I were exploring a drainpipe underneath the road going to Greenlake. At the beginning it was fine, but as we reached the middle, we'd both started feeling odd. Wally fell down on his knees, and I had to drag him by the hood of his coat to the other side.

As soon as my mother's head touched her pillow, she went straight to sleep. I didn't like being alone in the cot and I rolled onto my side to face the wall. Then I cried as quietly as I could for my aunt. I wondered where she was now. Even if she was dead, she still had to be somewhere. Solid things don't just vanish. Maybe she was up with God. Mrs. Pinsent talked about that sometimes in class, about having faith. So did Wally. His grandmother died when she banged her head in a slippery bathtub. He said his father told him she'd gone to "the Great Beyond," whatever that was, and Wally would see her again after he finished living his own life. Maybe I'd see Aunt Celia again, too. Maybe she was up there waiting for me. Maybe.

A heavy feeling rolled over me. I put my hands over my eyes and pretended Aunt Celia was sitting on the end of the cot. Her voice seeped into my head. "Everything always seems so much worse in the dark, Tommie, love. I always tell you that."

"But why?" I whispered.

"Because you can't see things clearly, of course."

"What should I do?"

"Take a gander in the morning, darling. When there's better light. Can you do that?"

"Okay." I lowered my hands and stared out the window at the moon. I remembered when I thought it was made of cheese. Wally never mocked me, but he did set me straight. "My father says it's nothing but a clump of dust."

"I'm sorry I didn't save you, Aunt Celia." My voice hitched. "I should've saved you."

She was quiet, but I could still hear her breathing.

"Was it him? Was it Dr. Henneberry you met at St. Augustine's?"

She never answered me.

"Who was it? *Who was it?*"

And then the sound of her breath was gone.

I waited for her to come back, but then I was opening my eyes and the room was sunny. My mother's bed was neatly made. The curtains were closed, but a breeze pushed its way in, making them flutter. George was there, on the windowsill, patiently swimming in slow circles. I sat up, put my feet on the cool floor. I wasn't so frightened anymore. What Aunt Celia said was true. Nothing ever seemed so terrible in the daylight. Even if Dr. Henneberry had stubbed his toe, that didn't mean anything. Tons of people bruise themselves every single day.

CHAPTER ELEVEN

A few mornings later, Martin Henneberry was sitting in my spot when I came into the kitchen for breakfast. On the counter in front of him, he'd set up glass tubes, eye-droppers, and a silver microscope. The cardboard box had a red-and-yellow picture of a smiling boy. Letters that said "Radioactive Ores Inside!"

I sat down next to him. "You're back," I said. My mother gave me a slice of cinnamon toast and a glass of milk.

"Yeah." He tapped brown powder into one of the tubes. "I hate those people."

"What people?"

"Old friends of my mother's parents. She makes us visit every year, but they're stuck up. Don't know how to have fun."

I laughed loudly, because I wanted him to know I was glad his trip was over. I wanted him to think I wasn't like them at all. I knew how to have a good time.

"Martin and Mrs. Henneberry arrived early this morning," my mother said. "Mrs. Henneberry ate some bad clams. It was fortu—"

"What's with that paper thing?" Martin asked, pointing at my chain. Already it seemed a little shorter.

"I made it. To count down."

"Count down to what?"

I still didn't know exactly what was going to happen at the end of the chain. "Just the days of summer."

"I bet a blind man could do a neater job."

My face got warm. Martin was right. Parts of it were sloppy and uneven. I was eleven years old. Not five or six.

"I'm kidding, Ware," he said, nudging my arm. "It's cool. It looks cool."

"Oh." I blew the air out of my lungs. "Thanks."

"Aren't you curious what I'm doing?" He lowered a pair of goggles down over his eyes and poured clear liquid into the tube.

"I was just about to ask," I said.

"Experiments. Highly advanced experiments."

"Neat."

"And this here"—he held up the tube—"makes things glow."

"Isn't that interesting," my mother said. She was wringing her hands in a towel. "Don't you think, Thomas?"

"Sure is."

Martin pushed a rubber stopper into a test tube and shook the contents. Then he popped off the stopper and offered it to me. "Take it," he said.

I put my toast down and reached for it.

Martin smiled. "Drink up."

I lifted up the tiny tube. It was filled with water, maybe, and a cloud of sandy brown bits. "Why's it so warm?"

Martin leaned his head to one side and his eyebrows went up. "That's science, Ware. Chemicals doing, you know, chemistry stuff."

"Sounds complicated."

"It is. I'll explain it to you later. Now drink up, I said."

The tube was getting warmer. I coughed. "Looks like dirt."

"Yeah. No. Why would I give you dirt?"

"Um." I switched hands. The glass was almost hot now.

My mother's mouth was open, and while no words were coming out, I could practically hear her saying, *Careful, Thomas. You have to be careful.*

"Those ores are pricey, Ware. And I don't have a ton." Martin shoved up the goggles. Red rings circled his eyes. "I don't want to waste them."

"But what if it—"

"C'mon. I double dare you!"

No one had ever dared me before. Let alone double dared. I put my nose near the opening. No smell. No fizzing or smoking. I wondered if Martin might think I was gutsy if I poured it into my mouth and gulped it. How bad could it taste?

My mother made a high-pitched coughing sound. She came over to me and removed the test tube from my fingers. "Martin Henneberry," she said. Really softly. "You are such a cutup."

He flipped the lid of his chemistry set closed. "I'm not a cutup. I just want to see him glow."

"Well Thomas doesn't want to glow today." She offered the experiment back to Martin. "But you're ever so kind trying to include him."

After I finished my breakfast, Mrs. Henneberry came into the kitchen. She held the edge of the counter with one hand. "It's Tom, right?"

"Yes," I said.

"I've scoured the entire house for you, young man."

"But he's been sitting right here, Mrs. Henneberry," my mother said. "Is everything okay?"

"Not in the least, Esther." She shook her head slowly. "Everything is certainly not okay."

"You're still feeling poorly?"

"*Poorly* is not a word to describe it. I'm in a terrible state of discomfort. But you needn't worry. Dr. Norton has just left and he's given me a little something to manage my symptoms." She touched my arm with icy fingertips. Her eyes were focused on my ear or my cheek. I couldn't tell. "Tom, darling. You're going to come sit with me. Keep me amused while I recover from this bout of indigestion."

I didn't want to go with Mrs. Henneberry. I wanted to catch up with Martin. He'd packed up his chemistry set and left. Perhaps he'd gone outside. Perhaps he'd take me swimming again.

"I'll sit with you," my mother said.

"Now, Esther. We're not girls anymore. Besides, you have your responsibilities."

My mother scratched at her neck. Then she said, "Go ahead, Thomas. Be a polite guest, please."

I followed Mrs. Henneberry as she swayed down the hallway. We went into the family room with the high slanted ceiling and the books and games. Through the open window came the sound of whistling and branches breaking. Mr. Green Thumb was working nearby.

She sank into the pink couch, patted the place next to her.

I eased in beside her. The material was soft. Maybe velvet. On the wall above the television was an ugly painting made with swirls of primary colors. Green. Red. Yellow. I could have painted it myself.

"Closer, Tom. You're much too far away."

I shuffled next to her. Our thighs were nearly touching. She took my hand in hers and squeezed my fingers. I wondered if this was what Mrs. Grimshaw meant about Mrs. Henneberry clinging to my mother. Like she seemed to be clinging to me now.

Her eyelids looked heavier by the minute. "I see you're admiring the artwork," she said, her chin drifting in that direction. "Are you familiar with the artist?"

I shook my head.

She giggled. "No of course you're not. How would you have been exposed to such creativity in Lower Washbourne?"

Why wouldn't I? Mrs. Pinsent made sure our class-room shelves had plenty of art books. And the library near the school received new material every month. Plus Wally's father was a living encyclopedia.

"He's very famous," Mrs. Henneberry said.

"For that?"

"You are so dear, Tom." She lifted my hand and, for a moment, pressed it to her cheek. "I hear you've been enjoying your stay with us."

"Yeah."

"You mean yes, ma'am."

"Sorry." I coughed. "Yes, ma'am."

"Martin says he's taken you under his wing."

"Sort of," I said.

"Do tell me all the wonderful things he's done for you."

He *had* done some nice things for me. "Well, we went swimming. And he pulled me around in a little boat."

"That sounds like such a romp." She yawned and closed her eyes. After a few seconds, she opened them again, took a sharp breath. "What else, Tom? What else has my son done to make you feel welcomed?"

"He gave me a bunch of those miniature cars."

When she touched my leg, my skin prickled up. "He's a very caring boy, Martin is. And I'm so pleased you boys are hitting it off."

I nodded.

"Can I share something with you, Tom? In strictest confidence?"

I nodded again.

"I'm sure you'd never guess, but Martin had a diffi-cult time making pals as a youngster." Her shoulder was against mine. "You see, he's sensitive, and his class-mates—well, his classmates teased him for whatever tiny reason they could find. Nothing, really." She laughed a little. "He was a tad uncoordinated. Couldn't run as fast or kick the ball like the others, but it was barely notice-able. Do you know what I think, Tom?"

"Um—"

"I suspect it had to do with my family. They were Gladstones." She touched my thigh again. "Of course you know who the Gladstones were."

"Yes," I said, even though I knew very little. Other than Mr. Gladstone had a factory, and many people worked there. Like Mr. King, before he got sick. And Wally's father.

"It was jealousy, you understand. Probably the par-ents' attitude filtering down to their children. So inde-cent, and poor Martin's feelings are still easily hurt, Tom. Those bullies did quite a bit of damage."

I picked at my fingernails. "That's not good," I said.

"Oh, but he has a pal now. An upstanding boy named Skip. And Genie. Has he mentioned Genie Bishop?"

"No, ma'am."

"She just adores him. A pleasant enough girl. Per-fectly fine for the moment." Her head tipped forward, and then she righted it. "And since you've arrived to visit with us, he's got you, too."

I tried to smile. "Yeah."

"He's delicate, though, Tom. You must promise to be gentle with him, do you understand?"

"I do, Mrs. Henneberry." Though I didn't really. Aunt Celia used to say Wally had a young soul and I had to be extra kind. But Wally and Martin were nothing alike.

"Perfect," she said. "You'll be a companion for him this summer." She drew her fingers through my hair. "You are so like him when he was younger, in his old clothes."

Martin's T-shirt seemed brand new. The shorts had a sharp crease where my mother had ironed them.

Mrs. Henneberry leaned back against the couch and sighed loudly. "Would you mind, sweetheart, helping me with my feet?"

"Your feet?"

"Yes, just giving them a rub."

With her toes she slipped off her shoes and closed her eyes again. She was very still, her chest barely moving. Her hands rested in her lap. Then she twitched her toes through her pantyhose. "Tom, dear? I'm waiting?"

I knelt on the floor in front of her. Her legs were like twigs. She lifted her left foot onto my lap and I held on to it, pressing my thumbs into the soft mounds. Beneath my fingers, her damp stockings slipped around. She made faint noises and covered her eyes with the crook of her arm.

I bent closer, smelled her ankle. I thought she'd have a flowery scent like my aunt, but instead it was sour. Reminding me of dark malt vinegar. I paused to sniff my hands. The smell had gotten onto my fingers.

Mrs. Henneberry's eyelids popped up. "Did I say you were finished, Tom?"

"Sorry."

As I pinched her feet, I wondered about the things Mrs. Grimshaw had told me. If Mrs. Henneberry had never forgiven herself about her little brother, was that why she acted so strangely? And would I ever forgive myself about Aunt Celia? I shouldn't have let her go anywhere with that man. I could've hollered out the window. I could've thrown a plate or a vase so it shattered on the roof of his car. He'd have slammed on the brakes. Gotten out, furious. Told my aunt he'd had enough. It was over between them.

"Between you and Dr. Norton, I'm beginning to feel restored." It was getting harder to understand her. It sounded like her tongue was too large for her mouth. She slid her hand over her chest and onto her stomach.

I pushed and rubbed and dug my knuckles into the flesh of her feet until my muscles started to cramp. Finally she sat up, her head seesawing on her neck. "Dear me. My vision has gone patchy." Then she dug around in the pocket of her dress. "For you." She pressed a silver nickel into my palm. "Buy yourself something sugary, darling. A little treat from me."

I locked my fist around the coin. This was the first money I'd ever earned in my life. Though I'd done chores around the apartment, my aunt had never given me an allowance. She told me I resided there, so I had to contribute to the upkeep.

The nickel felt warm. That tiny treasure, only enough for a chocolate bar, actually made me feel better. Stronger. Happier. I'd have to ask my mother who painted the picture above the television. I'd research his name next time I visited the library.

When I got back to the kitchen, my mother was lifting the lid on a pot and shoving an entire raw chicken inside.

"Where have you been?"

"Doing work for Mrs. Henneberry," I said. I sniffed my fingers again. "Who pain—"

"Good boy." She wiped her hands with the cup towel looped over the string of her apron. Then she reached for a yellow onion and with a long blade, sliced the end off it.

I'd ask later. I walked through the laundry room and into the bedroom. Then I froze. Something was wrong.

Something was wrong with George.

He was on his side, floating near the top of his bowl. His water didn't look clean. I rushed over to the window ledge.

He's dead, I thought. *George is dead.*

My second-best friend. He was the last thing Aunt Celia had given to me. I was supposed to take care of him. *I didn't do a good job. Again. I can't look after anything properly. What's wrong with me?*

George's fin lifted and fell against his side. He was still alive! He drifted through the water. His gills opened and flopped closed. I grabbed his bowl and carried it to the sink. After scooping him out, I dumped everything else. With a thin stream of water, I gently rinsed his orange scales. "You have to get better, George." I let water gush into his mouth. It came out the slits and spread over his body. Then I refilled his bowl and set it on the floor. I put in a few drops from the bottle of special solution that made his water safe.

"Come on, George," I said as I dipped him back into the water. "You can do it. She promised you'd live forever."

My mother came to the door. "What happened?"

"I don't know." I swiped my hands on my shorts. "His bowl turned brown."

"Did you overfeed him?"

"No." I wasn't a dunce. There was no pointy hat for me at school, like Martin had said. "I followed the rules exactly. No more than his eyeball."

"Maybe the sunlight, then. Having him up on the ledge made scum grow."

In the fresh water, his gills widened a little more. His fins seemed to be working harder. He wasn't on his side anymore, but he wasn't cutting around at his regular speed.

"George and I want to leave," I whispered. More than anything, I wanted to be home. Even with Aunt Celia gone, everything else would be safe. "Can I go back to my apartment?"

"No, Thomas."

"But what about my stuff?"

"I don't know. I think the police—"

"Have you called them? What are they doing? Have they found him yet?" As I watched George struggling, my questions were coming faster than I could get them out. I started to yell. "And when are we going? Where are we going to live? You said you were figuring things out. There's been loads of time. You should know by now. Unless you're not actually doing anything at all!"

"Thomas." She had her hand on her cheek. "How can you speak like that?"

I dropped my head. If Aunt Celia were there, she'd be so ashamed. Acting that way with my mother. I hadn't meant to. When I opened my mouth, the rudeness had just come spilling out.

"I'm sorry," I said. I couldn't look at her.

"That's okay, Thomas. I'm trying my best." Then she pointed at George. "I think you reached him in the nick of time." Her voice was cheerful. She bent down and lifted the wet bowl from the floor, slid it onto the dresser. "You should keep him here, though, from now on. To be safe. All that sunshine was too harsh for him."

I wasn't so sure about the sunshine part. The cloudy water had looked a whole lot like the liquid from a test tube. A test tube that had gotten hot in my hand and was filled with expensive ores that Martin Henneberry didn't want to go to waste.

EXCERPT

Testimony of Lt. Terry Hackman, First Precinct, Greenlake
Direct Examination by Prosecutor Clay Fibbs

A. Yes, I thought it absolutely necessary for me to participate in the interview, Mr. Fibbs. Given who the family was. Both the Gladstones and the Henneberrys have been generous supporters of our force over the years. We gave this the very highest priority.

Q. **Of course, Lieutenant Hackman. Can you describe how Thomas Ware was behaving?**

A. He seemed calm enough. Asked Detective Miller for a soda pop. Which he received.

Q. **And when you inquired about that afternoon?**

A. At first, he was silent. Then he kept repeating himself. A man in a black car. It was a man in a black car. When I asked about this supposed man's appearance, he said he was tall and wearing a beige coat. And one of those felt hats, a porkpie. If you can imagine it, in the August heat.

Q. **Did that seem unusual to you?**

A. It certainly did. And Mr. Ware couldn't remember much else. Nothing about the man's hair, or his face. If he had a birthmark or was left- or right-handed. He said he was just too shocked to notice.

Q. **What was your impression of Thomas Ware?**

A. The defendant wouldn't look me in the eye. He kept fidgeting with his fingers, wiping his nose. Every time he

was asked a question, he'd slurp his soda. Stare at the
bottle or twist it around. All those little actions, little
distractions, indicated to me he was being deceitful.

*Defense Counsel: Objection, Your Honor. The witness is
speculating. Drawing conclusions.*

*The Court: And a police lieutenant, with twenty-seven
years of experience, can't draw a conclusion,
Mr. Evans? Objection overruled.*

Q. **Did you also talk to Thomas Ware's mother? Esther
Ware?**

A. I did. No stretch to say she was hysterical. Not a
surprise, of course. Any lady would be, given what
she'd experienced.

Q. **Did you ask Miss Ware why she didn't call for an
ambulance? Call for help?**

A. We sure did. She said she wasn't permitted to use the
main line in the home. And she'd been responsible for
the costs of the second line. Her bill was in arrears,
so it'd been disconnected.

Q. **So her personal phone line was not operational,
and she didn't want to use the Henneberrys' phone
during this emergency?**

A. Claimed she wasn't allowed. We suspected she was
buying time, sir. To clean up. So her and the boy could
get their stories straight.

*Defense Counsel: Your Honor, objection. Again, he's
creating a narrative. A highly inflammatory one,
at that.*

The Court: Overruled.

Q. Does that inaction, not calling for help, indicate to you that she wasn't afraid of the shooter? Didn't feel her life was threatened?

A. I don't believe she thought she or the boy were in danger. It occurred to us early on that she knew the shooter and didn't view him as a risk to her.

Defense Counsel: Your Honor.

The Court: Enough, Mr. Evans.

Q. So instead of calling for help, she washed the defendant's clothing. Did you ask why she was doing that?

A. She didn't give a clear answer, but her efforts removed blood evidence from Thomas Ware's socks and shirt and shorts. She even scrubbed up his shoes.

Q. Did Esther Ware claim to have witnessed the murders?

A. She said she saw the whole thing through an upstairs window. Her words were nearly identical to Mr. Ware's. Generic male arrives in a generic black car, then he sauntered over, picked up Dr. Henneberry's gun, and shot the lot of them dead.

Q. After Miss Ware made these proclamations, did you investigate?

A. It was our job to follow up on every lead. We never made any assumptions, sir. But none of what she said made sense. I mean, why would a man, intent on killing a whole family, just expect a gun to be lying around? And leave two witnesses behind?

Q. Thank you, Lieutenant. And finally, what led to the decision to arrest Thomas Ware?

A. Every scrap of evidence pointed to him. And I soon came to realize this was not a child who was scared or distressed. This was an intelligent and disturbed young man, cold-blooded, the likes of which this county has never seen. Maybe even this whole country. I mean, what kind of kid can do something like that and then ask you for a flipping cherry soda?

CHAPTER TWELVE

After I ensured George was okay, I went outside and stayed by the rosebush for a while. Tucked underneath, I found the cardboard box, and when I lifted the lid, a handful of new matchbox cars waited inside. A Batman comic was rolled up on top. Martin must have put those there for me. Maybe he hadn't tried to hurt George. A friend wouldn't do something like that. I couldn't let my head keep pretending. I couldn't. Not about Martin. And not about Dr. Henneberry.

Two deep breaths. The storm that was brewing inside me did a hiccup and was gone.

I took out the comic. The cover was pristine, as though it hadn't yet been lifted, but inside several of the girls' faces had been scratched out. It was still fine to read, though. I liked to whisper all the noises that were written in big cartoon letters. "*Pow*." "*Crash!*" "*Sok*." "*Blap!*"

Through the window above my head came the sound of water splashing, dishes clanging. My mother was humming to herself. Bees buzzed around the drooping white roses. Mr. Green Thumb was pushing a lawnmower down by the pool. I didn't know where the Henneberrys were. I leaned against the side of the house. The stone was warm on my back. Sunlight drifted down on me and I closed my eyes.

Aunt Celia was there, standing behind my lids. Her hand reached for mine. "What do you say?" she asked. "You free?"

"Always."

We had a rundown theatre in Lower Washbourne, but Aunt Celia always insisted we take the bus to Greenlake so we could sit in the cooled air. She liked that the usher, with his round cap perched on top of his head, showed us to our plush chairs.

I wore shorts and a checkered dress shirt that had been Martin's. I even wore his socks. They went all the way up to my knees. My aunt had on a flowery skirt and a frilly white blouse. Her lips were red. "Don't we make a handsome couple," she said.

"We do."

As we walked past the popcorn stand, she slowed, then twirled around. Her skirt swung out and the tops of her thighs showed. When she grabbed my hand, pulled me away, I noticed she'd nicked a paper bag of freshly roasted peanuts. The front had a picture of a grinning monkey holding its own tail.

I snacked while I watched the cartoon that played before the western. Aunt Celia wormed her arm over my shoulder and reached into the bag. "This is one of my favorite things, you know."

"Peanuts?"

"No, silly," she said. "Going on a date with my little man."

"Really?"

"Yeah, really." She dropped the shells on the floor and crunched them with her new kitten heel. "Do you know, I was so thrilled when you were on your way."

"On my way where?"

"Oh, gosh. You are a card, Tommie. To this world, of course."

"You were?"

"Sure was. I knew you were going to be the hugest part of my life." Her right hand lifted into the air. "I had that feeling. Right from the get-go. You and me, two peas in a pod." Then she tossed a peanut into her mouth. "And I sure was right, wasn't I?"

My throat knotted up. "You were," I whispered. "Two peas."

And then I opened my eyes and sadness threatened to pin me to the ground. I was only one pea now, and the rest of the pod was empty. I had a feeling no one was even trying to figure out what happened to her. Who'd hurt her. Barely three weeks had passed, and everyone had already forgotten about it.

I couldn't hear humming through the window anymore. Mr. Green Thumb had disappeared. The bees were gone. I forced myself to stand up and I went into the kitchen for a glass of water. My mother was grating carrots into a silver bowl. Flour dotted the tip of her nose.

"What're you making?"

"Mrs. Henneberry's famous carrot cake."

"Mrs. Henneberry's?"

She continued to stir the mixture. Then she turned to me. "I've asked Mr. Vardy to find some chores for you."

"Mr. Green Thumb? The one you—"

"Please don't call him that, Thomas." Her cheeks turned bright red. "You've been moping."

"I haven't."

"Well, go see what he has in mind, and then I'll stop nagging. Deal?"

"Deal," I said.

I found Mr. Vardy on the front porch, clipping dead flowers from the planters. He was wearing a plaid shirt, sleeves rolled up. His face was tanned, and up close, he looked younger than I'd thought he was. Around the same age as Wally's father.

When he saw me, he put down the clippers. "You *are* your mother's son, aren't you?"

"What? I mean, pardon me?"

"Same. You and Esther." He tapped his face near his eyes.

"Yeah." Some of our features were identical. But some weren't.

I could see why my mother liked him. His eyes were pale blue, and he had thick brown hair. Kind of like mine was before Wally's mother had buzzed it off.

"Esther told me you're a hard worker?"

"I guess so." I wondered how she'd even know.

"Then you're exactly who I need." He smiled. His teeth were straight and white.

Without thinking, I asked, "Did Dr. Henneberry make your teeth so nice?"

He smiled again. Wider this time. "Nope. Not even close. Just blessed with a good set of chompers."

"Me, too." I remembered Mrs. King saying the exact same thing. She even used that word. *Chompers*.

As I looked at him out of the corner of my eye, I said, "How long have you worked here, Mr. Vardy?"

"Oh, forever. Too many years to count."

I scuffed my feet. Considered how embarrassed my mother was when I'd mentioned Mr. Green Thumb. Was it possible he was my father? We had the same hair and teeth. Was that enough to call it? I wished so badly Wally would appear. He'd size up Mr. Vardy in a flash and come to a solid conclusion.

"Esther thinks staying busy'll help you get better."

"I'm not sick. Haven't thrown up once."

"I didn't mean you caught a bug. I meant your chest. I'd guess that part of you is pretty sore right about now."

"Maybe." My chest did hurt. It hurt almost all the time.

Mr. Vardy pointed out at the front lawn. "You see the wet-a-beds?"

"Wet-a-what?"

"Those yellow flowers growing all down the sides of the drive."

"Sure. You want me to pick some for Mrs. Henneberry?"

He slapped the leg of his trousers and laughed. I liked those sounds. "She can't tolerate the sight of them. You need to dig them out. With this." He reached behind a planter and pulled out a long screwdriver. The end had two points. "Snag them by the roots and put them in there." He gestured toward a dented bucket beside the bottom step.

I examined the lawn. Hundreds of yellow flowers had bloomed overnight. "All of them?"

"That's the general idea." Then he leapt down the porch steps, jogged across the lawn, climbed into his dusty old truck, and rumbled away.

I squatted down on the grass and shoved the screwdriver into the soft soil. As I pressed backward, I felt a pleasing crack. The dirty root lifted up and up, and I plucked it out and tossed it in the bucket. Then I inched forward to the next one. The hot sun hit my head and sweat dripped down between my shoulders. I kept moving ahead a foot or two and stabbing. My fingers ached and my legs cramped, but I poked the ground over and over. Slowly I made my way down the driveway, and I decided I was going to show my mother's Mr. Green Thumb that I could do a proper job. For a little while, the sorrow that was gnawing at me opened its jaw and let go.

—

After I carried the full bucket back to the porch, I noticed the front door was open. Just a crack. Almost like an invitation. I turned my body sideways and squeezed right through.

At first, I couldn't see a thing. A moment later my eyes adjusted, and I realized I was in a large open area. In the middle a wide staircase rose upward, splitting in two at the halfway point. I slipped off my mucky shoes and tiptoed up the right side of the stairs, then down a hallway.

I knew my mother was in the kitchen and everyone else was gone. Perhaps I'd be able to find Martin's bedroom. I wondered what it would be like. The inside of a toy store? Or full of model airplanes and model cars? Maybe a record player or a stamp collection.

I tiptoed along. It was shadowy and quiet and there were several closed doors on either side. A smell hung in the air, like old lemon candy stale inside the tin.

At the end of the hallway was a dark wooden door. I held my breath and pushed it open. The room was bright, and the bed was covered with a yellow spread that had white pompoms decorating the bottom. A glossy nightdress lay neatly folded near the pillows. Instead of Martin's room, I'd discovered Mrs. Henneberry's.

On top of her dresser was a silver tray with jewelry, some coins, and two brown bottles of pills. Beside that was a light blue glass ball with a tassel. Mrs. Henneberry's perfume. I picked it up and sprayed it. I was reminded of those tiny purple flowers that bloomed in spring. My aunt would love that. I considered stealing it for her, and my fingers began sweating as I was trying to decide. Then it struck me. Again. Why did I keep forgetting she was gone? When were these shocks going to end?

I put the perfume down and pulled open a drawer in her dresser. Wally and I liked to hunt for hidden stuff. He could never find anything, but I was a hound dog. Like that book tucked in the back of his parents' bookshelf. Or the two chocolate bars my aunt had stashed under her side of the mattress.

Mrs. Henneberry's clothes were neatly folded and had striped paper beneath the piles. I searched in her night table next. Pulled on a red knob. I was hoping she'd have a secret bag of candy. But there were no Pixy Stix or Sugar Daddys, just a pencil, two more brown bottles, and a near-emptied tube of hand cream.

In the bottom drawer I found a notebook. As I picked it up, a squirt of fear shot through my guts. As though I was already nervous about what was written inside. Which was silly. It might only be blank pages.

I opened the cover. It wasn't blank. Mrs. Henneberry's writing was wispy and went over and under the lines. I leaned against the high bed and read.

Raymond thinks I'm naive, but I know. He likes it cheap. He likes it dirty. Daddy said never trust a man until you're introduced to his mother. How many years now? And I've never once met dear old mom.

Cheap and dirty? My aunt always talked about getting things on the cheap. It just meant finding a good deal. I flipped a page.

I no longer love him. I was a schoolgirl when I married him. Caught up in the uncertainty of war like the rest of those foolish, foolish girls. Getting hitched before their true loves shipped out. Sometimes I wonder if Raymond only wanted the Gladstone money. He tosses it around like it was his from the start.

I chewed on my thumb. I shouldn't be reading her diary. I should put it away and leave her room. But I couldn't stop myself. I flipped past more pages.

Thank goodness for Dr. Norton, he's the only person keeping me sane these days. And him. Him! I can't even bring myself to write his name. I won't do it, even though it rolls off my tongue when I say it at night and let my hands glide wherever they want to go. I think about him all the time.

Heels clacking in the hallway. I slapped the diary closed and dropped it into the drawer. Pushed the drawer closed with my leg. I didn't have time to crawl under the bed.

Mrs. Henneberry caught me standing there. Her hand very slowly floated up to her neck. "Tom," she said. "How . . . ?"

"I was trying to find the toilet," I blurted.

"You have your own facilities. Is yours not working properly? Should I have your mother call a plumber?"

"No. I got mixed up, is all."

"Of course you did. Why else would you be here?"

I curled my toes into the carpet. It was navy and covered with white squares. I wanted to leave, but I didn't know how.

"And you're a good boy, aren't you, Tom? I can just tell." She took a wobbly step.

"I try, Mrs. Henneberry."

"I know." Her eyes looked wet. "Mothers have an instinct about these things."

Her sweater slipped from her shoulders. She caught it with a finger and threw it on top of the nightgown. Then she lay down on a long chair and lifted up her feet. "Would you please, darling?" Inside her stockings, her toes flicked. "I am so exhausted. All that bother with my carrot cake. The women expect me to put in such effort, and then I'm forced to listen to them nattering at the church. They're all so crude." She put her arm over her eyes. "I mean, how can a lady lick icing from her fingers?"

I knelt down on the carpet and squeezed her left foot. She squeaked, then whispered, "Martin never wanted me close to him, Tom, when he was a toddler. Wouldn't let me touch him. Did you know that?"

"No," I said. *How could I?*

"Raymond was away, you see." She sighed. "That awful war divided so many families."

Like Aunt Celia, and my mother and grandparents. Three sides of a broken triangle. Though it wasn't just the war that separated them. It was the Gladstones, too.

"Martin fussed incessantly as a baby. It was quite stressful, Tom. Made me incredibly sad. He only settled when he was alone in his crib. And let me tell you, he spent the majority of his time there." She wiggled her right foot, and I switched.

"Did your mother help you?"

"My mother had no interest in her grandson. Thank goodness for Esther. Such a wonderful support. Believed in me when my own son didn't trust me at all."

I jabbed harder with my thumbs. "Why wouldn't he trust you?"

"I wasn't always— You see me now, Tom, as a woman who's very grounded. Very poised. But there was a time when I was, how should I put it? A titch more self-absorbed." She sighed. "But you can't visit the past. Adjust things to your liking."

"No," I said. "You can't." Otherwise, Aunt Celia would be alive. Maybe Mrs. Henneberry's little brother would be, too.

She was making more of those noises, like a baby mouse nuzzling around in its nest. I kept kneading and rubbing and pressing into her soles with my knuckles, and after a while she went quiet. I thought she'd fallen asleep, but when a man's voice came down the hallway, she sat up quickly, fluttering her eyes. "You need to scurry along, Tom, dear. Go see how Martin and Dr. Henneberry are managing. They're down by the dock. I believe Skip's with them. Oh, you must meet Skip. He's such a tremendous boy. You're going to really enjoy him. You can go, too."

"Go where?"

"Out for a row on the lake."

"I can?"

"Why not?" She poked another nickel into my hand. "But do be careful, dear. After your fun time, I want you back here. Not a hair out of place."

I shoved the money into my shorts pocket and ran out of her room. I passed Mr. Fulsome on the stairs, and he smiled at me. "Hey, champ," he said. My shoes were still by the front door. I forced them on, the backs folding down. I rushed down the path through the woods. After a few minutes, I could see the blue water twinkling through the trees. I came out on the sandy beach, the same spot I'd been with Mrs. Grimshaw. I slowed near some bushes, hesitated.

Dr. Henneberry and another man were standing on a long wooden dock jutting out into the water. The man was bent over, holding the side of a canoe as Martin and another boy climbed in. Both boys were wearing matching outfits. White T-shirts, white shorts, white sneakers. Martin was smiling at his father. Dr. Henneberry had his hands on his hips, foot tapping. I don't think he was smiling back.

"*You can go, too.*"

I wanted to, I really wanted to, but once I saw Dr. Henneberry out there, my legs began shaking so much, I couldn't step forward. At once, I needed to pee.

Don't be an idiot, I told myself. I made a fist and punched my thigh. Who cared about his dumb toe?

I retreated into the forest. I tucked myself down inside the shadows and watched from my hiding spot. When Martin and Skip began to row, their paddles moved with perfect timing. The two men whooped and waved as the boys disappeared into the long line of sunshine that was floating on the water.

CHAPTER THIRTEEN

I lay on my back on a blanket in the grass. I'd been trying to draw in the notepad my mother had given me, but the clouds kept drifting and changing. The rabbit turned into a spaceship. The fat man who was running became a stew pot with broken handles. The nurse in her uniform turned into nothing. The fluffy strings of white were impossible to capture on paper. It was better to simply watch them drift by and try not to think about anything. Aunt Celia, especially.

Then Martin's round head floated in front of my view, blocking out the sun. I sat up. I hadn't seen him in a few days. Not since George.

"You took that out of my garbage," he said.

I squinted from the sunlight. He had that red streak on his forehead again. "What?"

"My comic."

Superman was on the blanket beside me. "I didn't. You—" But I closed my mouth. I thought he'd been tucking surprises into the shoebox to cheer me up, but now I realized it was my mother.

"Who cares anyway, right? If I was you, I'd steal trash out of my garbage, too." A wide smile. I wasn't sure if he was being friendly or mean. Maybe both? "Hey, I heard about your fish," he said. "Some bad luck, hey?"

I rolled up the comic. In this one, every girl's face had been scratched out. Martin hadn't missed a single one. In some parts, he'd used a black pen to draw two circles with dots in the middle of their chests. Sometimes he'd drawn black triangles on the front of their pants.

When I looked up at Martin again, a soft yellow glow circled his head. He said, "You okay, pal?"

I put the comic back into the shoebox. I didn't understand why he ruined his comics, but that didn't mean he'd hurt George. "Yeah. It was algae. Being on the windowsill made gunk grow."

"Yup. I can see that. Some kind of exo-photo-light reaction." Martin unlatched the tongue of his belt and pulled it in tighter. "Don't forget, Ware. I'm a scientist. If you notice it again, I'll do some tests."

"I will."

"And just so you know, I'm not a cutup. I wish she never called me that."

"Who?"

"Your mother."

I'd forgotten all about it. "I don't think she meant anything."

"No?"

"No," I said.

"Alrighty." He kicked the grass with his sneaker. "Mother says you should come with me."

"Where?" I tried to act like I didn't care, even though I was excited to go wherever he wanted. I was tired of staying by the door with the rosebush. Tired of feeling that lonely ache behind my breastbone.

"Just climbing trees."

"Really?" I loved being in the woods around Martin's house. Maybe if we found four trees close enough together, we could drag in boards and build a platform high in the sky. We could nail wooden slats into one of the trunks so we could get up easily. Or even better, a rope ladder. We could haul it up so no one could reach us.

"Let's go if you're coming. I'm on a schedule."

"For climbing?"

He grinned. "Yup. That, too."

I left the magazine and the notepad on the blanket. He stomped down over the slope, and I stomped behind him. Past the pool and into the woods. As we walked under the leafy branches, Martin picked up several pine cones and tiny stones and put them in his pockets. I did the same. Perhaps I'd start a collection. The ground and the air around me hummed and crunched from all the summer bugs.

Over his shoulder, Martin said, "Mother says we have to spend time together."

"Why?"

"Because we're buddies, remember? You've got my back."

"Oh," I said. "Yeah. I do." I knew how to do that. I always had Wally's back if anyone was teasing him. More than once I'd gotten into fights at school because of him. Mrs. Pinsent said I was "acting impulsively," but my aunt told me I was gallant and understood how to be a loyal friend.

He checked his wristwatch again. "Come on," he grumbled. "We're almost late."

"For what?" I said.

He didn't answer. We went deeper into the woods. Martin was moving quickly, and I had to skip to keep up. We passed so many quality trees. Knobs and branches right for stepping, gripping. Martin never slowed down to check them out. Maybe he had his favorites.

Worn paths went left and right, but we were on the same one I'd followed the other day. We kept going until we'd nearly reached the hollow. "Here," Martin finally said. "Best two trees in the entire woods."

"Really?"

"Sure." He pointed at the trunk on the left. "You go over there. And I'll go here. Get good and high, now, Ware. So you can't be seen from the ground."

I scrambled up as far as I could. "Is this high enough?" I yelled over to him.

"Will you shut it?" he yelled back.

The tree swayed gently with the wind, and I hugged the trunk. A few feet away, a nest balanced on a branch.

A circle of twigs and strands of yellow grass with two blue eggs inside.

"What are we doing up here?"

"Guarding my land. This is Martin's Woods, remember?" He waved below him. "No person can enter without my say-so."

"Oh. Okay." I peered down through the leaves. "I see a squirrel."

"Shush."

Shuffling. Somewhere below us. I leaned and peered through the leafy branches. It was Mrs. Grimshaw. She must've forgotten her dress because she was only wearing a pink slip. An enormous glittery necklace looped around her neck, and her gray hair was poking out all over.

She came closer. I was about to call out, but I saw Martin press a finger to his lips. He winked at me.

"Abel?" she called. "Abel, are you out here?"

Then Mrs. Grimshaw was right beneath those two best trees. She made a sharp cry, as though she'd bumped a branch. She patted at her neck. I saw a pine cone bounce off her shoulder. Another snag in her hair. Her arms hacked through the air, and she scraped at her scalp, tugging out strands of hair.

Martin pressed hard against the trunk of his tree, hidden among the leaves. His tongue stuck out between his lips, eyes narrowing as he pulled things from his pocket. Aiming. He tossed a pebble. It popped off the path. A second one hit the hump on Mrs. Grimshaw's back. She cried out again and grabbed her ear. *Why is he doing that?* He tossed more, and they bounced off the top of her head. One smacked her cheek. She stumbled backward and rubbed at her face. "Damn birds! You rotten, rotten creatures!"

Martin cranked his hand back and threw a whole handful. Stones hit her backside, her thighs, her shoes. The cloth of her slip puckered and went smooth. "A bad day," she yelped. "Abel? Abel? It's a bad, bad day." Then the old woman looped around on the path and shuffled back the way she'd come.

Martin shimmied down his tree. He was laughing so hard, he snorted. "Did you catch that, Ware? Did you?" he called to me. "Do you know she never, ever looks up?"

My guts twisted into a hard knot. I wanted to stay up in the tree, but my hands held the right branches, my legs found the right bumps. I was back on the ground. "You shouldn't do that," I said.

"Well, she deserves it, you know." He flipped his pockets inside out, dust and seeds emptying onto the forest floor. "She was trespassing. Mother's plain sick of her."

"Still." I wanted to stand up for Mrs. Grimshaw like I did for Wally and pummel Martin so hard in his chest he'd fly back and land on his backside. But when he stared me straight in the eye, I couldn't do it. He was different from those boys in the schoolyard. His eyes held not a single drop of fear. He was proud of himself.

I swallowed. "You could talk to her?"

"My grandmother used to say she was a whore. Married a rich bastard, but she was still a whore."

I blinked. I didn't understand why he was talking like Mr. Pober. I thought Mr. Pober said disgusting things because he was sweaty and filthy and so poor he couldn't even buy soap. But Martin wasn't that way. His clothes were bright and clean and he had everything he could ever want.

"You crack me up, Ware. Like you're surprised or something. But a man's got a right—no, an obligation—to protect his property. Sure, it's written in the law books."

Martin talked and laughed, but I couldn't speak. As we followed the trail out of the woods, he slung his arm over my shoulder. He pulled me in close so I couldn't lag behind. Mrs. Grimshaw's cries still echoed in my ears. My own silence was there, too. I wasn't gallant. I just pretended to be when it was easy.

"Well that was a riot and a half," he said when we came out into the overwhelming sunshine of the yard. "Same time next week?"

"Is there any carrot cake left?" I asked my mother in the kitchen.

"No, that was devoured. I made a jellyroll, though." She took a platter out of the refrigerator. Vanilla sponge cake with a raspberry jam swirl.

"Could I have an extra slice?"

"You're hungry? You must be growing, Thomas."

Balancing the plate in my hands, I walked around the side of the house and down the driveway. When I reached the bottom, I saw that dusty old car again. I froze. It was slowly turning around.

The driver was only a few feet away from me. His window was rolled down, and he was wearing gold-rimmed sunglasses and a tattered straw hat. "You living up there, pal?"

My mouth was bone dry. "S-sort of?"

His hairy arm dangled outside the window, and with a loose fist, he bopped the side of his car twice. Then, without another word, he drove away.

I stood on the road, watching the car get smaller and smaller. Was that the same car? Was the hand the same? Could he have been my aunt's "sweetheart"? Was he checking up on me and my mother? Or was he just being neighborly? The more questions my mind spat up, the more uncertain I felt.

My legs were rubbery as I hurried toward Mrs. Grimshaw's, the first house on the right. Her place was dark brown stone, and nearly the same size as the Henneberrys'. The front door was partially covered with an overgrown shrub, so I went around the back. The woods came much closer to her house than at the Henneberrys', and except for a square patch of mowed grass, all the flowers and bushes looked wild. I knocked on her back door.

"I'll tell you right now, sonny," Mrs. Grimshaw yelled through the screen, "my Electrolux is in fine working condition and I can only wear one pair of shoes at a time."

"I'm not selling anything, Mrs. Grimshaw." I wanted

to get inside. In case that car circled around again. "It's just me. Thomas."

"Who?"

"Thomas, from next door. I brought you something from—" Then I blurted, "From Mrs. Gladstone."

"Ruth's trying to poison me now, is she? Well, I won't take it back, you tell her. I won't take back what I said."

This wasn't going very well. "No, I mean, from my— from Esther. She had extra cake."

"Oh, that poor dear girl. What a place to land." Mrs. Grimshaw pushed open the door. There was a blotch underneath her left eye and a piece of pine cone still stuck in her hair. "Come in, then. Let me take a look. Abel and I do love our sweets."

The kitchen was white and green. Tiny bits of dust floated in the sunbeams that came through the windows. A white cat was curled up on the countertop near a toaster and an orange one was asleep in a chair.

She took the plate from me and covered it with a cup towel. "I'll save it until Abel gets home."

I sighed. Abel Grimshaw would never get home. I'd done plenty of pretending since Aunt Celia had died, talking to her, seeing her so vividly inside my head. Once I came back to reality, though, my grief was a fresh burn. I wondered if it was the same for Mrs. Grimshaw. If she had moments where she remembered the truth, and it hurt like new each time.

"Do you want some apple juice?"

"Okay."

She pointed at the table and I sat down. The orange cat jumped onto the opposite chair.

"You're visiting next door?"

"Yeah."

"Poor boy. Not for long, I hope."

"I don't know," I said. I thought of my paper chain. It was only a quarter done, and I still didn't know what was going to happen when all the links were opened. What if my mother decided we should stay at the Henneberrys'? Or she planned to give me away to strangers? Exactly like she'd been when she arrived here with Aunt Celia. She kept telling me not to worry, but that was impossible.

"That Ruth Gladstone's viler than her husband, you know." Mrs. Grimshaw handed me a glass of juice. Small white things hovered near the bottom.

"How come?"

"Because she's a woman. And a mother, too."

What difference would that make?

"Since Alexander drowned, Ruth treats young Muriel like that girl's not worth two cents. Don't you think she suffers enough inside her own head?"

"I guess so," I said. Though I had no sense of what was happening inside Mrs. Henneberry's head. I imagined it was like a television set tuned to a fuzzy channel.

Tapping at the door, then. A woman with a handkerchief tied over her hair was outside on the step. Mop and bucket in her hand.

"Ma'am?" she called as she creaked open the door, stepped inside.

"What day is today?" Mrs. Grimshaw asked. "Another week gone already?"

"Certainly has." The woman went to the sink with the bucket. She clapped her hands at the white cat, and it got up, stretched, and dropped down to the floor.

"She's here to clean," Mrs. Grimshaw said to me. "Have you come to help her?"

"No." I stood up. The lady with the bucket smiled at me. "Thank you for the juice, though. I should head back." Mrs. Grimshaw wasn't alone anymore. She seemed okay.

"What did you say your name was?"

"Thomas."

"Don't go through the woods, Thomas. It's too risky."

I winced. "I—"

"The birds, dear. They get quite vicious if given the chance."

CHAPTER FOURTEEN

"It's freezing in here."

"Where? I can't see."

"Right in front of you, Tommie. Just lift up the branches."

I spun around. The woods were full of gloomy corners and dark green leaves and pockets of black. Icy drops of rain pecked at my scalp.

"Here! I'm right here!"

Flashes of white. A leg without stockings. Broken bluish veins forking over the calf. "That's not you! That's not your leg!"

"Of course it's my leg, silly. Grab it and pull me out!"

My hand reached forward. I touched her damp skin. *I can't! I can't do it!*

My eyes sprang open, but the bedroom was heavy with gray. Same as the morning my aunt never came home. I sat up in the cot. My mother was mumbling, but when I stared through the darkness, I couldn't see her shape in the bed. She had to be just outside the room.

Then I heard another person in the laundry room. Talking louder than my mother. Dr. Henneberry. I swallowed the spit pooling in my mouth and pushed back the blanket. I tiptoed across the bedroom and cracked open the door. Light from the moon was coming in the windows of the laundry, and in the glow I could see her. My mother had her back against the folding table. Towels piled behind her. And Dr. Henneberry was in front, leaning so close to her that my mother's back was bending away. His hand was on her leg. Her hand was on his wrist.

"Come now, Esther. Why must you be so difficult? I know you're not that innocent."

"I don't—"

"Haven't you gotten everything you wanted?"

"I wanted?"

"With the boy. I helped that along, you know. Didn't say a word when Muriel allowed him to stay for the entire summer."

"Thomas—"

My name hung in the air. I held my breath. Waited for my nerve to build. So I could dash out and push myself between him and my mother. Fists up.

"I know all about your little arrangement. There must be quite the nest egg built up by now."

What arrangement? What nest egg?

"Please. You don't understand. I'm tired."

"A woman who's tired. How novel. You should be grateful to me."

"I am, Dr. Henneberry," my mother said quietly. She turned her head toward the windows. She lifted her hand away. And then the tops of his fingers disappeared under the hem of her uniform.

My heart banged in my head, my arms, even in my ankles. Each beat making me smaller and smaller.

I closed the door quietly and rolled my back against the wall. I wanted to go home. I wanted to tell Aunt Celia what Dr. Henneberry was doing to my mother. And how horrible Martin was. And the odd things Mrs. Henneberry liked me to do. "I need help," I'd say. "I really need help. There are too many things to fix." And she'd stroke my back to calm me down. "Oh, Tommie. I told you already. Everything just seems scarier in the dark."

Everything's scarier in the dark.
Everything's scarier in the dark.
Everything's scarier.

I said it again and again, but it didn't help.

"Tell me what to do," I said. Nobody answered.

Outside the door, they were making noise. No, only he was. My mother was silent as a stone.

I had to get out of there. I dressed quickly and dropped all of the coins from Mrs. Henneberry into the pocket of my shorts. Martin's shorts. "I'll come back for you," I whispered to George, "I promise," and I climbed onto the cot, shoved up the window. The orange sun was rising. Not in a smooth way but like it was gasping for breath. Jerking upward, then halting. I dragged myself over the ledge and dropped onto the grass below. My aunt was gone, I knew that, but our apartment was still there. I looked after myself all the time. I could do it again. Mrs. King would bring me up supper, and I'd run to the corner to get her milk or bread. She'd know what to do about the Henneberrys. She'd know how to solve the problem. By the time I reached the bus stop, I was starting to feel stronger. Having a plan did that.

I waited a long time for the bus to arrive. Several ladies got off, in uniforms similar to my mother's, but no one got on except me.

"Heading to work this morning, son?" the driver said.

I smiled a little. "I'm going home, actually."

"After a weary journey, by the sight of you. But still, five cents."

With no cars and no passengers, I was in Lower Washbourne before I knew it. I wandered along the pot-holed streets with tall brown buildings lining either side. Morning laundry hung on the strings from win-dow to window and I inhaled the scent of detergent. Somewhere a baby was crying, and a woman was sing-ing a lullaby. Someone had burned their toast. I said hello to an old lady sitting on a stoop, her dress pushed down between her knees. Beside her, a cat licked its long legs. I took another deep breath. It felt good being cov-ered by shadows of everything ordinary.

I stopped into the drugstore on the corner. The aisles were narrow and I had to search the shelves. Rows of boxes and packets and metal tubes. I shook the coins in my pocket. I enjoyed the tinny clang when they bumped against each other. Finally, I found the bottle. Dark blue glass with white flowers on the label. I removed the cap and sniffed. That was her smell. Tonight, I'd put a few drops in my bathwater to make it feel like she wasn't too far away. I carried it to the front and spread some coins out on the counter.

A man in round silver glasses and a white coat counted out the money and then put the bubble bath in a brown paper bag. He twisted the top around the neck of the bottle. "Special lady in your life?"

"No," I said. "I just like it."

Over the top of his glasses, he looked me up and down. "To each their own, I guess."

"Mm-hmm." I smiled at him when he handed me the bag.

And then I was home. Just like that. The cement steps were the same. The railing on the north side was still missing. And grubby Mr. Pober, who'd watched my aunt's legs every day? He was still hunched down on the stoop. He had a lit cigarette in his brown fingers. Even though I could barely stand him, I was glad he hadn't changed.

I ran up the steps. Past Mr. Pober, through the door, and up the three flights of stairs. I went so fast, I nearly dropped the paper bag with the bubble bath. By the time I reached the hallway outside my apartment, I was out of breath.

Then I stopped short. The door was being held open with a pair of work boots. I edged forward and glimpsed inside. I checked the door again. The number was right.

But the rooms were all wrong. The entire place was empty. Not a chair or a book or a television set. Not a pencil case or lunchbox or cup towel. My birthday presents, both still in their boxes, were gone. The walls were now a dull, cold white.

"You! Kid!" A man with paint-specked overalls was coming out of our bathroom. "You can't be in here. Beat it!"

My fingers got tight around the paper-covered neck of the bottle. I wanted to scream, but I wouldn't let it out.

"Go on, I said. Get out of here!" He shook his fist in the air.

I turned and floated down the stairs. None of it was real. This was just another rotten dream and I'd wake up any second. I drifted past Mrs. King's apartment. Her door was ajar, too. She was puttering around her kitchen in a loose dress and flat shoes.

When she saw me in the hallway, an enormous smile spread over her face. I stepped inside, and she came toward me and tugged me into her chest.

"Mrs. King," I said. My throat was tight. I wanted to stay there and never move again.

"Oh, you're a treat for my soul, sweetheart," she said as she let me go. From the bedroom beside the kitchen, Mr. King was coughing and gasping, coughing and gasping.

"Should you get him some water?" I said.

"No, love. Water doesn't help anymore."

"Oh," I whispered.

"But look at you! Standing right here in front of me. Brightening my morning." She held my shoulders. "How did you get here? Is your mother okay? How do you find it living up there in luxury? Are you loving it?"

"I rode the bus," I said.

"And? And?"

Her face was so hopeful, I didn't want her to know my knees were about to buckle. "Everything is good, Mrs. King."

"Oh, I knew it."

"Except my mother doesn't make peanut butter cookies."

"If that's your gripe, love, then they're treating you well."

I crossed two fingers behind my back. "They sure are." I even managed to smile.

"Oh, I knew they would." Mrs. King lifted her chin. "Now, tell me everything."

"It's a huge place and there are tons of rooms. You wouldn't believe it, Mrs. King. They've got all this land and a pool and a small house for getting changed." I didn't mention the crack where someone could peek inside.

"And the Henneberrys? What are they like?"

"Mrs. Henneberry is . . . she's real soft, sort of. Sometimes we sit together and talk about art and bees and history. And Dr. Henneberry is . . . is alright, too. He works mostly, but he's taken me out paddling in a green canoe. He brought home a whole pound of hard candy, all different flavors. Me and their son split them, right down the middle. Fifty-fifty. He's older than me, but we still hang out together. Hiking, and we made a sandcastle on the beach by the lake. Must've been six feet tall, Mrs. King. His name's—" I paused. All the lies were making my tongue itchy. "His name's Martin."

She pressed a glass of lemonade into my hand. "Drink, love. You must be dried out."

"And I want to build a treehouse before the summer's up. I'll make pictures for the walls. If there's time."

"A resort style vacation, then. You got it made in the shade."

I nodded and took a long sip. The lemonade was tart and delicious. "I do, Mrs. King." I bit the side of my cheek, then pushed the question out. "What's going on up there?" I pointed at the ceiling.

She put her hand on her cheek. "Oh, Thomas. It's such a shame. Such a shame. I can barely think about Celia. I miss her so."

"All our stuff is gone. Did they move it?"

"I don't know, darling. All I saw was two men emptying it out not long after you left. Carrying down boxloads. I heard Mr. Pober tried to grab her nightclothes. I do hope he didn't get anything. Brazen, he is. I mean it was bad enough he was caught stealing ladies' laundry right off the lines." She sighed. "And now the paint fumes are really giving poor Mr. King a rough time."

"But our things were still there. My View-Master."

"Don't you be upset about that, okay? Promise me."

I nodded, though I was very upset.

"Why don't you ask Mrs. Henneberry to get you one? Explain what's happened. I'm sure she won't mind."

I would never do that.

"Oh, Thomas. How many times did I pop up to see you two? And then remember you weren't there. Dozens. Actual dozens."

I stared down at my shoes. The ends of the laces were frayed. I wondered if I should wrap a small piece of Scotch tape around them. Aunt Celia always used tape to trim my hair. She'd stick it to my forehead and then slide the scissors along underneath. It was never higher on one side than the other. As good as any barber could do. Even Wally's mother said so.

"Thomas? Are you daydreaming again?"

"Sorry, Mrs. King."

"I was saying I heard a young couple is moving in. No children though. Yet."

I knew Mrs. King was trying to be agreeable about things, but I didn't want to hear about other people moving into our apartment. I bumped the paper bag against my thigh. Mr. King was coughing again, and Mrs. King kept rubbing one hand against the other. I knew she needed to go and check on him. I handed her back the glass and wiped my mouth in my arm. "I should get on my way. So I don't miss my bus."

"Us, too. Mr. King has a checkup over in Greenlake."

She hugged me again, hard. One of my bones cracked and I buried my face in her dress. "It's so good to see you. Don't become a stranger, my love."

I didn't want to let go of her because what if I did become a stranger? What if, once I left, I never ever came back?

Mr. Pober was still on the front step. I could easily picture him trying to steal my aunt's clothes as they spilled out of an open box. His mustard-colored fingers touching the hem of her skirt. Pinching the belt of her robe. I wanted to spit on him. I wanted to stick my fingers into his pink eyeballs and jam them into his brain. I wanted to feel his ribs crumble like dead leaves beneath my feet.

"I know you," he said as I passed. "I know all about you!"

I stopped.

"She was a gorgeous broad, you know. Just gorgeous."

I turned and saw him push his hand between the legs of his trousers. He moved it up and down. "Thought she was too good, though. A gal too good for regular men. I tried to tell her, but she didn't listen. Got herself mixed up with the wrong sort, if you ask me. And look what happened."

"What? What wrong sort?" I yelled at him.

"That snooty rich guy. That's all I got to say about him, kid. Snooty rich guy thought he owned the god-damned world. Acted like he owned her, too. I'm not stupid. I know what's what."

"What do you mean, what's what?"

"I used to see her coming home. All hours. And not from her work. No, sir. Doll had other things going on. She reeked of it." Mr. Pober chuckled. His teeth were rotted. "A real life, Peter, Peter, pumpkin eater. But he didn't keep her very well, now, did he?"

I ran down the steps, along the sidewalk. *The wrong sort. The wrong sort.* She was mixed up with the wrong sort. *That snooty rich guy.* Who had a purple toenail from a paperweight. Mr. Pober knew who he was. Mr. Pober would recognize the man who'd killed my aunt.

I waited on the corner for the return bus. I passed the brown bag back and forth between my hands so many times, the paper was beginning to disintegrate. The stench of garbage was wafting out of a nearby can, and I tossed my aunt's favorite bubble bath in on top of it. I did not want to hold it anymore. To see it anymore. I bounced on my feet. My muscles were vibrating in a way that made me feel exhausted, but I couldn't calm down.

"Nice visit home?" the driver said as I climbed aboard.

I looked at him, but I couldn't see him.

"There, there, now. You're like a ghost, sonny. Take a seat, okay? This heat today would bowl a mammoth over. Let's take you back, shall we?"

I leaned my head against the window and the metal handle dug into my eyebrow. Each time we struck a bump, my teeth clanked, and the hurt inside began to drain away. Everything was pointless. Mr. Pober would recognize the man who'd killed Aunt Celia, but I knew by the way he'd laughed, he was never going to tell me. He was never going to tell the police. And even if he did, it wouldn't make her alive again. It wouldn't put our apartment back the way it was. My entire life was gone.

Something inside of me went flat then. Like a bottle of soda already opened, or a tire stuck with a rusty nail.

Testimony of Dr. Earl Simmons, Greenlake Office of the Medical Examiner

Direct Examination by Prosecutor Clay Fibbs

Q. **Dr. Simmons, you completed the autopsies on Muriel, Raymond, and Martin Henneberry, is that correct?**

A. Yes, sir. The bodies were transferred to Greenlake, and I examined them there.

Q. **Can we start with Mrs. Henneberry?**

A. Yes, a 36-year-old female, 61 inches tall, 111 pounds. She was wearing a yellow dress and white undergarments.

Q. **Your report is very detailed, but I'd like to focus in on a few particular areas. Particularly the gunshot wound. Can you describe that for the court?**

A. The entry point of the bullet was midpoint on the front of the victim's neck. It traveled through her trachea and then passed through a cervical vertebra. Which is to say, one of the bones in the back of her neck.

Q. **Observing the wound, what did you determine about the shooter?**

A. The shooter fired the gun at close range.

Q. **How do know that?**

A. Soot was evident around the wound. There were also minuscule marks in the skin from gunpowder. Those marks are called stippling and are actual burns. In addition, the bullet wound had a particularly ragged shape. Those factors indicate the shooter was within six to eight inches when he pulled the trigger.

Q. **Six to eight inches? That's something. And Dr. Henneberry?**

A. Yes. A 41-year-old male, 70 inches tall, 194 pounds. He was wearing a white linen shirt, gray linen shorts, and white briefs.

Q. **Did you make a determination on Dr. Henneberry's cause of death?**

A. Gunshot wound to the face. The bullet entered his body through his open mouth, piercing his palate, then traveling through his brain. It exited at the base of his cranium. The back of his skull.

Q. **How can you tell which direction the bullet went?**

A. You need to examine the wound. When the bullet pushes through tissue, it frequently produces a distinct hole, a clean hole, so to speak, but when it exits, the bullet can leave a messy gaping wound. It broke through bone and tissue on the back of Dr. Henneberry's head. In addition, detectives located the bullet embedded in the soil behind his lawn chair. They also recovered shards of Dr. Henneberry's skull on that same lawn chair.

Q. **Was this shot also taken at close range?**

A. No soot or stippling was noted around the entry point of the bullet. So the shooter had stepped back.

Q. **Stepped back?**

A. Yes, otherwise you'd still see that burn pattern I described.

Q. Thank you, Dr. Simmons. I just have a few questions about Martin Henneberry. He was recovered from the pool.

A. Yes, sir, he was. Martin was a 16-year-old male, 68 inches tall, and weighed 164 pounds. He was wearing only white cotton briefs.

Q. Can you describe the condition of his body?

A. The victim had a number of injuries. Of most importance was a single gunshot wound that entered to the left of his lower spine. The bullet went through his abdomen and exited just above his navel.

Q. And this led to his death?

A. Officially, Mr. Fibbs, he drowned. But the injury led to his incapacitation in the water. He could no longer swim. Couldn't get out of the pool.

Q. So it's possible the shooter may have been aware that Martin Henneberry was not dead? May have seen the boy drowning?

A. Drowning takes time. So it's possible. Likely, even.

Q. And you mentioned other injuries to his body. Can you detail those?

A. He had bruising on his right shoulder. Scratches to his upper body, and a long scratch on the front of his left shin. There were also some minor abrasions, irritation evident on his genital area.

Q. Let's start with the shoulder bruising. Did you determine when and how that came about?

A. Yes. Occasionally there can be discoloration or bruise-like marks on a body that occur after death.

This may happen when the corpse is handled. The bruising on his shoulder occurred postmortem when he was pulled from the pool.

Q. **The scratches?**

A. These were perimortem injuries.

Q. **Can you explain to the court what the term perimortem means?**

A. Occurring at or shortly before the time of death. My estimation is that these chest scratches were caused by Martin Henneberry's trying to drag himself out of the water. He came into contact with the tiles, the cement.

Q. **In your report, you also made note of some superficial abrasions to the, around Martin's—around his lower area.**

A. Yes, minor. Very minor. As I noted, those injuries were indicative of a youth—of a young man who was, who was being overly—I don't know quite how to phrase it—overly frisky with himself. I documented all damage to the body but didn't feel it deserved more than a cursory note in the report.

Q. **I understand. Just boyhood shenanigans, then.**

A. Exactly. Boyhood shenanigans. I strived to be thorough in my report, but in my opinion it's completely unconnected to the cause and manner of his death.

CHAPTER FIFTEEN

In the days after I returned from the vacant apartment, I didn't feel well. I was tired a lot. I couldn't think straight. I tried to get my mind to drift, go someplace fun or happy with Aunt Celia, but it refused.

"Your eyes are swollen, Thomas," my mother said. "Have you caught the sniffles?"

"No," I said. I hadn't sneezed once.

I couldn't sleep much at night, either. If I did doze off, all I did was dream. Sometimes about Mrs. Henneberry, stretched out on the sofa with her toes flicking. Or about Martin. He'd be hiding up in a tree, throwing radioactive chemicals down at Mrs. Grimshaw. Mostly, though, I dreamed about Dr. Henneberry. Him and Aunt Celia. In the dark. He wanted her to get in his car, and when she didn't, he got out and limped in front of the headlights. His slipper fell off and his entire foot was blue and purple as though it had been smashed by a hammer. He grabbed my aunt around her waist and clamped his hand over her mouth. When I screamed for him to let her go, he turned his attention to me. Hobbling closer, one bare foot slapping the ground, my aunt a wet paper doll in his arms.

I always woke up then. Choking and crying only seconds before he reached me. My mother would sit me up and get me a drink. "You're frightening me, Thomas," she'd whisper. "If you don't tell me what's going on, how can I help you?"

"You can't help."

"I can try." She'd bring the glass to my lips, so I'd take another sip. "We should know soon. Where we're going. Mr. Vardy thinks so too."

I couldn't explain why, but my mother was different when we were sitting side by side on that cot in the middle of the night. When I couldn't see her. And she couldn't see me. I would lean into her body, offer her the weight of my sadness, and she would hold it all.

"If you need to rest," my mother said as she sliced through a thick loaf of bread, "I don't mind."

I lifted my head up off the counter. "I'm good."

"Okay, but I might need a little assistance today. We've got company."

We didn't have company, of course. The Henneberrys did. My mother said it was neighbors from down the street. Mr. and Mrs. Gage, and their two children, Skip and his little sister. Also Mr. Fulsome, who seemed to be there nearly all the time anyway. He had no family and no wife. "I guess he feels at home with the Henneberrys," my mother said.

Somewhere down the hallway, a lady laughed loudly. Then a man said, "I really don't need any advice, Viv."

"James Fulsome! You certainly do need advice. What about my niece? Lovely, lovely girl. She's twenty-three, maybe twenty-four. Lives just on the edge of Lower Washbourne, but don't hold that against her." More laughter. "Let me introduce you two. Find some excuse."

"You're always the joker, Vivian. But I'm doing just fine on my own."

"Well, I for one can't believe no one's nabbed you."

Then Mrs. Henneberry spoke. "He does not need to be nabbed, Vivian. He's content being a bachelor. Aren't you, James?"

My mother was shaking her head. "Poor Mr. Fulsome." She cut another sandwich into triangles and scraped the crusts into the garbage. "They never leave him alone."

I shrugged. I didn't know anything about him. And I didn't care.

"Your skin's quite gray. Why don't you go get some sunshine on your face?"

"I don't want to," I said. I didn't want to play with Martin's old cars anymore. I didn't want to read his scratched-up comic books. I didn't want to do anything.

"Then could you bring this iced tea to them? Oh, and check to see if I've missed anything."

Carrying the cold pitcher, I followed the noise down

the hallway. I hesitated at the doorway, was relieved that the men were no longer there. Just the two women and a little girl. I placed the iced tea on a circular table in the corner. I stood beside it, unsure of how to determine if anything was missing. My mother had already brought the glasses. There were even sliced lemons floating in the tea.

"She's really become the worst bother, Vivian," Mrs. Henneberry said. Her dress was like a black-and-white checkerboard. "A daily torment."

"Come, now, Muriel. You're exaggerating. The woman's positively ancient. What could she do?" Mrs. Gage had red hair and was shorter than Mrs. Henneberry.

"Well, for one thing, she's always in our woods. Martin plays in there, you know."

"Oh, you can't be serious. Martin's too old to be cavorting about like a boy scout."

"Well, what if she falls and hurts herself? Is that my responsibility? And to see her!" Mrs. Henneberry waved her cigarette in the air. "A total state of disarray. Barely clothed, which is not surprising, given her reputation. Can you imagine if Martin caught her like that? Or Skip?"

Mrs. Gage was giggling. "I doubt Skip would even notice. Unless she's covered in those taffy candies he's always eating. Now that might catch his eye."

Mrs. Henneberry smashed the cigarette in an ashtray. "I'm glad you find some humor in this intolerable situation."

"Muriel, you're twis—"

"Poor Mother's rolling over in her grave."

I leaned against the wall. How would that work? Would Mrs. Gladstone roll fast? Or was it a slow circling? And didn't her shoulder get stuck on the roof of the casket? Or were there pillows inside and she could sink down? It probably wasn't a cardboard box like my aunt had. Mrs. Gladstone's was likely fancy with a whole lot of room to move and breathe. Was there a little lamp inside? I blinked and shook my head. No lamp. And no rolling or breathing. No nothing, because she was dead.

"But that was years ago, Muriel. Before I even lived here. I'd never have heard about the issues between your mother and Mrs. Grimshaw, except you told me."

"Issues? I'd say it was a tad more serious than that. I certainly won't forget."

Mrs. Gage frowned. "Well, maybe it's time you should."

"Maybe it's time you should," I repeated. I hadn't meant to speak. The words just went into my ears and slid out my mouth.

Mrs. Henneberry and Mrs. Gage were gaping at me. As though they were surprised to discover my presence. Had they not noticed me entering the room? Waiting there? Was I no different than a plant or a coat rack?

"I didn't know you had a guest," Mrs. Gage said.

"He's not a guest. He's just here for a week or two." Mrs. Henneberry touched the back of her hand to her forehead. "But his name, it escapes me." She wiggled her fingers in my direction, and when I approached, she handed me the ashtray. "This needs a refresh, dear. It's overflowing."

I nodded, took the heavy glass bowl from her. It was full of neat pieces of ash and bent cigarettes. Some were stained with lipstick.

"Thank you—"

"Thomas," I said.

"Oh yes. Of course. Thomas. Tom. How could I forget, seeing as we're such dear friends?"

As I started back toward the kitchen, she called after me, "Then you must hop up to Martin's room."

I was about to protest, but she raised her hand. "No buts about it, young man. Skip's already there. You're one of the boys, just as much as they are."

After I dumped the contents of the ashtray in the trash can, my mother took it from me and began to rinse the inside.

"Where's Martin's room?"

Her hands stopped. "Why?"

"Mrs. Henneberry says I should find him."

"Find him for what?"

"I don't know. It doesn't matter." Nothing mattered.

She rubbed the clean ashtray with a rag. The glass squeaked. "Don't use the main stairs. Go down the hallway behind the family room and use those. First room you'll see is Martin's. There's a sailboat hanging on his door."

As I turned to leave, she said, "Be careful, Thomas. Around that boy."

Be careful. She didn't need to tell me that again. I already knew what a terrible person Martin was. I'd seen it with my own eyes.

I followed her instructions and found Martin's room. The door was open, and Martin was perched on the side of his bed. Skip was there, too. I recognized him from the canoe. He was lying on the carpet, tossing a baseball up into the air and catching it as it dropped.

I knocked softly. "Mrs. Henneberry sent me up."

"Hey, look who's here," Martin said as I went in. Even though I was probably scowling, he seemed happy to see me. "Skip, this is my pal Ware."

Skip narrowed his eyes at me, tossed the ball higher.

Martin's room was enormous. His large bed had a navy bedspread, and the walls were covered in fighter jet wallpaper. Wooden shelves displayed model cars and shiny tin boxes and a set of burgundy encyclopedias. Off to the side, a low table was painted like a grassy field. It had a hundred or more red-and-blue tin soldiers arranged in neat rows. I reached my hand out, but Martin growled, "Don't even think about it."

A velvety bag full of marbles lay on the carpet. I got down on my stomach, tipped a few out. Glass swirls and cat's-eyes, cobras and orange flames. I flicked one across the carpet and it clinked against a second. I clinked another and another. Skip dropped the ball and sat up to watch me. I struck an aggie with my finger and it rolled away, banging a yellow swirly.

"Did you see that? He's got a real eagle eye, Martin.

Good thing he's not playing for keeps. He'd have you whipped in a flash."

"Who cares," Martin said. "He can have them if he wants. Marbles are for babies."

I wondered if I could do that. Collect them all into that soft bag and tighten the drawstring and carry them outside.

"Want to see what I found in Father's study?" Martin was holding a magazine, rolled into a tube.

Skip got up and pounced onto Martin's bed. When Martin opened the magazine, Skip said, "Whoa! This is your dad's?"

"Sure is. He's got a giant pile of them in the back of his gun cabinet. Didn't even have the door locked."

"Um. Wow. I guess." Skip cleared his throat. "I mean. Um. Check out the chassis on that one."

"I know, right?"

They were side by side, pressed tightly together, each one holding one edge of the magazine. Skip kept averting his gaze, but Martin gave it his full focus. He gnawed at his bottom lip like he was hungry. I stretched my neck and could see the cover. A woman, practically naked, her mouth in a surprised O. She was holding a fluffy pink towel to her chest. The sight of it made my heart skitter in an unusual way.

"You want some, Skip? I can get you a dozen. At least!"

Skip moved over on the bed. "Nah. Mother'd skin me alive if she found them."

Martin gazed at me and when our eyes met, he snick-ered, elbowed Skip. "You after a few of them, Ware?"

My mouth was full of saliva. "Nah. What would I want with that?"

"What's the matter? Don't like what you see?"

I swallowed. "I mean. It's just a person."

"Just a person, he says! Hear that, Skip? It's not a per-son, idiot, it's a *whore*. It's a stinking *whore*."

My fluttering heart worked its way up to my cheeks. He sounded just like Mr. Pober again. "Whores a-comin', whores a-goin'. Whores, whores, smutty whores." He used to sing that, and my aunt still said we had to forgive his shortcomings. She'd joke, "Women are allowed out-doors now, Mr. Pober!" But Mrs. King had called him a cockroach. "I had pity at first, when he got back from service. But now, I could crush him with my shoe."

I swallowed again. "How do you know?"

"What? If it's a whore?" He pushed the magazine toward me. "Look at it, for shit's sake. I know a whore when I see one."

Skip laughed a short laugh, and then cleared his throat.

Martin smiled at me. "You ever kissed a girl, Ware?"

I put my face on the thick carpet. Studied the marble in front of me. It was a popper, a whole lot bigger than the other ones. Inside had a green-and-amber cat's-eye. Wally had an identical one. I'd always wanted it, and even though he'd offered it to me several times, I couldn't take it. I knew it was his favorite, too. I rolled Martin's marble between my thumb and forefinger.

"Ever slide your hands inside her panties? Pop your finger in?"

In where? I thought. After Wally and I had found that book, we took the clothes off his little sister's doll. But all we saw was a tiny hole in the plastic bottom. Wally said it had to be wrong. "There's got to be more."

Skip was bouncing up and down on the mattress next to Martin. "Sure, he probably never even held hands."

"Don't be a drip, Skippy. I know that already. I just like seeing his face. He looks like he's going to upchuck."

I stood up. I put my hand in my pocket and dropped the cat's-eye marble inside. Martin didn't deserve to keep something so rare. "No," I said. "I haven't."

Skip stood up, too. His cheeks were really red. He tugged his T-shirt out of his shorts and let it hang down over his belt buckle. "And you haven't either, Martin," he said.

"What?"

"You heard me. You haven't done that stuff either."

"Have, too," he said.

"What? With Genie Bishop?"

"You bet. She's so easy. Lets me do whatever I want. Whenever I want to. She *asks* for it."

"Liar." Skip smirked and folded his arms across his chest.

I wondered if Martin actually heard him, because he just lifted up his mattress and tucked the magazine underneath. Then the mattress plopped down, and he said, "You two nosebleeds want to go for a swim?"

I followed them down the stairs. Even though I couldn't stand Martin, I did want to go for a swim. The hot summer air felt like it was stretched over my skin.

Dr. Henneberry and Mr. Fulsome were standing at the front door. They had their heads close together, and Dr. Henneberry was throwing his hands up in the air.

"He's hopping," Dr. Henneberry said loudly. "Hopping mad."

"How about a little getaway, Ray? Into the city. Might have better luck with things."

"Better luck? You can't have any luck at all when you got nothing to toss in the pot."

"Well, I guess we're up the creek." His fingers were touching Dr. Henneberry's elbow. "But we're up there together, buddy."

"If Muriel finds out, Jim—"

Martin paused beside his father, said, "Hey, Mr. Fulsome."

Mr. Fulsome's hand jumped like he'd gotten an electric shock. Then he said, "Hey, sport! How's the rowing going?"

"Great! I made the crew."

"Chip off the old block. Isn't that so, Ray?"

Dr. Henneberry sucked air through his teeth. "Yeah. Chip whose dippy mother bought every piece of equipment for the entire team."

Martin's shoulders fell. "Thanks Mr. Fulsome," he said. "See you later."

When we were on the front porch, Martin stopped, pointed at the glass jar left on the top step.

"Mother brought it for Debra," Skip said to him. Then to me, "My little sister. She's probably in a corner somewhere cutting paper into animals. She's such a yawn."

The jar gleamed. "Big Soap" was written on the label, and a blue plastic wand floated inside. Martin twisted off the lid and fished it out. Brought the dripping wand to his mouth and blew a bubble. Skip leapt into the air and clapped it with his hands. As the bubble burst, an explosion of tiny rainbow droplets fell down into his hair and eyes.

"Now you catch it, Ware," Martin said to me and blew a second.

I jumped, but the breeze had already lifted it too high. My fingers never even grazed it. Martin blew through the wand again. I stretched and hopped off the step, but still I couldn't reach.

Martin kept blowing bubbles. Each time I tried to smack it out of the air, I missed. When he blew one for Skip, Skip broke it easily. I sat down on the step.

Martin hollered at me. "I saw you with the marbles, Ware. You're not even trying!"

"I am. You're making them go way up when it's my turn."

"Am not. Listen, buddy. I'll give you a dime if you get this next one. A whole dime!" He put his head way back, and a gigantic bubble began to emerge from the wand. Then it was quivering through the air, full of Martin's breath.

Even before it had detached from the blue plastic, I knew I wouldn't be able to reach it. So I pulled the cat's-eye popper from my pocket. I felt the weight of it in my palm.

"Come on, candy ass!"

I threw the marble. As hard as I could. It tore through the air, and I yelped with joy when it ripped straight through that fat bubble. A soft mist of soapy water fluttered down onto my face.

But I hadn't considered that once the marble had done its job it would keep soaring, in a perfect arc, up and over and then curling down. Onto the front of Dr. Henneberry's mint-green car.

Smash! The windshield exploded into a million pieces of sparkly glass. We ran over. Glittering shards were everywhere. On the ground, on the hood, inside the car on the white seats. I backed up. Clapped both hands over my mouth. The round lights on either side of the hood got smaller. Or perhaps it was actually my eyes instead, squinting in shock.

"Oh. My. God." Martin was flapping his arms. "Father's going to go ape!"

"Why'd you do that for?" Skip said to me.

"I don't know."

Skip was shaking his head. "You're going to get a real wallop now, buddy."

My whole body went numb. I couldn't budge. I couldn't breathe. I couldn't even blink. The whole world was moving in slow motion.

Mr. Fulsome was outside first. "Well, isn't that the bite," he said.

I looked at Martin. And he looked back at me. There might've been a grin on his mouth. But he winked. I was sure of that.

Dr. Henneberry came down the front steps. "What in hell's name happened here? You boys. What did you do?"

My teeth chattered.

"It wasn't 'you boys,' Father," Martin said.

Mr. Gage had come outside now. Dr. Henneberry's hands were in fists. "Which one of you, then? Whose neck am I going to wring?"

Then his head turned in a tin-robot movement and his gaze locked on me. Same as he did in my dreams. His nostrils flared. Spit foamed at the corners of his mouth. My knees shook, and a thick, icy wave rolled through me. I wrapped my hands over my waist. I was going to be sick. Right in the middle of the gravel driveway.

"Now calm down, Ray," Mr. Fulsome said. "They're just boys, and you know how boys get up—"

I squeezed my eyes closed. But Dr. Henneberry was still there. In the headlights, his hand clamped over my aunt's mouth, lifting her off the ground. He was limping toward me. One slipper off. His toe purple. *You're going to get a real wallop now. This is it. This is it.*

"It was Skip."

I opened my eyes. Martin was pointing at his best friend.

"Yup. It was him. Skip did it."

Skip's mouth dropped open. "Martin! That's not—"

"He was throwing rocks, Father. Firing them at your car. I told him to quit it, but he wouldn't listen."

Mr. Gage said, "Apologize right now, young man. Un-be-lievable! Is this how we raised you? The costs are coming right out of your savings, you can mark my words on that."

Skip's mouth would not close. Tears welled up and spilled over. He spun around and raced all the way down the driveway. I watched until he disappeared around a bend in the road.

Martin was next to me then. "Remind me later to give you that dime, Ware." He wormed his hand around my back and gripped my shoulder. Then he pulled me in close like we were brothers. I could feel warmth coming out of his armpit. "Skip's a loser. And by the way, Genie really does let me do stuff to her. You believe me, right?"

EXCERPT

Testimony of Barry (Skip) Gage, Friend of Martin Henneberry

Direct Examination by Prosecutor Clay Fibbs

A. Thomas never talked much. I don't like quiet people.

Q. **Barry, were you—**

A. It's Skip. I hate Barry. No one ever calls me that.

Q. **Okay then, Skip. Were you upset with Martin for telling that little white lie? That you'd broken Dr. Henneberry's windshield?**

A. At first I was. But then I realized. Martin could be a jerk sometimes, but I knew he was trying to cover for Thomas. My father just made me pay for it.

Q. **Let's jump forward about a week or so. Did you get into an altercation, a fight, with Thomas Ware shortly afterward?**

A. It wasn't exactly a fight. The guy gave me a bloody nose.

Q. **Please tell us the events that led up to that.**

A. All of us were down on the beach. Me and Martin, and Genie Bishop. She was sort of Martin's girl. But she ended up leaving.

Q. **Why'd she leave, Skip?**

A. No reason. Martin told us to haul driftwood for a fire, and she probably didn't want her dress messed up.

Q. **So a couple of chums having some fun. Was Mr. Ware there?**

A. I saw him standing in the woods. He was wearing
   Martin's old clothes.

Q. **What happened next?**

A. I kept collecting up the branches, and then he marched
   onto the beach and came right up to me. Running fast.
   That's when he punched me square in the face.

Q. **Assaulted you? With no provocation?**

A. Provo—?

Q. **Did you egg him on, Skip? Torment him?**

A. No, sir. I swear I didn't.

Q. **Can you tell us what happened next?**

A. I was trying to hold the blood in, but it kept pouring
   out of my face and Martin told me not to defend
   myself. He said I shouldn't knock him back because
   people from that side of town didn't know better.
   They weren't taught right.

Q. **But did you?**

A. No, sir. I listened to Martin. Plus, I was way too
   surprised. My shirt was ruined.

Q. **After striking you, did Mr. Ware leave the area?**

A. He did not. The three of us built a fire.

Q. **Did he apologize?**

A. No.

Q. **When you arrived home, did you tell your mother?**

A. I didn't.

Q. **She didn't notice your bloody shirt?**

A. My mother never does laundry, Mr. Fibbs. Besides, she
   doesn't ask about stuff like that.

Q. Why didn't you want to tell your mother, Skip?

A. I don't know. I didn't want to make a big deal. He was barely eleven, so he was a lot smaller than me. I was a bit ashamed of getting smacked by a kid.

Q. Were you afraid of Thomas Ware?

A. You mean scared? He wasn't that ba—

Q. Be honest, Skip.

A. I steered clear of him, as best I could. You never knew what he was going to do. He wasn't like us. Martin said he was a freak. A real little weirdo.

CHAPTER SIXTEEN

I was kneeling on the floor with Mrs. Henneberry's feet in my lap when a lady blew into the family room. She had puffy hair and flushed cheeks, and was plump around the waist. "Oh!" she said as she clapped her hands together. "I found you!"

"I don't believe I was hiding, Joan." Mrs. Henneberry took a deep breath and said to me, "Tom, this is Mrs. Bishop."

"Her oldest and dearest friend, darling. Long overdue for some chitchat, hey, Muriel?"

"Hello, Mrs. Bishop." I stood up and, without thinking, smelled my fingers.

"Hello, Tom. I'm Genie's mother," she continued. "Genie Bishop. I'm sure Martin has mentioned her?"

Mrs. Henneberry patted her forehead. "I doubt the boys discuss that sort of thing."

"Oh of course they do. Don't you fool yourself, Muriel. Boys natter on just as much as the girls nowadays." She turned back to me. "And where do you come from, young man?"

I didn't know what she meant. Where *did* I come from? Probably St. Augustine's at the beginning. Or maybe from the apartment. Some of me was from Mrs. King's place, too. And a part from the classroom at my school.

Mrs. Bishop snapped her fingers in front of my nose. "My goodness, Muriel, it's like he's having some sort of spell."

"Sorry," I whispered.

"He comes from wherever he wants, Joan." Mrs. Henneberry wriggled her feet back into her shoes. "Don't you, Tom?"

I nodded. "Yes, ma'am."

"Hop down to the beach now, Tom."

"The beach?"

"Don't quibble. You need to lend a hand. Martin's doing a cleanup."

I dragged my toe over the carpet, and Mrs. Henneberry reached forward and slipped a nickel into my palm.

"You're going to enjoy yourself. Skip's there, too." Then she said to Mrs. Bishop, "And Genie?"

"You better believe it." Mrs. Bishop plopped down hard in a chair. The legs squeaked. She fanned her neck. "Not a second passes without some mention of Martin this or Martin that."

"Oh dear," Mrs. Henneberry said. "I hope she's not too serious about this little connection."

"I won't fib, Muriel," Mrs. Bishop said as I was leaving. "The girl's struck. Simply struck by that young man.

I don't know what magic your boy's doing, but I've given up trying to control it."

Before I reached the beach, I heard their voices. Hooting and hollering, bouncing off the trees around me. One of them was Martin's, but there was also a high-pitched squeal. I tucked myself down behind the bushes and peeked out. Skip was a long way down the beach trying to tug what looked like a giant white stump. Martin was closer, and he was with a girl. That had to be Genie Bishop. She had long brown hair and she was wearing a flouncy skirt and the hem of her button-up shirt was tied in a knot over her belly button. Martin had an unlit cigarette stuck to his bottom lip and he was jabbing at Genie with a stick. "Stop it," she said, but she was giggling and spinning. Then he tried to lift up her skirt with the stick. She twisted, shoved his shoulder. He grabbed her wrist and yanked so she nearly tumbled into the sand. When she righted herself, he tried with the stick again.

"Martin Henneberry." She had her hands on her hips. "You better quit it!"

"Or what?" he said, tossing the stick aside. He peeled the cigarette from his lip and poked it behind his ear. "I never even touched you."

I watched them. Doing their strange sort of dance. Her words said she didn't like what he was doing. But her face, all lit up, said she did.

Skip had come up the beach, and he caught me standing behind the bush. He elbowed Martin, and then

Martin saw me, too. I pretended I wasn't being sneaky. I started whistling, and stuffed my hands in my pockets, strolled out onto the beach. My eyes watered from sun reflecting off the lake. I tripped over a large log that was half-sunk in the sand and slammed down on my front.

The girl rushed over. "Did you hurt yourself?"

I jumped right up and spat out grains of sand. "No. I'm good."

"You're Thomas, right?"

I nodded.

"I'm Genie."

"I know. I saw your mother back with Mrs. Henneberry."

She rolled her eyes. "My mother talks about Mrs. Henneberry constantly." She sat down on the log, and I sat next to her. With the side of her hand she scooped up her skirt and pinched it behind her knees. She was wearing socks with white lace around her ankles. "You're living with them?"

"For a bit."

"Don't you get lost in that huge house?" The words sprung out of her mouth, almost like she was singing. "Whenever I visit, I do."

I shrugged. "I don't really wander around much."

"Where were you before? With your father?"

My throat tightened. "No, my aunt. We had an apartment on Gerald Street."

"You're joking! Lower Washbourne?"

"Yeah."

She clapped her hands together, the same way her mother had. "Me too! We used to live in the apartments right behind yours. Can you believe it? But now we got a real house. My mother likes to tell people we're in Upper Washbourne, but"—she lowered her voice— "that's really not true." She dug her heels into the sand. "It's dumb. Who cares, right?"

I shrugged again. It didn't matter to me where she lived.

Then she said, "My father's teaching me to drive. When I get my license, he's going to buy a car that's all mine."

"That's really something."

"Yeah. My mother wants me to be able to come over here if I want. When she can't take me. So me and Martin can, you know, be together." She coughed.

"Hey, Skip! Check this out!" Martin was dragging a forked branch. He climbed into the middle of the fork and lifted it so that the single end stuck out from his hips. Skip grabbed himself around the stomach, said, "That'd scare the girls away!"

"Why?" Martin replied. "I got so much to offer." They were both snorting.

Genie scowled. "They're so juvenile. Why do you hang around with them?"

Martin dropped the branch. He stared at me.

"Mrs. Henneberry told me I had to help. Clean up the beach. What about you?"

"Me and Martin are going steady. And my mother really likes him. Like this much." She stretched her arms out wide.

"Cool," I said. I didn't ask why.

"We've been a thing for a few months now. Mother's certain we'll end up married. Which is beyond ridiculous, but I still sort of have to be here, right?"

Were there rules about going steady? I didn't know anything about that. "If you want, I guess."

"Where's your aunt now?" Genie said. "Is she still on Gerald Street?"

"No." I kept trying to believe she was, but that trick hadn't worked in ages. "She's gone."

"Oh. For good?"

I hesitated. "Yeah. For good."

"Where'd she move to?"

"I don't really know. I—" Then I said it. Plain and simple. "She got off a bus in Greenlake and she got murdered."

Genie nudged me with her arm and giggled. "That's a weird joke, Thomas. You're really odd, you know." When I didn't laugh back, she said, "You're not joking. Oh wow. That's horrible. Was she the last one? That nurse at St. Augustine's?"

I looked out at the lake. No one was sailing today. "Yeah."

"I saw that in the newspaper, but my mother wouldn't let me read it. I'm sorry, Thomas. You must miss her a lot."

The white points on the water skidded over the surface then disappeared into the blue. New ones snuck up
behind those. The wind was soft, and I knew on a day
like today, my aunt would've worn a scarf over her hair.
Tied tight under her chin. Something bright. Maybe
flowers on the fabric. With her big sunglasses.

"Thomas? I asked if the police solved the case."

"I—"

"Boo!"

I jumped. Stepping over the log, Martin pushed in
between us and sat down.

"You're such a brat," Genie said, slapping his arm.
"Why are you always trying to frighten me?"

"I like to," he said. He put his head to one side and
lowered his eyelids halfway. "You're cuter when you're
scared."

"Am I?" She twirled a lock of her hair.

Then, in that twangy voice he used sometimes, he
said, "Isn't she purty? Just as soft as a pocketful of mice!"
Probably someone said the same thing on that show
he watched.

She slapped him again. Less force this time.

"So," he said. "You two are chums now, hey?"

"We're just shooting the breeze."

"About what?"

I thought Genie was going to tell Martin about my
aunt, but she said, "Nothing."

"Huh," Martin said. "Didn't look like nothing."

"I was telling Thomas I'm a real good driver. And he was saying he never saw a beach fire before."

Martin slung his arm over Genie's shoulder and jutted his chin at me, winked. "Ware never saw a lot of things before."

"It's no big deal," she said, and she leaned forward, turned her head toward me and smiled. "Everyone in the world doesn't have their own beach, right?"

Martin pressed his face into her neck and mumbled something. Then he pulled her even closer and let his fingertips rest on her collarbone. Those fingers inched their way down. She curled her shoulder so his hand was forced to lift. "Martin," she said in a low voice. "Don't."

He dropped his hand back down. I think he was trying to feel her chest. Then he put his other hand on the tip of her knee. Slowly, slowly, it slid up her skirt.

"I said stop it." She closed her knees, flicked his hand off her front.

"What?" he said again. But he sounded different. Harder, almost. As though he wasn't joking around anymore.

Skip had stopped picking up wood. He was staring at the three of us.

"C'mon," Martin said quietly. "Why do you act prissy all of a sudden? When my friends are around."

She laughed a weird laugh and lay her head on his shoulder. "I don't know, Marty. I guess. I just. I don't know. Maybe I'm coming down with something. A summer cold."

He pushed in at her again.

"Can you stop it?" Her voice was feather soft. "Please?"

Stop it. Please. The words echoed inside my head.

Skip let out a loud whoop. "You're so full of it, Henneberry!" he called out. "Always gloating, but you're chock full!"

"What? What did you just say?" Martin yelled back.

Skip waved his hand as though he'd had enough and went back to picking up bits of wood.

Martin let go of Genie and sat up straight. His mouth gaped wide open.

Genie patted his arm. "Ignore him, Martin."

And Martin grinned and said, "Ignore what? What do you mean?"

"Nothing. I thought—"

"Yeah. You thought a whole lot of nothing, right, Genie?" He leapt up from the log and yelled, "Listen up, fellers. New plan!" He turned to me. "You and Skip are going to fight."

"What?" Skip dropped his armload into the growing pile.

"Yup. We do it after school all the time, Ware. Like a boys' club. Don't sweat it."

"Yeah, sure," Skip said, "but I don't want to fight him. He's what? Fifth grade? Sixth grade?"

I could feel my heart speeding up and I put my hands down onto the log. The surface was warm and dry. Skip was a lot bigger than those boys who'd picked on Wally. The path through the woods was right behind me, but how could I leave?

Genie stood up then. "Are you for real, Martin?"

"I'm always for real, babe."

"Well, I'm not sticking around for this."

Martin waved the back of his hand at her. "Then go find your loser mother and leave. My mother says she's dull as toothpaste anyway. Chawing on about curtains or dumb mud flaps for that rust heap she calls a car." He wiped his mouth with the back of his hand. "Nobody cares, Genie. Nobody cares!"

She stomped off. Her hair flounced, and her skirt flounced, and even the lace around her socks seemed to flounce. She shouted over her shoulder, "You can be really mean sometimes, Martin Henneberry! Really, really mean!"

He hollered back, "Just be grateful I'm letting you walk through my woods! I could make you go all the way around, you know!" But before he finished, she was already lost among the trees.

I stood up, too. "I don't want to fight Skip." But still I stayed on the beach. I could've followed Genie, but I didn't.

"What? Are you two men? Or a pair of wet rags?" Martin hopped backward, and with his bare toe he scraped out a small circle in the wet sand. "Come on, Skip. Stand in the middle. You too, Ware. If you get pushed out, you lose."

I walked straight over and stepped in the circle. Skip did, too. I couldn't tell if he was angry or nervous. I lowered my head.

"Okay, get ready." Martin took the cigarette from behind his ear and stuck it back onto his lip.

As we touched knuckles, Skip whispered, "Just play along. I won't actually hurt you."

My heart was behind my eyes, blurring my vision. I stretched my fingers, then made a fist. Pulled back my hand and waited. Skip stood there, slightly hunched, with both palms open as though he was going to tackle me. Martin counted down. "Three. Two. One." Then, "Fight!"

Skip didn't move. I closed my eyes and pictured Martin. Then I shoved my fist forward with all my weight and I punched Martin Henneberry right in the very center of his face. Martin cried out. With joy. And I slit open my eyes to see Skip. Bright red was squirting from his nostrils, gushing down over his mouth, soaking his neck, his collar. He grabbed his nose, blood spilling out between his fingers.

"What the hell? What the hell?" Wet sobs came from his bloody lips. "Why'd you do that for? I said I wouldn't hurt you."

"I didn't mean it." I wished I could disappear. Skip hadn't done anything wrong. He'd only been gathering up wood. But my hand had acted like it had done with the marble. Almost by itself.

Martin whacked me hard on the back. The cigarette was hopping around in his lips. "What a strike, Ware!

Well done, buddy! Well done! Took care of him in one fell swoop." His eyes were sparkling. "You're like a secret weapon."

Skip wouldn't stop moaning.

"Buck up, old boy," Martin said to him. "Rinse off in the lake. And then we're going to build the biggest god-damned fire my guy Ware has ever seen."

CHAPTER SEVENTEEN

A couple of days after the beach fire, a storm blew in. First the sky turned purple, then gusts of wind rattled the windowpanes. Rain poured, and the branches of the rosebush bent to the ground. The storm continued all afternoon and through supper. During the evening, thunder was booming as the Henneberrys' guests arrived. Mr. and Mrs. Gage. Plus a second couple I'd never seen before.

"Cats and dogs," Mrs. Gage said as she handed me a dripping umbrella. My mother helped her with her dripping coat.

"I very nearly canceled," the other lady said. She wiped her shoes on the rug.

"Well you're safe now," Mrs. Henneberry said.

Dr. Henneberry gestured with his hand. "Come on through. Jimmy's already at the table. Arranging everything."

I examined a small puddle on the floor. If I looked at Dr. Henneberry, those ideas would spring into my head. It was easier to keep them locked away. Key gone.

Mr. Gage shook his finger in the air. "Arranging in

his favor, no doubt. Last time, Fulsome took every bloody hand."

Dr. Henneberry laughed. "In that case, I'll tell him to raise the stakes. What's the point in playing poker for pennies?"

As the six of them walked away, Mrs. Henneberry called, "Come along, Tom. You'll be Martin's partner."

I scuffed my feet. The last thing I wanted to be was Martin's partner.

My mother bumped me with her elbow. Her stockings were polka-dotted from splashes of water. "Go on," she said, taking the umbrellas I'd been holding. "I'll be close by."

I'd never been in the games room before. The carpet was like sponge under my feet and the walls were dark blue. A glass-and-gold table on wheels was pushed against the wall, with a dozen or so bottles on it, full of different-colored liquids. In the middle of the room was an eight-sided table, and a wooden fan attached to the ceiling above it turned in lazy circles.

Martin was seated at a much smaller table near the window. Mrs. Henneberry nodded in his direction and said to me, "Just a round or two of whatever he wants, Tom. Then make yourselves scarce."

When I slid into the chair opposite Martin, he swatted the wooden board. The colored balls shivered. "I hate this stupid game," he growled. "It's boring."

"Go grab something else, then."

Angling his shoulders toward the window, he picked
up a glass that was hidden on the windowsill. As he took
a gulp, his face tightened and relaxed. "Just so you know,
Ware. If I happen to lose, it's because I'm not trying."

My leg bounced up and down. I didn't plan on trying
either.

The adults settled around the big table. I heard the
slish-slish of cards skimming over the smooth wood.
My mother came into the room, and using a metal claw,
she dropped ice into glasses. She poured seven drinks,
placed them on coasters beside each person.

She kept drifting in and out, bringing in plates and
putting them on a table near the drinks cart. Cheese
with toothpicks. Little wieners stuck to something green.
Dips and vegetable sticks and crackers topped with a
swirl of brown paste. Finally, a pie with a woven pattern
of flaky pastry. I'd chopped the rhubarb myself.

"Oh Esther, you've outdone yourself yet again," Mrs.
Gage said. "Hasn't she, Muriel?"

"Can I have her?" the other lady said. "Can I steal her
when I leave?"

Mrs. Henneberry sniffed. "Not a chance. She's mine
forever." Then to my mother, "Thank you, Esther. We're
all set, so no need to flutter about. You can take time for
yourself this evening. A good book, perhaps?"

Before she left, my mother glanced at me and smiled.
I tried to smile back.

"Will you hurry up?" Martin said.

I studied the board. Moved a yellow ball closer to

Martin's triangle. He tapped a blue one. Rolled it over the ridge with his finger. Then he moved a second one.

"Does it go like that?" I asked.

"Like what?"

"You get to move two?"

"This is my house, isn't it? I can move a hundred if I want."

I bit my lip. "But you're not being fair."

"I've often been accused of being so," he said in that drawn-out way again, "and it sometimes makes for unpleasantness." Then he took another gulp from his glass and gagged. "Besides, Ware, I said I'd lose, didn't I? What're you so uptight about?"

I didn't respond.

I wasn't sure what game the Henneberrys were playing, but they kept hitting their knuckles on the table. The more rounds they played, the louder their knuckles knocked, and each time they struck the wood, an invisible string inside my stomach shook.

"Heck, you're twitchy. You got ants in your pants?"

"Hardly," I said, moving another ball. "Once we're done two games, your mother said I can go."

He lowered his head without breaking his gaze. "Do you have something better to do, Ware? Am I boring you?"

The hair on my back stood up. He was watching me like I was an insect trapped inside a jar and he was deciding if he was going to release me or crush me.

"No," I mumbled. "I like being here."

"Good answer, buddy." He sounded friendly again. Then he pushed his glass across the little table. "Here, have a sip."

"I don't want any."

He leaned forward. "I told you to take a sip, didn't I?"

I brought it to my face. I could tell from the fumes it wasn't soda. Just as I opened my lips to taste it, Martin pumped the bottom of the glass. The liquid shot into my mouth and I gulped it down. Sputtered. Heat spread across my chest.

"See? Jitters gone."

I wiped my mouth on my sleeve. After a few minutes, the string plucking in my stomach calmed. I didn't want to tell him, but it was better.

Mrs. Gage exclaimed, "You're an absolute terror, James Fulsome. A real scallywag."

"He's just lucky," Mrs. Henneberry said. "Like an enormous rabbit foot." I glanced over at her. She had her hand against the side of her neck. "Aren't you, James?" Her words sounded like a boot stomping winter slush. Her hand dropped and she undid an extra button on her blouse. Her skin was shiny.

"You might consider a bite to eat, Muriel," Dr. Henneberry said.

She tittered. "Dr. Norton says it's important to stay hydrated with my medication."

"And your dear Dr. Norton knows best, does he?"

"My dear Dr. Norton knows everything, Raymond."

"One day you'll take a few too many of those pills, Muriel."

"Stop bickering, you two," Mr. Fulsome said.

Cards snapping, skidding across the wood. More knuckle knocking.

"Dear god, he's won again," Mr. Gage cried. "Confess, Jim! How many extra cards do you have in your lap?"

"That's my cue!" Mr. Fulsome stood up, patted Dr. Henneberry on the shoulder. "If I'm going to keep winning like a champion, I'll need a few snacks to sustain me."

He had just picked up a plate at the food table when lightning cracked. A flash of white sliced through the black sky and the whole window glowed. Then a buzzing, like a housefly trapped behind a screen.

The lights clicked out.

Someone gulped. "What's happened?"

"Everyone. Calm down."

"The storm. This awful storm."

"Just when my luck was about to turn!"

"James? Did you orchestrate this?"

Mr. Fulsome laughed. A cracker crunched.

"It's gotten so dark," Mrs. Henneberry said. "How has—Martin, darling, are you toying with the switches again?"

A round light arrived in the open door. "I've brought flashlights," my mother said and began handing them out. "And I can get candles."

At once, several clicks, and beams of light crossed over each other in the room.

A chair scraped back. "I'll check out the cellar," Dr. Henneberry said. "Esther, you come with me."

When he said my mother's name, I leaned forward in my chair.

"Do you think it's electrical, Raymond?" someone said.

"Unlikely, but I'll check the fuses. We won't be but a minute."

My mother's mouth opened like she was going to say something, but when Dr. Henneberry left the room, she followed.

"We should really head home, Muriel." Mrs. Gage stood up. "Skip's babysitting Debra. She'll be frantic with this outage."

Then the other lady stood up. "And we should head home as well. It's been a lovely time, though. As per usual, Muriel."

"Of course, of course."

They all left the room, taking the light with them. I sat in the pitch blackness.

"Should we wait here?" I said.

Martin was panting in the dark.

"In case the lights come on? So we can finish our game?" *Until my mother comes back?* "Martin?"

Another flash zigzagged through the night. For an instant, the room lit up. And the seat across from mine was empty.

—

I crept out into the hallway. The dark was thick like a blanket around my whole body. I stuck my arms out in front of me, edging forward. I'd never been in this part of the house before and I didn't know how to find the kitchen or the laundry. I didn't know how to find the cellar. Genie was right. It was easy to get lost.

Somewhere in the distance Martin was snickering. A door opened, another slammed. I thought I heard my mother, but perhaps my head was making that up.

I tiptoed along, keeping the tips of my fingers on the walls. I could feel velvet ripples and bumps of wallpaper. Then my hand touched the smooth paint of a door.

Whispering. Very close to me. I froze.

"You've had too much, that's all."

"Please. You've got to."

"I don't *got* to do anything, Muriel."

It was Mr. Fulsome and Mrs. Henneberry. She sounded like her nose was plugged up.

"But wouldn't you like to, James? You *are* my lucky rabbit's foot, after all."

"We've had this conversation before. I can't do that to Ray."

"Well, he doesn't have a problem doing it to me."

He sighed. "Really, Mure. You can't possibly believe such nonsense."

"We could go, James. Start fresh. No one would be any the wiser."

I shouldn't be listening to this. I knew it was supposed to be private, but if I slipped past the room, the floor would groan, or they'd hear my footsteps. They'd know I was there. I pressed myself closer to the wall. I'd wait in the shadows until they left.

Mr. Fulsome chuckled quietly. "Come on. Let's be serious for a second." Air moving over teeth. "Even if we both went bananas and decided to take off, that sort of thing costs a sweet nickel, you know that. I'm barely making ends meet, and Raymond's not going to—"

"But I have an account he can't touch."

"You have a what?"

"My daddy made sure. He saw who Raymond was straight away. He predicted this might happen, so he set up an account that Raymond doesn't even know about."

A loud thunk. Something rolled over the wooden floor.

"That's awfully—I mean, I don't know what to say."

"Say you'll consider, James. Just consider it."

Mr. Fulsome sighed again. "But people would talk."

"They're already talking, aren't they? I'm a laughing-stock. If we left, Raymond wouldn't even notice. And Martin, he can finish up in boarding."

"Mure—"

She was snuffling now.

"Come, now. I need to get home, and I can't leave if you're crying like this."

"Then I won't ever stop."

"Even if your face swells up horribly?"

"Even if," she said.

They were quiet for a bit. Then he said, "I know you're

unhappy, and I know Ray can be a little gruff sometimes, but am I your answer?"

"You could be."

"In the daylight, you know, I'm disgustingly ugly."

She made a wet, sad laugh. "You are not." She hiccupped.

When Mr. Fulsome finally strode out of the room, I tried to slide away, but he bumped into my shoulder. Knocked me backward onto the carpet.

"What the hell!" he yelled. "Who's there?"

I scrambled to my feet. "Sorry," I managed. "It's me."

"Who the hell is *me*?"

"Thomas, Mr. Fulsome. I got lost."

"I'm sure you did. Devious little bugger."

I'd never heard Mr. Fulsome sound angry before. He'd always been nice to me. "Sorry," I repeated.

He didn't answer me, he just tromped down the hall. His foot must have caught a table. A smash of broken glass and then a whole string of curse words.

"Tom? Tom, dear? Is that you?"

I held my breath.

"Tom, where are you? I insist you show yourself at once!"

I eased around the doorframe. "I'm here, Mrs. Henneberry."

"Oh, thank goodness. You have to help me, love. I've dropped the flashlight and it simply vanished. The useless thing cut out."

"Do you want me to find it?"

"No, don't bother." I think she was yawning. "I'm positively spent, and I need to rest."

Her nails scratched at my hand, then she gripped it. Led me down the hallway, away from where Mr. Fulsome had gone. Her shoes were slipping over the carpet.

"I can get another flashlight, Mrs. Henneberry. Or a candle?"

She didn't say anything.

My ribs struck a table and I grunted from the pain. Something wobbled, but it didn't fall.

We reached a tiny twisty staircase, and Mrs. Henneberry climbed up and up, never letting go of my fingers.

"How I know this house, Tom. I don't even need to open my eyes. Do you know my father had it built for my mother as a wedding gift? It was a complete surprise for her. Daddy was the most romantic man. Was your father a romantic, too, Tom?"

I held the railing. My father? Lately I'd been imagining that it might be Mr. Vardy. Perhaps he'd clipped tulips for my mother. Brought a bunch tied around the stems with garden twine. That would be romantic.

"Oh, dear. I'd forgotten. Your mother is our poor, dear Esther." Mrs. Henneberry stopped on the stairs. "And your daddy was—how to put it? He was absent?"

"I guess so."

"But that's not your burden to carry, Tom." Then she whispered, "Women make mistakes. Poor judges of character, every single one of us. Sometimes a handsome smile is all it takes." She squeezed my fingers, started stepping up again. "And do you know she's not once spilled the beans?"

"What beans?"

"I've asked her plenty, you can be sure of that. And never a word. I was convinced it was Mr. Vardy for a time. He's been with us for ages. Daddy hired him on."

"Really?" I held my breath.

"But I realized it couldn't possibly be true. He had the most adoring wife. Died of pneumonia six or seven years ago. Very unexpected. If you'd seen how stricken he was. Positively broken. No, he'd never have strayed. That was just my childish mind."

I felt queasy. Maybe from Martin's drink. Or maybe from the letdown about my father. When was I going to stop making up stories? About the Henneberrys. About a stranger in a black car who I'd seen exactly twice. And now about Mr. Vardy. Like my head was an inky screen and the movie reel just rolled on.

We were in an upstairs hall now. I felt along the wall and found a light switch. When I flicked it up, nothing happened.

"Don't fret, Tom," she said. "I'll look after you."

We moved along inch by inch. Now she was holding my hand with both of hers.

"So much night sky," she said. "It's such a burden, isn't it?"

"I guess so."

"Engulfing us. Reminding us how vulnerable we truly are. Almost hard to draw air."

She opened a door. A small amount of light came in through the windows. We were back in her bedroom. One of the curtains billowed.

It was cooler in there, but it smelled. Like an orange that appeared fresh in the bowl, but underneath, the whole bottom had collapsed with green mold. "Do you want me to close that?"

"Close what?"

"The window. Rain's getting in."

"It doesn't matter." Mrs. Henneberry was shaking candy in a tin. Or perhaps it was pills. In another flash of lightning, I saw her gray shape beside her dresser, bringing a tumbler to her mouth.

Then the sheets crinkled and the bedsprings groaned. Shoes clunked to the floor.

"Come closer, Tom. A boy your age should be napping."

With my teeth, I pulled off a piece of my thumbnail and chewed on it. I was caught in her room again. I didn't know what I should do.

"Now, Tom! I won't ask again!"

My feet moved over to the bed and she pulled me down beside her. "Now, that's better," she murmured. I lay my head on the silky pillow and could feel my hair ruffle when she exhaled. Her arm was skinny, but it felt like a lead pipe across my stomach. She was so close, my back was touching her middle. Our knees were bent together. Her cold feet were under mine. My heart was striking so hard, I was certain she'd feel me shaking.

"Martin was always such a rough child." Her mouth was inches from my ear. I could smell cigarettes and sugar.

"He seems alright to me," I lied.

"The other children didn't like how he played. Always a pinch or a pull. I expect he was the loneliest boy in the world. Acting so vile all the time. I don't know why he didn't care for me."

"I'm sure he did," I said. "Maybe—"

"But you," she slurred. Her finger ran over the top of my ear, along my hairline at the back of my neck. "You've always been a doll, Alexander. A perfect, beautiful doll."

Alexander? Mrs. Henneberry was even more confused than usual. Or maybe she was already sleeping and was dreaming about years ago. I did not close my eyes. After a few minutes, she was snoring. I looked into the jet-black of the hallway. I couldn't be sure, but I thought somebody was standing there. Just a couple of steps away from the open door. Waiting. But after I'd finally wiggled out from beneath her arm and left the room, whoever had been there was gone.

EXCERPT

Testimony of Francis Brown, Firearms Expert

Direct Examination by Prosecutor Clay Fibbs

Q. **Mr. Brown, can you tell us a little about string method?**

A. It's a developing field, first used twenty years ago. It helps investigators get a sense of where a shooter was standing, and how tall he was.

Q. **Can you explain for the court how it works?**

A. First thing to understand is that unless a bullet hits an object to alter its path, it will travel in a straight line. It doesn't curve, or loop around, right?

Q. **Of course not.**

A. Let's say someone fired a bullet in your house. Through your kitchen wall, into your dining room. You're going to get two holes, one on each side of the wall. Imagine a piece of string connecting those two holes, and then you extend it. You've now got a nice clean line of string showing the path of the bullet. The shooter stood somewhere along that line.

Q. **That makes sense.**

A. Now imagine the shooter moves his arm and fires a second bullet a few feet away from the first.

Q. **Really doing a number on my house.**

A. Right, right. Now you've got two straight lines of string through the air. Two bullet paths. The shooter is standing where those two lines cross over each other. That point in space can also give you some insight into how tall the shooter was.

Q. Thank you for explaining, Mr. Brown. Let's start with the bullets. Did you examine them from the Henneberry scene?

A. Yes, three slugs were recovered, and they were consistent with bullets used in a Colt Python.

Q. And were you able to find some—I mean, string some bullet paths? To get an estimate of the shooter's height?

A. I was. It was a bit more complicated, as the assailant moved after shooting Mrs. Henneberry and prior to shooting Dr. Henneberry.

Q. Try to explain for the court.

A. I started with Mrs. Henneberry. Her wound was particularly telling. I knew the exact angle of her repose, and I had the photographs to assist me. There were three points along the string line as the bullet entered and exited her neck and lodged in the grass behind her. With Dr. Henneberry, there were actually four points along his line. Through his mouth, out the back of his skull, through the lawn chair, and the spot where the bullet struck the lawn. I knew the shooter had changed position at some point or another, but using some mathematical calculations, I was still able to estimate the height.

Q. What was the shooter's height?

A. Somewhere between 4 foot 10 and 5 foot 5. Not as precise as I would've hoped, but as I said this was a complicated case.

Q. So not a tall individual, by any means.

A.   Relatively short, actually.

Q.   **Thomas Ware at the time of the shooting was 5 foot
2. Would that height fit into your estimated range
for the shooter?**

A.   Absolutely.

Q.   **Would this estimate fit in with a tall mystery man in
a porkpie hat showing up in his black car?**

A.   Obviously, it would not.

CHAPTER EIGHTEEN

"You were fast asleep when I came in," my mother said the next morning.

"Was I?"

"The house was so quiet without all the humming from the fridge, the fans."

"I don't remember."

"I do," she replied. She rubbed a plate with a cloth. Over and over. Then she put the plate on the counter with a thunk. "Thomas? Would you mind darting down to the cellar? I don't— The stairs are so steep. I just need two jars of peaches."

"Where?"

"You'll see some wood shelves on the back wall. Bottom row to the left, there's about a dozen bottles. I was there last night helping with the fuse box and I noticed them. And the whole time I was there, I kept looking at them and thinking to myself, they've been sitting for nearly a year and I haven't used them. It's criminal, really."

"Okay." I put down my spoon. "But I meant, where's the cellar?"

"Goodness me," she said. "Through the laundry. Where I've hung Dr. Henneberry's dress shirts. Behind is a door. It's rarely locked."

As I brushed past her, she reached up and touched my arm. "Thank you, Thomas. I like having you with me, you know."

"Really?"

"Yes. I was just saying so to Mr. Vardy. I really do."

I skipped into the laundry. August was right around the corner, and soon the paper chain would turn into nothing. My mother and I would move away from the Henneberrys'. Things would get better.

Exactly as she'd said, I found a small door behind three of Dr. Henneberry's damp shirts. I'd never noticed it before, and when I turned the handle and pulled, the hinges creaked. Right at the edge of the doorframe, a narrow staircase went straight down. Those stairs *were* steep.

The cellar was like a long hallway of concrete. One end had a dim lightbulb shining above a strange recliner chair. Behind me was only shadows. Against the wall to my left was a pile of cardboard boxes. A knotted towel was shoved behind them and I tugged it out. Not a towel at all but a ball made of socks, a T-shirt, and shorts. Probably Martin's. He'd likely put them there so he could play that bizarre game with my mother. Knowing she'd find them and clean them and put them back in his dresser.

I heard claws scratching up ahead. Or maybe it was behind me. It was difficult to tell as the noises bounced off the concrete. I scanned the corners for a mouse or rat. But there was nothing.

"Am I invisible to you, Ware?"

A shock went through me. Martin was down there.

"Why are you so spooked? It's just me. Your friend."

"I'm not spooked," I said, even though I was shaking. "I just didn't notice you."

"Your mother didn't notice me either. When I went through the kitchen."

"She's busy," I said. "She's got a lot to do."

"No, I'm invisible, Ware. Sometimes I love it. And sometimes I hate it."

"Sorry." I wrung my hands. That tingly feeling wouldn't go away. "I wasn't paying attention."

"It doesn't matter. You don't count."

He was lying in that reddish chair near the back wall. I realized now that it wasn't a recliner but a dentist's chair. With armrests and a platform for feet.

"It's so hot, isn't it?" he said.

"Upstairs, yeah."

"Outside, too."

"Sure is."

"But it's better down here." One of Martin's long arms hung down by the side of the chair. "I can relax. I mean, just really relax."

He had a point. The air in the cellar, though dank, was pleasantly cool.

The leather screeched. Martin rolled onto his side and put his face close to the seat. "This stinks."

"What does?"

"My stupid chair. I told Father to bring it down here when he got the new one for his clinic. But now it smells like somebody else has been using it." Martin made a gagging sound. "I have heightened senses, you know."

I didn't know what to say. Just behind him was the wall of shelves. A row of jars sat on the bottom one. I could see the orange globes suspended behind the glass.

"I just need to grab something for my mother."

"I thought you might be searching for me. We never finished our game last night."

"Um. We can finish. Do you want to?"

"Nah. Not really." He sat up, so his long legs slid under the arm parts. His chair made an unusual shadow on the floor. Like a bug. "I only wanted to have a discussion."

"Oh?" A bead of sweat trickled down the inside of my arm.

"My mother said things, didn't she?"

"What things?"

"About me."

"No. I don't think so."

"I don't appreciate your dishonesty, Ware. Though I do understand it. You see, I heard her. She said I was a difficult child. She said no one wanted to play with me."

He *had* been standing out in the hallway.

"I was a lonely boy? I didn't care for her?" The chair screeched again. "Sound familiar?"

"I guess?"

"What was there to care for? Nothing. I mean, you've been there. Even when she's sitting right next to you, she's nowhere to be seen."

I'd thought the same thing about Mrs. Henneberry before. But I wasn't going to tell Martin that. "I don't remember exactly. I was real sleepy."

He hopped off the chair and came over and put his hand on my shoulder. "Oh, Martin is so much bother! But *Tom* doesn't want to make me sad. Wah wah." He rubbed his eyes like a baby. Then he straightened his neck and fluffed up my hair. "I like you, Ware. You're a good nut."

Being with Martin was like being shoved back and forth by a wave in the lake. I couldn't tell if he was having fun with me or if he was going to kick my feet out and push me beneath the surface.

I coughed. "I need some peaches. My mother does." I darted around the chair and squatted down to grab a couple of jars. My hands were sweaty on the glass.

"I'll help," Martin said. He took another jar. "I can do that. I'm capable of participating. My rowing coach says I'm a valuable member of our team."

I went up the stairs and through the laundry. Martin was so close behind me, the front of his shoes caught on the back of mine. In the kitchen, I laid the jars on the counter.

"You had trouble finding them?" my mother said.

I shook my head.

"No trouble at all, Esther," Martin said. My mother jumped slightly. "I assisted. He was completely lost down there. And, well, I'm the resident expert."

"I guess I didn't explain clearly. Thank you, Martin, for showing him."

"You're welcome, Esther." He put his jar next to mine. Straightened them so they were aligned, the labels both facing the same way. "It was my pleasure."

Mrs. Henneberry strode into the room. Her smelly perfume wafted over me.

"How is this even possible?" she said, inhaling deeply. "The bluest sky after such a downpour?"

"It's lovely, isn't it," my mother said. She twisted the lid on a bottle of peaches. A small pop.

"Well I, for one, feel completely invigorated by the downpour." For the first time since I could remember, her eyes were opened all the way. "And what's this I hear? About Martin helping?"

Martin cleared his throat. "Just being a mentor to our young guest, Mother. Showing him the ropes."

"How wonderful, dear. You're growing into such a generous young man, just like your grandfather." Then she turned to me. "Tom, dear? You have dirt on your chin."

I scratched my thumbnail near the corner of my mouth, stuck out my tongue, tried to lick the flakes away.

Mrs. Henneberry laughed. "He's like a small stray, isn't he? Adorably disheveled."

Martin folded his arms across his chest.

"Perhaps a sink, Thomas?" my mother said. "A little soap and water?"

"Oh, don't make such a fuss, Esther. He's only a child." She ran a finger along the countertop. "Now, boys," she said, "I'm sending you two down to the soda shop. I'm going to treat you both to a shaved ice."

"You're coming, too?" Martin said.

"With you two scamps? Most certainly not. I'm waiting for Dr. Norton."

"Why's he here again? You said you feel refreshed."

"Yes, but that can change on a dime, Martin." She held out a folded dollar bill. "You know these health problems are unpredictable. It's not my choosing, dear."

"Yeah, sure," he said. He grabbed the money and stuffed it into his shirt pocket. "Come on, Ware. Let's go eat some stupid ice."

As we were walking down the driveway, Martin stayed right next to me. Sometimes his arm would rub on mine, and when I moved over, he moved, too.

"When are you leaving?" He reached down and tugged out a weed. Stuck it in his teeth and chewed.

"You mean me and my mother?"

"Yeah."

"Not much longer." *August was getting closer.*

The fluffy bit on the end of the weed bobbed up and down. "Do you want to go? I mean, no one's saying you got to, right?" Martin watched me through his left eye. His right was shut from the sunshine. "You could actually stay."

"I don't know." The very last thing I wanted to do was stay. "I'm not supposed to be here."

"Oh yeah. Skip told me your aunt got done in by that Greenlake killer guy. I forgot all about that."

The words punched me in the chest. All my air was gone.

"They never caught him, did they?"

I shook my head.

"Damn," he said. He made a hissing sound and spat the weed out of his mouth. "And that messed up your life, didn't it, Ware? Messed up everything."

Heat pulsed through my head. I bit down on my lips. Everything was messed up. But my mother had made promises. Inside the paper chain. She talked about working together and time healing all wounds. She also said Mr. Vardy was guiding her, and though he wasn't my father like I'd wished, he was a still decent man. He hadn't barked at me once. Not like Mr. Fulsome.

"That's okay, buddy. You don't need to say anything." He slung his arm over my shoulder. He skipped his feet twice, so our steps matched. Like I used to do with Aunt Celia. "And you can look at the bright side."

"What bright side?" I mumbled.

"Well, at least she liked you. At least you got to live all those years with somebody you didn't hate."

He was right. But I wondered why he would say that. If he was trying to tell me something. That after all the terrible stuff that happened, I was still the lucky one. Maybe he didn't have a bright side.

Martin's hand fell off my shoulder. "Well, lookit." He halted his steps in the middle of the road and pointed. Mrs. Grimshaw was on her front lawn. Her dress was twisted oddly so that one sleeve was underneath her arm and the button and buttonholes didn't match up. She had a fistful of dandelions. But it seemed she was collecting them, not throwing them away.

"They're getting her kicked out," Martin said.

"Kicked out of where?"

"Her house. Our street. My mother says if all the neighbors agree, the town might take her away. Put her in the loony bin and strap her down."

"Why would they do that?"

Martin spoke in a lady's voice. "She can't keep on like this, darling. It's a health issue when she's unwell. And her modesty. We've seen everything she's got to offer."

Due to her hump, Mrs. Grimshaw looked up with her eyes. She wobbled closer to me in bare feet. There was a round purple mark on her forearm. I wondered if it was from Martin throwing things at her from up in the trees. Or maybe not. Maybe Martin only did that the one time and he wasn't as bad as I thought. Maybe he was just like his mother said. The loneliest boy ever.

"You're that sweet young man visiting those nasty people next door?"

I didn't say anything, but Martin gagged loudly and poked me in my side.

"What's your name?"

"Thomas."

"Oh yes. Thomas. I remember now." When she didn't ask who Martin was, his eyes narrowed. "Do you want some apple juice?"

"No, thanks," I said. "We're going to get an ice cup."

She picked another dandelion. "Before you go, I have to ask. Have you seen Abel this morning?"

Martin snorted. "Crazy bat."

I hoped she hadn't heard him. "No, Mrs. Grimshaw. I haven't."

"I need to tell him about the birds."

"Oh yes, those sneaky birds," Martin said, in that high-pitched voice again. "Quite the menace in the neighborhood." He rolled his eyes and grinned.

So it wasn't the only time.

"Abel will know how to get rid of them. I'll let him decide."

"Yes, ma'am," I said.

Martin tapped his foot on the pavement. "Come on, Ware. Enough wasting time."

"We should go, Mrs. Grimshaw."

"We?" She stared at the air around me.

Then Martin spat. A wet bubbly splotch at the very end of her driveway. "I told you to come on," he said. He grabbed my arm, and we jogged down Roundwater Heights. After we'd passed a few houses, Martin let me go. He took out his money, smelled it, then put it away again.

"I hate that dumb bitch. I hate her so much. Always ignoring me. Acts like I don't exist. She's cuckoo but she's sure as heck not blind. She knows I'm there. She can see me clear as day."

"Why would she do that? Pretend?"

"Probably wants me. Thinks about me all the time. Mother said she had the hots for my grandfather. Made trouble for him when he didn't like her back. And her lame husband didn't even get rid of her." Martin spat again. "Dirty old whore."

I looked down at my feet as we continued side by side. Martin once again skipped to match my steps.

"Don't you think so, Ware? Don't you agree with me?"

"I—"

"Sure, you've seen her. Out in the woods like that. *My* woods." He put his fist in the air. "Martin's Woods!"

"She might stop going. Stop wandering around."

"She better. It bugs me, whenever I find her in there. I'm trying to drive her out, but my methods aren't working. I'll need to fine-tune my game."

Martin didn't say anything else while we walked the rest of the way. I'd never been to Main Street before. Most of the buildings were brick, painted white. Behind the windows, mannequins had on stylish clothes and shoes, and there was a whole shop selling only hats. In the display, several were balanced on plaster heads. A tiny card in front of the brown one said "Porkpie," and the price was $12.98. That was a lot of nickels. A lot of foot rubs.

We came to an ice cream parlor, and they had a window open to serve people outside.

"Shaved ice is lousy," Martin said. He marched up to the window and waved his dollar. "We'll get cones. Two triple scoops," he told the boy in the red-and-white-striped apron. "And double-dip 'em, chum." Martin let the boy keep all the change.

We took our cones to the end of the street where the pavement turned into sand. The north part of the lake was right in front of us and the water glistened in the sunlight. Closer to the horizon, two boats drifted with bright white sails. Gray gulls circled overhead screeching at us. Or maybe they were screeching at our cones.

"Do you know what she does all day? In that giant house?"

I bit into my cherry chocolate scoop, and my teeth throbbed. Had Martin been thinking about Mrs. Grimshaw this whole time? "Probably nothing," I said.

"Nope. She wanders around with her load hanging out." With his free hand, he grabbed the side of his chest and shook the air. "Doesn't even close her curtains."

I coughed. I didn't want to ask him how he knew she was naked. Or that her curtains weren't closed. "It is a big house" was all that came out.

We ate in silence for a while. Then Martin said, "I wonder about that a lot, you know." He tossed the last bite of his cone up into the air and a hungry gull grabbed it before it hit the ground.

"About what?"

"Who's going to live there when that bitch is finally gone."

CHAPTER NINETEEN

One night when Martin and Dr. Henneberry were away, Mrs. Henneberry told my mother I would have my meal at the dining room table. "How will the boy ever learn proper manners? I've seen him eat, Esther. Slumped over like an animal."

Before I went in, my mother told me about the forks and spoons and how to tuck the corner of my napkin into my shirt. I needed to keep my back straight, and my mouth closed whenever I chewed. "And don't belch," she said. "I know," I said back. My aunt used to burp loudly sometimes when she was drinking soda. She was always trying to make me laugh. Once I did the same in front of Mrs. King, but she didn't care for it. She really let me know, too. I never did it again.

When I went into the room, Mr. Fulsome was sitting at the head of the table. Mrs. Henneberry was around the corner from him.

"Come, Tom, dear. You'll sit across from me."

I sat down on the chair. It was soft, like a cushion under my rear end.

"Stop bouncing, Tom."

I stopped bouncing.

Hanging on the wall behind Mrs. Henneberry was a portrait of a man. His face was white and round, and his nose was sharp. His dark hair had a widow's peak in the middle of his forehead.

"I see you've noticed Daddy," she said. "He insisted we hang him in here."

"Why?"

"He never wanted to miss a single meal with Mother. So there he is."

The man in the portrait was staring straight at me. I shifted in my seat.

"And have you greeted Mr. Fulsome, Tom?" she said.

I hadn't seen Mr. Fulsome in a few days. Not since he'd gotten angry at me during the storm. "Hi." I waved my hand a bit.

"Well hello there, chum," he said. "Seems Mure's made you her pet project, hey? Scraping down your edges."

"What?"

Mrs. Henneberry laughed. "Pardon me, you mean, Tom. It's 'pardon me.'"

I sat up taller. "Pardon me, Mr. Fulsome?"

"Never mind, sport. I'm only yapping."

Mrs. Henneberry reached across the table and touched the top of my hand. "So nice to see you two getting acquainted."

My mother never looked at me when she came into the room, just ladled hot soup into the wide bowls.

"It's good to have you here, James." Mrs. Henneberry

stirred the soup around with her spoon. "Raymond has been swamped at the clinic."

"He has," Mr. Fulsome said. "I've dropped by a time or two and I can't get through the sea of youngsters in the waiting room. The whole scene makes me shudder, if I'm honest."

Mrs. Henneberry laughed again. "Raymond always did manage well with children."

"Are we talking about different Rays here?" Mr. Fulsome said after he'd slurped some soup.

She put down her spoon and reached over to slap his forearm. Then she opened one of two metal tins next to her plate and removed a pill. Swallowed it with a sip of water. "Dr. Norton," she said, and smoothed down her hair. "A small tweak for my nerves."

"Right," Mr. Fulsome said. "The good Dr. Norton."

After a while, my mother came back in and took away the bowls. Mrs. Henneberry never even tasted her soup. Then my mother returned and put pork chops on our plates. A scoop of potatoes with flecks of parsley. Carrots that smelled like brown sugar and butter.

"This looks divine, Esther," Mr. Fulsome said. "Are you sure I can't tempt you away? The accommodations won't be near as pleasant, but you'll get all the adoration you deserve."

My mother's face went red.

"Didn't you know?" Mrs. Henneberry said. "I've decided to let Esther find a place of her own. End of this month. Can you believe it's the first of August already?"

My mother placed a bowl of peas in the middle of the table. She glanced at me and she offered the tiniest smile. My back went even straighter.

"Well that's wonderful news, Esther. You should've done it years ago. Do you need some suggestions?"

"That's kind of you," my mother said, "but Mr. Vardy is helping me find something suitable. I'll still be here, though, bright and early every day."

"She's deserting me." Mrs. Henneberry stuck out her bottom lip and wrinkled her forehead. "We've hardly been apart, the two of us, for so long. I don't know how I'll manage. Why I've agreed to it."

"Nonsense, Muriel. You don't own the woman." Mr. Fulsome stabbed his fork into a pork chop. Pink juice spread over his plate. "Long overdue, if you ask me. It'll be an adjustment, Esther, I'm sure, but you'll find your footing. These Henneberrys will devour you whole if you let them."

Mrs. Henneberry was laughing again, but this time her laugh flowed out. Like thick liquid.

"Thank you, sir," my mother said.

I tried to hold the knife the right way, but it wasn't working. I wanted to pick the pork chop up and tear into it with my teeth. But that would be rude, so I ate a carrot. Mrs. Henneberry poked a single pea with her fork and put it in her mouth. She nibbled and nibbled for a long time.

"James," she said after she'd finally swallowed. She was blinking slowly.

"What is it, Muriel? You've barely touched your plate."

"I was just thinking," she said.

"About?"

A foot tickled up my leg. I jumped. Then Mrs. Henneberry's head went back and she covered her mouth with her hand. I think she was giggling, but she wasn't making any noise. The foot went away, and Mrs. Henneberry shifted in her seat. A couple of seconds later, Mr. Fulsome pushed his chair back from the table. "Now, Muriel," he said. "Be a good girl."

"Tell me," she slurred. "You've got his confidence, haven't you?"

"Whose confidence?"

"Why, Raymond's, of course. You know what he's doing?"

Mr. Fulsome dug his fingers in around the collar of his shirt and pulled. "What do you mean?"

"You know exactly what I mean, James Fulsome. He tells you everything, doesn't he?"

"We're friends, Mure."

"Friends," she said. She tapped her pork chop with the point of her knife. "Close friends."

"Sure."

"Then you know why so much has vanished. You know where it's gone."

Mr. Fulsome shook his head. "Vanished? Gone? What are you talking about?"

I wriggled in my chair. This was adult conversation, and I didn't think I should be hearing it. Mr. Fulsome kept glancing at me, but for Mrs. Henneberry, it was as though I wasn't even there.

"Gladstone money, of course." She took a cigarette out of the other metal tin and lit it. "Piddled away, James. I don't know how else to put it."

"I can't say, Mure. I mean. You'll have to have a discussion with Ray about all that business."

With her fingernail she snapped the end of her cigarette and ashes dropped onto her potatoes. "I was wondering if it had to do with your little weekend getaways. He always comes home in the foulest of moods."

Mr. Fulsome cleared his throat. "Not at all. I'm sure it's nothing. Really. Maybe he just moved funds around."

"Moved funds?"

"You know. For better investments?"

"Oh," Mrs. Henneberry said. Smoke was making her eyes water. "Perhaps you're right."

"I'm sure whatever he's doing, his family's at the forefront of his thoughts. And he probably doesn't want to bother you with all those details. I mean, how boring, right?"

"Of course. But still. It's such a sneaky thing to do. And to learn about it from Daddy's friends at the bank." She pushed the cigarette into the middle of her pork chop. "Well I can be sneaky, too. Right, James? With our plans? You and me. And Tom, too, of course. A perfect little trio."

I stopped chewing.

Mrs. Henneberry shifted her chair again and then Mr. Fulsome shifted his. He smiled and shook his head. "Now, Muriel Henneberry," he said. "Nothing is happening. With me and you. Or Tom here, who's just trying to eat his supper. Just because you ask me something doesn't make it a plan."

I stared down at my plate. With the tines of my fork, I mashed the carrots into orange mush.

Mr. Fulsome kept moving his chair. "Your toes are being very naughty this evening. What if Ray came in?"

"Ray? Who's Ray?" She banged her curled fingers on the table and her mouth opened and her eyes crinkled. But not a sound came out. As though her volume knob had been twisted all the way down. Finally, she said, "Have you ever experienced such a good life, Tom? Have you ever had such times? It's non-negotiable, James. Tom will join us. All I ever wanted was a darling boy."

My heart sank like a loose ball of wet paper. I did have a good life—before I'd moved to Upper Washbourne. I had a just-fine life. I didn't want to go anywhere with Mrs. Henneberry and Mr. Fulsome. I wanted exactly what I had before. Just now, it would be with my mother. She'd told them we were leaving. I tried very hard to believe her. But even though my chain was shrinking every morning, the end of August still seemed a long, long time away.

Transcript of Radio Report
KGLB – 1470AM, Greenlake Station
March 20, 1959

News out of the courthouse today in the Ware trial.
Defense Counsel William Evans cross-examined firearms specialist Francis Brown. Brown used a scientific technique called the string method to determine
the shooter's height in the Henneberry slayings. He
testified that his calculations were a clear match
for Thomas Leon Ware, the boy who stands accused.
During questioning, Evans poked holes in Brown's
science, and Brown admitted the estimate did not
account for shoes, a sloping ground, or an assailant
who was crouching. Most shocking, though, were doc-
uments admitted in court that showed Brown had
worked closely with members of Greenlake PD and
had already been made aware of the accused's height.

Dr. Silas Fedder is with us in the studio today. He's a
professor of legal studies at Slipton College.

—*What do you think of this newfangled approach,
sir? Strings and angles and mathematics?*

—It's solid science, no doubt. And working with the
police to reconstruct a scene is pretty standard, but
there has to be a division between law enforcement
and scientific experts.

—Division?

—Simply put, police may desire a specific outcome. They have a suspect in mind. But a scientist should only know the facts, the data. Remain impartial. It's highly unusual for police to reveal details of a suspect to an expert.

—How would that affect Mr. Brown's numbers?

—I'm not suggesting he purposefully skewed his results, but he could have unwittingly made minor adjustments. Knowing Thomas Ware's height was unnecessary for him to complete his tasks, and frankly, it now strains his credibility.

—Well, I'm sure the country will be talking about it this evening. And while I have you here, Dr. Fedder, can we chat about the shooting itself? Three bullets. Three kills. All in a few seconds. Would you say a trained man committed that crime, or a child who'd never handled a gun in his life?

—An experienced shooter, certainly. But still, that boy could've been a damn lucky shot.

CHAPTER TWENTY

I counted back ten steps and threw the beanbag. It dropped straight down through the small hole in the wooden board. Mr. Vardy had found the game in the shed, and he'd dragged it over near the door with the white roses. The paint was peeling, and the beanbags were damp and musty, but it still worked fine.

I ran and collected the beanbags from under the propped-up board. Then counted back eleven steps. I threw again. *Flump.* It went right through. This was too easy.

"You've got quite a knack, Tom, dear," Mrs. Henneberry said. I turned around and she was standing behind the screen door. Her neck and waist were thin as pipe cleaners. "Mr. Vardy made it for Martin, but he wouldn't bother with it."

Just a few minutes earlier, Martin had come around the back corner of the house, all out of breath like he'd been exercising. When I tossed another ringer, he'd rolled his eyes. "Don't bother begging me to play with you, Ware. I've already got plans."

"Why didn't he like it?" I asked Mrs. Henneberry.

"He just couldn't hit the mark. I didn't want him to think poorly of himself, so I insisted Mr. Vardy store it away." With her fingertips, she pushed open the door. Stepped onto the patch of dirt. "Now. The reason for my intrusion."

"Your what?"

"Just listen, please, Tom. Without interrupting."

"I didn't mean—"

"There you go again, dear. Cutting me off. I do forget sometimes you were raised in Lower Washbourne." She lifted her foot and looked at the heel of her shoe. "Where was I? Oh yes. Dr. Henneberry is working today, of course, and Martin has gone to meet his rowing team. I have the rest of my afternoon entirely free. We're going to spend it together, Tom. Just you and I."

"But my mother," I said. I didn't want to rub Mrs. Henneberry's feet for all those hours. Whenever I slowed down, she'd get cross. "She might need me for—"

"It's all arranged. I've already spoken with her. She's cleaning the bookshelves in the family room, so that's quite a chore she's set for herself."

"But—"

"I'll be in the car." Then she went back through the screen door. After a while I heard the front door slam and then a car engine sputtering. The toot of a horn.

I threw another beanbag. This time it missed and slid over the wooden board. I wanted to stay in the sunshine and play. Or go inside and help my mother with all those books. Or find some paper and colored pencils and draw something for George. He had to be tired of swimming past a plain wall. The horn tooted again, and I hurried to the front of the house. Stopped short.

Mrs. Henneberry was behind the wheel of an older dark-colored car. I'd never seen it before. Her pale arm was dangling out the window. Tapping the side panel. Exactly like *his* hand had done.

"Come on, Tom," she called. "You really are a dawdler."

My fingers were sweating as I opened the door.

"Shall we get going, then?" She looped the car around, driving over the lawn, then down the driveway and out onto the smooth pavement of Roundwater Heights.

I chewed my thumbnail.

"Quit that this instant, Tom." She reached over and smacked my hand so hard it stung. "Children raised with proper nutrition don't eat their own fingers."

I hunched down in the seat. "Sorry," I said.

"Never mind that now, dear." She was calm again. "I've got a delightful afternoon planned for us. Do you like Daddy's car?"

Daddy's? "Sure," I managed.

"I had Mr. Vardy bring it out from the garage."

I wanted to chew my nails again. "Does Dr. Henneberry drive it, too?"

"Oh sure. We both do. Even Mr. Vardy takes it sometimes. Daddy used to call it his old beater. We use it when we want to be a little less conspicuous."

I wasn't sure what "conspicuous" meant. I leaned my head against the back of the seat and closed my eyes for a minute. I put myself back on the fire escape. Peering down through the holes in the metal to watch Aunt Celia waiting on the step. Mr. Pober beside her, his back and neck curled like a snake about to strike.

Then the car arriving. Was it as low? Or as long? Was the back as sloped? Or the wheels half-hidden?

My head began to throb as I tried to recall the exact features. But they were lost. My mind kept straining to create a connection where most likely there was none. It couldn't be the same car. I opened my eyes and tried to relax.

As Mrs. Henneberry drove through Upper Washbourne, she leaned forward in the seat and held on to the steering wheel. Her chest was close to her hands. "It's so difficult to keep all these signs straight," she said, staring out through the windshield. "But we will get there, Tom. We will. You've got my word."

"Where are we going?"

"Such an eager beaver. You'll see!"

After about half an hour, we passed a sign for Greenlake. "Look, Tom, we made it." She patted my thigh. "You were trembling. So full of worry."

I wasn't worried. I looked down where her hand had touched me. I wasn't trembling either.

We drove through the town. There were smaller homes on smaller streets, and we passed St. Augustine's Hospital. Mrs. Henneberry didn't slow down, and I was glad because I didn't want to see the empty bus stop. Or the forest just behind it. Then we were on a busier street that had businesses on both sides. A barber. A bookstore. A drugstore. A hardware shop. Suddenly she braked and pointed to a red brick building. There was a sign in the shape of a square, and a shiny white tooth hanging from a post. The sign said "Painless Dentistry."

"That's Dr. Henneberry's clinic," she said. "I chose the tooth myself. Isn't it the cat's pajamas?"

"It's a fine tooth," I said. I held my breath, waiting for her to tap the brake.

"I know you'd love to see the inside, Tom, but we mustn't. He can't abide a drop-in. I did it once and he was positively incensed. Threw his entire day's schedule off."

I stared straight ahead as we drove past. Only a few more weeks and my paper chain would be finished. I'd never have to worry about Dr. Henneberry again.

We parked in front of Belbin's Toy Shoppe.

"Did you know I organize a toy drive here every year?" she said. "During the festive holidays."

"No, ma'am." When I stepped onto the sidewalk, heat waved up around my legs.

"Oh, we nearly clear the shelves. Such a feeling to give to those less fortunate. You've probably met the families, Tom. Mostly in those cramped apartment buildings, if you must know." The bell above the door tinkled as we went in. Mrs. Henneberry yawned. "Anything you want, darling. Don't be shy."

A saleslady came over. "So lovely to see you, Mrs. Henneberry. And who's this?"

"Tom. Tom Ware. He's Raymond's nephew, but I've claimed him for the summer."

"Such a handsome boy."

"Isn't he, though?" she said.

The lady bent down and put her hand on my shoulder. "What suits your fancy today, young man?"

"Something you've pined for," Mrs. Henneberry said as she waved at the boxes beside her. "Something that would make your heart float, dear."

I'd been in Belbin's a couple of times before, but only to "browse," as my aunt had said. She'd watched me carefully, and if I was really lucky, a toy I'd touched would end up wrapped under our Christmas tree. But I'd never been allowed to choose an item and actually leave the store with it in my hand. I glanced about at everything. Now that I could pick whatever I wanted, I didn't care very much. Nothing in that store would make my heart float. The only thing I pined for was gone.

"Perhaps one of those roll things you push and pop? Or that monstrous head that looks like a dirty potato?"

The saleslady shook her head. "That certainly won't do. He's such a big boy, aren't you? I'm guessing a volcano kit or army men, or even a pogo stick?"

Mrs. Henneberry frowned when the saleslady guided me toward a different section of the store. Airplane models, transistor radio sets, painted wooden yo-yos. A box of magic tricks with a clown on the cover. I saw Slinkys and View-Masters, but I didn't want new ones. I wanted to get my birthday gifts back.

When Mrs. Henneberry looked at her watch for the third time, I grabbed a heavy magnifying glass with a shiny white handle.

"That's marble," the saleslady said. "A stone, but it's very soft. You can dissolve it."

"I'll be careful," I said. I didn't want anything dissolved. I thought of Martin's chemistry set. I thought of George sitting on the dresser in the bedroom.

"Is that it, Tom?" Mrs. Henneberry said, frowning again. "Really?"

I nodded.

"He's got the mind of a naturalist, I suspect," the saleslady said. "Shall we wrap it?"

Mrs. Henneberry waved her hand, and moments later we left the store. I was carrying a small parcel underneath my arm.

"You're hungry, Tom."

I wasn't hungry at all.

"What might a young boy like you want?" She tapped her chin. "Of course. The very basics. I know just the spot." She smiled at me and took my hand in hers. "Too bad Dr. Henneberry is so overwhelmed today. This is one of his favorite places to lunch. He likes the basics, too."

We walked to a diner, and when we went inside, the smell of frying grease hit my face. Mrs. Henneberry chose a spot by the window, and within seconds the waitress came over. She stuck her tongue through the ball of pink chewing gum in her mouth and blew a bubble until it popped. After she grabbed the pencil from behind her ear, Mrs. Henneberry ordered two double cheese-burgers, two fries, a large slice of blueberry pie, two root beer floats, and a cup of coffee, no cream, no sugar. Soon food was crowding the table. The glasses of soda were wet and bubbling over with creamy foam. A red-and-white straw stood in the middle of a scoop of vanilla ice cream. Only an hour earlier, I'd eaten most of the grilled cheese my mother had made. Now I had to work through the mountain sitting in front of me.

"Go on," Mrs. Henneberry said as she poked at her fries. "This is what you love." She lifted the top bun off her burger and shuddered. After she lit a cigarette, she stared out the window, sipping her coffee. Strands of smoke squiggled up from her hand.

I ate slowly, and after each bite I took a sip of the float to force it down. Mrs. Henneberry's seat was in shade, but mine was in full sun. I started to feel sick. Sweat dripped down under my hair and between my shoul-ders. The stink from her cigarette went right into my nose. Behind me, a cook dropped another beef patty onto the grill.

Suddenly Mrs. Henneberry was frantically waving her arms. "Goodness!" she exclaimed. She smushed the cigarette in the ashtray and was half out of her seat. The table squeaked when her thighs bumped the edge.

A lady appeared on the other side of the window. She was waving back at Mrs. Henneberry, and then she rushed through the door and over to our table.

"Muriel, darling. I haven't seen you in an absolute age!"

"How has that happened?"

"So strange to find you here. In a place like this."

"Oh, it's just for the boy," Mrs. Henneberry said. "I can barely tolerate a leaf of lettuce these days."

"Oh yes, I've heard all about it. Feeling better, then?"

"Day by day. Dr. Norton is a lifesaver."

"My sister says the same thing." Then in a hush, "Five children, Muriel. The racket! She couldn't manage a day without the dear doctor."

Mrs. Henneberry gestured toward me. "This is Tom. Ray's cousin's son. He's come in on the train just this week. From out east."

"Oh really? Where?"

Mrs. Henneberry touched her throat. "They've just moved. And for the life of me, I can't recall the town. Picturesque, I'll tell you that. Their property is simply magnificent."

The lady smiled at me. There were wrinkles around her eyes and her lips. "How he puts me in mind of your Martin, don't you think? So soft-boned."

"It's the clothes, really. He's had to borrow some of Martin's after his luggage was misplaced. I suspect it was stolen, though."

"Nothing would surprise me with all the hooligans these days."

"But we haven't let the mishap put a damper on

things. Have we, Tom, dear?" Mrs. Henneberry patted my hand. "He's such a lamb. We've been making a day of it. Showing him what life is like in our little neck of the woods."

"Couldn't hook Ray into joining you?"

She shook her head. "His clinic. It's positively over-booked. You'd think he was the only dentist in Greenlake."

The lady laughed and put her hand on her stomach. She was wearing a pair of white mesh gloves. "And I can't get Rusty off that boat of his. Fussing over every inch of her. I do believe he's infatuated."

It was Mrs. Henneberry's turn to laugh. I tried to sit up straight and push another fry into my mouth. The salt burned my tongue.

"You're very lucky to have such agreeable company, Muriel. I've been saddled with Rusty's mother. Bringing her all the way out here to another seamstress. She fired our last one as the sorry woman insisted she was going to sew a size twelve, not a size two. She wasn't bright enough to play along."

"Oh, dear."

"Well, love, I do have to dash."

Mrs. Henneberry stood up again. "We'll see you at Martin's sixteenth? You've gotten the invite?"

"Did I not call you? Rusty and I wouldn't miss it for the world."

"I've invited the whole circle. It's going to be absolutely perfect."

"Your parties always are, Muriel."

Mrs. Henneberry gave her a loose hug, and then the lady went out through the door. I watched her run across the road.

"Are you making it through, Tom, dear?" Mrs. Henneberry said as she sat back down. She lit another cigarette.

"What?"

"Pardon me."

I stared at her. My stomach was flip-flopping. I wished I had dropped some of the food under the table while she was distracted. "What?" I said again. "I mean, pardon me?"

"Shall I ask for our pie?"

"Okay." I tried to burp quietly.

Mrs. Henneberry signaled to our waitress. She took another sip of her coffee. Then the cup slipped from her hand and banged against the table. Brown liquid sloshed out. She was twisting in her seat and her fingertips were pressed to the window. Her mouth was wide open. I looked outside, and I knew right away what had made her turn pale. Dr. Henneberry wasn't in his clinic with a sea of kids, like Mr. Fulsome had said. He was meandering along the sidewalk. And he wasn't alone. A pretty woman with wavy brown hair and bright red lips was walking right beside him.

Mrs. Henneberry's cigarette was fixed in the air. She gaped straight out that window, eyes wide open. Dr. Henneberry got closer and closer. He was chatting and grinning, and the lady kept bending at the waist. Whatever he was saying, she was finding it incredibly funny. Her dress was blue and white stripes and the fabric swayed. It had a wide neck. Sunshine fell on her shoulders.

Arm in arm, they swept right past the window. If Mrs. Henneberry smashed her hands through the glass, she could have grabbed Dr. Henneberry's sleeve. But she just sat there. Glued to her spot. She didn't even tap her fingernails to get his attention. And then he was gone.

I leaned around to watch him. He was already a distance along the sidewalk and his hand had curled around the lady's waist. Then it stopped to rest lower than necessary on her hip. No, that was wrong. His hand shouldn't have been there at all.

The waitress plunked the slice of pie in the middle of the table. Blue filling glopped out over the pastry. "Will there be anything else, ma'am?" she said as she scooped up our plates.

Mrs. Henneberry giggled in a weird way and shook her head. "Nothing at all, thank you, dear. It's been marvelous." Then she said to me, "Sometimes faces look so familiar, don't they?" She picked up a fork and squished one of the berries. Blue juice burst out onto her fingers. "But the mind plays tricks on us."

The mind plays tricks on us. Was that why I kept picturing Dr. Henneberry's hand? And his purple toenail? And the top of a car that was no different than thousands of others?

"Tom? Are you listening to me?"

"What?"

"Pardon me! Did you see which direction Mrs. Johnson went?"

"Who?"

"My friend," she said, a new cigarette pinched in her fingers. She unclipped her pink purse and took out the smaller metal tin. She had tremors in her hand, and it took her three tries to open it. "She was standing right in front of you, for pity's sake. Plain as day!" She pushed a tiny white pill into her mouth. Then she took a second pill and cut it in half with her front teeth. Powder stuck to her lipstick. She took a quick drink of water. For a second, her eyes bulged, and she wrapped her fingers around her neck. Then she was fine.

"Across the street," I said.

"That way?"

"Underneath that big tree over there. I think she left."

"You think? You *think*?"

"No, ma'am." I squared my shoulders. "I saw her leave."

Mrs. Henneberry clicked the tin closed and dropped it back in her purse. She sucked hard on the cigarette and bit the powder off her mouth. Lipstick smeared her front teeth. She chewed on her thumbnail, but I didn't think it was a smart idea to say something about being properly raised.

"Thank you, Tom," she finally said. Then she reached over and smoothed my cheek. Smoke stung my eyes. "We're having a nice time. We really are."

Puffs of gray came out of her nostrils. I sat and waited, clicking the heels of my shoes together underneath my chair. It seemed like only yesterday I was out on the fire escape with Wally, burning my name into the strip of wood. How could my whole world have changed so quickly? There was so much troubling stuff to keep inside my head. Each horrible thought like a grenade. One false tug, and everything was going to explode.

After a little while, Mrs. Henneberry stood up. She gripped the side of our table with one hand. With the other, she shoved her cigarette into the top of the blueberry pie.

Her head kept falling forward as we drove back.

"Mrs. Henneberry? Are you okay?"

"Peachy keen, dear. Couldn't be better."

I gnawed the inside of my cheek as the car kept going onto the gravel shoulder, then back over the yellow line. In my lap, I held my small package from Belbin's. I reminded myself it wasn't that far.

"Are you sure?"

"Kneeees bees, really, darling."

We left Greenlake and took a road through Lower Washbourne.

"Oh, why did I come this way? I do loathe these tiny streets." She squinted out the windshield. "Barely enough room to get by. And the potholes. They might chew up an entire wheel." She looked over at me and smiled a slow, flat smile. "You've got no reason to be nervous, Tom, love. No one can jump in at us while we're moving."

We turned onto Gerald then. My actual street. I tried to take a deep breath, but even with the windows opened, there wasn't much air in the car. The brown apartment buildings rose up around us. I didn't see Wally, but some younger kids from my school were lining up to play leapfrog. Mrs. Henneberry slammed her horn over and over. "Who owns those children, for heaven's sake?"

I didn't tell her kids were always outside. Or that cars never drove fast like she was. I stared out my open window. Other than Aunt Celia and me being gone, nothing had changed. My apartment window was right there. And Mrs. King's. Directly below. There was our front step, with the wide crack in the cement where weeds always grew. Mr. Pober was sitting where he always was. His face had turned red-brown from the sunshine, and the armpits of his short-sleeved shirt looked wet.

Got herself mixed up with the wrong sort, he'd said. *That snooty rich guy*.

Out of the corner of my eye, I saw a ball rolling into the street.

"Mrs. Henneberry! Watch out!"

And right behind the ball was a boy.

Her foot pressed the brakes. The tires slowed. Her head first, then her hair drifted forward in slow motion, covering her face. She wiped it away. The boy was standing in front of the bumper, holding his ball. He burst into tears before he took off back to the sidewalk.

"Is everyone okay? Are we okay?" She was panting. Her fingers were spread wide.

Then a woman was screaming. Maybe the boy's mother, but I didn't recognize her. "You trying to murder someone, lady? Go on! Keep moving! Get out of here and don't come back!"

Mrs. Henneberry put her hand on her chest. Her mouth was open, and air was going in and out fast. She reminded me of George moving water over his gills. "Is she speaking to me, Tom? With that tone? Surely she's not?"

"I think so."

"Lock your door, darling. Quickly. Push down that little knob there." She tapped the gas and the car leapt forward. She sped up. When she glanced over at me, her eyes were not seeing straight. "It's vulgar, isn't it, Tom, dear? These neighborhoods? A lot of these people are so poor and unstable."

"I—"

"No wonder, living that close. No better than, than barn animals. Pure squalor."

I stared straight ahead.

As we drove out of Lower Washbourne and into Upper, the sun bounced off the hood of the car. "I've left my glasses, Tom. My sunglasses. I left them at that diner."

"Can you see?"

She fluttered her eyelids. "I do hope so." Her hand slipped off the steering wheel. The windshield wipers began slapping back and forth in a blur.

"Oh my," she said. Slowly she reached around behind the wheel. "I banged something I shouldn't have."

"Mrs. Henneberry?"

"It's been a tremendous day, Tom." Her words were rubber bands stretched thin. "I can rely on you. I know that."

"Yes," I whispered.

The car went side to side.

She braked hard. I flew off my seat and the small package I was holding nearly fell out the window. I tucked it under my leg.

"The drive is so much longer going home, isn't it? How can that be?"

I kept my palms braced against the dashboard. After what felt like hours, we turned onto Roundwater Heights.

"If only I could have a short spell. To rest. I've grown quite weary all of a sudden, Tom. Everything is so scattered. All the outside won't stay still."

"But we're almost there," I said.

Mrs. Henneberry blinked. Blinked again. She was like Mrs. Grimshaw's cat dozing next to the toaster. Then her eyes were completely shut.

"It's all confusing. We should be home just a sec—"

"Mrs. Henne—!"

The car skidded off the pavement. This time she didn't swerve the wheel. She didn't brake. We drove straight into a mucky ditch, the nose of the car smashing into dirt and rocks and grass. Metal crunched. The door to the glovebox slammed down and my knees scraped beneath it. My head and then the fronts of my shoulders rammed into the dashboard. A blast of pain went through my front teeth, through my brain, through the back of my neck. I cried out loud. When I pushed myself back onto the seat, blood from my forehead was leaking down over my right eye. Blood filled my mouth.

Mrs. Henneberry was holding tight to the steering wheel. "Goodness, Tom," she said. Branches and leaves covered the windshield. "What have we gone and done?"

CHAPTER TWENTY-ONE

"Possums," Mrs. Henneberry told my mother after we had crawled out of the car and walked the rest of the way home. "A mother with her fluffy babies on her back. It was adorable, Esther. What was I to do—squish them flat?"

Then she went to use the other telephone line. The phone in the hallway just outside the kitchen didn't work anymore.

My mother guided me to a stool and with a warm, wet cloth, she wiped blood from my head and face. She made me swish my mouth with salty water, and then she peered inside. "You've bitten yourself," she said. "What really happened?"

"Possums," I lied. I didn't want her to worry. "A mother and a bunch of babies. Six, maybe. They were up on the road."

"I thought they were only out at night."

Mrs. Henneberry came back into the kitchen, told my mother she was absolutely not to be disturbed by Dr. Henneberry or Martin, but Dr. Norton was to be sent up the moment he arrived. "Mr. Fulsome, too," she said. "He's coming a little later to help me with my problem."

"Is everything going to be okay?" my mother said.

Mrs. Henneberry closed her eyes. She wobbled back and forth like there was a breeze. I counted. One. Two. Three. Then her eyes fluttered up. "Oh yes, Esther. Things will be fine. I'll just be taking charge now."

She insisted, once my mother had washed the "unsightly blood" from my face, I should find my way to her room and wait. When Dr. Norton had finished examining her, he would check me over as well. "Just to be on the safe side. Those possums gave you quite a knock, Tom."

"Thank you, Mrs. Henneberry," my mother said.

"You know where my room is, right, Tom?"

My mother rubbed the top of my arm. "I do," I said.

"I don't know what I was thinking," my mother said when Mrs. Henneberry was gone. She went to a drawer and fished out a bandage. "Letting you go like that. I thought it would be—I thought—" Her face turned pink as she tore open the bandage and tried to stick it on my scalp. My hair got snagged in the tacky parts. "I should never have let you go."

I thought she was going to start crying. "It's just a bump," I said. "I've had worse at school."

My mother wiped the tip of her nose. "The doctor will know. He'll have tests and things, I'm sure."

When I went into Mrs. Henneberry's bedroom, she was coming out of her bathroom in a nightdress. It was the same color green as the moss that grows up the bottom of trees. With a shaky hand, she pulled back the covers and climbed into her bed.

She wagged her fingers at the curtains. "Pull those across, please Tom."

I yanked them and the room turned a dark, sleepy orange. It was stuffy in there. Then came a low growl from outside. Mr. Vardy was using the electric mower again. He said I could try it if I thought I could handle it, though I had to be careful on the slopes. If I slipped, it wouldn't think twice about slashing up my legs. I sat in a chair and waited in the shadows.

"Are you there, dear?"

"Yeah," I said. "Over here."

Her head shifted on the pillow. "When I was a young girl, I had a line of suitors. Did you know that, Tom?"

"No," I said. *Of course I didn't.*

"Sons of Daddy's friends. Nice boys. Handsome boys. Appropriate choices."

My hands were sticky with sweat. I wormed them under my thighs.

"But I wouldn't listen. I wanted Raymond. As soon as I saw him with that candied apple stuck in his mouth. I was at a carnival with Joan Bishop. You remember Genie's mother? And when everything shut down, Raymond convinced me to climb up one of those rides. He thought I was so daring. So reckless. He fell for that girl."

My head and mouth were whomping. Though I'd told my mother it didn't hurt, the bump was way worse than anything I'd ever gotten at school. I wanted to go to my cot and sleep. It was hard to keep listening.

"And then Martin came, and he looked so, so like my little brother. Did you know I had a little brother?"

"No," I said, even though I did.

"Well the sight of him, the sight of Martin, so small, so fragile, it flooded me with fear. I couldn't manage it. Being his mother. So many things could go wrong. Millions. And just like that, all my spunk was gone." Her hands stretched over the bed. "Raymond left me then. He's still here, of course, but he left me behind."

The mower choked and sputtered. I'd try it next time. I'd tell Mr. Vardy I could be responsible.

"Such a hideous feeling to be forgotten. As though I was discontinued."

"That's too bad," I said, because I didn't know what else to say.

"No need to be dramatic, Tom. I've had Dr. Norton to lean on. Seeing me through. He's been by my side as far back as I can remember." She took a deep breath. "Say my name, Tom."

"What?"

"Pardon me. I told you to say my name."

"Mrs. Henneberry?"

"No. Miss Gladstone."

"Miss Gladstone," I said.

She sighed. "Again."

"Miss Gladstone."

"And again."

I whispered her name over and over, until I thought she'd gone to sleep. But then she said, "I need you to stay close by, Tom. Very close. I can't do this without you."

"Do what?"

"I'm going to be strong. For once in my life, I'm going to stand tall. Do you understand?"

"Sort of. Sure," I said. The room was changing. Light turning soft and gray as the sun slipped down behind the trees. The lawnmower noise had long since stopped. I tapped my mouth. It felt like someone else's top lip was attached to my face. Even though I'd washed my hand, my skin still smelled like pennies. I laid my head against the side of the chair.

The creaking door woke me up, and an old man poked his head inside. He had thick black glasses, and even though it was stifling, he wore a knitted vest.

"You hiding in here, Muriel?"

"Oh, Dr. Norton," she said. She sounded half-asleep. "Yes. I'm not far."

"Why are you alone in the dark?"

"Alone? I have my Tom here with me."

He didn't make a sound as he stepped over the carpet and put his rectangular bag on the night table. The same table that had her diary in the bottom drawer. Where she wrote about Dr. Henneberry liking something cheap and dirty. "Shall I ask him to wait outside while we converse?"

"No," she mumbled. "Of course not. Why would you?"

"Well, I do insist on a lamp," he said as he reached beneath the shade. "Mind yourself."

With the sudden brightness, my eyes stung and watered. Dr. Norton glanced over at me and smoothed the top of his wide tie. He was bald except for a ring of gray hair around the back of his head. It curled down over the collar of his shirt. "Muriel, you were in such a state of distress when you called."

"Yes, distress. Tom and I. We've had a slight mishap."

"In your car?"

"Ducklings on the road, Doctor. It was like an assembly line at one of Daddy's factories."

He got close to her. Then he lifted the blanket. "I don't see any obvious injuries, Muriel. Is it your neck, then? Your back? Tell me, how might I put you at ease?"

"Pain. I'm experiencing so much pain."

"Where, dear?"

She tried to push herself up in bed, but her arms buckled and she tumbled back.

"Just stay still, Muriel. You can point."

Her hand dropped on her chest. "In here."

He undid the clasp on his black bag. The top opened like a pair of jaws. He removed a stethoscope, put the ends in his ears. "I'm going to have a listen. Inhale, please. Good. Now exhale. Very good."

"Is there anything else you can give me?"

"Muri—"

"Anything at all, Dr. Norton? I just can't. Can't manage this churning in my head. It's simply too much for me."

"Well, I could offer some—"

"Yes, yes," she said. Her head fell to the side, chin touching the tip of her shoulder. "Thank you very much."

The doctor rummaged around in his bag and withdrew a small bottle. "Only until you're on firmer ground, Muriel."

"Positively no longer. I promise."

He sat on the side of her bed and opened the bottle. I watched him tip one, then two pills out into his hand. He helped Mrs. Henneberry sit up so she could take the medicine.

"A quick exam for Tom, please, Doctor," she said as she lay back down. "I believe he struck the dashboard."

The doctor twisted on the bed and nodded at me. "Given your skull a crack, have you, sonny?"

"Yes sir," I said.

"Three times three."

"Um. Nine?"

"What is bread made of?"

"Bread? Um, flour and wa—"

"Spell river backward."

"R-E-V-I-R."

He stood up and closed the mouth of his bag. He threw the flap over the top and buckled it. "Perfectly healthy, Muriel. No need for concern. A child's head is like a boulder. Practically indestructible."

"Thank you, Dr. Norton."

"Call if you need me. Day or night." He picked up his bag, clicked off the lamp, and left.

It was quiet in the room after that. Mrs. Henneberry's breaths came in soft puffs. I waited and waited but did not move from the chair. My tongue kept prodding the raw holes in my cheek. My head slipped forward onto my chest. I may have dozed off again.

It could've been minutes, or hours, but Mrs. Henneberry woke up with a loud gasp. My eyes popped open. My neck and shoulders were stiff. Through the dimness, an arm crept upward from the bed, then waved about like it was searching the air.

"Tom? Tom, dear? Are you still here?"

"Yeah," I said softly. I didn't know if I was allowed to leave. My stomach was empty, but at the same time, I felt like vomiting. Shivers went up and down my spine.

"I've just had the most wonderful dream," she said. "About what things could be like. They will be like. If I do everything properly." Her mouth opened and closed. The sound like peeling tape. "Has James—has Mr. Fulsome arrived yet?"

"I don't think so."

"Oh," she said in a flat voice. "We have something so important to discuss."

"Do you want me to go and ask my mother?"

"No, dear. He'll be here. I know he will." She yawned. "Why don't you run along. Have Esther make you something nourishing." She reached for Dr. Norton's bottle and twisted off the lid. "But before you go, another blanket for my legs, Tom, please. They aren't getting any blood at all."

EXCERPT

Testimony of Mrs. Alice Grimshaw, Neighbor

Direct Examination by Prosecutor Clay Fibbs

Q. Can you state your name for the court, please, ma'am?

A. Alice Everly Grimshaw.

Q. How long have you lived next door to the Henneberrys?

A. I live next to the Gladstones.

Q. Of course. They were the Gladstones originally.

A. I've been in my home for fifty-nine years. The only way I'm leaving is in a box, sir.

Q. Okay, Mrs. Grimshaw. Now, the court wants to understand what happened on the afternoon your neighbors were shot.

A. They were shot. Yes. That was a terrible day.

Q. Can you tell us what you saw and heard?

A. I remember it. I do. I saw a man driving past my house. Pulled into the Gladstones' driveway. Him right there.

Q. Can the record show Mrs. Grimshaw has indicated Mr. James Fulsome. Do you recall what time, ma'am?

A. Maybe three o'clock. Before my walk. I needed to find Abel.

Q. Abel is . . . ?

A. My husband. Abel Grimshaw. You know him, I'm sure you do.

Q. Your Honor?

The Court: Just carry on, Mr. Fibbs.

Q. What time did you see James Fulsome leave?

A. You're going to have to ask the policeman, sir.

Q. Excuse me?

A. The policeman told me what time the car left. I didn't see it. I already explained that.

Q. That's not what's in your statement, ma'am. But let's move on, shall we? Did you hear gunshots that afternoon?

A. I did. I did. I heard them. So close together. Like one loud bang in my ears.

Q. After the gunshots, did you see Dr. Norton arrive?

A. Oh, I know who he is. Visited me once when I had a flu. Didn't take so much as my temperature before he opened that bag of his. Offered me pills. Abel showed him the door. Knew a scoundrel when he saw one.

Q. I'll ask my question again, ma'am. Did you see Dr. Norton arrive?

A. I went for my walk and then I went home. A thousand cars could have come and gone. How would I know? I didn't see a single one.

Q. When you went for your walk, did you happen near the Henneberry property?

A. I—

Q. Where did you go that afternoon, ma'am?

A. I don't want to talk about it. I don't.

Q. Mrs. Grimshaw, you've sworn an oath to tell the truth. Please tell us where you went.

A. I was in the woods.

Q. Did you see anyone in the woods?

A. The birds. All those little houses didn't help.

Q. Ma'am? In your statement, you said you saw Thomas Ware prior to the shootings.

A. Thomas? A lovely name, isn't it?

Q. Do you see Thomas Ware in the courtroom today?

A. That's him right there. He's so well mannered. I don't know why he'd be staying with the Gladstones.

Q. The Henneberrys, Mrs. Grimshaw. He was residing with the Henneberrys for the summer. When you saw Thomas Ware in the woods, how would you describe his demeanor?

A. I don't want to talk about the woods. Why aren't you listening to me?

Q. We're trying to establish—

A. Bad things.

Q. Was he doing bad things? Did you witness something, ma'am?

Defense Counsel: Objection, Your Honor. Clearly the prosecution hasn't learned to ask one question at a time.

The Court: Can you try again, Mr. Fibbs?

Q. Sorry, Your Honor. Mrs. Grimshaw, did you see Thomas Ware acting unusually in the woods?

A. No, no. No. No. I couldn't see at all. I fell and hurt my hip.

Q. You never mentioned a fall to the officers. When they stopped by, you told them you weren't injured.

A. I wasn't anymore. I couldn't find Abel, so I'd taken
    care of myself.

Q. Your Honor, I think we need to disregard the
    witness's testimony. Her memory isn't— She's
    deviating significantly from the account she gave
    police. We may have overestimated her lucidity.

*The Court: I tend to be in agreement, Mr. Fibbs.
    Mrs. Grimshaw, we are grateful for your time this
    morning, ma'am. You may return home now.*

Defense Counsel: But Your Honor, we haven't had—

The Court: Can someone help her on the steps?

CHAPTER TWENTY-TWO

"Mrs. Grimshaw thinks the birds are biting her."

"Oh," I whispered. "That must hurt."

I was sitting in the passenger seat of Mr. Vardy's truck and he was backing into Mrs. Grimshaw's drive. "Not near as much as your noggin, I doubt."

He meant the egg on my forehead and my shiner and my fat lip. Mr. Vardy told me he'd tied a cord between his bumper and Mrs. Henneberry's car and pulled it up out of the ditch. Besides some scratches to the hood, there wasn't much damage.

"It's no big deal," I told him.

Mr. Vardy parked near the trees, and when we got out, he opened the back gate. I shoved my new magnifying lens into the back pocket of my shorts.

"Of course, the birds aren't *actually* biting her, Thomas. Probably just flitting about making her nervous." I knew they did more than flit about. "But if she believes it, why not try and help her?"

I nodded. "Yes, sir."

Mrs. Henneberry didn't know Mr. Vardy did occasional chores for Mrs. Grimshaw. Mrs. Gladstone and

Mrs. Grimshaw were like water and oil, he'd said. There'd been a rift for years, well before he started working there, but he'd never gotten involved in it.

He tapped my arm. "Did you hear me? No need to advertise we're here."

"I won't," I said.

Together we took everything out of his truck. Mr. Vardy laid out some newsprint on a patch of grass beside the house. The miniature houses were already hammered together, and he spaced them out on the pages. Then four tiny tins of paint. Red, yellow, blue, and white. He gave me a bucket, and at the hose, I filled it with clean water.

"Your mother tells me you're something of an artist," Mr. Vardy said.

"She said that?"

"Sure did."

"How would she even know?" It came out like an insult, though I hadn't meant it to.

Mr. Vardy scuffed up some gravel with his work boot. "You got good reason to be angry, Thomas. And confused.'"

"I'm—" I started, but he put up his hand.

"I shouldn't, but I'm going to say this anyhow. That place, that house, and everyone in it? For as long as your mother can remember, it has surrounded her. And while I won't say the reasons she gave you to her sister, I can tell you this. She certainly didn't do it for herself."

I stared at the wooden houses on the newspaper. I remembered what Dr. Henneberry had said to my mother. About some sort of *arrangement*. "You know why?"

"Like I said, it's not my place. She'll explain when she's ready." For a second, Mr. Vardy put his hand on my shoulder. A heavy hand. Then he passed me two paint-brushes. "This should keep your mind busy for a while. Even though they're going up in the trees, I know you'll take pride in your work. Don't rush it."

"I won't," I said. While Mrs. Pinsent said I was the best in art, I was also the slowest. I never rushed it. "How should they look?"

"Completely up to you." Mr. Vardy smiled. "They're just birdhouses, Thomas. You can't make a mistake."

I crouched in the sunlight and dipped one brush into the red. I made a thick coat over the roof and rinsed the hairs. Yellow and blue stripes for the panels. I painted around the circular hole where the bird would stick its head for seeds. Then I painted the wooden perch where the bird would sit. Finally, I mixed yellow and blue and painted tiny flicks of green around the base, so the house appeared to be sitting in grass. I rinsed my brush again.

Many evenings, when my aunt was gone to work, I'd sit at Mrs. King's kitchen table and paint with water-colors and thick paper. Mrs. King always put a warm cookie on a plate and a tall glass of milk. I'd paint forests and sunsets and funny faces and dancing bears. Mrs. King taped every picture I made, whether it was good or not, to the wall across from Mr. King's bed. "Something to distract him from his cough," she said. The paintings went from floor to ceiling and they would lift and shud-der with the breeze from the fan.

When I shifted over to the next birdhouse, I had an uneasy feeling, as though someone was watching me. Martin was likely sneaking up behind me, would grab me any second. I peered over my shoulder, but no one was there. Mr. Vardy had already left, and the driveway was empty. Then I noticed that dark, dusty car turning around out in the road. I hadn't seen it in a while, but it was definitely the same one. The front light on the right side smashed in. It crept past the Henneberrys' and it kept creeping along past Mrs. Grimshaw's. The man driving stretched out his neck like he was curious what I was doing, and then he tipped his hat and waved. Without thinking, I lifted my brush to wave back.

"You'll be wanting some apple juice."

I jumped. A gob of white paint landed on my bent knee. Mrs. Grimshaw was right beside me, wearing a dress with yellow flowers. I couldn't see any parts I shouldn't.

"Here," she said. She handed me a warm glass and I gulped it down.

"I guess I was thirsty," I said as I gave her back the glass. When I checked the road again, the car was gone.

"You're that nice boy from next door, right?"

"Yes. Thomas." I adjusted my hair, hiding the lump on my forehead.

"Now I remember." She put her hand up to block the sunlight from her eyes. "You're staying with the Gladstones."

"Sure. Yeah. I guess so."

"Not for long, I hope."

"Until the end of August. Then me and my mother are getting a place. And my goldfish, George. He's coming too."

"That's better news. They're rotten people, especially Ruth. She's getting worse if what I hear is true."

"What did you hear?"

She lowered her voice. "Oh, you wouldn't understand, dear. Esther's in a sticky situation, and Ruth's already scheming, of course. I've seen that horrid Dr. Norton visiting. I do hope nothing's done to her. I do hope."

Mrs. Grimshaw was right. I didn't understand. What sort of "sticky situation"?

"She's trying to get rid of me, too." Mrs. Grimshaw's words were like a croak.

"Who is?" I asked, even though I knew.

"I shouldn't have to leave when I'm waiting for Abel."

"No," I said. My paintbrush was getting dry so I dipped it in the water bucket. "No, you shouldn't. You're not doing anything wrong."

"You're a sweet boy," she said, and she smiled at me. Her eyes were round and brown with white eyelashes, like an old doe's. "Do you think those will help with the birds?"

"I hope so."

As she went back into her house, I took a big breath and squeezed the water out of the paintbrush. Only one bird was causing problems. I had to find a way to stop him, but I couldn't think how. I used to just bolt forward, fists up, and do what needed to be done. But over the past couple of months, I'd changed into a different person. As though all the braveness had seeped out of me. I kept trying to catch it, but it kept slipping through my fingers. Like dry sand.

Once my mother and I found a place, things would get better. I'd go back to being me again and I'd figure everything out. What to do about Martin and Dr. Henneberry. How to help my mother find a new job.

I stuck the paintbrush in the white and dropped some on the newsprint. Then I took some blue and swirled it through to make it lighter. I scooped the paint off the newsprint and started on another roof.

Another scoop of paint, and as I leaned closer, I saw a news article mostly hidden behind the birdhouse. I dropped the brush, shoved the house to the side. There was a row of black-and-white photographs. Four women. Three strangers, and then my aunt in her nurse's uniform. She was beaming, a white cap balanced on her head. In the bend of her arms, she was holding a bunch of gray roses. The headline read "Predator Stalking Streets of Greenlake." My eyes skimmed over the article. All young, unmarried females. Murdered in identical ways. Tossed away like trash near footpaths in the woods. Police had no leads. Not a single one.

I tugged my new magnifying glass out of my back pocket. I angled it until I found the exact spot to capture the sun. The point of light struck the word "Predator." Smoke began to rise up. The light ate a hole through the paper, and brown edges began to curl backward. The entire headline was eaten away next, and then the light chewed through the graduation photo of my aunt. A small yellow flame crept across the faces of the other women, and it moved out and out until the news article was completely gone. I stood up. Lifted my foot and stomped on it. Ashes fluttered up, landed on my shoe. On Martin's shoe.

CHAPTER TWENTY-THREE

The next day, I was at the kitchen counter when Mrs. Henneberry called out to me from down the hallway. She was waiting by the front door.

"Perfect," she said. "You're all ready." She had on a long pink summer coat. Her hair was different, all clipped to the side and curled under in a blond roll. "We have business, Tom," she said in an almost chirp. "Extremely important matters to attend to." She tapped her watch. "And time's a-wasting. We should get going."

"I need to tell my mother first."

She clutched my arm and I yanked it back. Then she giggled. "You're quite peppery today. What if I told you we're picking out a surprise for Esther?"

"Really?"

"Yes, of course. Totally top secret."

Mrs. Henneberry led me out the front door and I climbed into her car. Her father's old beater. It had been washed and waxed, and I couldn't see the damage. Most of the swelling in my face was gone, too. Mrs. Henneberry hadn't even noticed it.

"And so you're aware, I'm feeling very clear-headed, Tom," she said as she slid in the driver's side. "Clear on all fronts." She dropped a piece of paper, covered with numbers and bad handwriting, onto my lap. Mrs. Pinsent would've called it chicken scratch.

As we looped around in the driveway, I saw my mother at the side of the house. She was waving both arms.

"Oh no," I said. "She's caught us. It'll ruin the sur—"

"Now, now. That was just a little fib." Mrs. Henneberry patted my knee. "What we're actually doing is changing lives, today. So much more vital than a silly surprise, don't you think?"

I twisted around. My mother was framed inside the back window of the car. Her hand was on her head, like the sun was burning her. I made a thumbs-up, so she wouldn't worry, but I couldn't tell if she saw me or not. I slumped down in my seat and picked at a loose thread on my shorts.

"Don't brood, darling," Mrs. Henneberry said. "We'll find no roosters on the road today!"

We passed through the wide streets of Upper Washbourne until she stopped in front of a brown brick building. I went inside with her. At the tall wooden counter, a man with a skinny mustache made us go talk to a different man, whose stomach was so round it touched the desk. Mrs. Henneberry said, "Yes, I'm certain. Absolutely certain, in fact," a whole bunch of times. She had to sign about a dozen papers and then the man disappeared and came back with a large stack of bills. Mrs. Henneberry was smiling and nodding so I knew it wasn't Monopoly money. The man counted it out and pushed it inside a brown envelope. He folded the flap over, and when he stuck his tongue out, Mrs. Henneberry's hand leapt up. "No, thank you, Mr. Simms. I don't need it sealed." She dropped the envelope into her purse.

"Step one!" she said when we were outside. "Isn't this exhilarating?" Huge sunglasses covered half of her face and her eyes were hidden. I knew the lids were beginning to droop, though. I could tell by the way she spoke.

We were almost back to the car when a lady called out, "Muriel? Muriel, is that you?" The lady's heels clicked on the pavement.

"Of course it's me, Joan," Mrs. Henneberry said when the woman reached us. "Tom, you remember Mrs. Bishop? Genie's mother?"

"Hello, Mrs. Bishop," I said.

"Were you banking, Muriel?" Then Mrs. Bishop shook her head. "My Bill does our banking. I just haven't got the head for numbers and such."

"I was hardly banking. We have someone for that." She glanced at me. "You seem awfully flustered, Joan."

"Oh, I'm just winded after my mad dash." She bent at the waist and laughed. "And—and I wanted to let you know, we got the invite. Received the invitation, I mean, and it's an absolute yes from the three of us. Genie can barely contain her excitement. To be at Martin's side on his special day. Could we have planned it any better?"

"Planned it?" Mrs. Henneberry put her hand on her throat. "What plan do you mean?"

"No, no. I just meant . . ." She straightened up and smiled. "You and me being like sisters, and now our youngsters. What a thrill it is seeing this bond growing between them. Should I stop by later?"

"I would love that, Joan, I really would, but these days are so cramped. Isn't that right, Tom?"

I nodded because I knew that was what I was supposed to do.

"Not to worry. I understand cramps!" Mrs. Bishop hooked her thumb inside the belt around her dress.

Once she'd gone, Mrs. Henneberry said, "Of all the things I needed to witness today, Tom, Joan Bishop's doughy face was the very last." Then we got back in the car and drove away. We went along the outside of Lower Washbourne, but we didn't go down Gerald Street this time. Instead we stayed closer to the trees. Sometimes I could spy patches of lake water where the leaves weren't as thick. Finally we turned onto a dirt road with forest on either side. A green sign, nailed onto a wooden post, had painted white letters: "Lark's Lane." At the very end, we came to a spot where the trees opened up. Mrs. Henneberry drove her car down a gravel bank and onto a narrower path leading straight into the woods. "Does this seem normal, Tom?"

No. This does not seem normal.

"Can you read that note, dear?"

I picked the piece of paper off the seat. "It says Lark's Lane, Mrs. Henneberry. I think."

"You think? Well, you're going to have to do better than think, young man. We're not scooting to the general store for nails."

"It's messy. But I think— It says keep going."

"Then that's what we'll do." In a snap, she was relaxed again. "Not so difficult to follow a few instructions, is it?" Her chin was over top of the steering wheel, her fists almost touching her chest. Branches scraped hard against the car as she kept tapping the gas, and the car kept wedging through the woods.

As we drove further in, the path got thinner and thinner. The trees were closer together. No sunlight. I couldn't see them, but up above birds were crying.

"Could he have, Tom? Could Mr. Fulsome have made a mistake? Maybe I'm going the wrong way. What if I get stuck? You're a terrible copilot, Tom. Simply the worst." She stopped the car, the engine still chugging. Then she sat back. Her hands slapped the steering wheel and she yelled out, "I can't lose confidence. I won't lose confidence! Dear James would not lead me astray." She pressed down hard on the gas. I grabbed the sides of the seat. A branch bent backward on the windshield, whipped through my open window, and swatted me. I yelped. Ripped leaves tumbled onto my lap.

We tore through the woods, and then the car shot up over a small hill. We flew out of the blanket of trees,

landing with a jolt on some gravel. I let out my breath
and looked around. Ahead of us was a yellow sand
beach and all that clean, blue water. We'd reached the
southernmost part of the lake. Nothing was there except
a camper. And a car half-hidden by the growth of flow-
ering shrub. As we drove a few feet closer, a dog, with its
lips snarled, yanked against a chain.

Mrs. Henneberry squealed. "We're here! We did it,
Tom. Step two success!" She cranked back the key in
the ignition. The engine sputtered and went quiet. She
peered out. "Can a person actually reside in such a
contraption?"

"I don't see why not," I said. "It's like a cozy apartment."

She took Dr. Norton's bottle from her purse and nibbled a pill. "Well I, for one, will never understand the
appeal. Trapped inside a tiny tuna can? Surely it would
make you unstable. Don't you think, Tom?"

"I don't know." My aunt and I had lived in a small
place. So did Mrs. King and Wally and Wally's family.
Probably Mrs. Pinsent, too, though I never knew exactly
where she went after school. Were we unstable? Mr.
Pober was, though. But Aunt Celia said that was from
the war, not the size of his living room.

With her fingernail, she picked white dust from her
bottom lip. "Come along, then. You shouldn't dilly-dally,
Tom. We'll lean on each other, won't we?"

As we got out of the car, a lady in a red-and-white
polka-dotted bikini came around the side of the camper.
She stood there with her hands on her hips.

"Well, hello there," Mrs. Henneberry said, but it was hard to hear her over the barking dog. "We're so sorry to intrude without making a proper appointment."

The woman kept gaping at us.

"Is now a good time?" The handles of Mrs. Henneberry's purse were balanced on her left forearm. "I'm looking for your— I'm a friend of James Fulsome?"

The lady slammed the side of the trailer with her palm, then lifted the end of the dog's chain. The dog lunged but couldn't reach us, and the pair of them jogged down the beach.

The metal door swung open. A heavy man with shiny black hair was standing there. His shirt was unbuttoned, and more black hair covered his chest. Thick like an animal's pelt. He looked almost familiar to me. Like I'd stood behind him at the grocery store, or watched him deliver the milk. When he stepped onto the piece of cement that was his front porch, I could smell coconut. Or perhaps it was pineapple. Like Aunt Celia's upside-down cake.

Mrs. Henneberry pinched my wrist as we walked closer. The heels of her shoes sunk into the sand. My sneakers did, too. When we reached the low fence that went all around the camper, she let me go and pushed at the gate, but it didn't open. She pushed again. "Can you see to that, Tom?" she whispered. I pulled up a metal wire, and we went inside the yard.

"High security round here, huh?" the man said.

"Is it? Oh, dear. We've shown up unannounced. But we were assured it was fine."

"And who did all this assuring?"

"Your friend James? Mr. Fulsome?"

The man moved his fingers through his chest fur and laughed. "Jimmy Fulsome. That good-for-nothing? Calling me a friend now, is he?"

"An acquaintance, perhaps? Yes, that might be more apt." She pushed her sunglasses further up on her nose. "He said you'd be expecting me."

"You?"

"Yes." She unclasped her purse and withdrew the brown envelope. "This is what's required, I believe, for— To fix the problem?" She shoved it at him.

When he took it, he licked his lips and lifted the paper flap. He scraped his thumbnail over the bills, and then laughed again. It seemed like he was in a good mood.

"Don't worry. It's all there. Right down to the dollar."

The man closed the flap. Used the corner of the envelope to itch his bellybutton. "Oh, I never worry. Makes you age, don't you think?"

"I never considered that." Mrs. Henneberry coughed. "I expect those funds will help you with some repairs. Get your car running again."

I hadn't paid attention to the man's car. It was dusty and partly covered by a bush. Now I took a closer look. The front right light was smashed out.

I understood then why that man seemed familiar. He was the one who kept driving around Roundwater Heights. Slowing to a crawl when he passed the Henneberrys' house. I stared at him. The straps of his sandals were hanging open and he had streaks of what might be ketchup on his beige shorts. No way was he Aunt Celia's sweetheart. She'd never have tolerated someone so grimy. And nobody would ever mistake him for a proper gentleman, or a *snooty rich guy*, for that matter.

"Oh, it runs just fine," the man said. He caught my eye and winked.

"Mr. Fulsome's been in touch?"

"Oh yup. He sure has."

"Explained everything precisely?"

"That's all he's been doing, trying to explain. Full of wacky ideas. That one's dumber than a bag of hammers. I can't get him to shut his trap."

Mrs. Henneberry took my wrist again. Her finger-nails dug into my skin. "That's exactly James. Doesn't like to bother. He just wants everything settled. Everyone happy."

"Well," the man said, waving the envelope, "this should settle things up proper."

"Yes," she said. "I do hope so. And—and, I should say, I don't need any details about your plans. What you're going to do."

"I don't see what it is to you. At this point."

She teetered on the sand. "Might I add something about timing, sir?"

He looked her up and down. Like Mr. Pober had looked my aunt up and down. As though he were hungry for a fried fish supper. "Honey, you can add whatever you want. Wherever you want."

"It needs to happen on August eighteenth. It has to be that date. I'm adamant about it."

"You want a date, lady?"

"I mean, I'd prefer. My son, Martin, you see. He's having a birthday on the sixteenth. And he's actually turning sixteen, too. It's kind of a big deal. Invitations have already gone out." She was talking quickly. "I mean, surely you can appreciate what it's like planning a party for a teenager these days. It's no small feat, believe you me. And then of course, my family and I will take the Sunday to recuperate. Do you understand?"

"A party, hey?"

"I wouldn't want to spoil it with any nastiness. Not with so many friends coming for a swim. We actually had the pool installed closer to the front of our grounds. Off to the side, of course, as the backyard is so dreary. Doesn't see a moment of sunshine." She glanced up at the sky. "Oh, I don't know why I'm chattering on. Surely you're not interested in our landscaping."

As he dragged the side of the envelope over the hair on his stomach, it made a crackling noise. "And I'm not invited to your shindig?" He grinned at me.

"Heavens, no." She giggled. "Positively not." When his grin faded, she cleared her throat. "Not to offend you, sir. It's—well, it's just our close-knit circle, really. Just a little cookout. And a quick splash. Besides, I wouldn't have a clue how to introduce you."

He shook the envelope again. "I was only pulling your leg, lady."

"Oh." She breathed out hard. "You've got a sense of humor, Mr.—" But he didn't offer his name. She let go of my hand and clutched me around the shoulder. Then she cleared her throat, said, "So that date's set, then?"

"Whatever you want, doll."

"The address is in that envelope. Tucked in front. Roundwater Heights in Upper Washbourne. You may have heard of it?"

"Oh yeah. I've passed by there a time or two."

"We do get lollygaggers." She scratched her neck. "Not to say you're one of those sorts, sir. Not at all. It's just they're a bother. I don't know why I even mentioned it. I mean, you'd feel the same way if dozens of sightseers just happened to show up here, wouldn't you? Thankfully that's unlikely, given the trouble we had finding your residence. Tom was an expert navigator, though."

"Was he, now?" The man opened the envelope and withdrew a single crisp dollar bill. "There you go, kid."

He reached out, and my hand reached forward. Then I had an entire dollar bill locked in my fist.

"Oh, that's very generous of you," Mrs. Henneberry twittered. "Tom? What have I taught you to say?"

"Thanks, sir. Thanks a lot."

"You bet, kid. Anytime."

Mrs. Henneberry had long pink marks from her ear to her collarbone. "We'll be heading along now. We wouldn't want to take another second of your precious time."

The man laughed. "You got yourself a sense of humor too, huh?"

We got back into the car, and she reversed, went forward, reversed, went forward, until the car was turned around. Then she pushed the shiny nose through the bushes again. When we reached the gravel bank on the other side of the woods, she pressed hard on the gas, and rocks popped out from the spinning back tires as we climbed onto Lark's Lane.

"And that, my darling Tom," she said when we were passing a field with two spotted cows, "is how a job is done. Figuring out the best approach. Finding the correct people. I can't believe how easy it all was." She took her hand off the wheel and tapped my kneecap with a cold fingertip. Her smile was huge. "We'll pull in for a strawberry cone along the way. A treat for you."

EXCERPT

Testimony of Dr. Jermone Neville, Neuropsychologist
Direct Examination by Prosecutor Clay Fibbs

Q. Dr. Neville, have you had a chance to review the
    police files on Thomas Ware?

A. Yes, sir. I did.

Q. Can you summarize his statement detailing his
    version of events?

A. It was simple. A man drove onto the Henneberry
    property, exited his automobile, retrieved the gun,
    shot the family, and then departed.

Q. Did you give it any credibility?

A. Not an ounce.

Q. Can you explain for the court why you formed that
    opinion?

A. For the past seventeen years, I've been studying the
    shift in family structures across our country. It's had
    a devastating effect on the population, and what I
    can tell you is the inner workings of these children is
    different than those youngsters brought up in a nuclear
    family. Mom, dad, and tot.

Q. What sort of differences?

A. An internal disruption, I like to call it. Imagine a child
    is like a bottle of water and sand. It gets shaken up at
    times, of course, but Mother and Father are able to
    soothe it, to help that sand settle so the water is clear.
    In those children without a true family unit in place,

the sand never settles. Their worldview remains muddied, confusing. They become prone to acting out, defiance, lying, stealing. Of course, this escalates as the child develops.

Q. **Sounds serious.**

A. It sure is. Thomas Ware is being raised without the input of a father figure. Without a male moral backbone. The behavior patterns are the same, sir. Deviance and deceit.

Q. **Above and beyond Ware's family history, was there anything specific about his statement that caused you to dismiss it?**

A. For starters, his account lacked any specific details. Given the impactful nature of the incidents—

Q. **What do you mean by impactful, Dr. Neville?**

A. A bicycle accident, for example. That instant your dog was struck by a car. Your first kiss. A circus with a fire-blower. It really depends on age and life experience. Studies have shown that we all have an aptitude for negative memories. We might not remember what flavor the batter was, but we sure recall the paddling after we stuck our fingers in the bowl.

Q. **I can believe it.**

A. Witnessing a shooting would obviously be a negative occurrence. I would have expected his memories to be very focused, very detailed. Not simply a tall man in a long coat and a hat tilted over his face. I suspect it was an image he saw in a comic book.

Q. Officers did find plenty of those in his possession. Did you examine them?

A. I did. Many pages were damaged. Faces had been scratched out. Predominantly those belonging to women.

Q. So an issue with the ladies, perhaps?

A. Yes, sir. And some inappropriate doodles, we'll call it. Likely due to a weakened maternal bond. Issues with the female form. He doesn't want a woman to actually see him. To see his true self.

Q. So your opinion on the accused, Thomas Ware?

A. Given everything I've read and seen, Mr. Fibbs, I'd say he's a boy who's not only a liar but one with a troubled conscience. Deeply troubled, sir.

CHAPTER TWENTY-FOUR

The next morning, my mother was humming in the kitchen. "I've got two pieces of good news, Thomas. I don't want to say too much, in case something happens, but Mr. Vardy has found a place he thinks will make you very happy."

"Really?" I climbed onto my stool and picked up the spoon next to a bowl of cereal. I used to notice how heavy it was, but I didn't anymore.

"End of August, like I told you. It won't be ready until then." She smiled at me and wiped away the milk I'd spilled.

My heart did a flip-flop. Everything was going to work out. I could tell. I counted the links on my paper chain and the end of August was only eighteen days away.

"And my second bit of good news."

I held my breath. I was ready.

"I've spoken to Dr. Henneberry."

Hearing Dr. Henneberry's name, my head suddenly felt light on my shoulders. "You did?"

"Yes. About the accident. How you hit your mouth. Your teeth."

"They just clanked together," I said. "Not even a chip."

"Well, just to be sure. He's agreed to take you to his clinic and give you a checkup."

"But I don't want to go to his clinic. I don't need a checkup."

"It's a huge favor to me, Thomas. I had to go to him and ask him." Her voice changed. "I had to ask."

"But I saw the school dentist in April. Or May, maybe."

"Yes, and I doubt he did much. Dr. Henneberry is the best in Greenlake, they say. Difficult to even get an appointment."

"No, it's not! He goes out. He goes out and—"

"Thomas! Why are you being so obstinate?"

"I don't want to go."

"I'm sorry, but you're going. He'll make sure you don't have injuries. Most of those teeth need to last you a lifetime."

I kicked the panel beneath the counter. "Well, *she* never bugged me about my teeth. The school check was good enough for *her*."

For several seconds, my mother stared at me like I'd stomped on her foot. Then she said in a soft voice, "It doesn't matter what Celia did or didn't bug you about. I'm responsible for you now, Thomas. These are my decisions to make."

I dropped my spoon and it clattered in my bowl.

"You're upset," she said, wiping up milk for the second time.

"No, I'm not," I lied. "I just don't want you going near him. I don't like him. I don't— He's got guns here. In the house."

"So do a lot of men, I assume."

"And—" But I couldn't say the rest. Why would she even believe me when I barely believed myself?

My mother picked up my bowl. "Hurry and brush before he leaves. He's taking you with him."

I got off my stool.

"Try to be grateful, Thomas. I know going to the dentist is not enjoyable, but how bad can it be?"

When I came around the side of the house, Dr. Henne-berry was already in his mint-green convertible. I hurried over to the passenger side and climbed in. The windshield had been replaced, but a tiny piece of broken glass was still on the floor mat. I put my shoe over it and didn't budge the entire drive to Greenlake.

We parked in front of the red brick building with the hanging tooth. Without a word to me, Dr. Henneberry slammed his car door and went inside. When I got out, I stood directly beneath that tooth. The molar Mrs. Henneberry had chosen. Four sharp roots pointing down. Then I forced myself to go inside.

The walls of his clinic were light green and the air was heavy with the scent of cleaners and metal. I stood behind Dr. Henneberry. He was getting mail from a lady's desk near the front door. A nameplate said "Mrs. Audrey Mapps."

"Isn't it such a beautiful day today, Doctor?"

"It is, Mrs. Mapps. Other than the storm last week, we've barely had a cloud all summer."

"Got everything watered in one fell swoop." Her laughter was like tinfoil crunching. "Would you like a coffee?"

"I'm fine, Mrs. Mapps. Just had one at home."

"Okey-dokey." She straightened some papers. "Oh, and I nearly forgot. Where is my mind? You've got a visitor."

Dr. Henneberry's shoulders lifted. "Visitor? Now who might that be, Mrs. Mapps?"

"Just Mr. Fulsome. A cordial pop-by, I'm sure. He's been waiting for roundabout ten minutes in your office."

Dr. Henneberry blew out a loud gust of air, then went around a corner and I couldn't see him anymore. I waited beside Mrs. Mapps's desk.

"You're lucky he could squeeze you in, love," she said. "Just follow on through, and you'll find a seat in the hallway."

I didn't move.

"I've got a booklet of word searches. Would you like to try one?"

"No, ma'am."

"Okey-dokey. Well, go on, then. Be brave. We aren't called 'Painless Dentistry' for nothing."

I did as Mrs. Mapps instructed and found the chair. The hallway floor was made of black and white squares. On the wall was a framed picture of two dogs, both on their hind legs. One was wearing a beige coat and the other was wearing a checkered golf shirt. The top half of the office door was made of milky glass, but I could still see the shapes of Dr. Henneberry and Mr. Fulsome shuffling around. I could hear them talking.

"No more pressure, Jim. I told you. I need time, goddammit. To straighten things out."

"Ray, stop. Just listen to me."

"What do you want me to say? It was an asinine thing to do. I went all in for the both of us, and now we're sunk."

"Ray?"

"I'm sorry I ever got you involved. Putting our necks on the line. I am sorry as can be."

"All this fuss is turning you into an old man, Ray."

"You better believe it."

"Really got you edgy, hey?"

"That's an understatement."

"Makes you want to tear out all those gray hairs you've been sprouting."

"I thought you were him, Jimmy. So many times he's been up to the house. Driving past, watching us. It's a threat, really, isn't it? A goddamned threat." He was quiet for a few seconds. "Why are you grinning? For god's sakes, why are you grinning like some wild fox?"

Mr. Fulsome was laughing then. "Come over here. Let me rub your shoulders."

"I don't need my shoulders rubbed."

"Fine, then. I'll give you the news."

"What news?"

"Not just news. Spectacular news. Everything's smooth now. You don't have to give him another thought."

"What are you talking about?"

"It's all squared up. Our debt. Taken care of."

"How?"

"Now, I can't get into particulars, Ray, so don't press me on it, but I had a stroke of good fortune."

"You got the money?"

"That I did. Right down to the last copper. Delivered straight to his one-room accommodations out on the beach. It was all rather unexpected, trust me, but there you go. Sometimes an opportunity presents itself. And you're partly to thank, you philandering piece of trash."

"I don't understand."

"You don't need to. But we have to agree. No more of those places, alright, Ray? Not another bet as long as we live. I like my knees attached to my legs, thank you very much."

They were both laughing then. Through the cloudy door, it looked like they were hugging. Clapping each other on the back. Then Dr. Henneberry said, "Oh, come on. Get out of here, Jimmy."

I swung my feet back and forth under the chair. When the door opened and Mr. Fulsome came into the hallway, he gave me a mean look. "Well, you just keep showing up everywhere, don't you? Worse than crabgrass."

"Lunch later, Jim?" Dr. Henneberry called out.

"You betcha," Mr. Fulsome called back. "Best part of my day, Ray. Best part of my day." I heard Mrs. Mapps say goodbye and then the bell jingled as the front door opened and shut.

"Hurry up, then," Dr. Henneberry growled as he brushed past me. "In here." I followed him into an examining room. He slammed the door behind us. Mrs. Mapps seemed very, very far away.

The room had a chair that reclined and a tall metal tube with a tiny white sink attached to its side. There were pumps and pedals and shiny silver trays. I caught the faint smell of vomit. I tried to stay calm, but my guts knotted. *A place he thinks will make you very happy.* My mother had said that. I tried to focus on what sort of place it might be, but it was hard to hold good things in my head.

Dr. Henneberry pulled on a stiff white coat and did up a row of buttons on the left side, all the way up to his neck. Then he picked up a wide wooden block that was lying against the wall. Tossed it onto the seat.

"Get in," he said.

"In?"

"On the damn chair, kid."

I crawled up onto the block and lay my head back. Dr. Henneberry pulled open a drawer and took out what looked like two leather belts. He placed my right arm up on the armrest and tugged a belt over my wrist. He yanked it tight and buckled it. Then he did the same with the other arm. I lifted my head to look down. My hands were tingling.

"What are those?" I said.

"Safety precautions. For special cases."

"What?" I cleared my throat. "I mean, pardon me?" I wanted to tell him I wasn't a special case. I'd already seen the school dentist three times, and when I'd opened my mouth, he'd just clanged a tooth or two with a metal stick and said, "Beautiful smile." Last year, he even gave me a lemon lollipop after I was done.

"I don't want you flinging your hands up and hurting yourself. Or getting in my way."

He rolled a chair close to me and reached up to flick a switch. Three bright lightbulbs shone straight into my eyes. Dr. Henneberry's breath was hot, and it smelled like coffee and cigarettes. I tried not to breathe. As he grabbed my cheeks, my mouth opened by itself. He pushed in a piece of metal, then I heard a hard click and I could not close. I felt his fingers poking around my gums. I tasted soap. My throat swallowed and swallowed all by itself.

While he was examining my mouth, he spoke right into my ear. "Your mother told me about her sister," he said, as though he were reciting a boring headline. "Single girl. Living on her own. Never a good situation."

"Unurh uhn o," I said. Drool spilled down my chin. *She wasn't on her own.*

"What a story that was." A sharp instrument was in his hand. "Out like that by herself at such an hour."

"Uh-urrrh." *A nurse.* "Ur-ing." *Working.* Coming and going late at night was part of her job.

He started scraping and scraping. Hard bits of I don't know what pecked the roof of my mouth. My arms and legs burst out in gooseflesh.

"First time I met her, I could tell." *At the hospital? Did he meet her at work?* "Within minutes—no, seconds—I knew exactly what she was like." He dropped that instrument and picked up a different one. "That pert little smile. The way she lowered her eyelashes after catching my eye. Any man could tell what she wanted."

Angry tears trickled out of my eyes. Dribbled down into my ears.

"Sometimes girls invite tragedy, you know. By the way they act. Dress. That sort of thing. Some girls ask for it. And they get what they want."

I gagged, choked, tried to wriggle my arms free. He did not slow down. His words were a tornado inside my skull. And then, when his hands were stretching the corners of my mouth, I knew for certain. I'd tried to convince myself otherwise, but now I had no doubt Dr. Henneberry was the man who'd hurt my aunt. He'd picked her up from the bus that night in Mrs. Henneberry's old beater. He'd dragged her into the woods and done whatever he wanted. He told himself she'd asked for it. She'd invited the tragedy. Then he left her naked and cold and never coming home.

Dr. Henneberry was the proper gentleman. He was that *snooty rich guy.*

That was the truth. It was fixed in my mind.

"Ah ai!" I cried. *Stop it.*

I hated him. I hated his face and his shoulders and his sharp, sprucy aftershave. But most of all, I hated his hands. His thick hands that had no trace of hair. If I rolled my eyes down, I could see them. White and clean and pudgy. Those hands killed my aunt.

Then he was drilling. Grinding into my teeth. Electricity zapped in my jaw. My skull. My ears. My eyeballs. My wet back came up off the chair. His knee pumped and pumped, working a pedal. And that noise. A worn-down knife scraping against stone.

I struggled, pulled, twisted, cried, and eventually I went away. I floated up to the ceiling and hovered there, gazing down at myself. My head was pushed back onto the headrest. The leather bands sliced into my wrists. My fingers curled, and the corners of my mouth appeared red and hot like they were going to split in two. His hands moved the drill in and out of the new holes in my teeth. From down below, he said, "You got a poor mouth. You got a poor mouth, boy."

But I didn't feel it anymore. With my spine against the ceiling, I closed my eyes. I could leave if I wanted. My whole body could drift away. With my fingernails, I dragged myself forward. Inch by inch. I went past Mrs. Mapps and out the main entrance, but the bell forgot to jingle. I eased down the street. I passed Belbin's Toys where I got my magnifying glass and I found the diner where Mrs. Henneberry and I had our cheeseburgers. I coasted over, and next thing I knew, my mother and I were at a table. She was holding her purse with two hands and had a blue hat pinned to her head. Mr. Vardy roller-skated past and gave me a foaming root beer float. *He's found it*, my mother said. *A perfect place for us.* I nodded and took a sip. It tasted so much better this time. *We'll go fishing, hey?* Mr. Vardy said. *Get you a pair of waders. Take your best friend, Wally, along.* I smiled and nodded, then I took a long gulp, and a wave of icy pain punched me right in the jaw. Then another stab. And another. I shook my head. *I want to leave now*, I said. Soda and melted ice cream poured from the sides of my mouth.

Customers around me were whispering.

"Filthy," one said.

"Never seen more rot."

"You'd never find that level of decay outside Lower Washbourne."

The dripping glass in my hand vanished, and when I opened my eyes, Dr. Henneberry was straightening the tools on his silver tray. He undid the belts around my wrists.

"Get up," he said. "Go see Mrs. Mapps."

When I stood, the room went sideways. Black splotches roiled around me.

"Don't you dare throw up in here."

I held the side of the chair.

It was over.

It was over.

It was all over.

Mrs. Mapps drove me back in Dr. Henneberry's convertible. "Now that wasn't so rough, was it?" she said. "Youngsters get all in a tizzy, but that man has the lightest touch." When we got there, I opened the car door, tripped out into the driveway. My cheeks were full of slimy bloody tissue. "Remember, love," she called. "Tell your mother soft foods for a day. And then you'll be right as rain." She turned the car around and drove away.

I tiptoed past our side door and tucked myself in beside the rosebush. Thorns scratched me, but I could barely feel them. Even though I pushed in on my eyes, tears still spread over my fingers. All of the sadness had returned.

I couldn't go find my mother. I couldn't tell her about soft foods, or anything else. I closed my eyes. Sobbed without making a sound. I tried to think about her good news. That it wasn't much longer before we could leave. But even if the new place did work out, it wouldn't be the same. Nothing ever would.

CHAPTER TWENTY-FIVE

I woke up with my face and shoulder slumped against the stone of the house. As I sat up, my head grew woozy and my whole chin ached. I spat out the bloodied gauze still crammed into my cheeks and crawled out from beside the rosebush. I was actually hungry. Maybe I could have a peanut butter and jelly sandwich on my mother's fresh bread.

Over my grumbling stomach, I caught another sound. I held my breath and strained to listen. There it was again. Two branches rubbing together. No, a newborn kitten, whining softly. As though its paw or tail was nipped.

I had to find it. If it was really small, I'd sneak it into the kitchen under my T-shirt. Fill a saucer with fresh milk and carry it through to the bedroom. I'd have to make sure it couldn't get up on the dresser, though. George would get a shock if he swam into five sharp claws.

I searched among the patch of mint Mr. Vardy had planted. Pulled back the longer clumps of grass. Checked the vines that were clinging to a crisscross of lattice. There was nothing there, only soil and shadows and two rusted toy cars. The whining was getting louder, more frustrated. I stepped cautiously over the grass, following the side of the house. Perhaps it was in the vegetable garden out back. Or trapped beneath a bedsheet that had blown off the clothesline.

As I turned the corner, I saw a tall shrub shiver slightly. I crept closer, but instead of finding a kitten, I discovered Martin. He was balanced on top of a milk crate, wedged among the dark leafy branches. His shorts were bunched around his ankles. I could see his white backside. I took another step. The fingers of his left hand were spread against the wall, and his other hand was yanking between his legs.

I craned my neck. Martin kept looking up and down. Taking glimpses through a small square window, then leaning his forehead against the stone sill.

It struck me. That was the window of the bathroom I shared with my mother. She must be in there. Washing herself in the tub, like she often did in the afternoons when it was extra hot. And Martin was disguised among the bushes, watching her. Like a thief. Or a trespasser. His grunts were getting worse and worse.

Burning liquid came up in my throat and I gagged and spat. Martin jerked his head around and scanned the yard behind him. He didn't startle when he saw me. Instead he slowly lowered his hands and hauled up his shorts. He fixed his belt and tucked in his shirt and smoothed away the blond curls that had fallen into his eyes. A red mark on his forehead. "Hey, Ware," he said quietly as he stepped down off the crate. "I can see you standing right there, buddy. Do you think I can't?"

I turned and ran out of the backyard, past the side door and the roses. Every stomp made pain shoot through my jaw. From behind me, Martin was still calling out. "Hey, pal! Why'd you take off?" He sounded so friendly. So cheerful. Like he'd done nothing wrong. "Where are you going? You want a game of checkers?"

I raced down over the slope. Past the pool and into the woods.

It was darker among the trees. Branches poked my sore jaw, my arms and legs, but I tried to stay on the right path. I thought I'd come out on the beach, by the log where Genie and I had talked, but instead I came to the edge of a backyard. I recognized it.

Mrs. Grimshaw was sitting on her patio. She had a bowl in her lap. She might have been shucking peas.

"Who's there?" she said. "Is someone there?"

I walked out of the trees so she could see me. "Just me, Mrs. Grimshaw. Thomas."

"Strange way to show up at someone's house, don't you think?"

"I'm sorry," I mumbled. Tears were waiting, but I held them in.

"Oh, I'm not fussy, dear." She put the bowl near her feet and stood up. "Since Abel passed, I do like company."

Since Abel passed. Did that mean Mrs. Grimshaw wasn't confused anymore? That she didn't think her husband was wandering in the woods?

The screen door creaked as she opened it and she went inside. Then she opened it again and called, "Well, are you coming?"

I followed her into her kitchen. Everything was neat, and the floor shone. It smelled like sliced oranges. She pointed to the table.

"By the looks of your face, you'll want some buttered toast," she said after I'd sat down. She didn't wait for me to say yes or no, just dropped a slice of bread into a toaster. "A cut of bologna, too. Oh, and apple juice. All children love apple juice."

"Okay," I said. I was dizzy and hungry, and the bottom of my face was beating at the same time as my heart.

When she put the food in front of me, the sight of it made my chest ache. In a different way than my teeth ached. "Thank you," I said.

"My pleasure. Hardly no one visits anymore, other than the girl who straightens up. She was here all day. Did my hair, too." Mrs. Grimshaw patted the bulging scarf covering her head. The end of a blue roller was sticking out. With a sigh, she settled into the chair across from mine. She was wearing a dress buttoned up and stockings and a white sweater over her shoulders. She seemed normal. Perfectly normal. When she lifted her head and smiled, her eyes were lost in her face.

"Now, tell me, what's got your goat?"

"I don't know."

"Surely you've got something troubling you."

I took several breaths, then I said quickly, "Everything here is wrong. It's awful. I miss my aunt." I wasn't crying, but snot was dripping out of my nose and down over my swollen mouth. "I miss my home."

"There, there." She reached a warm, dry hand over and patted mine. "You feel like you're breaking in two. Trying to figure out how you can get going when there's nothing under your feet."

I nodded.

"I was the same. When my Abel died. You never met him, but he—Abel was my home. Do you understand that?"

I did. I really did.

"And now, even though I live here, my home is gone." Mrs. Grimshaw pulled her hand back. "That might not make sense to you."

"It does," I said.

"Then you and I have something in common."

I ate slowly, trying to use my front teeth to bite through the toast. I slurped some apple juice to turn it into mush. With my tongue I worked the food against the roof of my mouth.

"You lived with her?" she asked. "This aunt of yours?"

"Yeah. But now I'm with my mother."

"Ah, yes. You're Esther's boy. I'd heard about it. Worst-kept secret in Upper Washbourne, your mother having a baby. I always thought that must have been so hard on her. Giving you over. Though I doubt she had much choice in the matter."

I could feel the lump of bread and meat going down my throat. Mr. Vardy had said the same thing. *She certainly didn't do it for herself.*

"Without Esther, Muriel would have flown straight off the rails. Your mother kept her grounded. Well, grounded enough so that the talk stopped. And then she had her hands full with Muriel's boy."

"But how could they do that? How could they make her give me over?"

"Those people have their ways. Do you know how old she was when she came here?"

"Thirteen, I think. My aunt was fifteen. They came from England, to get away from the bombing."

"Ah, yes. The sisters. We would have taken the pair of them, you know." She adjusted the curler in her hair. "But Esther went to the Gladstones. They always got what they wanted. We inquired about your aunt, but Ruth didn't want her next door. It would be a distraction, she said, because Esther was meant to be a friend to Muriel. A friend to help her after what had happened with Alexander."

I shifted to the edge of my seat.

"The Gladstones were supposed to take care of Esther. To be like her family. That was the agreement. See that the girl got a proper education. Raise her into a young woman. Surely they could afford that."

"I don't understand."

"For a few weeks, it was fine. We saw the two of them being driven back and forth to school. Then it was only Muriel. We'd thought Esther had been sent back to the church and we got our hopes up. But then Abel saw her in the yard. She was wearing a maid's uniform."

I put the toast back on the plate.

"Abel was mad. Oh, he was livid. Like I've never seen. They'd taken away her opportunities. And a young woman, no matter her circumstance, should still be given every chance to succeed. She was very bright, your mother. Curious, too. Abel and I could see that when we met her at the church. A real crackerjack with numbers."

"That's not fair," I said. "Did Mr. Grimshaw tell Mr. Gladstone to fix it?"

"Oh, no. They couldn't even look at each other, those two. But Abel spoke to the group who'd placed her."

"And that worked?"

"It didn't. They thought as long as she had a roof over her head, what did it matter?"

"Why didn't my mother leave? Why wouldn't she just run away?"

"At that age? I'm sure her sister'd been placed elsewhere. Where was your mother to go?"

"But when she got older?"

"Probably didn't think she could, Thomas."

"But why? What stopped her?"

"Walls, I'm sure."

I shook my head. "What walls? There's a hedge, but—"

Mrs. Grimshaw touched the side of her head. "There are plenty of walls. Just because you can't see them, doesn't mean they aren't there."

That didn't make any sense.

Mrs. Grimshaw put her elbows on the table. She edged closer to me. "And this aunt who was lucky enough to have you. What was she like, dear? Tell me about her."

I wasn't sure what I should say. When I thought about her now, all I could imagine was the bad stuff. Her waiting in the rain next to Mr. Pober. Or driving away, and Dr. Henneberry's arm hanging out the car window. Or her legs, spotty blue and crooked on the ground, an earwig crouched on her ankle. But that was not who she was. That was not my aunt. Finally, I said, "She was a nurse. A good nurse. She told jokes all the time. Dumb jokes, but they were still funny. She liked to dance and dress up and read mystery books and doodle. She made the best spice cake you ever tasted in your life. She was really afraid of bugs, and I had to catch them for her. And she was always kind to everyone." Kind to the wrong ones sometimes. People who didn't deserve it.

I couldn't tell Mrs. Grimshaw the best part about my aunt, though. That even though she had to remind me a hundred times to close the refrigerator door or turn off the tap or finish my sums or wipe my shoes, she still thought I was special. She'd loved me.

"Hm." Mrs. Grimshaw leaned back in her chair. "Sounds like quite a woman."

"She was."

I ate the rest of my sandwich. I didn't want to think about my mother never going to school. Never having a real friend. The Gladstones had taken her in, and even though they had that enormous house, they'd stuck my mother inside a closet next to the laundry room. She'd probably gotten so used to being confined, it was going to hurt to stand up and finally stretch. To leave the Henneberrys and live in a place with me.

What if, when I'd opened the last ring on my paper chain, she wasn't strong enough? What if she changed her mind? What if she sent me to the church and they had to find me another family? What if I wasn't allowed to go back to school?

My head was heavy with questions. But all the answers were the same. Everything that had gone wrong with my life, my aunt's life, my mother's life was because of the Gladstones. And now the Henneberrys.

I gulped the rest of my apple juice.

"Are you feeling better, Thomas?"

I shook my head. I wasn't feeling better. I was feeling confused. I was feeling scared. Mostly, though, I was feeling very, very angry.

I wanted them gone.

CHAPTER TWENTY-SIX

I'd made a decision. I knew what I was going to do.

The next morning, as soon as my mother went outside to pick beans from the garden, I snuck into Dr. Henneberry's study. Heavy curtains blocked the windows, but I felt along the wall until I found the switch. A dull light spread over everything.

The walls and floor were made of polished wood, and the glass on the doors of the gun cabinet gleamed. I glanced inside. Several rifles and a few smaller pistols were on display. If Wally were here, he'd know the exact names of each one. The dates they were made, too.

In the middle of the room was a large wood desk. On top, there was nothing but a lamp and a small pile of papers. A solid brass bird sat right on top, weighing them down.

There had to be something in here. Proof of what Dr. Henneberry had done. As soon as I found evidence, real evidence, I was going straight to Greenlake to see Detective Miller.

I yanked at the top drawer. A box of pencils. More papers. A glossy red stapler. The bottom drawer. Some paperbacks. What looked like a photograph of a younger Dr. Henneberry and Mr. Fulsome, wearing uniforms. A model of a set of teeth and gums.

In the middle of his desk was a thinner drawer. If he was sitting in his chair, it would be right above his thighs. I lifted the metal handle and tugged, but it was stuck. Peering closer, I saw a small keyhole, and I rattled the handle back and forth as hard as I could. The latch inside wouldn't let go.

I searched his desk and the bookshelves. The windowsills behind the curtains. I picked up the lamp by its neck and shone it on the floor. Nothing. But when I went to put the lamp back in its place, I saw it. Hidden where the base had been. A tiny golden key. From the other side of the house, my mother was calling. "Thomas? Where are you?"

My hand shook as I stuffed the key into the hole and twisted. The drawer slid open, but there was not much there, either. A few hairpins, but those might have belonged to Mrs. Henneberry. An old newspaper article from the *Greenlake Chronicle* with a snapshot of Dr. Henneberry and Mrs. Mapps posing outside Painless Dentistry. One of those lady magazines. The cover had a naked woman talking on the telephone, the black cord stretched across her bare stomach. Two packets of cigarettes and the empty wrapper from a Butterfinger. Just garbage.

I swept my hands along the back, into the corners where I couldn't see. I pulled out a piece of broken metal. A hollow silver square with a circle with white gems, several of them missing. A brooch, maybe, or the clasp on a belt. Just more junk.

I turned it over on my palm. The underside was tarnished and I noticed a streak of brown. I didn't know why, but my fingertips started to tingle. As though they realized they'd found the exact thing they shouldn't have. Not garbage at all, but something important. Maybe even evidence.

I jammed it into the pocket of my shorts and locked up the drawer and tucked the key back under the lamp. Then I bolted out the front door and down the driveway. I could still hear my mother, her voice distant, calling out to me. I didn't slow down.

With another nickel earned from Mrs. Henneberry's foot rubs, I boarded the bus at the end of Roundwater Heights. Twenty minutes later, I got off in Lower Washbourne. I didn't go back to my old apartment, though. I waited with a bunch of people who were dressed in work clothes, and with my transfer ticket, I climbed onto a second bus to Greenlake. We traveled down the main street, past that stupid hanging tooth. I stared at it as hard as I could, but the chains holding it up still wouldn't snap. *They soon will though*, I told myself. I meant that things were about to change. Troubled times were coming for Dr. Henneberry. Mrs. Pinsent would have said I was using figurative language.

I rushed up the painted steps of the police station. Inside a lady stood behind a long wooden counter. A tight brown curl was stuck to the side of her forehead.

"Another scorcher," she said, fanning the air under her chin.

Behind her was a cabinet with dozens of tiny drawers. Each one had a white label stuck to the front, and I wondered if one of them had my aunt's name written on it.

"Can you hear me okay, dear? I asked, what can I do for you?" She was staring at the bruise on my forehead. Ten days had passed since I'd hit the dashboard, and it was now mostly green and yellow. "You collecting for the Scouts?"

"No," I whispered. Then I said louder, "I need to talk to a policeman."

"Anyone at all, or you got someone special in mind?"

"Special. Detective Miller."

"An officer won't do?" She dropped a pencil into the white mug on her desk. On the mug was a picture of a sleeping lady and the words "Dreaming of Mr. Perfect."

I shook my head. "No, ma'am. It's about my aunt. Miss Celia Ware."

She stared at me. With two fingers, she wiggled the top button of her dress. "Oh sweetie. That's dreadful."

"It's important," I said. I patted the side of my shorts. The brooch clip thing was still in there.

"Well, he's not around, but his partner is. Detective O'Connor."

I hesitated. Detective O'Connor hadn't seemed as friendly as Detective Miller. "Can I wait?"

"Of course not. Why would you when you don't got to? I'll get you right in."

She stood up and went to a heavy wooden door. When she tugged it open, she called out, "Ernst? A youngster's here to see you." Then she tapped my shoulder and pointed. "That's him, love. That tall feller right there. He'll help you with your questions, I'm sure."

When I slid into the wooden chair beside his desk, he pointed at his own face. "You get in a fight? That why you're here?"

"No, sir."

"A little tour around, then? You want to see a real jail cell? I can lock you up for a couple of minutes, like the crooks. That's always a thrill."

I shook my head.

"Then what? Come on, now. Don't be afraid, lad. Spit it out. A policeman is your pal, you know."

I was starting to sweat. I tugged at the neck of my T-shirt.

Detective O'Connor put his hand on my shoulder. "It's okay, son. Did something happen? You can trust me. But I can't sit here all day and guess. I got cases to work on."

I had to do it. I had to try. "My aunt," I whispered.

"Aunt?"

"She was in the woods. They found her." My words shivered.

"Who found her, son?"

"A man and a lady. They just got married. They went for a hike near St. Augustine's Hospital."

He leaned back in his chair and pinched high up on his nose. "I knew you looked familiar. That was a sorry business, the whole terrible thing. But unfortunately I haven't got much to offer," he said. "Wish I did."

I closed my eyes. I had to push the words out of my throat. "Dr. Henneberry."

"Henneberry? Yes, that's right, that's right. You're out at their place, yeah?"

"Yeah."

"It's all coming back to me. I spoke with . . . with who? Was that your mother a few weeks back?"

I nodded. "She works there."

"And you're staying with her?"

I nodded again.

He whistled. "Boy oh boy. What a spot to spend the summer. I mean, I've never seen such a property. We were there for some blowout last year. The grub, the pool, the sand, the lake. It's incredible. Living like that." Then he sat up, slid his chair closer. "You heard if they're planning, you know, another afternoon for the force?"

"No, sir."

"Hm. Maybe next year. Well, I hope you're counting your blessings, young man. They're good people. Good, good people."

He took a big gulp from his mug and wiped the back of his mouth with his hand. Then he said, "Now, what can I do for you, friend?"

All of a sudden, the room was spinning. The air was warm and thick. It was hard to breathe. I squeezed my eyes closed, straightened my spine, and I told Detective O'Connor everything. How my aunt had treated Dr. Henneberry at St. Augustine's. I didn't understand why they'd missed the chart to prove it. I explained how his toe looked when the slipper fell off. That was easy enough to check. I told Detective O'Connor that my aunt had bruises on her arm. Five little ones. And I told him I was nearly certain Dr. Henneberry had borrowed Mrs. Henneberry's old beater to pick up my aunt at our apartment. "His other car is kind of flashy, but in Mrs. Henneberry's, he wouldn't even stand out." And finally, I said Dr. Henneberry's hands were the exact same hands as the man who came to get her. Everything made sense. I didn't have a shred of doubt. "Dr. Henneberry is the Greenlake Predator."

Detective O'Connor didn't say anything at first. He plucked up a toothpick from his desk, jabbed it between his lips and wiggled it. Then he examined a white gob that was stuck to the end. After he tossed the toothpick in the trash can, he smirked at me. "You got any solid evidence to back that up?"

Yes, I'd almost forgotten. I dug into my pocket and put the clip on the desk. "I found that in Dr. Henneberry's desk. He's got a locked drawer. He keeps secret stuff in there."

"Had a bit of a snoop, did you?" Detective O'Connor poked the brooch with his finger.

"Look," I flipped it over. "See that brown stuff? I mean, it could be blood, right? I don't think it's my aunt's, but I'm sure it belonged to one of those other ladies."

"Ladies?"

"Yes, sir. I saw the photographs in the newspaper when I was painting birdhouses."

"When you were painting birdhouses, hey?" He scratched at the blood, then brought the metal to his nose and sniffed. "My bet's on rust, pal. Not blood."

"But still. It's not Mrs. Henneberry's because it was hidden away."

"Right. So let's pull it all together, shall we?" Detective O'Connor put his elbows on his desk, knotted his fingers together. "We got the brooch as a solid clue. The car might be the same. And that accident with the toe, right? Oh, and the hand. We can't forget that. All this leading you to believe Dr. Henneberry did away with your aunt. And a couple of other ladies. You could've just cracked the case wide open." His mouth was a white line. His eyes had gotten smaller. I could tell he was taking me very seriously.

"And there's a man who sits on the front stoop of my old apartment building on Gerald Street. That's in Lower Washbourne."

"Yeah, I know where it is."

"His name's Mr. Pober. He says mean stuff, but he knew my aunt was mixed up with the wrong sort. He told me. He saw him. You just need to show him a photograph of Dr. Henneberry. Like they do on television."

"Oh, right." Detective O'Connor nodded slowly. "Like they do on television."

"Exactly," I said. I took a deep breath. It was such a relief to finally get it all out. And to have someone really care.

"Seems you got all this sorted. Detective Ware, is it?"

I smiled a small smile. "Sort of."

Detective O'Connor's bottom teeth were scratching at his top lip. "Warped sort of fellow, Dr. Henneberry, hey? Real sicko."

I kept nodding. "It was him. I just know it. Mr. Pober knows it, too."

Detective O'Conner brought his face closer to mine. "Are you a good listener, sonny?"

"What? I mean, pardon me?"

"Does your teacher at school say you're good with learning?"

I coughed. "Sure," I said. "Sure. Yeah." *Sort of. Not exactly.*

"Well, I'm going to give you a few directions, and I do hope you cleaned out your ears this morning."

I tried not to even blink. "Okay." I'd do whatever he said. Maybe he'd let me ride in the police car to talk to Mr. Pober. Then we'd go straight over to that swinging tooth, and I'd help arrest Dr. Henneberry. Clamp the cuffs around his wrists myself. I could almost picture his face.

"You know how much his family, his wife's family, has done for the police?"

"No, sir. I—"

"An awful, awful lot." He was so close now, I could see the tiny veins on the tip of his nose. "Did you see the plaque outside?"

"No, sir."

"Land this building stands on? Donated by the Gladstones. Any officer hurt on the job? His wife, his kids—all taken care of. How?"

My knees jiggled. My muscles were itching to leap up and get things done.

"A fund created by the Gladstones, and now kept up by the Henneberrys." He pulled a pencil from behind his ear and twirled it in his fingers. Then he pointed the sharp end at me. "And who probably paid for this? I'm sure I don't got to tell you."

"Oh," I said. What difference did those things make?

"Now, do you know what fabricating means?"

"No, sir."

"It's the same as lying. Lying! You like to make up stories, don't you?" He smacked his hand on the top of his desk. I jumped. "Don't you!"

My head nodded all by itself.

"I'll tell you this," he said.

I sat on my hands.

"Make-believe is for prissy little girls. Are you a prissy little girl?"

He didn't believe me. All the things I'd explained. And the clip I'd found in the desk drawer. All the hope I'd had suddenly drained out of me. Same as if Detective

O'Connor had drilled holes in my back and it just flooded out.

"You listening to me?"

He wasn't going to drive over to my old apartment and talk to Mr. Pober. Or show him a photograph. He wasn't going to throw Dr. Henneberry in a real jail cell. Where they lock up all the crooks.

He snapped his fingers so close to my face, the air puffed into my eyes. "You hearing me, kid? Keep at it, and you're going to find yourself in hot water, buddy boy. Real hot water."

EXCERPT

Testimony of Mrs. Joan Bishop, Family Friend
Direct Examination by Prosecutor Clay Fibbs

A. Our families have always been close. Not with
Dr. Henneberry. We never really knew his people. But
Muriel and I grew up together, vacationed together.
She was a Gladstone, then, and I was an Easton. We
were just girls.

Q. And do you— Mrs. Bishop? Can someone offer the
lady a tissue?

A. Sneaks up on me, that's all.

Q. I want to ask you about a specific event. A specific
afternoon. Did you attend Martin Henneberry's
birthday party?

A. I did. We all went. My husband, Bill, and my daughter,
Genie. She was ecstatic. It was quite the bash. That
was Muriel's way. The only thing she ever did with a
budget was toss it aside. She had streamers and
balloons around the pool. A huge white umbrella
thing. She even had these adorable paper balls,
lanterns or some such, hanging from the branches.
Though we never got to see them lit. Things went sour
well before the sun went down.

Q. Most of the afternoon, though, was an enjoyable
party?

A. Flawless. Muriel planned it all, right down to the
napkin color. She made this lovely spinach dip. Tiny

carrots pulled straight from her own garden. Raymond was grilling. James Fulsome, too. My Bill offered to help, but they were all set. Do you remember, Bill?

Q. **Mrs. Bishop, please don't direct your responses to your husband. Only to the court.**

A. I'm so sorry.

Q. **There was an upset, as you mentioned?**

A. An upset? That's an understatement.

Q. **Can you tell the court what happened?**

A. It started right after Muriel was carrying Martin's birthday cake down from the house. It was a triple-decker. Enormous. Of course, that was pure Muriel. She'd made it herself.

Q. **Then?**

A. Martin was nowhere to be found. He and my daughter, Genie, had gone for a stroll. I try not to be a hindrance, Mr. Fibbs, if you know what I mean. It's hard to control young love. I always dreamed Martin and Genie would get married. I was so thankful my Genie—

Q. **Mrs. Bishop, if we could stick to the disruption?**

A. As I was explaining, my Genie and Martin had stepped away, and Mrs. Henneberry had the cake in her arms. Then that boy, some wayward child under the care of a housekeeper—

Q. **You mean Thomas Ware?**

A. Yes. Right in the middle of the backyard. He started wailing. Wailing like someone had stabbed him with a hot poker.

Q. **About?**

A. Poor Martin, of all people. When that young man couldn't possibly have been more gracious to his guests. I was stricken by it all.

Q. **What happened after that?**

A. Muriel got such a start with the screeching, the cake toppled right out of her grasp. I could have cried for her, it looked so delicious. And then the maid, I don't remember her name, she'd been steps behind Muriel with plates and forks. Didn't she go ahead and drop the lot of them on the flagstone path. Everything just shattered. I nearly fainted.

Q. **Go on, please.**

A. And then Raymond rushed over to that boy—

Q. **Dr. Henneberry attended to Thomas Ware?**

A. Yes, that's correct. He took him into this sort of tight embrace. Just hugged him. Well, the boy calmed right down. Just like that. Went completely silent. Maybe Raymond squeezed the madness out of him.

Q. **And then—**

A. Ray led him up to the house. No doubt to get him a cold drink. They were beyond kind to him. Treated him like one of their own. I would have lost my marbles over it, if it were me. But I guess they understood he had his challenges after being uprooted. And that unspeakable business with his aunt, Mr. Fibbs. Maybe that's at the bottom of this whole thing. We all just finished our drinks, our snacks, just to be sociable, and then everyone scattered.

Q. So after Thomas's outburst, his episode, everyone went home?

A. Pretty much. The wind had changed, if you know what I mean. And my Genie was in such a state. She'd never encountered that sort of uncouth behavior before. Or since, Mr. Fibbs.

Q. Mrs. Bishop, how did you feel around Thomas Ware?

A. Terrified, sir. My whole body was quaking. Tip to toe.

Q. Can you explain why?

A. Watching him, that boy was so vicious, I thought he was going to kill someone.

Q. Kill someone?

A. That's exactly what I said, Mr. Fibbs. Kill someone. And then he went and did it, now, didn't he?

CHAPTER TWENTY-SEVEN

The phone was ringing somewhere deeper in the house, and then it stopped. After a moment, Mrs. Henneberry's shoes clacked down the hallway. "The canopy is on its way, everyone!" she called. "Oh, what a glorious day for a soiree!"

"Someone's chipper," my mother whispered as she spread icing over a triple-layer chocolate cake.

She was right. Lately, Mrs. Henneberry was always chipper. Ever since we'd gone to see that hairy man in the camper, she'd stopped talking. Now she only hummed or sang.

"Doesn't it look delicious, Thomas?" my mother said.

I didn't reply. That birthday cake was much fancier than the iced ginger one my aunt had made for my birthday, but it could never taste as good. I went to the wall under the cupboard and ripped off another link in my paper chain. Every day it was shrinking. After today, only fifteen more days and we could leave. Then I'd never, ever come back. And no matter what, my mother wasn't going to come back either.

"Are you okay? You've been out of sorts since Thursday. It's Martin's big day, you know."

"So what?"

She put down the spatula. "I've already talked to Mrs. Henneberry, and you're welcome to join in. Is that what's bothering you?"

"Yeah," I lied. "I wasn't sure."

"Well, you can put it right out of your mind."

She offered me the icing-covered spatula, but I shook my head. Then Mrs. Henneberry came into the kitchen. She was wearing a pink dress with huge white dots and a white belt, and she was carrying a flat box under her arm. "I had a sneaky sense you needed some boosting up, Tom. With all this attention on Martin, I just knew you were bound to feel a little left out."

"I've just let him know he's invited," my mother said. "Can play with the other children." She moved dishes into the sink, then cleared away my untouched breakfast.

"It's a celebration, Esther. What do you think, we'd exclude him?" Mrs. Henneberry pushed the box in front of me. It had a thick blue ribbon, neatly knotted. "And you're going to be pleased to have this, Tom, darling. Very pleased."

I touched the corner of the box. It was covered in a pattern of tumbling baby bears.

"Tom?" Mrs. Henneberry put her hand on my shoulder. "You act like you've never seen a present before. Martin would have already torn it to shreds."

I tugged the ribbon. Even though my insides were one big snarl, my mind still skipped through all the possible things that might fit inside. A large model car, a record player, a train that looped around and around. Hours and hours of distraction from being stuck in a place I despised.

The ribbon slithered to the floor and I lifted the top. I peeled the tissue paper back to reveal a white shirt with a round collar. And matching shorts with a navy line going down the side. A red handkerchief folded on top.

"Oh, it's lovely, Mrs. Henneberry," my mother said. She reached over to feel the shirt. "Such fine stitching."

"I had it sewn specially," she sang. "A sailor's suit. All the rage these days. Do you like it, Tom? Do you?"

"He does," my mother said. Her hand pressed down on my arm. "Right, Tom?"

"Yeah," I said. The lies continued to roll off my tongue. "I love it."

"Wonderful. Hurry and change then, dear. Do you need help getting out of your nightshirt?"

"No, he'll manage, Mrs. Henneberry," my mother said quickly. Then to me, "Do as you're told, Thomas. Don't dawdle."

In the bedroom, I threw the box on the cot. I stripped off my pajamas and tugged on the new shirt and shorts. Underneath everything were a pair of navy knee socks, and I yanked those on as well. As I stared at myself in the mirror over the sink, my face went hot with shame. Why should I have to wear such a ridiculous outfit? I wasn't a baby. I was eleven years old.

"Tom, dear?" Mrs. Henneberry was waiting in the kitchen. "How does it fit?"

I had no choice but to feed the triangle of red fabric under the wide collar and tie it in the knot.

I dragged my feet over the tile in the laundry room. When I reached the kitchen, Mrs. Henneberry gave me a loose hug. "Oh, I should have gotten that smart hat to finish it off." Her hand touched my chin. "My mistake."

My mother was frowning, but she said, "Thomas? Your manners?"

"Thank you, Mrs. Henneberry."

"Oh, you're so welcome, dear. You look very clever, indeed." She bent close to me. Her blond hair fell forward, and I could feel her breath in my ear. "You might just steal the show today, Tom. You might just."

Then she went out through the side door. She was yelling again. "Nearly, nearly! A few feet to the left, please. Yes, that's it. Perfection achieved!"

I followed her outside. Mr. Vardy and another man were down near the pool, hammering posts into the lawn. A huge square of white lay on the ground between them. They hoisted it into the air. Mrs. Henneberry made her way down the slope, pointing this way and that. Another man sliced open a bag, dumped chunks of coal into the round stomachs of two shiny barbecues.

My mother appeared behind the screen. "Can you keep yourself clean until the party?"

"I'll try," I said.

I knelt down by the rosebush. Underneath it I found a matchbox car partly buried in the dirt. With a stick I picked and picked at the dirt around the wheels until they could spin. I glanced back down at the pool. Mr. Vardy had carried a ladder over to the trees and he was hanging colorful balls among the leaves.

I knew my mother liked him. Anytime she said his name, she flushed and turned away. Mr. Vardy always treated me nicely, too. Why couldn't he have been my father? If he was, he'd insist I take off that foolish sailor suit. "If you need me to set Mrs. Henneberry straight, I'll do it. Can't have my boy dressed like a laughingstock."

The men were finished up. Soon people would begin arriving. I threw the car back under the bush and got up. How many times had Martin strolled around the back corner of the house when I was playing there? Sneaking up on me and making me leap out of my skin. Fixing his belt or smoothing down his hair. A red mark in the middle of his forehead. Was he watching my mother at night, too? Was he ever watching me?

I followed the path and found the window of our bathroom. The milk crate was still there, and I grabbed it, threw it as far as I could. It didn't crack, though, just landed on the grass with a sturdy thump.

The sun overhead was blazing. When I looked down

at myself, the sailor suit seemed even brighter. There wasn't a breath of wind.

My mother was in a different uniform. The everyday buttercup-yellow was gone and now she was wearing a short-sleeved black dress with a crisp white apron. A young girl, about the same age as Martin, was with her. I'd never seen her before. She was wearing the same outfit as my mother. Her black hair was in a loose bun at the bottom of her neck.

Under the white canopy, there were three tables covered in red-and-white-checkered tablecloths. My mother and the girl kept going back and forth from the house to the pool. They carried down plates and napkins and forks and knives and bowls and bags of chips and Cheezies. Big round tubs of ice were full of soda bottles and beer bottles. Blown-up beach balls floated in the pool. On the other side, one of the men had arranged a row of lawn chairs. A fluffy colorful towel was placed at the end of each one.

"That's exactly what I was thinking," Mrs. Henneberry said, though no one had asked her a question. "Nothing too splashy. I mean, he's a teenager. Just a perfect summer cookout to mark the occasion."

Cars began to show up. They filled up the driveway first, then overflowed onto the lawn. Guests wandered over the grass, down the slope toward the pool. There were men and women and little children and some teenagers around Martin's age. Mrs. Henneberrys' friend from the diner in Greenlake. And her husband. Everyone wore light summer dresses and ironed shorts and sandals. No one else had on a sailor suit. The gifts they carried were enormous.

Mr. and Mrs. Gage arrived, and Skip and his little sister, Debra. Skip scowled at me. Mr. Fulsome was there, too, and Mrs. Henneberry ran over to him. Their heads went together, and she whispered in his ear. He laughed and slapped his leg. "Oh, Mure, your wacky ideas. You crack me up." Then he strode over to Dr. Henneberry and rubbed his hand between Dr. Henneberry's shoulders.

I took a couple of steps back. That was the first time I'd seen Dr. Henneberry since he had his hands stuffed inside my mouth. At the sight of him, the muscles in my legs turned to jelly. He was chuckling when Mr. Fulsome locked his arm around his neck and pulled him in. Knuckles grating over his scalp. There was no guilt on Dr. Henneberry's face. He wasn't bothered about hurting my aunt. Or the other women. He was grinning and shaking hands when he should be in a jail cell in Greenlake. He'd gotten away with it.

I'd tried. I did. But Detective O'Connor refused to do his job. I loathed myself then. For being just a boy. A weak, useless boy in a goofy costume.

Another car drove in and parked at the end of the driveway, far away from the others. A man opened the door and bent to flip the front seat forward. Genie

Bishop crawled out from underneath his arm. Her brown hair was shimmering, and she had a large blue bow on the top of her head. When she saw me, she waved. Before I could wave back, her mother, coming around from the other side of the car, grabbed her wrist and tugged her into the growing crowd. The box her father was carrying was the biggest. It looked like it was wrapped in aluminum foil.

"Where's the man of the hour?" Mrs. Bishop called out.

And at that moment, everyone turned toward the house. Martin had appeared at the top of the slope as though he'd just done a magic trick but without the smoke. He had a wide smile and was holding a rope. At the end of it was a black puppy with a pink ribbon tied around her neck. She was leaping and straining, and Martin was yanking at the rope. Together they jogged down the stone path to the pool, and Martin pumped the air with one fist. The crowd whooped and cheered. They wrapped around him. Clapped his back and fluffed up his hair and patted his new pet.

"By jumpings, you've really shot up, Marty."

"Taller than Ray, now, isn't he?"

"What a gorgeous pup, Martin. Is she purebred?"

"Sixteen. I remember those years. Caught yourself a girl yet?"

"Anyone ever tell you you're the spitting image of your granddaddy Gladstone?"

I glanced over at Genie. She was perched on the edge of a chair and was chewing on a strand of her hair.

Mrs. Bishop, squeezed in behind her, was shoving her hand against Genie's lower back. "Go," she said. "Go on, for god's sakes! Stand next to him. Where you belong."

Mrs. Henneberry floated past me. "Tom, love. Why haven't you joined the other boys?" She already sounded drowsy. "Come, I'll bring you over. You can meet Martin's new friend. She's a birthday gift from Skip. I do hope he'll take care of her. And all that puppy clean-up isn't left to Esther."

She slid her arm through mine and we wove our way through all the guests. "Have you wished Martin a happy birthday?" she said when we reached him.

I took a deep breath and pushed it out. "Happy birthday, Martin."

The puppy was fighting against the rope and Martin dropped it. He punched my arm. "Hey, thanks, Ware." Then his head went side to side like a puppet's, and with his hands, he tightened an invisible tie near his neck. "You're really styling, aren't you, buddy?" The puppy was near my feet. Jumping on my leg, licking my calf. Then she sat back on the grass, staring at me with her brown eyes, her tail flicking back and forth.

"Isn't he, though?" Mrs. Henneberry lifted her eyebrows at me, like she was saying, *See, Tom?*

I took a step back. Martin watched his puppy as she stepped back, too. She pawed at my foot and whined.

"Seems she's taken a shine to you, Tom," Mrs. Henneberry said.

I shrugged, but I couldn't stop myself from reaching down and scratching the little gal between her two floppy ears. Her fur was so soft.

"Hey, you!" Martin waved at the girl who was helping my mother. When she came over, he scooped up the end of the rope and handed it to her. "Take this up to the house. No one wants a dog drooling all over them while they're trying to eat."

"Yes, sir," she said as she tugged the puppy away from me. "Come on, girl. Come on!"

"*Yes, sir*," Martin repeated. "I like that."

"Open for business!" Mr. Fulsome hollered. He stabbed some meat and dropped it onto a paper plate. "Line up, line up! Who do you trust with your grilling? Me or Scorch-It Ray?"

Dr. Henneberry snapped his tongs at Mr. Fulsome's hip. "Come on. You can't trust Jimmy Fulsome. No one trusts Jimmy!"

Mrs. Henneberry wobbled on her heels. She whispered, "I trust you, James," but I think I was the only one who heard her.

Everyone was eating and drinking. My mother and that other girl were rushing about, adjusting things on the table, stooping to pick up dropped food or tossed-away napkins. I moved around, too. Mostly no one seemed to notice me, except for a few of the older boys who pointed at me and snickered. Then Mr. Fulsome came up beside me. "Nice seeing you again, mate," he said. "Captain gave you day leave?" Behind him, Dr. Henneberry was still leaning over his barbecue. He hadn't looked at me all afternoon. Which was a relief. Mr. Fulsome offered me a hot dog with mustard and relish. I took it and sat on the grass near the pool house. The wiener was black, and the bun was soggy, but I still managed to eat most of it.

Mrs. Henneberry marched past me. In her arms she held a bunch of big plastic hoops. "They've just gotten these at Belbin's," she announced. She gave a pair to two smaller girls, who climbed into the middle of them and tried to swing them around. "Hula-Hoops," she said. "Aren't they a hoot?"

She dropped the rest in a pile. Then she was trying to clap her hands together, but sometimes the left one missed the right. "Young ladies first. Come along, now. Time to get into your swimsuits."

Genie Bishop glanced at her mother before she got up and took the paper bag from under the lawn chair. A few other girls went into the pool house with bathing suits balled up in their hands.

Martin was whistling as he wandered around. He had his fists stuck deep in his pockets. I watched him go to the corner of the pool house. He stopped whistling. He patted the front of his shirt. "Huh?" he said to nobody, and then he bent down on the grass and combed his fingers through the blades like he'd lost a coin. Then, quick as a flash, his eye was up at that tiny crack in the wooden boards.

I stopped chewing. "Can you keep a secret?" he'd said when he showed it to me. No one else paid him any mind. He could do what he wanted, because he was a Henneberry. That was what my mother told me. I never knew what she meant at first, but I knew now. Martin pretended to find what he'd lost, held his two empty fingers up to the sunlight, and said, "There you are!" I tossed the end of my hot dog into the grass.

When the girls came out, the boys went in. And then the pool was full of teenagers splashing and screaming. A small boy wearing an orange life vest floated among them on top of a Styrofoam whale. His cheeks and neck and arms were fire engine red. Genie climbed onto Martin's shoulders. He gripped the tops of her thighs, which were wet and glossy in the sunlight. Another girl climbed up on Skip. They were yelling and giggling and tossing a beach ball back and forth between them.

"Everyone's already in, Tom." Mrs. Henneberry knelt next to me. "Don't you want to cool down?"

"No," I said.

"Have you had some snacks?"

"Yeah. I mean, yes, ma'am."

"That's good. I can't eat in this heat. Dr. Norton says I have a delicate system." With a jiggling hand, she picked up the tails of the red knot and let them drop. "It's all a tad much, really. The clamor. The silly fuss to please Martin, when he is never pleased." She yawned. "What I wouldn't give for an icy cloth over my eyes and one of your special foot rubs. Come find me later, Tom."

Dr. Henneberry was very close to the young girl who was helping. His open mouth was inches from her neck and his hand touched her waist. That same hand. My heart ticked faster. I licked my upper lip. It tasted of salt.

"Tom? Are you listening? A foot rub. My feet are throbbing. Once our guests leave, I'll need you immediately."

Another five cents. "I guess," I said.

"So agreeable." Mrs. Henneberry nipped my cheek. "How did I ever survive without you?"

When I looked back over to the barbecues, Dr. Henneberry and the girl were gone.

After a while, everyone climbed out of the pool. A mother bundled the sunburned child in a towel, and when he cried, arms sticking out, she let him drag the whale from the water. Carry it around. Martin was lying on a towel. Genie tried one of the Hula-Hoops, but she couldn't get it to spin, so she left it and lay down next to Martin. He edged closer to her. Their bare skin was touching, and he kept plucking at the straps of her swimsuit. Mrs. Bishop grinned. She bumped her husband with her elbow and said, "Mark my words, Bill. Those two'll be engaged before this year is over."

"Calm down, Joan," he said. "She's barely fifteen."

"So?"

Not a single cloud hung in the sky. The sun beat onto my skull and the hot dog sat in my gut like a fistful of gravel. I wanted to go indoors. I wanted to lie on the cold tile floor of the laundry where everything smelled clean. I wanted to get away from all the noisy guests.

Away from my mother who was now working alone. Away from this woolly ball of dread that wouldn't leave me alone.

I was about to get up and go when Martin started crawling like a bug over the grass away from Genie. He spoke to Skip. Then he was nodding and grinning and Skip said, "Yeah, right, Henneberry. No chance, pal." Martin held up five wiggling fingers, and Skip yelled, "You're on!" Then Martin crawled back to Genie. I sat up straighter. He was up to something. Probably something rotten. How could Genie like him?

He was whispering in Genie's ear. The ends of her hair were wet and stringy, and her bow had already fallen off. He kept talking and talking, and she was chewing her fingernails, and he put on a sad face and twisted his fists into his eyes like he was play-crying. She kept peering over at her mother. Mrs. Bishop was flicking the back of her hand at Genie and nodding. "Go on, sure, go!"

Then Mrs. Bishop turned to Mrs. Henneberry. "It just fills my heart. They're so taken up with each other."

Mrs. Henneberry frowned.

"Remember when you and me were like that? With Bill and Ray? Those sweet strolls through the woods?"

"Of course, Joan." Mrs. Henneberry folded her arms across her chest. "Such nice times. Lasting about ten seconds."

Genie hesitated another moment, then got up. She took her towel and went into the pool house. I guessed she was going to get changed. I guessed Martin was going to creep around and spy on her again. Mrs. Bishop hadn't seemed to notice.

But it wasn't Martin who went to the hole this time. It was Skip.

I went, too. I stood right behind him. When he saw me, he pressed his finger to his lips. "Shut it," he said. "I got five whole bucks riding on this."

Five dollars was a lot of money.

"It's . . . birthday," Martin mumbled from inside the pool house.

"I know," she said. "Why do . . . a party, silly."

"Oh my god," Skip whispered.

"I'm ready . . . present now."

"My father . . . name's on it. So you'll know . . . me." He coughed. "I don't mean that."

"I don't get it." Then quiet. "I don't—"

"You act . . . innocent, but I know . . . in the pool. Shaking your . . . plastic circle."

". . . just having fun."

"I want . . . fun, too."

"We are, aren't we?" she said.

". . . stuff with other boys. Messed around."

". . . haven't . . ."

". . . leave me out? Treat me . . . ?"

"I'm not, Martin."

My heart was beating fast. Skip had both hands cupped around one of his eyes. "She's letting him. She's letting him! Darnit! I'm going to lose my five bucks!"

But then Genie said, "That hurts, Martin . . . That . . ."

"What?"

". . . said don't."

"You . . . a selfish bitch, Genie . . . sixteen . . . give . . . me."

I could hear her crying. Skip shook his head and he brought his mouth to the crack. He hollered, "That's cheating. You're a cheat!" He was laughing. "What a milksop. Marty Milksop."

My fingers and my feet and my lips were full of pins and needles. The grass was not flat anymore. Everything was filing my ears and my nose. Hiss of soda opening. Sharp crunch of celery between teeth. A polite belch. The shivering fringe on the canopy. Burnt meat. And each time I blinked, my aunt was right behind my eyelids. I saw her on the ground in the woods. *That hurts!* Blink. *That hurts!* A bug crawled over her shoulder and, blink, she was screaming and couldn't get away, and blink, my legs were so heavy and—

I ran from the pool house and tripped. My knees smacked the ground and tore the grass. I got up fast. Martin was already coming out that perfect painted door. Everyone started singing "Happy Birthday" really loud. I yelled at Mrs. Bishop, "Genie's upset!" but her mouth was wide open and she was singing louder than the rest. "It's Martin!" I yelled again. There were so many colors. So many sounds. No one could see me. The red handkerchief was too tight around my neck. I pointed.

"It's him!" Martin winked at me. He bowed his head at all the visitors and pressed his hands over his heart. "Happy birthday, dear Maaarrrrty!"

I opened my mouth and I hollered. "Martin Henneberry is a pig!"

The singing stopped. Everyone went quiet. No one was moving except Mrs. Henneberry, who was baby-stepping down over the stone steps carrying the three-layer chocolate cake my mother had made. She slowed, and through her half-closed eyes, she gazed out at everyone. Her head was bent to the side. The cake started sliding and sliding. I yelled again, as loud as I could.

"A pig!"

In a squeaky voice, Mrs. Henneberry said, "Have you planned a roast, James? Do you need an apple for its mouth?" The cake left the platter and plopped onto the stone path. My mother was right behind her. There was a loud crash of plates, clatter of cutlery. Mrs. Henneberry took another step and the heel of her shoe sunk deep into a mound of icing.

Time slowed down. People surrounded me. Someone hissed, "Out of the way. I'll handle this."

Arms wrapped around me then, squeezing me tight. Fingers poked deep into my armpit. Yanking me forward, my ankles banging together as I flew up over the grass and in through the side door. A fist gripped the back of my sailor shirt, dragging me into the laundry room. My chest cut into the steel sink and a hand clutched the hair at the back of my head, pushing me down, down, into the icy water gushing from the tap. A soft cake of soap was forced between my lips, scraped over my tongue, filling all the new silvery grooves in my molars.

Dr. Henneberry's gritty voice arrived inside my head. I could see his neck. The bottom of his chin. He was bright red.

"Got a call . . ."

I sputtered and shook and sputtered and shook.

". . . from the police." In and out went the soap. Strands of his greased hair fell over his forehead. "Telling them I'm some type of what? A murderer?"

Acidy vomit erupted from my nose, my mouth. Hard bites of wiener. Smooth knots of bun.

"Stealing a piece of cheap jewelry from my desk. Do you know who owned that? Do you?"

Strings of yellow slime dripping into the sink.

"My goddamned dead mother, that's who."

I tried to cry out, but I kept gagging. The soapy chemicals burned my nostrils, my throat.

"How in hell's name could you have come from Martin Gladstone?"

What?

"Oh, I know all the dirty secrets. Your dear daddy was an old bastard who took a run at your mother."

What?

He let go of me. "She's a typical woman, though. Lets things happen."

What? What?

Then he slammed the soap into the bottom of the sink. "How could a man like that make something so useless. So lame."

Above me, he was panting hard. But it slowed down, as though his body was gathering calm with each breath. He dried his hands in a folded towel. "Well, then," he said. "That's been taken care of." He smoothed his hair back into place. He turned around and his soft footsteps got quieter and quieter until he was gone.

My knees buckled, and I slumped into the sink and spat and spat.

What did he mean? It couldn't be true. How could it be Martin Gladstone? The man who'd taken my mother in. He was supposed to be her family. He was supposed to be her father.

EXCERPT

Testimony of Mrs. Grace Pinsent, Elementary School Teacher

Direct Examination by Defense Counsel Mr. William Evans

Q. How long did you teach Thomas Ware?

A. Three years in total, Mr. Evans. Minus a month.

Q. In that time, did you get to know him well?

A. Very well.

Q. What kind of boy was he?

A. Thomas is a good, quiet boy. Always clean and nails trimmed and properly dressed. A bit of a chronic daydreamer, though, to be honest. Some educators think that indicates a child is slow or not capable, but if you ask me, it just means he's got a lot going on up top. Bright and creative. Someone beyond his years.

Q. How so, Mrs. Pinsent?

A. In his academics. He has some challenges staying on task, but he's still best in class for his mathematics. Art as well.

Q. Was Thomas ever rude or aggressive?

A. Not a once. When I was teaching him, he was sensitive and very aware of those around him. Gentlemanly, too.

Q. Can you explain what you mean?

A. Holding the door open for me, or if I dropped a book, he'd hurry to pick it up. I recall when he saw two boys tormenting a second grader. Messed up her hopscotch

squares just for fun, and it led to a little scuffle.
Occasionally, his best friend, Wally, was the brunt of
cruel jokes. Wally has some troubles with his pronun-
ciation, but Thomas wouldn't let anyone pick on him.
That led to fights as well. Fights is probably the wrong
word to use, Mr. Evans. Thomas isn't a fighter. But he
won't shy away from a skirmish. He always did have a
rather strong reaction if he saw someone being
treated poorly.

Q. Did you get a sense of his family life?

A. I did. A child's behavior usually reflects what's going
on at home. Mothers have changed, too. Much more
permissive now. Children do as they please. But not
Thomas. He was well loved, and his aunt always had
high expectations of him. She was a devoted care-
taker, which really makes the difference, especially if a
father figure is absent. It was a disgrace what
happened to Celia Ware. In this day and age, a woman
should be able to wait for a bus, without risk of—I
can't even say it.

**Q. Did you ever feel Thomas was a danger to you? Or to
other students?**

A. No, sir. Absolutely not. Never. In fact, I'd say I was
more worried about Thomas hurting himself.
Sometimes he rushed headlong without thinking.

**Q. Based on your close interactions with Thomas for
those three years, do you feel he could have
committed this crime?**

A. No, I do not.

Q. Why do you feel that way?

A. Because during our time together, I've gotten to know his heart. And that kind of destruction, that type of violence, is not in there, Mr. Evans. It simply isn't.

CHAPTER TWENTY-EIGHT

"Right when I laid eyes on him, Esther, I knew he was a nuisance. You and Muriel mollycoddling him. No control. And now he's calling my son—my son!—names at his own goddamned party."

I was sitting on the cot in the bedroom with my mother, and Dr. Henneberry was just outside. Hollering at us through the open door. He told my mother I was to pack up my belongings—my worn toothbrush, the drawer of Martin's hand-me-downs, George and his fishbowl—and get the hell out of his home. As he yelled and waved his hands, my mother cried. She said she was sorry for what I'd done. It wasn't like me. I was a nice boy. Her face was pink and puffed. There were smears of chocolate icing on her apron. "We won't have a place until the end of the month, Dr. Henneberry."

"Not good enough," he said.

"I'll keep him out of sight. You won't see a hair on his head."

"Still not good enough."

Then Mrs. Henneberry slid past Dr. Henneberry and stood in the middle of the bedroom. She kept her back to him. "That's completely unnecessary, Esther," she said. "Tom's hair is lovely. And you're my family, aren't you? We've agreed until the end of the month, and we'll keep to that. Besides, Tom has become very dear to me."

"Muriel!"

She smiled a small smile but didn't look over her shoulder. "I won't let him bully you a second longer, dear. All this fuss over a cake. It wasn't even my best effort. And Martin barely eats sweets!"

Dr. Henneberry jabbed the air with his hands. "It's not over a cake, for Christ's sakes! Didn't you see him outside? That's not normal behavior. Shrieking at the top of his lungs. If I had my way, I'd stick him in a cage!"

"Too much sun on your head. Is that what happened, Tom?" She put her cold hand on my cheek. "I knew I should've bought that adorable straw hat. None of this would've happened."

"Muriel! I've spoken."

After she'd cleared her throat, she turned to face him. "Well, I'll be speaking too, Raymond, dear. I'll be speaking very soon."

My mother wiped her face with a tissue. Mrs. Henneberry told her to take me upstairs to the blue room. "All he needs is some rest and recuperation. Perhaps he's still shaken up from the car. You know, from that tiny slip up with those furry little—what were they again?"

As we were leaving, she said to Dr. Henneberry, "And by the way, Raymond. Martin doesn't want that silly puppy anymore. It's tied to the front porch and has already made a mess. Take it back to Skip. What a pre-posterous idea."

My mother kept her arm around my shoulder as we climbed the stairs. She led me past Mrs. Henneberry's room to the one right next door. After she folded back the blanket, I climbed between the cool sheets. I pulled my knees up to my stomach. My head was still spin-ning, and my scalp stung, too. The skin where my hair parted was burnt. My mother found a bucket and put it near the side of the bed.

"Thomas?" she said quietly. "It's time we talk."

I turned away, pushed my face into the pillow. "Are you angry?"

"Never mind that. I heard what Dr. Henneberry said to you. In the laundry."

"What part?" I whispered.

"The last bit. About where you came from. He had no right to tell you. I meant to, long ago, but I was too ashamed."

I rolled onto my back. "Martin Gladstone." There. His name was outside of me. Wavering in the gap between us. "Is it true?" Then behind my eyelids, the old man's face appeared. Same as the portrait hanging in the din-ing room downstairs. I could see his ears. They were small, with attached lobes. Similar to mine.

"Mr. Gladstone—um, Mr. Gladstone could be very demanding sometimes."

I wanted to ask what she meant by "very demanding," but I couldn't. I just said, "With you?"

She smoothed her hands over the bedspread. "Yes."

Her voice shook, and I understood that whatever happened was wrong. Wally and I had gone through every single page in that book from his apartment, and nothing mentioned *very demanding*. Or mentioned an old man who was already married and had taken a girl into his home. A girl who was meant to be like a daughter.

"That doesn't make sense."

"No, it doesn't make sense. But that's it."

I looked at her hands that could push. Her feet that could walk. Her mouth that could say whatever it wanted to say. I didn't understand why those parts of her hadn't done something.

"You could've left."

She frowned. "It might seem so. But I was alone. I was young. And then, you were coming."

I heard Mrs. Grimshaw in my head. What she'd said about walls. *Just because you can't see them, doesn't mean they aren't there.*

"Martin Gladstone was your father, Thomas." The blue room got very dark. The only thing I could see was my mother. "And I know you've probably thought otherwise, but I wanted to keep you so badly. You were the best part of me. I don't think I can ever forgive myself."

My throat was dry and tight. "Why'd you do it, then?"

She took a deep breath. "When I couldn't hide my condition anymore, Muriel found out. She thought I'd met someone in town, and she was delighted. At first. Despite everything, I was delighted, too."

"Why didn't you stay delighted?"

"I'll try to explain, okay? Mr. Gladstone made arrangements to bring me here because of Muriel. She was very unwell when I arrived. In her head, I mean."

"What does that matter?"

"In the first couple of weeks, she became distressed if anyone spoke to me. Approached me, even. If she went out, I was made to sit and wait in her bedroom until she returned. She'd dress me up and plait my hair like I was a doll. It was strange and suffocating, but eventually it got better. Mr. Gladstone became convinced I was the key to keeping his daughter healthy. To keeping her from hurting herself."

"That's bad," I said.

"It was. Eventually Muriel met Dr. Henneberry though, and the two of them married. The Gladstones could barely tolerate him, but I was pleased. Her mind was occupied with someone else, and for a while, she didn't bother with me at all. Within the year, Martin came along. But Dr. Henneberry had already joined the war effort, and he was away. Would be for some time. Muriel came to rely on me. Even more so, as Martin was a difficult child. I looked after him."

"So? What did that have to do with me?"

"When I learned that I was expecting you, I told Muriel I wanted to find my own place. She was beside herself. Became hysterical at the thought of it."

"What do you mean?"

My mother was quiet for a moment, then she said,

"I can't even describe it. She was frantic. Agitated. There was no way to calm her. Mr. Gladstone had to bar her down in the cellar until she exhausted herself. Muriel thought I was going to wander away and vanish."

"Oh," I said. I blinked. Like her little brother, Alexander, had.

"Of course, Mrs. Gladstone soon found out what had caused Muriel's relapse. I wasn't certain, but I suspect she knew what Mr. Gladstone had done. She brought Dr. Norton to examine me, but that man always made me so nervous, I refused any treatment. You were born downstairs, you know. It was peaceful. You and me in that little room." She sighed. "It was Mr. Gladstone who decided Muriel was too fragile to be without me. And so was Martin. He was only four. Even though Mr. Gladstone did some terrible things, I believe he loved his daughter. And his grandson." She sighed again. "I wasn't allowed to leave."

"Not allowed? People can't stop other people from going out a door. They just can't."

"Oh, they can, Thomas. Mrs. Gladstone explained what would happen if I pushed things. I had no schooling, and she'd make sure I never found another place to work. Celia was already in nursing school, and Mr. Gladstone would see to it that she was expelled from the program. Mr. and Mrs. King, who'd cared so much for Celia, would lose their apartment. Mr. King would get fired from his job at the Gladstone factory. The list went on and on. Mrs. Gladstone wanted you put up for adoption. Offered to a family far, far away. But Mr. Gladstone permitted me to give you to Celia, so I could still see you growing up. We made an arrangement. No one was ever supposed to know. They were a proper family, the Gladstones. That sort of thing didn't happen under their roof."

"How could they do all that?"

"Oh, they could, Thomas. That and much, much more. The Gladstones were generous to a lot of people, a lot of organizations. The police. The hospital. And for some, generosity creates debt. Creates power. I tried to leave more than once. But the threats always came. I knew I could never take care of you. And then, when Mr. and Mrs. Gladstone were gone and Muriel seemed better with Dr. Norton's help, and Martin was a bit older, I thought I could finally go. No one would miss me. But you and Celia were so content. Like you belonged together. I didn't fit into that picture. It was better to leave things as they were."

"No," I said. "No. You could've told us. Aunt Celia would've helped. Mrs. King, too."

"We can't go backward. Mr. Vardy knows everything, and he's been very supportive, encouraging me to stand up for myself now. I'm going to do that. I'm finally going to find out who I am. I've always belonged to someone else. First to my parents. Then to Celia when we came over here. Then to the Gladstones. And now the Henneberrys." She took another deep breath. "I've never just belonged to me."

My mother had always seemed so solid. Like her feet were sunk deep into the ground. And the wind, no matter how hard it blew, couldn't topple her. But that wasn't who she was at all. She'd been pretending all this time.

"I'm sorry, Thomas. You're only eleven, and I've burdened you with all these things. I don't want you to be upset."

I shook my head, even though I couldn't tell if I was upset or not. If I wanted to cry or not. If I wanted to stomp and punch and break something. Or not. It was like a huge boulder was standing in front of me that wasn't there before. About my mother. About my father. I thought about all the questions I'd asked Aunt Celia. And Mrs. King. How often I'd thought my mother didn't want me. Didn't really even like me. And now I knew. She'd loved me when I was born. She probably still did. Even though "very demanding" Martin Gladstone was my father. "It doesn't even matter," Mrs. King had said when I'd bugged her too much. "Whoever he is. You're not him. And he's not you."

It doesn't even matter.

It doesn't even matter.

I rolled onto my side and closed my eyes. I was tired and wanted to sleep, but before I did, I examined the boulder. I touched it with my fingertips. It was warm and solid, and the stone was shot through with anger and fear and loneliness. But it was made of something else, too. Relief.

I could see its edges.

I could see my mother standing close.

I could see a path, a thin path, that wound its way through the grass around it.

CHAPTER TWENTY-NINE

When I woke up, the room was dark. A gray shape hovered near the closed door. A ghost? No, Mrs. Henneberry was in the room. She floated over and placed a tray on the night table.

"I've been watching you nap," she said. Her words were so feathery, part of me wondered if I was still asleep. "You're on the mend, I can tell. Sit up."

I pushed myself back in the bed, and she plumped a pillow behind me. Then she eased the tray onto my lap. Everything looked fuzzy. A glass of milk, maybe. And a wide bowl that was filled with black. I smelled tomatoes. I felt around for a spoon.

"I can't see," I said.

She flicked the switch on the lamp. The black in the bowl turned red. A small pile of soda crackers sat in a dish next to it. The clock ticking on top of a dresser showed it was three o'clock in the morning.

"It's your favorite. I prepared it myself."

It wasn't, but my mouth still watered.

"None of this was your fault, Tom. I'm not displeased at all. I should have let Esther carry the cake down. She's strong, your mother is. She's always been strong, you know. That's why I've kept her so close to me. I couldn't manage on my own. The weight of it."

I couldn't tell if Mrs. Henneberry still meant the cake or something else. She nudged the bucket away with the tips of her fingers, then sat on the edge of the bed.

"You were distressed." Her shaky hand smoothed my hair. "All that hullabaloo. You're just a little boy, Tom. A small child."

I picked up the spoon and stirred the soup, but I couldn't bring it to my mouth.

"Martin can be quite rambunctious. I already know. And this whole thing with Genie. I mean her swimsuit was . . ." She put her finger on her chin and sighed. "Well, it was a bit much, wasn't it, Tom? Very ill fitting. I found it quite distracting."

I stirred the soup some more.

"They hurried right out behind you, did you know that? The Bishops. Genie was especially unsettled."

It hurts. Genie's voice was still inside my head. I didn't help her. I'd wanted to help her. I tried not to cry.

"Now, now, Tom. That's okay. You don't need to tell me what was bothering you. We both have our closets, don't we? And our little skeletons tucked inside."

Her eyebrows were lifted. In the light from the lamp, the blue of her eyes was nearly gone. All that was there were the black middles, and bright white circles around them.

—

I was sweating. Someone had opened the curtains, and even though a breeze came through the window, the room was sweltering.

Through the open window, I could hear an engine idling out front. I slid out of the bed and took a look. Martin was sprinting down the gravel driveway to the waiting car. Directly below the window was a police car, parked very close to the front steps. It had a red gumball light on its roof.

Dr. Henneberry's car was gone. So was the old beater. I left the room and tiptoed downstairs, to the hallway that led to the kitchen.

"I'll need to tell Thomas," my mother was saying.

"Best to face it head on," a man said. "Not sugarcoat."

My skin went cold. That voice belonged to Detective O'Connor.

Chairs were scraping and then he was in the hall-way. My mother coming behind him. She had her fingers knotted up and pushed into the band of her apron.

"And there he is," he said, smacking me gently on the shoulder. "Going to be a writer someday, hey, sport? That's my guess."

My mother's face was pale, and I was certain he'd told her what I'd done. My legs turned stringy, but I still tried to stick out my chin. *So what if she knows? I didn't do anything wrong.*

"I'll leave you to it," Detective O'Connor said. "Pass on my best to Dr. and Mrs. Henneberry."

He let himself out. Slam of the screen door, and he slowed at the rosebush, inhaled the scent of white flowers. Then he was gone.

"Come, Thomas," my mother said. "Into the kitchen. I'll make you some cocoa."

"I'm too hot for cocoa."

"You'll need something sweet in your stomach."

I followed her and climbed onto my stool. Waited while she got down the yellow container, a mug from the cupboard, milk from the fridge, and then heated it in a small saucepan. She gave me the heel from a fresh loaf of bread, and I tore off a piece, dipped it in my mug.

"Did you sleep okay? After what we discussed?"

"Mostly." I didn't tell her that Mrs. Henneberry had brought me soup in the middle of the night.

My mother turned the radio, with the low music, all the way off. She sat on the stool next to mine. "Detective O'Connor came with news."

The lump of chocolaty bread ached as it slid down to my stomach. "Did he tell you I was there? I went to the station in Greenlake?"

"He did."

I pushed the cocoa away. "It was the truth. I know what Dr. Henneberry did."

She pushed the cocoa back toward me. "More, please." I managed a small sip. Then she said, "He did do some things, Thomas. But not what you imagine."

"What, then?"

My mother looked down at her hands. "These past two days. I never thought I'd have to share such things with you. You're only eleven."

"Yeah. But I'm done being a kid." I was done back in June, when my aunt died.

She picked at the ragged skin around her fingernails. "I had a feeling Celia was spending time with him."

"What?" *I was right! That was him in the car. That was his white hand.*

"When she told me about the paperweight, it was just too much of a coincidence. It happened here at home, in his study. He knocked over that brass bird on his desk. He thought he'd broken a bone, so he went to St. Augustine's. And that's where he saw Celia. Of course he'd met her before a time or two, when she'd visited here."

"She never told me she came here."

"I'd asked her not to mention it. I didn't want you to be upset. I never thought this was a suitable place for you to be."

"Then why didn't you say anything?" I said. "About him? Why'd you act like you didn't know?"

"My sister had to make her own decisions, Thomas. Celia was headstrong, ever since we were children. If I'd said a word, it would have pushed her further the wrong way. I figured she'd lose interest in him in a week or two."

"But that never happened."

"And I didn't know the whole story."

I stared at my mother. "What whole story?"

"That Dr. Henneberry had gambling debts. Serious ones. He told me about it that night the power went out."

"So what?"

"Well, he found out about you, for one thing. When he went to the bank. He learned that Mr. Gladstone had set up a monthly payment for a child with the last name Ware. I'm sure it didn't take long to put two and two together."

"I don't get it."

"A savings account. Dr. Henneberry thought Celia could access it. I suspect that was why he took up with her. There's quite a sum of money there now and he wanted it. He pressured me to close the account, or sign it over to him. He was furious when I explained that the documentation was very clear, that no one could touch that account. Just you. When you're older."

"You should've warned her. Warned her what was going to happen."

"Thomas, enough. He may not be a good husband to Mrs. Henneberry, but he didn't hurt Celia."

"He did. I just know it."

My mother rubbed her eyes. "No. He hasn't murdered a woman. Let alone four. That's why the detective was here." My mother reached into the neck of her uniform and took out a tissue. She blew her nose. "Drink your cocoa," she said. "And finish the bread."

She waited while I did as I was told. It was hard getting it down.

"What did he tell you?" I said.

Her mouth opened. Then closed. Then opened again. "That man, Thomas. That man who was always on the front step of your apartment building."

"Mr. Pober?"

"It was him."

"No," I said. "It couldn't be. He said she got mixed up with the wrong sort. Aunt Celia didn't even like him. He'd seen Dr.—" Then I remembered what else he'd said. *Thought she was too good, though. A gal too good for regular men.* He'd sounded angry. Like he was jealous, almost.

"She didn't like him, no. That didn't matter. He followed her on the bus. She probably never even heeded him. I'm guessing she was planning to meet Dr. Henneberry, as she wasn't on duty that night. But she was gone when he got there."

"That's wrong," I whispered.

"He died some days ago. Mrs. King noticed he wasn't on the front step. She thought he might've been sick. Or had fallen. When the superintendent went to check on him, he'd been gone for a while."

"Gone where?"

"Gone, Thomas. Dead."

"Oh," I said.

My mother folded over the tissue and pushed it back inside the front of her uniform. "The police came, of course. And when they found what they did, they called Detective O'Connor."

"What did they find?"

"Ladies' things. A yellow scarf that belonged to Celia. Some panties and such. And writings."

"What do you mean, writings?"

She sighed and rubbed her eyes again. "Stories, sort of. Of what he'd planned. Or done. Or wanted to remember. I don't know exactly. Enough that the police are confident he was the man hurting those women in Greenlake."

It was all too much to take in. Mr. Pober was the Greenlake Predator? I'd made a bad mistake about Dr. Henneberry. But I didn't feel any better. Maybe I even felt worse. I slid off my stool. When I got to the door, I said, "I'm glad Mr. Pober's gone. I hope it hurt when he died. I hope it hurt really, really bad."

My mother stood up. Her eyes were pink, and her lips were tight. With the side of her hand, she smoothed away breadcrumbs that had fallen onto the counter-top. "I can't say my mind's any different, Thomas. I hope it hurt bad, too."

Greenlake Chronicle
March 24, 1959

LOCAL DOCTOR ACCUSED
OF SHODDY PRACTICES

Dr. Arnold Eugene Norton of Greenlake has been called before the Medical Board. He was reported for improper prescribing of medication causing deliberate harm to multiple patients, as well as accepting inflated payment for services rendered. Sources indicate that he targeted the wealthy families of Upper Washbourne. If these accusations are proven, Dr. Norton could lose his medical license and his medical practice. Notably, Dr. Norton was the personal physician to murder victim Muriel Henneberry, and also a key witness for the prosecution in the trial against 11-year-old Thomas Leon Ware. When asked for comment, Prosecutor Clay Fibbs stated, "While the allegations against Dr. Norton are disturbing, they in no way affect his credibility in this case."

CHAPTER THIRTY

"It's a very important day, Tom!" Mrs. Henneberry's yelling was so loud and shrill, it echoed all the way down the hallway and into the kitchen.

"You'd better go see," my mother said. "She sounds delighted about something."

After I broke another link off my paper chain, I went up to her bedroom. I stood outside her open door and waited. My head still felt sore and empty from everything that had happened over the past two days. Like I'd fallen from the swing set at school and banged my head on the ground. After my mother had told me about Mr. Pober, I went to see George. I moved his bowl down onto the floor and I lay next to him. I watched him going around and around in his bowl, his orange fins flicking. I cried for a while about what I'd learned but seeing him made me feel better. Doing the same thing. He never went any faster, but he never went any slower either. And he was content enough with that.

"Come closer, darling," she said when she saw me standing there. "Now, I don't bite. Not you, especially!"

I went into her room. She was wearing shoes and

stockings, but also a long robe, even though it was getting close to dinnertime. Three boxes were opened up and three different black hats were sitting on her bedspread. She was taking turns trying them on and gazing at her reflection in a tall mirror with carved wood legs.

"What do you think?" See-through black lace covered part of her face. Her breath hitched and she sniffed. Dabbed the corners of her eyes. Then her face was pleasant again. "Tom, dear? Will this do?"

"It's pretty," I said. I took another couple of steps. Her calendar book was wide open on her writing desk. Her notes were written in black ink, but there was the tiniest red x scratched on today's date.

"Such difficult choices." She paced in front of the mirror. Her heels slipped on the carpet and she was more wobbly than usual. "I don't know if it says the right thing." Then she ripped the hat off and flung it across the room. "No, this won't do. It won't do at all. It has to be perfect!"

I held my hands together behind my back. Her window was open. I could hear Mr. Vardy singing outside.

"I said sit down, Tom." She stretched her neck at me. Her eyes were fuzzy again. "Aren't you paying attention to me?"

"Sorry." I mustn't have been listening.

I hurried to the chair by the window. I stared through the glass, at the front lawn and the long driveway. Mr. Vardy was near the road, standing on top of a small ladder. He was using pointy clippers to give the hedge a flat top. I wished I was out there helping him.

"What could possibly be taking so long?" She tugged open the bottom drawer of her night table and pulled out the bottle Dr. Norton had given her. With her fingers, she pinched the lid and twisted, but the cap wouldn't come off. "How is this so difficult?" She twisted again. "I can't do it. I can't do it!" She threw in into my lap. "Open it, Tom. At once! I can't wait a second longer."

I clutched it, but the lid was stuck tight.

"Oh, for god's sakes. For god's sakes, Tom! You're useless! Just give it to me." She snatched it and dropped it on the carpet. Then she slammed the heel of her shoe on it.

The bottle splintered. Mrs. Henneberry got down on her knees and flicked through the pieces of brown glass with her finger. She picked out two white pills, brushed them off, and put them in her mouth. As she sat back on her heels, her robe fell open. Her chest was covered in bright red blotches. Hives, maybe. Like Wally got when he had to answer a question in class.

"My hands are clammy," she said, laughing a little. "I haven't had clammy hands since Raymond and I were courting." She turned and swiped them on her bedspread. "How absurd is that? Tom? Why are you gawking out the window like that?"

"Maybe you're worried?" My hands got sticky when I was scared.

"Worried? Oh, you are such a scamp." She puffed out air and laughed. "Not in the least. Why would I be worried?"

Mr. Vardy stepped off the ladder and shifted it to the left. He climbed up again, and his clippers went snip-snip-snip. If he had been my father, everything would have been different. I'd have grown up with him and my mother. My aunt would have met someone nice a long time ago. I might even have had a cousin. We'd probably be best friends. Or second best, because Wally would still be number one.

"Mrs. Bishop called me this afternoon, Tom. Did I tell you that already?"

Maybe to tell on Martin. Martin the Pig.

Mrs. Henneberry stood up and straightened her robe. "They're leaving on some dreary holiday, but she wanted to tell me what a *stupendous* time she'd had at the party. What a *stupendous* time Genie had. She actually used that silly word."

"Oh," I said. *Oh.*

"Never even mentioned the fuss, she didn't. Or the cake. So we're both in the clear." She tapped the tip of my nose. "She told me Genie is enthralled with Martin."

I swung my legs back and forth beneath the chair. "Does that mean she's scared?"

"Oh dear, Tom. You are on a funny roll today." She laughed again, and then went to her bed and sat down. "But I'm not quite sure about it all, really. He's getting to be quite skilled at rowing. Even his instructor says so. He shouldn't be, you know, frenzied by someone like her." Her words were coming out slower and slower. "They are dear people, mind you. Dear, dear people. I didn't want to upset the apple cart at the onset, but I just don't think she's the right fit. Genie, I mean. Not Mrs. Bishop." She grabbed the fabric on her chest and giggled. "Such a shocking thing to imagine." Then she took a deep breath and sighed. "I do feel quite relaxed now. So much more like myself."

With his arm, Mr. Vardy was brushing away the leaves and twigs he'd clipped. When I closed my eyes, I could practically feel my arm going over the top of the hedge. The sharp bits sticking out, scratching my skin. I was whistling.

"Tom?"

"Huh?"

"Pardon me, Tom. Oh, we are slow to catch on, aren't we? But that's not your fault, dear. Considering your background."

"Sorry," I whispered again.

"I said I'm glad you're here with me. You'll stay when they arrive."

"When who arrives?"

"The police, of course."

"Detective O'Connor's coming back?" My hands were suddenly sweaty, too.

"Oh, I don't know who they'll send. It doesn't matter. But I will be devastated, Tom. You can be sure of that. Genuinely devastated. Do you know what that's like?"

I did. When they knocked on my door and I saw Mrs. King with her face so full of pain, it was then that

I understood that word. In a flash, everything turned into steam. Rainwater on hot pavement.

She lay back on the bed. Her elbow bent over her eyes. "You'll have to help me find a seat. My knees should undoubtedly go weak, but not quite to the point of collapse. Can you remember to do that?"

"I will," I said. "I'll help you find a seat."

"Of course I'll have to ask what happened. I'll have to inquire. That would be the natural thing to do, right?"

Mr. Vardy shifted the ladder again and then he was clip-clip-clipping a fresh spot.

"Oh dear." She gathered the front of her robe in her fist. "Oh dear. I can't believe it. I simply can't believe it." Her head rolled around on her neck. "Do I sound like I've been taken aback by the news, Tom? Really alarmed by it?"

"Yes," I said, but that was a lie. She did not sound alarmed. More like a small breeze caught behind a heavy curtain.

"You can help me sit down." Then her mouth opened and out came a slow, sleepy laughter. The one that didn't make any sound. "Foolish me. I'm already sitting down."

Mr. Vardy took a red handkerchief out of the back pocket of his trousers. He patted his neck and his forehead. Then my mother was walking toward him with a tall tumbler in her hand. Iced tea, I guessed. He drank it down and gave her back the empty glass. They spoke for a moment or two, and my mother covered her mouth to hide her smile. She put her hand on her cheek. He said something else, and she wiped her eyes and nodded. As she was walking back to the house, she turned her head and looked back at him. Twice. I liked seeing her do that. Her Mr. Green Thumb.

Mrs. Henneberry sighed. "The afternoon is passing so slowly. Tom? Tell me something. Tell me what you want to be when you grow up."

"I don't know, ma'am."

"If you could be anything in the world. Plumbers are never short of work. Or a handyman. You could drive a taxicab in Greenlake. You're personable enough, and you might meet the most interesting people. Or you could even work at the movies. Just think—all the popcorn you've ever wanted."

I closed my eyes for a second. What had Aunt Celia always said to me? *If you work hard, you can be a scientist, or a race car driver, or someone that designs bridges or skyscrapers. But do you know what's most important when you grow up, Tommie?* I did. I remembered.

"I'd like to be a good man, Mrs. Henneberry. More than anything. That's what I want to be."

She sobbed loudly. She was sitting up again, her feet dangling over the side of the bed. Her shoes had fallen off and her robe had fallen open even wider, and I could see the clip at the top of her pantyhose. She dropped her face into her hands. I thought she was crying, but when she lifted her head, her eyes were dry.

"Oh, Tom. You are such a sweet, sweet child. You know why? Because you've suffered. You've surely suffered. Tell me how you've suffered, darling. Tell me what's happened to you. Everything. Before you came here to live with me."

"I don't know," I said. "I'm not sure what to—"

"Go on."

"I liked living in Lower Washbourne."

"Ugh. How utterly depressing, dear. No wonder!"

I shifted in the chair. "The air used to smell like soap and wet sheets. And you could always hear a baby crying somewhere. Or someone hollering out the window about some news. And there were cats that nobody owned that would follow you home if you let them. Sometimes me and Wally would play hopscotch even though it was just for girls."

Mrs. Henneberry gave her head a quick shake. "Well you won't find those sorts of diversions here, Tom. Chalk all over the streets? And strays? Dear god."

"I didn't mind. I—"

"That's enough, Tom. You—" She was pacing again and breathing faster. Her face was greasy. "You do like to chatter on, don't you? Puts me on edge, it does. On the very edge! I thought I was calm, but, but now there's this strange fluttering in my chest. Do you know what that is? I can't call Dr. Norton." Her fingers were curled, and she clicked her nails together. "Get me another, Tom. Please, dear. Just watch the glass. Last thing I need is to ingest a shard. Oh, just break it in half. No, don't. The whole one. I'm just so terribly unsettled."

I crouched down near the mess on the carpet. I was careful and took out a pill and brought it to her. She crushed it with her teeth and lay down again.

"I do feel unwell, Tom," she said, lifting her head. "Why are you not in your chair? I told you to sit down. Didn't I tell you that? Why are you giving me such a vicious headache? Today of all days?"

I went back to the chair by the window and tried to stay still. Maybe my mother would come find me. Maybe Mr. Vardy would glance up from his work and wave me down to him, so I could help like I wanted to.

Mrs. Henneberry was groaning on the bed. "Oh, Tom. This fluttering will not go away. I do believe it's getting worse."

I touched the window with my fingertips. I wished hard for something to happen, but my mother never called me. Mr. Vardy didn't look up.

"Are there clouds coming in?"

"There are, Mrs. Henneberry. Outside is going gray."

"I knew it. I can feel it in my head. It's gone all cottony. And what is that monstrous sound?"

"Sound?"

"Snipping. Something snipping. Am I dreaming that, Tom?"

"No," I said. "Mr. Vardy is fixing your hedge."

She huffed. "That man is always up to something. This or that. It needles me so much to hear him working."

The clock ticked and ticked. I tried to count the seconds, but I kept losing my place. A fly crawled over the outside of the window screen. I looked it in the eyes, but then it flew away. Each time Mrs. Henneberry talked, her words were more and more like mud. "Do you ever feel," she mumbled, "like your hands aren't quite right? There should be mittens or gloves or claws or something, Tom, at the ends of your wrists. Soft, smooth shells." Then she was up again and weaving over to the mirror. From her pocket she removed a little gold tube and she got close to her reflection, applied red lipstick. She gazed at herself. "Of course you can come in, Officer. What? Something happened to my husband?" She pulled her eyebrows together. "That simply can't be. Who'd want to hurt Raymond?" Then she put the back of her hand over her mouth. Lowered her head.

When she looked up again, her eyes were even glassier, her lipstick smeared.

"Tom!" she hissed. "Stop slouching like that. Sit tall, young man."

My throat gulped by itself. I straightened my back.

Then gravel crunched. Dr. Henneberry's car was coming up the driveway. He rolled past Mr. Vardy, and when Mr. Vardy lifted his clippers in the air, he toot-tooted the horn.

"He's home," I said. Finally. Mrs. Henneberry would stop worrying.

"Pardon me?"

"Dr. Henneberry's home. I see his car."

Her face changed in an instant. Brighter. She wiped the corners of her mouth. "James is driving it? Mr. Fulsome?"

I squinted. "No. Dr. Henneberry is."

"What?" The color in her cheeks went down to her neck. Tons of those red blotches now, all joining up, but her face was white as a sheet.

"Do you want me to help you sit now?"

She didn't answer me. She limped over to the window. She'd only put one shoe back on. She peered down. Dr. Henneberry was winding a crank, and the roof of his car was rising up and over. "No. It's not supposed—" She put both hands on the glass and then her fingernails scraped as her hands tightened.

Downstairs, the front door slammed. Dr. Henneberry was inside now, and his booming voice reached her room. "Esther? A gin and sin, could you? I'll be in the study."

"Noooo," Mrs. Henneberry said again. "Is it true, Tom? Tom! I'm talking to you!"

"Esther!" Dr. Henneberry called out again. The muscles in my back got tight. "It's been a day! My drink?"

"I can see it in your slitty eyes, Tom. You're judging me. You are." She stepped closer, and then she squealed. When she raised her foot, a sliver of glass stuck out of the bottom of it. Blood was spreading over her stocking.

She hobbled back on one foot until she could lean on the bed. "Get it out," she cried. "Pick it out."

I leapt off my chair and knelt down in front of her.

With my fingernail, I scraped out the glass. It dropped onto the carpet.

"You've made such a mess of things, Tom. You've ruined everything." Her mouth was in a wet snarl.

I didn't know my heart could beat so fast without exploding. I backed away, and she limped toward me. Each time she took a step, her foot left a dark red stain on the carpet.

"After you insinuated yourself into my life. Did I ask for you?"

I shook my head.

"Who do you think you are?"

"Nobody."

"You think you know what's happened to me? You think you should have an opinion?"

"No," I whispered.

"You're an insolent little boy."

Then she brought her hand back and struck my cheek.

The pain was a pop of white behind my eyes. I couldn't help it, I started to cry.

Then she slapped me again. I curled my arms over my head.

"You brazen child."

I squatted down on the carpet. She kept hitting me. She got down on her knees and she hit my back and my head and my shoulders. I thought I would be pounded into that thick carpet. Pounded until I disappeared.

"Esther!" she screamed. "Esther! Where are you? I need you here now!"

It took my mother forever to reach the room. I opened my eyes and looked up at her. She looked down at me and then she looked at Mrs. Henneberry. Mrs. Henneberry's hands were in fists close to my back. Her lipstick made lines across her cheek, and her hair was in tangles.

"What's happened? What's happened?"

"That thing, that's what. Look at him! Look at his face! Have you ever seen anything so smug? I was careful with my plans."

"What plans, Mrs. Henneberry?"

"The man. Living in the trailer. We had an understanding, and now everything is ruined. Because of your son."

My mother got down beside me and helped me to my feet. "I don't—"

"He'll have to be rehomed, Esther, do you hear me? Dr. Henneberry was correct. I should have heeded my husband's caution. But no. I thought I knew better."

"We have a place, Mrs. Henneberry. Mr. Vardy just let me know. I've only got to sign the papers."

"I've been very tolerant, Esther. Indulgent, even, as you very well know. But I won't bear it a second longer. Not under my own roof."

My mother had her lips pulled in over her teeth. Her chest was moving up and down. "Mrs. Henne—"

"I'm going to keep you, though. I hope that's very clear. I've changed my mind about your leaving. But I don't want him anymore. I don't want him in my sight."

"I ca—"

Mrs. Henneberry put her hands up. "Don't answer me back, Esther. Not another word."

My mother kept her hand on my shoulder as we hurried along the hallway, down the stairs, through the rest of the house, and into the kitchen. She didn't let go of me until we were in our bedroom with the door closed.

"What on earth, Thomas?"

I was sobbing so hard, I could barely get the words out. "Dr. Henneberry."

"I don't understand. What happened with Dr. Henneberry?"

"She didn't want him coming home."

EXCERPT

Testimony of Miss Esther Ware, Defendant's Mother
Direct Examination by Defense Counsel William Evans

Q. I'd like to go back to that day. Do you remember
   what you were doing?

A. Yes, I do, Mr. Evans. I was washing windows. I was on
   the upper floor, in a corner bedroom.

Q. What caused you to look outside, ma'am?

A. I heard an automobile arriving. Then a door slammed.
   At first I wondered if Mr. Fulsome had come back. Or
   if Dr. Norton was early. I checked to see. That's when
   I saw a car sitting there. And a man.

Q. Could you identify the type of car, Miss Ware?

A. I don't know too much about cars, sorry. Black and
   shiny. The front was rounded a little, maybe?

Q. What about the man? Could you describe him?

A. When he got out, I could see he was tall. I would say
   slim, too. He was wearing a beige coat and a hat.

Q. What sort of hat?

A. Brown. Maybe a dark tan. I don't know much about
   men's fashions either.

Q. Did you see his face?

A. No, sir. I couldn't see who he was.

Q. But you had a good view of the grounds from
   upstairs.

A. Yes, sir.

Q. What did the man do after he exited his car?

A. He cut across the grass at the side of the house. Toward the pool. Then he— I saw him reaching for something on the little table where I'd put the lemonade. It happened in seconds, Mr. Evans. He shot them. He killed the three of them.

Q. **You witnessed this man using Dr. Henneberry's gun to commit murder.**

A. I did.

Q. **And what happened after that?**

A. The man turned around and he was leaving.

Q. **Did he take the gun, Miss Ware?**

A. I think so. It was hard to see, but that's the only explanation. I was panicked, as you can imagine. I rushed outside as fast as I could. I had to get to Thomas. I needed to make sure he was safe.

Q. **Was he?**

A. Yes. He wasn't injured. He wasn't hurt. Of course, he was in shock, but he was okay.

CHAPTER THIRTY-ONE

A mug of milk sat on the night table. It smelled sour. Since I'd woken up, I'd been wandering around the bedroom I shared with my mother, wondering what I should do. Outside the sun was shining, but I couldn't tell what time it was. My head was groggy, but my back wasn't sore. When Mrs. Henneberry hit me, it hadn't been hard enough to bruise me. Though I could not forget the surprise of it. How she was wailing at me while staring at nothing.

The night before, my mother had asked me a bunch of questions. Then she went and found Mr. Vardy, and he asked me even more questions. It was weird seeing him standing there inside our small room. He was much taller when he was indoors. But I didn't mind. In fact, having him and my mother standing side by side in front of me made my heart calm down. As though together, they could be a wall. Not to hold me in, like those my mother had inside her head, but to keep things out. A good wall.

I told them everything I could. I told them how much I hated rubbing Mrs. Henneberry's feet. I told them how she was always eating those white pills. I told them that we'd seen Dr. Henneberry outside the diner and there were no possums in the road. I told them how much it hurt when I went to Dr. Henneberry's clinic, and the disgusting things he'd said about Aunt Celia. I told them about the naked magazines under Martin's mattress and how he'd climbed up in a tree and threw stuff down at Mrs. Grimshaw. I told them how he was being rotten to Genie at the beach. And what he did in the pool house. How Martin had made a bet with Skip, and Skip had watched through the crack.

I didn't say anything about Dr. Henneberry pushing my mother against the folding table. Or Martin spying through the window while she was in the bathroom. I didn't want Mr. Vardy to hear those parts.

My mother sat on the bed and put her arm around me. "I thought you were managing," she said. "I didn't know things were like this."

Mr. Vardy had his hands on his hips. The room was going gray, but no one turned on a light. "I can take him, Esther."

"Take him?"

"He'll come to my place. That's what I'm going to do."

"You wouldn't mind?"

"Not at all. There's not much space, but then, he's not very big, now, is he?"

"If it's no trouble." My mother rubbed her hands together. "That might be best. Muriel will calm down in a couple of weeks and I'm sure she won't make an issue when I leave."

As I thought about that conversation, my shoulders relaxed. I'd take my paper chain with me. It'd be easy to pack up as it was now quite short.

I paced some more. Bed to cot to sink to dresser to bed to cot to sink to dresser. I paused to sprinkle some food in George's bowl. He darted up to the top and snapped at the flakes. His tail wavered, and I wanted to believe he was grateful.

I fixed the blanket on the cot and read some comics. I went through every page and I couldn't find a single face that Martin hadn't scratched away. A couple of times, Martin had drawn hairy animals sitting on the ladies' shoulders. Reaching down with their claws. It was hard to tell what they were. Mrs. Pinsent would say he'd made a poor effort.

I got dressed and then decided to gather up my things. I pulled my aunt's blue suitcase out from beneath my mother's bed. From the bottom drawer, I removed my pants and shirts and put them neatly inside along with my comb and George's container of food. When everything was all packed, I finally creaked open the door and tiptoed into the laundry room. My mother was in the kitchen. She grunted, and then a sound like she was slapping skin.

She flinched when I came to the doorway. "You startled me, Thomas." She was hunched over a bowl on the counter and her hands were covered in flour. Music was playing quietly on the radio in the corner. "You slept a long time."

"I wasn't sleeping. I was getting ready."

"I know you're uneasy, but we'll figure everything out. Mr. Vardy will be back around dinnertime to take you. Stay close by me until then, okay?"

I nodded. I opened a loop of my paper chain. It was a sketch of a frog sitting on a person's palm. Wally said his father told him they won't give us warts, so it was fine to touch them. Gently, I tugged off the remaining loops from under the cupboard. I would put that in my suitcase, too.

"I don't want you worrying anymore about Martin or Dr. Henneberry or Mrs. Henneberry. Do you understand?"

"Okay," I said.

She worked the dough in the bowl. "Things changed so slowly. So very slowly. How could I not see?"

I think she was talking to herself. Or I would have told her that things didn't change slowly. They'd changed very, very fast. "Like swimming in a soup," I said instead. Aunt Celia used to say that when the whole world seemed murky and difficult to understand.

She smiled at me. "Yes. Like swimming in a soup."

Tapping, then, at the side door. My mother sighed and wiped her hands in a cup towel. When she went to check, I peeked out into the hallway.

"Mrs. Grimshaw. How can I help you?"

"Is Ruth home?"

"Ruth? You mean Mrs. Gladstone? No, she's—"

"I do need to talk to her. It's time she knew what was going on."

"What? What's happened?"

"In the hollow in the woods."

"Um. I can let Mrs. Henneberry—"

"You'd think he'd leave me alone," she said. She pushed past my mother and came into the hallway. "But the birds. They don't want the little houses that boy"—she pointed her finger at me—"built."

"But—"

"Martin Gladstone. He's done this. I can't tell Abel. Oh, I can't tell Abel. He'll be so distraught."

She was only wearing white panties and a white bra. Her legs were a crisscross of blue veins, and a thick fold of her stomach hung over her underwear. I knew right away which Mrs. Grimshaw she was. The lost Mrs. Grimshaw. The other one, who could talk and remember and laugh, was someplace else.

"Oh dear," my mother said. "Just a moment. I'll find you a shirt to cover yourself."

My mother rushed past me. I could hear her sorting things in the laundry room, cupboards opening and closing, the crunch of a basket.

"You know about the birds?" Mrs. Grimshaw said. Her eyes narrowed. Sunlight came through the screen and turned her body into a round shadow on the hallway floor. "Come here, young man."

I took a step.

"What's your name?"

"Thomas."

"Oh yes. Thomas. That's a good name." She pulled the skin down on her cheek. "They pecked at me. Do you see? When I was out looking for Abel. I tried to fight them off, but they kept swooping down." Two tiny purple bruises marked her face and another one marked her arm. She touched a scrape on her leg. Her fingernails were dry and yellow. "That man, you see, is trying to torment me."

"That's not good" was all I could say. I wanted to tell her the truth, but how could I explain? This Mrs. Grimshaw didn't even know Martin Henneberry existed.

"Have you seen Abel? My husband? He's been gone for so long." She pushed her finger into a cut on her neck. "I'm going to find him. I'm going to find my husband today."

My mother was back in the hallway. She was holding a faded nightdress in her hands. "Nothing else was loose enough," she said. "Mrs. Henneberry's so slight."

We turned back to the door, but Mrs. Grimshaw was already gone.

"Who's going to fix things?" I said to my mother.

"I don't know, Thomas."

"Who's going to punish Martin?"

"I don't know."

"Mr. Vardy?"

"Mr. Vardy has a job here. Like me. It's complicated."

"So he won't do anything?"

My mother sighed again. "I don't know what will happen. I don't want to say for sure."

But she was saying a whole lot. Nothing was going to happen to Martin Henneberry. Mr. Vardy would take me to stay with him until my paper chain went down to zero links. Eventually my mother and I would move into our new place. She'd then travel every day to the Henneberrys' on the bus with those other ladies in uniforms. Martin would still climb the trees and still watch my mother. Mrs. Henneberry would still be acting like a lunatic and Dr. Henneberry would do whatever he wanted, even if it hurt other people.

"Try not to get undone about it. We've got everything all sorted for you and—"

But I didn't hear anything else she said. Martin's mop of yellowish hair was bobbing past the window over the kitchen sink. Sunlight snagged in the ends of it, making his head appear golden.

"Are you paying attention, Thomas? Mr. Vardy—"

I went into the hallway and out through the screen door. I stood in the patch of dirt near the white roses. That rusted matchbox car was stuck in the ground again. The roof crushed into the seats.

Martin was already halfway down the sloping lawn. His hands were in his pockets and his elbows flapped in and out. He was heading toward the woods. Probably to play his sick game.

No one else was going to set him straight. I'd have to be the one to teach him a lesson. Like I'd done with those boys from school picking on Wally. Punched the biggest one right in the stomach and knocked the wind out of him. That stopped them. I'd do the same to Martin. Even if he was five years older than me and a whole lot stronger.

As I passed the pool, I heard a car pull into the driveway. I turned around and saw Dr. Henneberry climbing out of his mint-green car. The roof was down. He dashed around the front and then opened the passenger door for Mrs. Henneberry. She was wearing her huge sunglasses and had a scarf over her hair. Slipped over her arm was a pile of shopping bags. Dr. Henneberry pushed his face into her neck, and Mrs. Henneberry's head went back and she shrieked with joy.

A light blue car drove in behind them and parked beside the convertible. It was Mr. Fulsome.

"By the pool, Jimmy!" Dr. Henneberry hollered. He waved his hand. "We'll be there in two shakes."

Dr. and Mrs. Henneberry went inside the house. As Mr. Fulsome was wandering over the lawn toward the pool, I slipped into the woods. I could hear Martin's whistling up ahead. Twigs cracked and insects buzzed. On a low branch, a crow bent forward and cawed and cawed like its whole body was forcing the noise from its beak.

Even though he didn't slow down, Martin surely knew I was behind him. I wasn't trying to be quiet. Leaves crunched under my shoes. I tripped over a knobby root, and when my hands and knees smacked the path, I yelped. But he didn't turn around. He kept walking and walking, swinging his arms. Then he slowed next to those two trees, the ones he and I had climbed only weeks ago.

I stopped, too, and watched him. He didn't leap to catch the lowest branch and then pull himself up. He just leaned his back against one of the trunks and didn't budge. He kept chewing the sides of his fingers and spitting on the ground. When there was nothing left to bite, he folded his arms across his chest and starting whistling again. Martin seemed in a very good mood.

And then, in an instant, she was teetering down the path. One foot after the other, inching closer and closer.

"Abel?" she whispered.

Martin peeled his back off the tree and stood right in front of her. I held my breath and waited for my legs to do what my brain was telling them to do. *Hurry. Get over there fast. Hit him. Go and shove him down.* My muscles twitched. I repeated the words, but my muscles weren't following instructions. Martin was so much older. Martin was so much taller. Martin was so much scarier.

Mrs. Grimshaw kept scuffing along as though Martin wasn't there. She was still only wearing those white panties and white bra. She had on a pair of black shoes with thick heels. Her gray hair stuck up like a fan on the back of her head.

"Abel?" she called. "Abel? You need to come home right now."

Martin blocked her way. When she came upon him, she stopped and shook her head, like she'd found a tree in the wrong place. He widened his legs and bumped her backward.

"I'm right here," he said. "In front of you."

But her neck remained bent. She didn't lift her eyes.

"Why can't you see me?"

She wiped a hand across her forehead. "Abel? Where are you?"

"You're in Martin's Woods, you know. This is my hollow. You don't belong here."

Mrs. Grimshaw tugged at her hair. "The birds."

"There's no goddamned birds, you crazy old coot."

She tried to get around him. She stepped off the path and her feet skidded on the damp moss. Martin scooted sideways and got in front of her again.

"Too many birds," she said. "Nasty things." Her hands were up around her head.

"You haven't got a clue." He spat on the ground near her feet. "You're insane, you know that?"

"Abel will shoot them. Abel?"

"Yep. Your dead husband." Martin tapped his silver watch. "Expecting him any minute."

As he laughed out loud, her face changed. Her features twisted. He was still smiling, but at the same time he looked angrier than I'd ever seen him before. My head kept saying, *Go, go, go!*, but my legs would not move.

"Everyone knows you're a whore. Even my mother says it. Got that house from lying flat on your back. Making up lies about my grandfather. I can't wait until they lock you up. A home for wackos."

"Abel? I need you, Abel!"

She scuffed again, and Martin's stomach struck out, pushing her. "Look at me! I'm right here!"

Her hands chopped at the air and he knocked her again, harder this time. She fell down on her side. She cried out, lying on the ground. Her arms and legs moved, and her stomach shook, and her head was stuck between the roots of a tree. Martin stood over her, staring down at her.

And then, and then, and then he was on top of her. Squishing his body into hers, his back going left to right. His hands were reaching, grabbing under him, and her white panties were down at her ankles. She made choking sounds like a hand was covering her mouth. Her knees were bent, and the heels of her shoes dug into the ground.

Martin. I tried to yell it.

Martin. I tried to go over.

Martin! I tried to stop him.

But I couldn't move a single muscle.

His naked rear end was in the air. Poking, poking. How many times? Nine. I don't remember counting, but I knew the exact number. It was over in seconds and it also went on forever. I could not breathe. I could not look away. I could not even close my eyes. Mrs. Grimshaw scratched at him, and Martin cursed but did not slow down.

He brought his head down to his chest and his rear end and his shoulders tightened. A quiver went through him. I saw it and I heard it.

And then he sprung up from the ground and landed on his feet. He reached down and pulled his shorts up over his hips. He did up the buttons and brushed away some dried leaves sticking to the front of his T-shirt. Then he wiped his hand across his mouth. When he stepped back onto the path, he shook his arms and legs, and with his hands, he tugged his head to one side like he was stretching. Or cracking the joints in his spine.

Once his clothes were arranged, he turned to stare straight at me. He knew I'd been standing there all along. He grinned. And I did nothing. My time to move ahead, to fly at him, to pummel him with my fists, to chop him at the knee, had come and gone. I didn't help Mrs. Grimshaw. With my silence, with my stillness, I'd become a part of the attack.

Then Martin was whistling again. As though nothing at all had happened. He wandered away, taking a different path.

Mrs. Grimshaw groaned and rolled onto her hip. She got to her feet. Wavering back and forth, she gripped her knees. With one thick hand against the bark of a tree, she pulled her panties up her legs. The elastic made a snap. She dragged her feet as she went away. Dirt stuck to her back. Leaves and sticks clung to her messed-up hair and on the bare skin of her shoulders. She left her shoes behind.

EXCERPT

Testimony of Miss Esther Ware, Defendant's Mother

Cross-Examination by Prosecutor Clay Fibbs

Q. Miss Ware, I know this is difficult. Being up there, talking about your son.

A. It's not easy, no.

Q. Unfortunately, I have some serious issues with your testimony.

A. I told the truth, sir. Same as Thomas told the truth.

Q. The man was wearing a beige coat. In the summer heat?

A. Yes. I know it's strange. But that's what we both saw.

Q. You witnessed all this from where? The kitchen?

A. No, sir. As I told Mr. Evans, I was upstairs, in a corner bedroom. I was looking out through the windows.

Q. Understood. So, when this man arrives, dressed for a crisp fall day, does Dr. Henneberry get up to greet him?

A. No, sir. I never noticed that.

Q. What about Mrs. Henneberry. Did she put her lemonade down?

A. I don't know.

Q. Let me answer it for you. No one budged an inch. Don't you find that odd?

Defense Counsel: Objection, Your Honor. Is Mr. Fibbs testifying?

The Court: Move on, Mr. Fibbs.

Q. Another sticky point, Miss Ware. This unknown individual, clearly with intent to harm, doesn't bring a gun himself? But just happens to get lucky, exceedingly lucky, finding Dr. Henneberry's gun sitting next to some refreshments? And then, by golly, he's able to get his hands on that gun with no struggle whatsoever?

Defense Counsel: Again, Your Honor?

The Court: Mr. Fibbs.

Q. Okay. Let's talk a little about your relationship with your son. You gave Thomas up as a baby, is that correct?

A. I did.

Q. Did you feel some sense of guilt over abandoning him?

A. I made a mistake. I—

Q. So you felt guilty that you were not in your son's life.

A. I told you, Mr. Fibbs, I'm telling the—

Q. And now you're trying to protect him.

Defense Counsel: Objection, Your Honor. He's badgering her.

The Court: I'm not going to warn you again, Mr. Fibbs. Ask your questions.

Q. Of course, Your Honor. Miss Ware, what were you using to clean the windows?

A. The windows? Rags. Water and vinegar in a bottle. Old newsprint.

Q. Right. Now, you said you were near some windows on the upper level. The side closer to the pool. And you had a great view?

A. Yes. I had the bottle in my hand and—

Q. Well, maybe you'll explain for the court why police discovered your cleaning supplies in Mrs. Henneberry's room? On the very opposite side of the house?

A. I don't—

Q. You're not able to see through walls and wood and stone, now, are you, Miss Ware?

A. I was—I went—

Q. Miss Ware? We can't hear you.

A. I'm sorry. I'm so sorry.

Q. You're admitting you lied, Miss Ware. There was no black car. No man in a coat and hat.

A. Thomas told me, and I was, I tried—

Q. You tried to deceive the court.

A. I'm sorry. I want to help him. Thomas is my son.

Q. The court understands, Miss Ware. You wanted to be a good mother. You were figuring out what that was.

CHAPTER THIRTY-TWO

I don't know how I got out of the woods. I was there, then I wasn't there. All at once, soft grass was beneath my feet. My forehead was aching. I must have banged it against a tree. My heart was missing from behind my ribs, and all that was left was skin and hair and teeth and bones. That was the way cowards were built. With nothing on the inside.

Mrs. Henneberry and Dr. Henneberry were on the other side of the pool. They were lying back on lawn chairs. Mrs. Henneberry was wearing a yellow dress, and a huge straw hat covered her face. A dripping jug of lemonade sat on the wooden table between them. Lively music played from a transistor radio beside the jug.

Mr. Fulsome was there, too. He was perched on the end of Dr. Henneberry's chair. "Come on, Mure," he said. "I'm too handsome to be ignored like this." But she didn't lift up the hat. Her eyes were hidden.

Mr. Fulsome smoothed the inside of Dr. Henneberry's knee. "A round of golf next week, Ray?"

"But Raymond," Mrs. Henneberry said, "we're organizing our couple of days. Remember we're making a fresh start?"

Dr. Henneberry laughed. "Are you two fighting over me?"

They hadn't noticed that I was there. Or else they didn't care.

Mr. Fulsome stood up and climbed the slope toward the driveway. Dr. Henneberry called out, "Golf sounds great, Jimmy. Why don't you drop by the clinic on Thursday?"

"Raymond! What about me?"

Mr. Fulsome yelled over his shoulder, "Don't forget to put your gun away, Ray. Before Mure shoots me in the back." He looked right through me. I wondered if a person could turn into a ghost. Just like that.

Dr. Henneberry adjusted the volume on the radio.

"Oh, I like this tune, don't you?" Mrs. Henneberry said. She flicked her toes.

Floating over the grass, I slowed several feet from their lawn chairs. I watched Mr. Fulsome leave in his light blue car. He tooted his horn. When he was gone, Mrs. Henneberry lifted the front of her hat and took a sip of lemonade. "Esther's made it too tart. Like she's forgotten the sugar. I do hope she's not squirreling away our supplies for when she leaves."

"What's that, dear?" Dr. Henneberry reached over and tickled her arm. "You're completely hidden under that abomination."

"I know. Such a luxury to disappear for a spell, isn't it, darling?"

"I want to say again, Mure, how terrible I feel for all that business. I don't know what came over me. My father was like that, as you know. A gambler of sorts. I should've learned."

Mrs. Henneberry waved her hand. "Not another word about it, Raymond. The entire ordeal was so unpleasant. I'd prefer to put it behind us."

"Agreed." He pointed at a silver gun, glinting on the table next to the jug. "I should put that away. Like Jim said."

"Oh, just call Esther. I don't want to miss a single second of the afternoon with you."

I drifted even closer, standing behind them, then. I could see the backs of their heads. Dr. Henneberry lifted his newspaper and started reading the front page. It had a large photograph of Mr. Pober in his military uniform. The headline said "Streets of Greenlake Safe Again."

Then, as calm as could be, Martin breezed out of the woods. He peeled off his T-shirt and threw it onto the grass. He kicked his shoes high up in the air and they plopped onto the concrete near the pool. He wasn't wearing socks.

"Hey, champ," Dr. Henneberry said.

"Hello, Father!"

"Enjoying the afternoon?"

"Sure am," he said. He sounded cheerful.

"What've you been up to?"

"Oh, just taking some air in my woods."

"Us, too. This weather is amazing."

Mrs. Henneberry lifted the floppy front of her hat again. "Oh, there you are, love. I wondered where you'd gone off to. We have lemonade if you're thirsty. Though I warn you, it's quite bitter."

Martin took long strides toward his parents and stood between the two lawn chairs. Even though I was on the other side of the small table, he never glanced at me.

Mrs. Henneberry looked up at Martin. "What's that scratch on your face, dear?"

"Just a twig, Mother. Don't worry, I cracked it off."

He took the glass from Mrs. Henneberry. Gulped most of it.

"Oh, you've reached that age, haven't you?" She fanned her hand in front of her nose.

"What age is that, Mother?" he said, and crunched a chunk of ice.

"You positively reek, dear." Mrs. Henneberry giggled. "Raymond? Can you talk with him? That sort of thing is boy territory. Man territory, I should say."

"I will, I will. But not right now."

"And Martin, love? We do need to chat about the Bishop girl. I'm afraid she's worn out her welcome. After the party. She's just . . . How can I put this delicately. A bit coarse?"

Martin rubbed a hand across his stomach. "Yeah. It

was getting pretty dull, Mother. But you were friends with them, and I didn't want to—"

"That's because you're so thoughtful. Don't worry another second about it. You're my priority, darling. I'll talk to Joan and we'll let her down easy, hey?"

Martin gave her back the empty glass. The brim of her hat dropped back over her face. Then he wiped his mouth on his arm, leaned in my direction, and whispered in that nasally drawl, "Oooh! That's just as smooth as a widow's kiss."

With a flick of his wrist, he cranked up the music on the radio. Then he strode toward the pool, fiddling with the button on his shorts. They dropped to the ground, and he kicked them away with his toes. Running, he leapt into the pool with his knees up to his chest. Water splashed in a giant ring around him.

I drifted closer to the lemonade. Sunlight bounced off the gun and stabbed me in the eye.

"Can you adjust that, dear? It's far too loud." But Dr. Henneberry never moved. He was focused on the newspaper.

I took another step. The table was right in front me.

Martin was swimming under the water. He came up for air, his hair plastered to his forehead like a helmet. When he shoved it back, he was grinning at me.

You can't tell.

He just moved his lips, but I knew what he said.

You can't say a word.

Birds were crying up in the trees. I was so ashamed of myself. How could all of my courage have evaporated? I wanted the grass to split open and the ground to swallow me down.

The music pumped into the backyard. I reached the tip of my finger out. The metal on the gun was warm.

I yanked my hand back. Someone else was in the backyard.

EXCERPT

Testimony of Mrs. Alice Grimshaw, Neighbor

Direct Examination by Prosecutor Clay Fibbs

Q. Mrs. Grimshaw, we appreciate your coming back. And we appreciate the court's indulgence, so we can get to the bottom of things.

A. I want to help, sir. I have things to say. About that boy.

Q. About Thomas Ware?

A. Yes, sir. He's told some lies.

Q. Let's start at the beginning then, ma'am. Your statement to police. Did you see Mr. Fulsome's car leave?

A. The blue one? I saw a blue one drive down Roundwater Heights. I was getting myself cleaned. After I fell in the woods. I saw it out my window.

Q. And a black car?

A. No, sir. No black cars that afternoon. That was one of his lies.

Q. Thank you for confirming that, Mrs. Grimshaw. You mentioned in your previous testimony that you encountered Thomas Ware in the woods. That something happened. Can you tell us what he was doing?

A. Watching.

Q. Watching what?

A. That was the worst part. His face. His eyes. I could tell he was broken.

Q. Can you explain what you mean for the court? Do
   you mean he was breaking things? Being aggressive?

A. No.

Q. You were afraid of him, then?

A. No. Of course not. I was only afraid of Martin
   Gladstone. He was in the woods, too.

Q. Martin Gladstone? He's been— Your Honor? I fear
   we're venturing into—

A. I should've known better. I tried to get around him,
   but he pushed me down.

Q. Mrs. Grimshaw. Martin Gladstone has been dead
   and buried for a number of years. Clearly, we've
   wasted more of the court's time.

*The Court: Let's not be so hasty, Mr. Fibbs. I've allowed
   your witness to take the stand again. Let's see what
   she has to say.*

*Mr. Fibbs: I know you're not from this area, Judge, so
   you're unfamiliar. But to say a dead man pushed her
   down? Smearing Mr. Gladstone's good name, when
   that family has done so much for the whole—*

*The Court: I don't care what they've done, Mr. Fibbs.
   They're not above the law.*

Mr. Fibbs: I don't know what law, sir. They're dead.

*The Court: That may be, Mr. Fibbs, but I've learned a
   thing or two after thirty-three years on the bench.
   There's a thread of truth in every story. And if you'll
   be so kind as to allow me, I'd like to find out what
   that thread is.*

Mr. Fibbs: *But. Yes, sir. Sorry, Your Honor.*

The Court: *Mrs. Grimshaw, what do you mean, he pushed you down?*

A. In the hollow. I was just trying to get by, but he was very rough with me, and he climbed on top of me, and—

The Court: *Are you trying to say that Martin Gladstone— that he violated you in the woods?*

A. Yes, sir. And it wasn't the first time. He's done it before. I told Ruth. I told her. And what she did—it was even—

The Court: *Who is Ruth?*

Mr. Fibbs: *That was Martin Gladstone's wife, sir. But like I said, she's been—*

The Court: *Mrs. Grimshaw? Can you tell the court what Mrs. Gladstone did?*

A. She did the worst thing possible. She—

The Court: *Ma'am?*

A. Ruth Gladstone didn't believe me.

The Court: *About the assault?*

A. She told our neighbors that I'd chased after him. They should mind their husbands because Abel had brought trash back from the dump.

The Court: *There's a dump?*

Mr. Fibbs: *She's from Lower Washbourne, Your Honor, sir. The entire place is pretty much—*

The Court: *Thank you, Mr. Fibbs. I never asked for your input. Mrs. Grimshaw, what happened after your experience in the woods?*

A. I went home. Then I went right over there.

The Court: Where?

A.　To talk to Ruth again. She had to know. What that man was doing.

The Court: You went over to the Henneberry property?

A.　I went to see Ruth Gladstone.

Mr. Fibbs: Your Honor, this is absurd.

The Court: Mr. Fibbs, I'm asking the questions now.

Mr. Fibbs: But—

The Court: And what happened when you arrived at the Gladstones'?

A.　Ruth still wouldn't listen. Martin Gladstone was in the water. Swimming. He looked so young, but I still knew exactly who he was. And there was that other man. I knew he was one of them, yelling after I'd—

The Court: What exactly do you have there, Mrs. Grimshaw? In your purse.

A.　My dress. The dress I was wearing. It's very, very dirty.

The Court: And is there something sticking out? What's rolled up—

A.　It's that gun. I found it on the table, you see. And right away, I knew Abel put it there to help me. So I could set things right on my own.

The Court: Order. I'll have order in my court. I won't tolerate another outburst! How did you do that, Mrs. Grimshaw? How did you set things right?

A.　I killed them, sir. I killed them with the gun. I wanted the birds to be quiet.

CHAPTER THIRTY-THREE

Mrs. Henneberry lifted her hat, reached over, and picked up the radio. She fumbled with the black dial, changing the station. Then she noticed the visitor. "Oh, she's back, Raymond. When are we going to get this sorted?"

"We will. Just ignore her, Muriel. She'll go on her merry way."

Mrs. Grimshaw had changed her clothes. She was wearing a black dress but her feet were still bare. I couldn't tell for sure if she was normal or not, but when she looked at me, I don't think she knew who I was.

"Abel's gone," she said as she came across the lawn.

From underneath her hat, Mrs. Henneberry said, "Oh, not this Abel nonsense again. Another afternoon disrupted."

"I need to talk to you, Ruth."

Mrs. Henneberry crossed her legs at her ankles. "Do you hear that, Raymond? She wants to talk to my mother. You need to do something."

"Yes, Muriel. As soon as I'm finished reading my article."

Martin was floating in the water on his back. He had

his hands behind his head, watching us. Smirking, as though we were part of a comedy show on television.

"I can't tolerate all her madness. After everything she's said about my family. Tormenting my dear mother with her lies. Now she's wandering freely onto our property. Raymond? Raymond, do something!"

"Don't give her any attention, love. That's what she's after." He turned the page. "It says here Packard cars are ending production."

Mrs. Grimshaw stood between them. "You need to listen to me."

"I don't have to listen to a single thing."

"Abel's gone," she said. "I understand that now."

Maybe the clear Mrs. Grimshaw was there after all.

"At least we've made progress," Mrs. Henneberry mumbled.

Martin squirted a line of water out of his mouth. It went up into the air and splashed down around him.

"And he's not coming back. That's why the birds are so loud. In the hollow. That's why they—"

"Birds in the woods! How utterly unique." Mrs. Henneberry started chirping.

"Stop," Mrs. Grimshaw whispered. "I want to talk to you."

More chirping.

Dr. Henneberry chuckled. "Yes, Muriel. Come now. That's beneath you."

But Mrs. Henneberry kept on chirping and giggling.

"Stop it!" Mrs. Grimshaw yelled out this time. She

started rocking back and forth on the spot. Her hands were shaking. "Abel's gone. Abel's gone. Abel's gone."

Mrs. Henneberry's sounds got even louder. Her arm was bent over her stomach and she kicked her feet up into the air, as though her bird calls were the funniest thing ever.

"Abel's gone."

"That he is," Dr. Henneberry said from behind his newspaper. "Means you'll need to start taking care of yourself, I'm afraid."

Dr. and Mrs. Henneberry didn't even move when Mrs. Grimshaw picked up the gun. As she held it out in front of her, her arm no longer shook. Her finger squeezed the trigger. A click, then a blast. The radio tumbled from Mrs. Henneberry's hands. Dr. Henneberry dropped his newspaper. His feet slapped the ground. He was yelling and reaching. And before the first shot had left my ears, Mrs. Grimshaw fired the second.

Martin was trying to swim to the side of the pool, his arms striking the surface of the water. Mrs. Grimshaw turned and took two steps. The third bullet hit Martin's back. At first, he was flailing, but slowly, he began to sink. A cloud of blood coloring the water around him.

My hands came up to cover my eyes. My limbs were trembling, and the front of my T-shirt was sticking to my chest. Mrs. Henneberry was quiet. Dr. Henneberry was quiet, too.

The only thing making noise was the transistor radio, crackling and sputtering in the grass.

Transcript of Radio Report
KGLB – 1470AM, Greenlake Station
March 26, 1959

Bombshell revelations out of the Greenlake court-house this hour in the trial that has captivated the entire country. All charges against eleven-year-old Thomas Leon Ware, of Lower Washbourne, have been dismissed. Details are scant at this time, but Judge Elias Ricker has released the jury of ten men and two women, stating their services are no longer required. The courtroom erupted today when a credible confession was extracted on the stand. According to sources, the triple murder of the Henneberrys was the result of an ongoing neighborly dispute. We will keep you updated as information is released.

CHAPTER THIRTY-FOUR

When my lawyer, Mr. Evans, finally led me out the side door of the courthouse, my mother was waiting there with Mr. Vardy. He'd brought his truck, so we didn't need to take the bus. It was chilly outside, and the sky was a dull gray. My mother hugged me. "Oh, Thomas," she kept saying. "Oh, Thomas." Her breath made clouds in the air.

"Come on," Mr. Vardy said. "You've wasted enough time already these past months." I could tell he meant it in a lighthearted way. Probably to make things easier. As we walked to the truck, he laid his hand on my shoulder. It was heavy sitting there, and it felt warm.

"Where are we going?" I said as we left the parking lot.

"You'll see," my mother said. I sat between her and Mr. Vardy, and she wouldn't let go of my fingers. She kept squishing them and lifting them up and down. Spring snow was falling on the windshield and the wipers pushed it away.

We drove through Greenlake. We passed Belbin's toy store. It was all lit up inside. We passed the red brick building where Dr. Henneberry's clinic had been. The tooth had vanished, only metal strings remaining, and the windows now had displays of ladies' wigs on white plaster heads. We passed the hospital where my aunt had worked. And the bus stop where she probably last stood. I looked because there was nothing special to see. I wasn't afraid anymore. We drove along the water for a while and passed the hidden road where Mrs. Henneberry and I had met that man in his camper. Then we turned right toward Lower Washbourne.

Brown buildings came up on either side of the street. There were no lines of laundry as it was still too cold. Steam puffed up from a grate in the road. We turned onto Gerald Street. We were getting closer to my old apartment building. "What's going on?" I asked. "Why are we here?" Mr. Vardy stopped the truck before we reached it.

"I couldn't get a place at the same building," my mother said. "But they had one available half a block away."

It was very nearly the same, except the front steps didn't have a crack and the railing on one side wasn't missing. And instead of filthy Mr. Pober, a woman sat there in a plaid coat with a baby on her knees. He was wearing a woolen sweater and a hat with a pompom and his cheeks were bright pink. She kept bouncing him up in the air and each time he came down, he squealed. "Only time he quits fussing," she said to my mother. "When he's half-froze."

The apartment was on the second floor. If we were in my old building, we would have been straight across the hall from Mrs. King. It had two bedrooms, and a brown rug and a green couch. The cushions had enormous buttons in the middle. Next to the couch was a bookshelf with a few paperbacks, a 500-piece jigsaw puzzle, and a deck of cards wrapped with an elastic band. The fringe on the lampshade shuddered as heat lifted off the radiator. Near the kitchen was a white table and two white chairs. George was swimming in his bowl in the middle of the table. He hadn't changed a bit.

"Our centerpiece." my mother said.

"He's a nice one," I said.

My mother waved her hand. "I'm sorry Thomas. There's not much here."

I shook my head. "But there's everything here."

In the days after I returned home, I slept for hours on end. Mr. Vardy told my mother I shouldn't rush things. He said I'd been through an ordeal that would damage most grown men, let alone a child. My mother made pancakes for breakfast and grilled cheeses at lunch and vegetable soup at night. One afternoon she went out and came back with a bulging shopping bag. Trousers and two white T-shirts and a knitted sweater with a diamond pattern on the front. She even got me a new pair of black rubber boots that had a red band around the rim. "This last blast of cold won't last long," she said. "And I don't want you wearing those clothes anymore." Martin's clothes.

Mrs. King came by with a plate of oatmeal raisin cookies. She said seeing me was a "salve for her soul." I didn't know what that meant, to be a salve, but it sounded like something good. When I asked her about Mr. King, her eyes got wet. She told me he'd stopped coughing in his sleep about two and a half months earlier. "It was his time," she said, patting my hand. "I'll need you to come visit and brighten things up."

Mrs. Pinsent brought over two canvas bags filled with schoolwork. I'd missed a fair amount of my grade seven year. She'd decided to move over to the middle school, so she was going to be my teacher again for the last few months of the year. "I never had a single doubt, Thomas," she said. "And now that you're back home, I expect you back in my classroom in short order."

Once the news about what happened got out, stories began appearing in the *Greenlake Chronicle*. People were giving interviews about the Henneberrys. My mother said she couldn't tell what was gossip and what was true. "It doesn't seem right to dredge things up. No matter how you slice it, three people are dead." She still allowed me to read them, though. Women from the church said Mrs. Henneberry "had always been erratic. And a little uppity." Martin's schoolteachers said, "The boy knew no bounds, and he took delight in observing other children struggle." I saw a quote from Mrs. Bishop: "Martin Henneberry treated my girl, Genie, like a toy for his amusement. A repulsive young man. I tried to put an end to it, I did." There were strange rumors about a relationship between Dr. Henneberry and his best friend Mr. Fulsome. Mr. Fulsome said, "Absurd! Of course I loved Ray. Loved him like a brother. He didn't deserve this.

He'd done nothing wrong." There was an article about Martin Gladstone's legacy. How it had been tarnished.

My mother didn't look at me when she said, "Thomas? Do you want to ask any questions?"

I shook my head. I didn't want to talk about anyone named Martin ever again. I'd never be able to forget what he'd done to my mother, to Mrs. Grimshaw, and maybe even others. I didn't want to think about him being my father. Maybe I'd have questions tomorrow, or the next day. Or maybe not ever. Maybe I'd just be the boy who appeared in the world in a big sploosh, like Aunt Celia had said. That could be true if I thought it enough times.

One day, my face was in the newspaper, too. Smack in the center on the front page. A photograph that was taken in grade five. They used the word *chivalrous*, and my mother had to explain that meant I was being courageous or big-hearted. For trying to protect Mrs. Grimshaw even though she'd done an unthinkable thing.

The newspaper said Mrs. Grimshaw was "no more than an ailing widow who was pushed and pushed.... An upstanding woman who'd been assaulted by two generations of a family whose reputation was built only on cold, hard cash.... She was being forced from the home she'd shared with her beloved husband Abel Grimshaw." Mrs. Gage, Skip's mother, said, "Sure, Alice was a little muddled sometimes, but we all lent a hand. Except Muriel Henneberry. She was affronted by the sight of her. Wouldn't stop talking about past slights and did her best to get the whole street in her corner.

Doesn't a woman have a right to protect herself? While I never condone violence, and I'm sorry for what happened, clearly poor Alice had simply had enough."

"Is she going to jail?" I asked.

"No," my mother said. "I don't think so." She went to the table and opened the container of George's food. Pinched up a few grains in her fingers and sprinkled it over his water. "Mrs. Grimshaw, she's elderly, and well, her health. She wasn't in her proper mind when she did what she did. She'll get help."

"So no jail?"

"No jail, Thomas."

"That's good," I said.

My mother came and sat on the couch next to me. She smoothed the hair off my forehead. "Can I ask you something?"

I nodded.

"On that afternoon. Why did you lie to me?"

I didn't know how to explain it. When I saw what happened to the Henneberrys, memories of Aunt Celia flooded through me. I heard her asking me, "Do you know what's most important when you grow up, Tommie?" I kept thinking about what she said. I was supposed to be a good man. After I moved into the Henneberrys', all that summer, I'd seen so many shocking things. But I never once stood up. I never fought. I didn't ask for help. I did nothing. After Mrs. Grimshaw shot the Henneberrys, I only had a second to decide. Was I going to tell the truth about what she'd done?

I decided to be good again.

I decided to be brave again.

That was why I lied.

Even though I didn't answer my mother's question, she was nodding like she understood. Then she said, "You don't always have to look after people, you know. Sometimes you have to let others look after you."

I swallowed. "Did you think I did it?"

"I didn't know what happened. I thought you were being honest. And I tried to tell them, the police, the same thing. I worried they wouldn't believe you, but I thought perhaps they would believe *us*. And I only ended up making things worse. If only . . . I don't—"

"Do you love Mr. Vardy?" I didn't know why that burst out of my mouth. I guess some quiet part of my brain had been wondering.

"What?" My mother sniffed in air and put her hand on her cheek. "I really— I'm not sure if I should—"

"It's okay if you do, Mom."

She smiled then. Shook her head. "Yes, Thomas. You're right. It's okay if I do."

The next morning, as I was eating a late breakfast, my mother said, "Oh, I nearly forgot. The superintendent from your old apartment dropped by. He brought some things he'd collected. Before they cleared the place out."

I jumped up from the table. "Stuff from my birthday?"

"I don't know. It's in a cardboard box behind my bedroom door."

I rushed into her room and knelt down on the floor. There were two boxes, and I popped the lid off the one closest to me. But my things weren't inside.

"Oh, Thomas, not that one." My mother was peering around the door. "The other box. Close that up quickly."

But I had already reached in and touched the red leather purse. Thin handles that went over my aunt's wrist. A navy leather shoe with a silver buckle. And a slippery pink scarf.

"Those are from Detective Miller. He thought we might want to keep them."

I pushed the scarf aside, and beneath it, I found the second shoe. I picked it up. When I turned it over, I saw threads sticking out where the matching silver buckle had been torn off.

A silver buckle.

My skin prickled, and I opened my mouth, but no words came out. A missing silver buckle. I blinked. Then a picture flashed behind my lids, and my mind remembered what my body already knew.

"You've gone pale. I should've brought it out to you. Close the lid."

"Her shoes," I whispered.

"Detective Miller said she fought. Fought hard. The clip came off in the struggle. They never recovered it."

No, they hadn't. I'd recovered it, though. Hiding in the very back of a locked middle drawer. Dr. Henneberry had called it cheap. But it hadn't belonged to his mother after all. That hollow silver square with tiny white gems, a few missing, belonged on my aunt's shoe. It broke the night she died. When she'd struggled with Dr. Henneberry.

"Thomas? Are you okay?"

I placed the shoes back in the box and closed the lid. "I'm good. I wasn't expecting it, is all."

In the kitchen, I pulled one of the chairs over to the window. I put my elbows on the sill. The sun had been shining, and most of the snow was gone. The remaining stubs from the icicles were dripping. Kids were running around in the street. I pushed up the window and leaned out to see. The air was cold and warm at the same time. Down on the sidewalk, Wally was playing kick the can. It was the first time I'd seen him since I got back. He was taller, and the sleeves of his sweater came up over his wrists. He was wearing a blue hat. When he noticed me, he waved both hands.

"You coming down?" he called up.

"Not sure," I called back. I didn't know if I was ready for everyone to see me.

"My father told me not to be bugging you after everything. He wouldn't let me go knock."

"You could've. I wouldn't have minded."

"That's what I told him." Wally's arms went up in the air as though he were exasperated. "Hey—I still got your nameplate. I hung it on my door right next to mine. Sunny keeps calling me Wall-Tom. You'd think I was a fish or something."

My mouth opened and laughter burst out. Effort-
lessly, like it was the easiest thing in the world.

"Hey," he said. "Speaking of fish, you want to go this
weekend? My dad says they're starved in the spring and
they let their guards down."

"Sure," I said. "Fishing sounds good."

I closed my eyes and put my head down on the windowsill. I remembered the proof Detective O'Connor
had described to my mother. The clothes they'd found in
Mr. Pober's apartment. The stories he'd written. But the
panties were probably stolen from the strings of laundry around the apartments. The stories, just fiction. I
couldn't think of a single nice thing about that man,
but I knew he did not commit those crimes. I also knew
what it meant to be falsely accused. It didn't matter that
Mr. Pober was disgusting or that he was gone. I still
had to set things right. I needed to think carefully about
who I could tell. Who would understand. I took a deep
breath and blew it out. Nothing bad could happen
while I decided, because Dr. Henneberry was gone, too.
I had time.

A cool breeze brushed over my face. I pretended it
was my aunt spinning around in a sparkly dress. She was
giggling. "What do you think, Tommie? Is it too much?"

"No," I whispered. "It's just right."

"How do you always know what to say?"

Then I heard a loud "Oh!" I opened my eyes. My
mother was leaning over the sink in the bathroom, a

bucket and rags on the floor next to her. She called out, "Can you come here, Thomas?"

I hurried over. Her hands were clasped together, and she reached them out to me. "Do you mind letting this little guy loose outside? I want to finish my cleaning."

I nodded. I could smell bleach. Our hands touched, and the insect slipped from her cupped hands into mine. Inside the darkness, I felt it tiptoeing over my palms.

"They're coming up through the pipes," she said. "We'll keep the plug in. That'll solve that problem."

I stared at my mother.

"Why are you looking at me like I've got two heads?"

"I don't—"

"It's nothing to be afraid of. It won't hurt you."

"I'm not afraid," I said.

I carried it across our apartment and reached out the window that led to the fire escape. The earwig raced away on blurry legs. Down below, that lady was back on the stoop, bouncing her baby. Two girls crouched nearby, playing jacks on the sidewalk. Then Wally was running across the street, my name board tucked under his arm. "I got it!" he cried. "I got it for you." He was clomping up the fire escape stairs.

I looked back at my mother, in bright yellow rubber gloves, humming in the bathroom. Mr. Vardy was coming over later, and she was going to make a roasted chicken and candied carrots. A caramel pudding cake for dessert. When she caught me watching her, she smiled at me. *We'll keep the plug in.* She hadn't solved the hugest problem. But she'd still solved a tiny one. And that mattered. It mattered a whole lot.

I didn't have to do it alone.

EPILOGUE

Over thirty years have passed since that summer afternoon when Mrs. Grimshaw shot and killed the Henneberrys. Over thirty years since those cold spring days when I stood trial for those crimes. Even though the memories have softened, I still spend a great deal of time considering the enormity of it. How a moment, a finger snap, altered the direction of my life.

After a while, the news articles about the case began to slow down. People's fascination moved on to other scandals and tragedies. As my mother had predicted, Mrs. Grimshaw was not incarcerated. Instead, she was treated for senility at a private facility in Greenlake. My mother heard that she proved to be a challenge for the staff. She continually escaped. I was saddened to learn of her death some years later, but I liked to believe she wasn't searching anymore. She'd finally found Abel.

As the sole surviving heir of Martin Gladstone, I eventually received a considerable inheritance. But instead of making any immediate decisions, my mother and I decided it was best to be still for a while. We remained in the apartment in Lower Washbourne. I completed high school, and she completed her high school equivalency. Both of us received some tutoring from Mrs. Pinsent. While I accepted my offer from Slipton College, my mother declined hers. However, she did accept Mr. Vardy's marriage proposal. He currently owns several gardening supply stores, and my mother manages all of the accounting.

Sometimes I'd run into Genie Bishop at the college. We had coffee together once or twice. We never spoke of Martin Henneberry, but she did confide that after the trial, her mother had tried to arrange a date between Genie and Skip Gage. Genie had refused. The last time I saw her, she'd just become engaged to the son of a store clerk. She told me, with a wry smile, that her mother would never recover from it.

I continue to live in Lower Washbourne. A house, now, no longer an apartment. I married Wally's sister, Sunny, when I was twenty-eight, much to my mother's delight and Wally's consternation. I have a child named David who is very nearly the age I was when the Henneberry killings took place. For the most part, my son leads a charmed life, though he complained bitterly when I wouldn't permit him to watch the *Gunsmoke* special on TV.

Over the years, I have tried to use that immense Gladstone wealth to improve people's lives. My mother was denied her right to schooling as a child, so I established the Esther Ware National Scholarship that provides education for underprivileged girls. I also funded the construction of the Celia Ware Wing at St. Augustine's Hospital. I wanted my aunt's name to be associated with what she loved instead of how she died.

Doors opened in 1972, and it quickly became the country's leading facility for research and treatment of lung disease. I have invested heavily, but silently, in the amenities of my community. Improving the library, building a youth center, renovating the schools, cleaning up the beach around the lake. Lower Washbourne has long since shed its reputation as an undesirable place to reside.

I also quietly arranged for an extensive investigation into Dr. Henneberry. I needed to determine if he was indeed the Greenlake Predator. The man who'd murdered my aunt and multiple other women. Nothing much came of it until recently, when I learned of a new method that scientists are using to examine crimes. While most of the evidence had been lost or returned to families, some had been neatly stored away. Panties and bras. A silk slip. Torn stockings. A cracked pair of cat's-eye glasses. I hired a laboratory to use this technique to compare those items to personal belongings I'd kept from the Henneberry estate. Dr. Henneberry was matched to three of the four murder cases, Aunt Celia's and two others. He could not be excluded from the fourth, as the biological material had simply degraded.

My original goal was to find closure for both myself and the victims' families, and in that, I was mostly successful. I also wanted to have Mr. Pober's name cleared. Even though years had passed, the *Greenlake Chronicle* still printed a retraction. Wally was the journalist who wrote it.

Each year on the anniversary of the shootings, I return to the house at the end of Roundwater Heights. A dozen or more young children reside there now. Running and tumbling over the grounds. They all have unique, sometimes devastating, circumstances, but are getting the best of care as they await permanent placement in good homes.

After I park, I always walk down the slope toward the woods. The pool has long since been backfilled and the pool house demolished. I take a leisurely stroll through the woods alone. I think about Aunt Celia and my mother, and the burdens they'd carried throughout their lives. I think about the dysfunction and the deviance of both the Gladstone and Henneberry families. I think about that afternoon. Even now, when I close my eyes, I can still hear the gunshots, feel the warm splatter of blood and bone on my skin. I think about the trial, too, and how very close I came to losing my freedom.

As I reach the end of my walk, I always spend time reflecting on Mrs. Grimshaw. The bottomless gratitude I feel for what she'd done. And I don't mean shooting the Henneberrys. When she was testifying at the trial, she omitted a small, but very important, detail. For her, it changed very little. For me, it changed everything.

On that afternoon, Mrs. Grimshaw and I were standing on opposite sides of the wooden table that held the lemonade. The air was thrumming with Mrs. Henneberry's giddy chirping. Dr. Henneberry was grumbling and cracking the pages of his newspaper. Martin was gliding around in the pool.

Mrs. Grimshaw only noticed the gun when I grabbed for it. She knocked my hand out of the way so she could clutch it herself.

At eleven years old, I couldn't grasp the seriousness of what I was about to do. The terrible mistake I very nearly made.

I would have shot them. I would have shot them all.

ACKNOWLEDGMENTS

An Unthinkable Thing is my eighth novel and I can say, without a doubt, it was the most complicated and challenging writing process to date. More than any previous book, *An Unthinkable Thing* is the result of teamwork, and would never have taken shape without the expert guidance and enduring support of multiple people.

First and foremost, a heartfelt thank-you to my agent, Danielle Egan-Miller. She approaches every interaction with exceptional knowledge and unwavering positivity. I'm so glad to have found her and her amazing team at Browne & Miller.

I have immense gratitude for my editor, Lara Hinchberger, at Penguin Canada. With tremendous expertise, and a bottomless well of patience and care, she helped me fully discover the story I was supposed to tell. I'm so pleased with the end result.

Thank you to Aniko Biber, who got the first peek at the manuscript. At that point, I was flooded with doubt, and cannot express how much I appreciated both the feedback and encouragement.

A special thank you to two friends, Palmina Ioannone and Tania Madden, who knew just when to swoop in with rib-cracking laughs. Those moments were so needed during these past months of uncertainty and anxiety.

Being creative during the pandemic has sometimes been difficult and sometimes impossible. I'm grateful to my three children, Sophia, Isabella, and Robert, who inspired me every day with their remarkable resilience.

Lastly, I would like to express my appreciation to the Ontario Arts Council for supporting this project at its earliest, messiest stage.

© AnnaLena Seemann

NICOLE LUNDRIGAN is the author of several critically acclaimed novels, including *Hideaway*, which was shortlisted for the Arthur Ellis Award for Best Crime Novel, *The Substitute*, and *Glass Boys*. Her work has appeared on "best of" selections from *The Globe and Mail*, Amazon.ca, *Chatelaine*, *Now* magazine, and others. She grew up in Newfoundland, and now lives in Toronto.

nicolelundrigan.com
Facebook.com/njlundrigan
Instagram @nicolejlundrigan

Don't miss Nicole Lundrigan's chilling, page-turning new psychological thriller, *A Man Downstairs*, in which memories prove dangerously deceptive and it is never too late for revenge . . .

Coming soon from Viking Canada

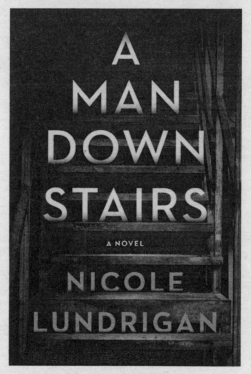

TURN THE PAGE TO READ AN EXCERPT

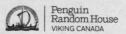

Penguin
Random House
VIKING CANADA

www.penguinrandomhouse.ca

PROLOGUE

I've come to realize there is nothing sweeter than a second chance.

Of course, I knew I'd never see her again. But you and I are together now, and that's what counts. The first moment you smiled at me, all the missteps I'd made in the past were swept away. Forgiven and forgotten.

Most evenings, I am content to gaze at you through the window. My actions feel comfortably familiar, and each time I linger in the backyard, I automatically envision a dozen ways in. Cheap locks or forcible doors. That worthless plastic clip securing the bedroom window. But I won't do that this time. With her, I played a different role for different reasons, and now I have other ideas.

Though tonight, as I stand on the grass beneath a milk-white moon, I feel worried. You are pacing about the kitchen, a phone pressed to your ear and concern on your face. I wonder if you are safe. If you are happy. As I follow your steps, my left leg buckles from pain. Glancing down, I catch the glint of metal. Fingers gripping the splintery shaft of an axe, its dull blade jabbing my calf. I can't recall picking it up. And I take a moment to remind myself that I am like everyone else. Choking with apprehension. Prone to dark thoughts.

I rest the axe against the side of the house. I will remain measured this time, and not rush ahead. Second chances don't come along very often.

NOW

•

CHAPTER ONE

Molly

"What if it's a scam?"

"It's not a scam."

"But it could be, Mom. You don't know everything."

There was a sneer in Alex's tone, and Molly realized her teenaged son was baiting her. Instead of responding, she gripped the steering wheel, focused on the curving road ahead. She still hated this stretch of the drive. These last few miles before they passed the mouth of that narrow dirt trail. When she was a child, someone had erected a white cross in the ditch beside it. A glaring reminder for her, her father, and the entire town of what happened there.

"If it's real, this place better not be a total dump," Alex mumbled as he unwrapped a hard candy, tossed it into his mouth.

This place was a cheap furnished rental that Molly had found online. Several overexposed snapshots suggested it was bright and clean. In no way luxurious, but choice was limited in a town this size. The owner was flexible with dates, mid-September to whenever, and the location was ideal, only about a twenty-minute walk from her childhood home.

"There's a roof and running water. How bad can it be?"

"Are you serious?" He slumped down in his seat. "I should've stayed with Dad."

A pain prickled through her chest. Since Leo left a year ago, Alex had seen him only a handful of times. At first calls were sporadic, unreliable, and before long they tapered off altogether. Then last spring, Leo purchased a one-bedroom condo with his latest girlfriend. Purposefully, Molly suspected, so there was zero room for a sweaty sullen teenager. Especially one who needed to monitor his food intake, his blood sugar, his insulin.

"I was joking," she said. "If it's awful, we'll pack up and head over to your grandfather's."

"We should have done that anyway."

She sighed. If they stayed with her father, she knew she'd be swallowed by the sadness of him. He'd had a massive stroke six weeks earlier. A passerby found him crumpled on the front step of his home and called for an ambulance. He was rushed to the hospital in the city, and when Molly arrived, doctors explained that the damage to his cerebellum was extensive. Even so, Molly had fully believed he'd recover. That he was simply hidden beneath some gauzy layers of confusion. But when he finally opened his watery eyes, there was no glimmer. No recognition. Just a blankness that broke her in two.

"I thought it was better," she said. "For us to have our

own space. You'll hardly be around, anyway. What with school. And, well, your hours." Two hundred of them, to be exact. Community service for a terrible error in judgment involving his cellphone camera and a girl.

Alex turned his head toward the window, folded his arms over his ribs. "You always do that."

"Do what?"

"Bring it up when I'm trapped. Not like I can get out."

She glanced at the silver handle inches from his fist. Her mind spat out a scene. One fluid movement, unsnapping his seatbelt, shoving open the door, and rolling sideways. The dullest thud as his slender body hit blacktop.

"Fair point, darling. I'll try to speak only when you have a viable means of escape."

He didn't laugh, just unwrapped a second candy. The hard edges clinking against his teeth. She wondered if his blood sugar might be low. She wondered if she should ask. Nothing about their interactions seemed straightforward anymore.

Just ahead, a faded wooden sign said "Welcome to Aymes!" Beside the words was a ghost of a corncob with a bandana knotted around its kernel neck. Even though she tried to control her reaction, the sight still made her palms grow slick. They were nearly there.

Around the next bend, the yellowing fields gave way to a dense belt of trees. It was jarring, the sudden shift from vast openness to towering branches, rising up, pressing in, covering the road in leafy shadow. On the north side, the ground began to angle steeply, climbing higher and higher.

As though on cue, Alex bolted upright, pointed out the window. "And that's where it all went down."

The white cross had long ago decayed, and the once obvious road was now nothing more than an overgrown path, its entrance blocked by a red metal barricade. Years ago, men would drive through the brush to a drop-off point called the overhang. They'd lower their tailgates, toss trash into the deepest part of Rabey Lake. Bottomless, locals used to say. Things simply disappeared.

"I guess so," she said.

"Nobody really knows the whole story, but that dude still went to jail?"

Molly sighed again. They'd had this conversation innumerable times. "Yes, Alex, he went to jail. Until his conviction was reversed."

He was right, though, about no one knowing the entire story. A clear determination was never made about the location of her mother's death. It was possible she'd died in the garage at their home. Or was killed on the overhang. She could have been dumped over the side while still alive, drowning in the lake. And her skeleton remained there, bare bones tangled up with stained mattresses, pieces of scrap, torn chairs with wild rusted springs. Nearly forty years had passed, and Molly still thought of her mother every day.

"How's that fair?" he said. "All because you 'guessed so.'"

Her spine stiffened. He was being cruel now. Itching for a fight. He knew she'd witnessed her mother's death when she was a child. And that the following year she'd testified during the trial. Though proceedings were a blur, there was one moment she recalled with absolute clarity. The entire jury leaning forward as she'd whispered, "There was a man downstairs."

Later, of course, she understood that the individual who'd entered their home was not a man at all but a skinny boy. A year or two older than her own son was now. She could still picture Terry Kage, seated beside his attorney, shaggy hair and acne-scarred cheeks. His gangly form floating inside a beige suit with massive lapels. He might have worn that outfit to his high school prom. If he had gone.

When Alex was younger, he'd often peppered her with questions about his grandmother, the boy, the murder, but it was out of concern for Molly's well-being. Lately, though, his interest had intensified. He'd been snooping in her home office and found the one box she'd kept hidden. Her legs weakened when she discovered him sitting cross-legged on the floor, surrounded by pages of the police report, crime scene photos, trial transcripts. "Some of this is bullshit," he'd said. "You know that, right?"

As they rounded another turn, Molly slammed the car brakes. Alex lurched, smacking his palm on the dashboard.

"What the hell, Mom?"

"Oh, honey, look."

On the road in front of them, two deer had stopped. One larger, and one slightly smaller. Heads lifted to stare at them, the undersides of their tails white and flickering. Perhaps mother and son.

The doe stood her ground until her fawn had trotted down the shallow embankment on the other side. Then she darted behind him, the pair vanishing into the woods.

"Now you don't see that in the city, right?"

"Whatever," he growled. "Can we get going?"

"Doesn't hurt to pause and appre—"

"I told you a million times already. Quit trying your shrink garbage on me."

Annoyance bubbled inside her. How could this be the same boy she'd birthed, wore on her chest, played with for hours? Even slept on the floor of his bedroom when he was afraid of monsters. She'd desperately wanted to give him the intense dedication her own mother had once given her. Her father had often described it in detail when she was young, so Molly knew exactly how much she was loved. But instead of a similar bond, she could barely talk to her son.

Alex lay his cheek against his seatbelt. Hard crunch then, like crystal shattering, as his molars pulverized the sugar down to dust.

CHAPTER TWO

When Molly pulled into the driveway of the rental, a man was standing in the middle of the lawn. He was tall and gangly, the buttons of his plaid shirt misaligned. Behind him was the tiny bungalow she'd seen on the rental website. The wood siding had a deep chestnut stain, and the front was shaded by a steep roof.

As soon as she parked, the man began striding toward them.

"I guess that's our landlord, Mr. Farrell."

Alex groaned. "Why does he look pissed?"

"No clue." She rubbed at the dry patch on her left elbow. A tiny spot of psoriasis that persisted, no matter how many treatments she tried.

"Finally made it," the man said, as they stepped out. The lenses of his glasses were riddled with scratches, and it was difficult to see his eyes. "I'd expected you much earlier."

"Oh?" Though they'd been slow getting on the road, she couldn't recall giving him any indication of when they'd arrive. "Sorry about that."

"Well, we won't dwell. How was your trip?"

She glanced at Alex. "Blissfully quiet, thank you, Mr. Farrell."

"No need for formality, Molly." He tugged off his glasses and rubbed them with the hem of his shirt. "I prefer Russell. Or Russ. Not Rusty, though, if you don't mind."

"Got it," she said. "Russ, but not Rusty." She put her hands on her lower spine and stretched. A joint in her back popped.

Russell clapped his hands together. "Should we get you folks unpacked?"

"We can manage. Thank you though. We'll just need the keys."

He put up his palms and shook his head. His comb-over was a pale and unnatural color. Like butterscotch smeared on his scalp. "I wouldn't dream of it," he said. "Consider it part of services provided." Then he reached for the trunk latch.

When Russell turned his back, Alex rolled his eyes at her.

The screen door creaked when she opened it. The place was exactly as pictured online, though it appeared smaller. Cramped. The cupboards were basic brown, the countertop an uncluttered white. Pushed into a corner was a square table large enough for her and Alex to have dinner. It could also serve as a desk for when she connected with her young clients who'd opted to continue therapy through remote sessions.

When she walked through the kitchen and into the living room, she immediately took note of the oversized painting hanging above the couch. A basic landscape to most everyone else, but for Molly, the sight of the over-hang on canvas was disturbing.

"Impressive, right?"

She jumped. Russell was right behind her, and she could feel the warmth of his breath on her skin.

"Did it myself," he continued. "I'm a beginner, as you can tell."

Molly could recall going there when she was a teen-ager. Traipsing through the woods until she reached that clearing. Always alone as friends were few and far between during those years. She'd usually stay until darkness rose around her, perched near the edge of the rock, wondering how it might feel to slip through the air the same as her mother had. Would she flail? Would there be a jolt of terror when she struck the water?

"You've certainly captured it," she said, turning her back to it.

"I hike over there fairly often. Set a few snares. Take in the view of Rabey Lake."

"I bet it's really something," she managed, as she envisioned a rabbit caught in a wire noose.

"Sure is. Especially in the fall."

"Which room's mine?" Alex yelled from the hallway.

"You choose," she called back.

While Russell went outside again, she continued exploring. Opened a closet to find a stackable laundry. Peeked into the bathroom. The fixtures were dated, but the shower curtain still had folds from the packaging.

"No pets, as I explained," Russell said over the top of the box he was carrying. "And I can't tolerate rowdiness." He glanced at Alex, who was dragging a bulging suitcase across the tiled floor. "If you could try to be light on your feet, that would be appreciated. Seeing as I'm in the apartment below."

He'd mentioned that in their email exchange. After his divorce, he'd created a "lower-level suite" and let out the upper level. Which was, he said, "much more appealing to clients."

"We'll do our best, won't we, Alex?"

Alex offered no reply as he went out for another load.

"Well, then. You'll notice I've provided a few basics so you won't have to rush out this evening. Seeing as you arrived late and all."

"That's very thoughtful, Russ."

Alex bustled back inside and dropped the last box on the ground. "Trunk's empty." Then he dug his phone out of his back pocket. "What's the Wi-Fi password?"

Russell pursed his lips, examined Alex over the top of his glasses. "A word about that, young man. As you may have surmised, the internet is shared by the entirety of the home. I expect you to be judicious with your streaming."

"Of course," Molly said, taking a step closer to Alex.

"And there are restrictions on the modem. Filters. To keep things appropriate, if you know what I mean."

"I'm sure that'll be fine, right?"

"Yeah, whatever. So, password?"

Russell nodded toward the fridge. There was a sticky note with writing on the front panel. Alex tore off the small paper, went into the bedroom on the left, pushed the door closed with the tip of his sneaker.

Russell raised his eyebrows. "I do hope we're not off on the wrong foot, Molly?"

"Don't worry. He's a good kid." Or he used to be. And she hoped he still was. "Besides, we're not in town to watch endless hours of porn."

Molly's attempt at lightness made Russell scowl, and he brought his hand to the highest shirt button, twisted. "I wasn't insinuating such a thing. I know you've got a lot on your plate. Regarding your father's health."

Her throat tightened. She'd have to get used to strangers with awareness. Aymes was no larger than a thimble, and most residents knew her father. He'd been the town pharmacist, retiring only a few years ago. As a teenager, she'd spent innumerable afternoons at his drugstore, retreating from the cruelty of her peers. Her mother's death had given her an indelible stamp of otherness that did not fade as she grew up. "You're right," she said. "I do have a lot on my plate."

"Well, keys are on the counter. Garbage day is Wednesday. Make a note because I don't do reminders." Russell's mouth widened into a line. A smile, perhaps. "I'll be close by if you need anything."

Then, instead of going outside, he opened the door beside the fridge.

"That's not your actual entrance, is it?" she asked.

"Oh, I'm just being lazy. I have a proper door on the far side of the house."

After he'd gone, she went behind him and pressed her ear to the wood. His footsteps grew softer and softer, and then a distant click from below. She turned the knob, eased the door open a crack. A steep set of steps with another door at the bottom. The light switch had to be in his apartment, as the single bulb suddenly flicked off and the space dissolved into blackness.

Grabbing the keys from the countertop, she locked the door.

When Alex came back to the kitchen, he'd changed into a different hoodie, different track pants. "Can we order an extra-large pepperoni? I'm starved."

Opening the fridge, she saw apples and juice, bread and eggs. A package of hot dogs and one of ground beef, dripping blood onto the empty shelf below. After Russell had gone through the trouble to make their first night comfortable, he'd surely be offended at the sight of a pizza delivery man. "Give me five minutes."

She filled a pot with water and put it on the stove. Slit open the hot dogs, dumped them in. Waited for it to boil.

"Mr. Farrell seems friendly." She peeled the safety foil off a bottle of ketchup.

"Yeah, if you vibe on weirdos."

"That's a bit harsh, Alex."

"So what?"

He flumped down at the kitchen table and screwed

a needle cap onto the end of his insulin pen. Lifted his T-shirt, injected the clear liquid into his abdomen. They ate their hot dogs in weighted silence. The instant he'd shoved the last bite into his mouth, he scraped back his chair, cleared away his plate, and returned to his room. Molly kept chewing, swallowing. Barely managing half before discarding the rest.

Before getting up from the table, she took several slow, purposeful breaths. Hoping to calm the sensation inside her head. It reminded her of the rising hum in railway tracks, well before a train barreled into sight. As she taught her clients to do, she tried to identify a single concrete thought that was causing distress. Then examine the evidence to determine if the thought was fact, or if it was a distortion rooted in emotion.

What Alex said in the car had really bothered her. *"Because you 'guessed so.'"*

Perhaps he didn't realize that was a trigger point for her. Perhaps he did.

She'd attended many therapy sessions as part of her training and gone over and over the afternoon her mother died. Relayed the events, answered questions, processed feelings, and reviewed. Her recollection of what occurred was pristine. And therein lay the problem. Though the psychologist had not explicitly mentioned it, Molly believed her movie-like memory was suspicious. The way each detail neatly stacked on top of the one before, and nothing ever altered in her retellings. Based on Molly's experiences with her young patients, people often forgot aspects of a traumatic ordeal, or simply made mistakes. She, however, did not.

As she'd already completed the intensive work to heal, she tried to ignore baseless concerns when they crawled into her mind. That stone of grief hammocked inside her chest would be there for the rest of her life, but why continue to poke at it? Sometimes she told her patients that it was okay to simply accept aspects of a trauma and put those bits away. It was not avoidance; it was a strategy to cope.

Even so, she could still close her eyes and find her mother's killer there. In that moment he was standing in their driveway, he'd reminded Molly of a squirrel. A lock of black hair falling over his eyes, and both fists, like paws, pressed into his chest.

The trial made national news. Not so much for the murder; more for Molly's involvement. *Feisty girl takes down killer. Wonder child wows jury.* In newspapers, Terry Kage's droopy-eyed mug shot often appeared alongside her nursery school photo. Pigtails, plaid smock, crooked, nervous grin. The owner of a local diner clipped an article, slid it into a plastic frame, and hung it on the wall until Molly's father asked him to take it down.

Due to depth, debris, and murky conditions, divers had been unable to locate a body, but there had been overwhelming physical evidence. Copious amounts of blood in the garage, in the car, stains in the soil on the overhang. Even smeared on the boy's hands, face, neck, T-shirt. A clump of long dark hair was tangled in a button on his jacket, and two straight lines marked the dirt, where her mother's heels were undoubtedly dragged toward the edge.

But when it came to the decision those twelve people made in a stuffy room, were Molly's words the most damning? Did hearing those vivid details slipping from the innocent mouth of a four-year-old decide a young man's fate? It took less than an hour before Terry Jerome Kage was convicted in the death of Edie Margaret Wynters.

Several years later, that conviction was overturned. The appeal was based on the argument that the defendant had had ineffective counsel. Terry Kage's lawyer had opted not to cross-examine Molly. When prosecutors angled for a retrial, Molly's father refused to have her testify again, and they declined to proceed. Terry, then twenty-one years old, returned home to Aymes.

As she recalled what happened next, her muscles tightened. She was determined not to think about it, and took several additional deep breaths, exhales slightly longer than inhales. Then she got up, washed the few dishes from dinner, and made herself a cup of chamomile tea.

Carrying the mug into the living room, she sank into a worn wingback chair. Russell had placed a neatly folded wool blanket over the arm. Dry-cleaning tag still stapled to the frill. As she sipped her drink, she examined the enormous artwork again. When she'd told Russell he'd captured the overhang, she wasn't exaggerating. The glistening trees, the clearing, the sharp edge of rock in the foreground. And in the background, an expanse of murky water. A handful of colorful cottages dotting the shoreline on the other side.

Though Alex had labeled Russell a weirdo, she figured he was just a kind but quirky man. Still, she could not understand why he would choose this as his subject. If he knew her father, then surely he knew what had happened to her mother. What type of person would spend hours painting the exact place where a local boy had disposed of a dead woman's body?